A HOUSE
A-HAUNT

A HOUSE A-HAUNT

CLASSIC STORIES OF HAUNTED HOUSES, HORRIFIC ROOMS, AND OTHER GHASTLY ABODES

EDITED BY
CHAD ARMENT

COACHWHIP PUBLICATIONS
Greenville, Ohio

A House A-Haunt
© 2019 Coachwhip Publications

No claims made on public domain material.
Cover image: 'Haunted House,' by Thomas Moran
   (1858)

CoachwhipBooks.com

ISBN 1-61646-482-8
ISBN-13 978-1-61646-482-0

CONTENTS

THE GHOST STORY OF PLINY THE YOUNGER   7

THE TAPESTRIED CHAMBER   11
    Sir Walter Scott

THE HAUNTED MANOR-HOUSE OF PADDINGTON   33
    Charles Ollier

THE HAUNTED AND THE HAUNTERS   47
    Edward Bulwer-Lytton

AN AUTHENTIC NARRATIVE OF A HAUNTED HOUSE   109
    Sheridan Le Fanu

THE GHOST AT LABURNUM VILLA   131
    Anonymous

THE SPOOK HOUSE   151
    Ambrose Bierce

THE LITTLE ROOM   157
    Madeline Yale Wynne

THE RED ROOM   177
    H. G. Wells

THE HOUSE THAT WAS NOT   193

   Elia Wilkinson Peattie

A CASE OF EAVESDROPPING   201

   Algernon Blackwood

THE SOUTHWEST CHAMBER   225

   Mary E. Wilkins Freeman

THE EMPTY HOUSE   269

   Algernon Blackwood

THE TOLL-HOUSE   297

   W. W. Jacobs

AFTERWARD   313

   Edith Wharton

THE BECKONING FAIR ONE   363

   Oliver Onions

THE ATTIC   469

   Algernon Blackwood

THE DECOY   479

   Algernon Blackwood

THE GHOST HUNTERS   511

   Allen Upward

THE GHOST STORY OF
PLINY THE YOUNGER

When was the first ghost story told? At what period
in the world's infancy did the minds of man first
feel the dread delight, the awful attraction, which
modern scepticism has deprived us all of, except
children and village lasses? We confess we cannot
tell. And instead of collecting scattered fragments
from antiquity, we subjoin a translation of a ghost
story, perfect and complete, of the respectable age
of eighteen centuries, which so terrified the calm
philosopher Pliny, of Christian-hating reputation,
that he wrote to his friend Sura, the consul, to ask
whether it could be true. So exactly does this story
correspond in all the ghostly elements to authentic
narratives, which inundate the waste-paper baskets
of magazine editors every Christmas, that we cannot think it the first attempt of the invention in
this direction. Poets must have lived before Homer,
and dealers in the supernatural must have traded
on man's love for the marvellous long before the
time of Pliny's informant. We meet with ghosts in

the "Iliad," and Æschylus twice introduces them on
the stage. Indeed, the belief in their appearance
naturally arose from the idea that, until a man was
decently buried, old Charon would not convey his
soul across the slimy Styx, but left it to squeak and
gibber on this side the stream. Hence it was considered a greater crime at Athens to leave a parent
unburied than to allow him to starve to death. And
that beautiful play of Sophocles, in which Antigone
suffers death rather than leave her brother's corpse
unburied, had a far greater charm in Pagan Athens
than it can have in Christian England. But we are
digressing. Here is the promised story, from the
twenty-seventh epistle of the seventh book of Pliny,
the younger:—

There was, at Athens, a house, large and spacious,
but with a bad name. In the silence of the night,
there was wont to be heard in it the rattling of iron,
and, if you listened more attentively, the clash of
chains, first at a distance, then hard-by. Presently
there appeared a ghost—an old man, lean and squalid, with long beard and rough hair. He carried fetters
on his legs and gyves on his wrists, shaking them as
he walked. Hence every night was spent in wakeful
terror by the inhabitants. Sickness followed vigils,
and death sickness. For even during the daytime,
though the phantom had departed, the recollection
of it clung to them, and the terror lasted longer

than that which caused it. Accordingly the house was deserted, condemned to solitude, and entirely given up to the spectre. It was advertised, nevertheless, to be let or sold, in case anyone, not knowing the circumstances, should be willing to purchase.

Athenodorus, the philosopher, came to Athens, read the notice, asked the terms, and, having his suspicions roused by the low price, made inquiries, and heard the whole story. So far from shrinking, he took the house all the more eagerly.

When evening drew near, he orders his couch to be placed in the front room, calls for a writing-tablet, a style, and a light, dismisses all his attendants, and devotes his attention—eyes, head, and hands—to writing, lest his mind, being unemployed, should conjure up fancied sights and sounds.

At first there was the silence of night, deep as elsewhere; then the clash of iron and the rattling of chains. He neither raised his eyes nor relaxed his style, but fixed his attention upon his work. The clink grew louder, came nearer, and sounded, now at the door, now within the room. He looks up, sees and recognises the spectre described. It stood and beckoned with its hand, as if calling him. He made a sign with his finger for it to wait a little, and again settled down to his tablets and style. It rattled its chains at his head as he wrote. He looked up again, making the same sign as before, and without further delay took the candle and followed. It walked with slow step, as if weighted with the chains. After turning into the courtyard of the house, it suddenly slipped into the earth and disappeared. He piled some weeds and leaves to mark the spot, and, the next day, going to the magistrates, advised them to order the place to be excavated. A skeleton was found, the flesh all wasted away by putrefaction, and the bare bones bound in fetters and chains. It was taken up and publicly buried; and after that the house was no more troubled.

(From *Once a Week*, 1869)

THE TAPESTRIED CHAMBER; OR, THE LADY IN THE SACQUE

Sir Walter Scott

(1829)

About the end of the American war, when the officers of Lord Cornwallis's army which surrendered at
Yorktown, and others, who had been made prisoners
during the impolitic and ill-fated controversy, were
returning to their own country, to relate their adventures and repose themselves after their fatigues,
there was amongst them a general officer, to whom
Miss S. gave the name of Browne, but merely, as I
understood, to save the inconvenience of introduc-
ing a nameless agent in the narrative. He was an
officer of merit, as well as a gentleman of high consideration for family and attainments.

Some business had carried General Browne upon
a tour through the western counties, when, in the
conclusion of a morning stage, he found himself in
the vicinity of a small country town, which presented a scene of uncommon beauty and of a character
peculiarly English.

The little town, with its stately old church whose
tower bore testimony to the devotion of ages long

past, lay amidst pasture and corn-fields of small extent, but bounded and divided with hedgerow timber of great age and size. There were few marks of modern improvement. The environs of the place intimated neither the solitude of decay, nor the bustle of novelty; the houses were old, but in good repair; and the beautiful little river murmured freely on its way to the left of the town, neither restrained by a dam, nor bordered by a towing-path.

Upon a gentle eminence, nearly a mile to the southward of the town, were seen amongst many venerable oaks and tangled thickets the turrets of a castle, as old as the wars of York and Lancaster, but which seemed to have received important alterations during the age of Elizabeth and her successors. It had not been a place of great size; but whatever accommodation it formerly afforded, was, it must be supposed, still to be obtained within its walls; at least, such was the inference which General Browne drew from observing the smoke arise merrily from several of the ancient wreathed and carved chimney-stalks.

The wall of the park ran alongside of the highway for two or three hundred yards, and, through the different points by which the eye found glimpses into the woodland scenery, it seemed to be well stocked. Other points of view opened in succession; now a full one, of the front of the old castle, and now a side glimpse at its particular towers; the former rich in all the bizarrerie of the Elizabethan school, while the simple and solid strength of other parts of the building seemed to show that they had been raised more for defence than ostentation.

Delighted with the partial glimpses which he obtained of the castle through the woods and glades by which this ancient feudal fortress was surrounded, our military traveller was determined to inquire whether it might not deserve a nearer view, and whether it contained family pictures or other objects of curiosity worthy of a stranger's visit, when, leaving the vicinity of the park, he rolled through a clean and well-paved street, and stopped at the door of a well-frequented inn.

Before ordering horses to proceed on his journey, General Browne made inquiries concerning the proprietor of the château which had so attracted his admiration, and was equally surprised and pleased at hearing in reply a nobleman named whom we shall call Lord Woodville. How fortunate! Much of Browne's early recollections, both at school and at college, had been connected with young Woodville, whom, by a few questions, he now ascertained to be the same with the owner of this fair domain. He had been raised to the peerage by the decease of his father a few months before, and, as the General learned from the landlord, the term of mourning being ended, was now taking possession of his paternal estate in the jovial season of merry autumn,

accompanied by a select party of friends to enjoy
the sports of a country famous for game.

This was delightful news to our traveller. Frank
Woodville had been Richard Browne's fag at Eton,
and his chosen intimate at Christ Church; their
pleasures and their tasks had been the same; and
the honest soldier's heart warmed to find his early
friend in possession of so delightful a residence, and
of an estate, as the landlord assured him with a nod
and a wink, fully adequate to maintain and add to
his dignity. Nothing was more natural than that the
traveller should suspend a journey, which there was
nothing to render hurried, to pay a visit to an old
friend under such agreeable circumstances.

The fresh horses, therefore, had only the brief
task of conveying the General's travelling-carriage
to Woodville Castle. A porter admitted them at a
modern Gothic lodge, built in that style to correspond with the castle itself, and at the same time
rang a bell to give warning of the approach of visitors. Apparently the sound of the bell had suspended the separation of the company, bent on the various amusements of the morning; for, on entering
the court of the château, several young men were
lounging about in their sporting-dresses, looking at,
and criticizing, the dogs which the keepers held in
readiness to attend their pastime.

As General Browne alighted, the young lord came
to the gate of the hall, and for an instant gazed, as

at a stranger, upon the countenance of his friend, on which war, with its fatigues and its wounds, had made a great alteration. But the uncertainty lasted no longer than till the visitor had spoken, and the hearty greeting which followed was such as can only be exchanged betwixt those who have passed together merry days of careless boyhood or early youth.

"If I could have formed a wish, my dear Browne," said Lord Woodville, "it would have been to have you here, of all men, upon this occasion, which my friends are good enough to hold as a sort of holiday. Do not think you have been unwatched during the years you have been absent from us. I have traced you through your dangers, your triumphs, your misfortunes, and was delighted to see that, whether in victory or defeat, the name of my old friend was always distinguished with applause."

The General made a suitable reply, and congratulated his friend on his new dignities, and the possession of a place and domain so beautiful.

"Nay, you have seen nothing of it as yet," said Lord Woodville, "and I trust you do not mean to leave us till you are better acquainted with it. It is true, I confess, that my present party is pretty large, and the old house, like other places of the kind, does not possess so much accommodation as the extent of the outward walls appears to promise. But we can give you a comfortable old-fashioned room, and I venture to suppose that your campaigns have taught you to be glad of worse quarters."

The General shrugged his shoulders, and laughed. "I presume," he said, "the worst apartment in your château is considerably superior to the old tobacco-cask, in which I was fain to take up my night's lodging when I was in the Bush, as the Virginians call it, with the light corps. There I lay, like Diogenes himself, so delighted with my covering from the elements, that I made a vain attempt to have it rolled on to my next quarters; but my commander for the time would give way to no such luxurious provision, and I took farewell of my beloved cask with tears in my eyes."

"Well, then, since you do not fear your quarters," said Lord Woodville "you will stay with me a week at least. Of guns, dogs, fishing-rods, flies, and means of sport by sea and land, we have enough and to spare: you cannot pitch on an amusement, but we will pitch on the means of pursuing it. But if you prefer the gun and pointers, I will go with you myself, and see whether you have mended your shooting since you have been amongst the Indians of the back settlements."

The General gladly accepted his friendly host's proposal in all its points. After a morning of manly exercise, the company met at dinner, where it was the delight of Lord Woodville to conduce to the display of the high properties of his recovered friend, so as to recommend him to his guests, most of whom were persons of distinction. He led General Browne to speak of the scenes he had witnessed; and as every word marked alike the brave officer and the sensible man, who retained possession of his cool judgement under the most imminent dangers, the company looked upon the soldier with general respect, as on one who had proved himself possessed of an uncommon portion of personal courage—that attribute, of all others, of which everybody desires to be thought possessed.

The day at Woodville Castle ended as usual in such mansions. The hospitality stopped within the limits of good order; music, in which the young lord was a proficient, succeeded to the circulation of the bottle; cards and billiards, for those who preferred such amusements, were in readiness; but the exercise of the morning required early hours, and not long after eleven o'clock the guests began to retire to their several apartments.

The young lord himself conducted his friend, General Browne, to the chamber destined for him, which answered the description he had given of it, being comfortable, but old-fashioned. The bed was of the massive form used in the end of the seventeenth century, and the curtains of faded silk, heavily trimmed with tarnished gold. But then the sheets, pillows, and blankets looked delightful to the campaigner, when he thought of his "mansion, the cask."

There was an air of gloom in the tapestry hangings which, with their worn-out graces, curtained
the walls of the little chamber, and gently undulated
as the autumnal breeze found its way through the
ancient lattice-window, which pattered and whistled
as the air gained entrance. The toilet too, with its
mirror, turbaned, after the manner of the beginning
of the century, with a coiffure of murrey-coloured
silk, and its hundred strange-shaped boxes, provid-
ing for arrangements which had been obsolete for
more than fifty years, had an antique, and in so
far a melancholy, aspect. But nothing could blaze
more brightly and cheerfully than the two large wax
candles; or if aught could rival them, it was the
flaming bickering fagots in the chimney, that sent
at once their gleam and their warmth through the
snug apartment; which, notwithstanding the general
antiquity of its appearance, was not wanting in
the least convenience that modern habits rendered
either necessary or desirable.

"This is an old-fashioned sleeping apartment,
General," said the young lord; "but I hope you will
find nothing that makes you envy your old tobacco-
cask."

"I am not particular respecting my lodgings," replied the General; "yet were I to make any choice, I
would prefer this chamber by many degrees, to the
gayer and more modern rooms of your family mansion. Believe me that when I unite its modern air of

comfort with its venerable antiquity, and recollect that it is your lordship's property, I shall feel in better quarters here, than if I were in the best hotel London could afford."

"I trust—I have no doubt—that you will find yourself as comfortable as I wish you, my dear General," said the young nobleman; and once more bidding his guest good night, he shook him by the hand and withdrew.

The General once more looked round him, and internally congratulating himself on his return to peaceful life, the comforts of which were endeared by the recollection of the hardships and dangers he had lately sustained, undressed himself, and prepared himself for a luxurious night's rest.

Here, contrary to the custom of this species of tale, we leave the General in possession of his apartment until the next morning.

The company assembled for breakfast at an early hour, but without the appearance of General Browne, who seemed the guest that Lord Woodville was desirous of honouring above all whom his hospitality had assembled around him. He more than once expressed surprise at the General's absence, and at length sent a servant to make inquiry after him. The man brought back information that General Browne had been walking abroad since an early hour of the morning, in defiance of the weather, which was misty and ungenial.

"The custom of a soldier," said the young nobleman to his friends: "many of them acquire habitual
vigilance, and cannot sleep after the early hour at
which their duty usually commands them to be
alert."

Yet the explanation which Lord Woodville thus
offered to the company seemed hardly satisfactory
to his own mind, and it was in a fit of silence and
abstraction that he awaited the return of the General. It took place near an hour after the breakfast-bell
had rung. He looked fatigued and feverish. His hair,
the powdering and arrangement of which was at this
time one of the most important occupations of a
man's whole day, and marked his fashion as much as,
in the present time, the tying of a cravat or the want
of one, was dishevelled, uncurled, void of powder,
and dank with dew. His clothes were huddled on
with a careless negligence, remarkable in a military
man, whose real or supposed duties are usually held
to include some attention to the toilet; and his looks
were haggard and ghastly in a peculiar degree.

"So you have stolen a march upon us this morning, my dear General," said Lord Woodville; "or you
have not found your bed so much to your mind as I
had hoped and you seemed to expect. How did you
rest last night?"

"Oh, excellently well—remarkably well—never
better in my life!" said General Browne rapidly, and
yet with an air of embarrassment which was obvious

to his friend. He then hastily swallowed a cup of tea, and, neglecting or refusing whatever else was offered, seemed to fall into a fit of abstraction.

"You will take the gun to-day, General?" said his friend and host, but had to repeat the question twice ere he received the abrupt answer, "No, my Lord; I am sorry I cannot have the honour of spending another day with your lordship; my post horses are ordered, and will be here directly."

All who were present showed surprise, and Lord Woodville immediately replied, "Post horses, my good friend! What can you possibly want with them, when you promised to stay with me quietly for at least a week?"

"I believe," said the General, obviously much embarrassed, "that I might, in the pleasure of my first meeting with your lordship, have said something about stopping here a few days; but I have since found it altogether impossible."

"That is very extraordinary," answered the young nobleman. "You seemed quite disengaged yesterday, and you cannot have had a summons to-day; for our post has not come up from the town, and therefore you cannot have received any letters."

General Browne, without giving any further explanation, muttered something of indispensable business, and insisted on the absolute necessity of his departure in a manner which silenced all opposition on the part of his host, who saw that his

resolution was taken, and forbore further impor-
tunity.

"At least, however," he said, "permit me, my dear
Browne, since go you will or must, to show you the
view from the terrace, which the mist that is now
rising, will soon display."

He threw open a sash-window, and stepped down
upon the terrace as he spoke. The General followed
him mechanically, but seemed little to attend to
what his host was saying, as, looking across an extended and rich prospect, he pointed out the different objects worthy of observation. Thus they moved
on till Lord Woodville had attained his purpose of
drawing his guest entirely apart from the rest of the
company, when, turning round upon him with an
air of great solemnity, he addressed him thus:

"Richard Browne, my old and very dear friend,
we are now alone. Let me conjure you to answer me
upon the word of a friend, and the honour of a soldier. How did you in reality rest during last night?"

"Most wretchedly indeed, my lord," answered the
General, in the same tone of solemnity; "so miserably, that I would not run the risk of such a second
night, not only for all the lands belonging to this
castle, but for all the country which I see from this
elevated point of view."

"This is most extraordinary," said the young lord,
as if speaking to himself; "then there must be something in the reports concerning that apartment."

Again turning to the General, he said, "For God's sake, my dear friend, be candid with me, and let me know the disagreeable particulars which have befallen you under a roof where, with consent of the owner, you should have met nothing save comfort."

The General seemed distressed by this appeal, and paused a moment before he replied. "My dear lord," he at length said, "what happened to me last night is of nature so peculiar and so unpleasant, that I could hardly bring myself to detail it even to your lordship, were it not that, independent of my wish to gratify any request of yours, I think that sincerity on my part may lead to some explanation about a circumstance equally painful and mysterious. To others, the communications I am about to make, might place me in the light of a weak-minded, superstitious fool who suffered his own imagination to delude and bewilder him; but you have known me in childhood and youth, and will not suspect me of having adopted in manhood the feelings and frailties from which my early years were free." Here he paused, and his friend replied:

"Do not doubt my perfect confidence in the truth of your communication, however strange it may be," replied Lord Woodville. "I know your firmness of disposition too well, to suspect you could be made the object of imposition, and am aware that your honour and your friendship will equally deter you from exaggerating whatever you may have witnessed."

"Well then," said the General, "I will proceed
with my story as well as I can, relying upon your
candour; and yet distinctly feeling that I would
rather face a battery than recall to my mind the
odious recollections of last night."

He paused a second time, and then perceiving
that Lord Woodville remained silent and in an attitude of attention, he commenced, though not without obvious reluctance, the history of his night's
adventures in the Tapestried Chamber.

"I undressed and went to bed, so soon as your
lordship left me yesterday evening; but the wood in
the chimney, which nearly fronted my bed, blazed
brightly and cheerfully, and, aided by a hundred
exciting recollections of my childhood and youth,
which had been recalled by the unexpected pleasure
of meeting your lordship, prevented me from falling
immediately asleep. I ought, however, to say that
these reflections were all of a pleasant and agreeable kind, grounded on a sense of having for a time
exchanged the labour, fatigues, and dangers of my
profession, for the enjoyments of a peaceful life,
and the reunion of those friendly and affectionate
ties which I had torn asunder at the rude summons
of war.

"While such pleasing reflections were stealing
over my mind, and gradually lulling me to slumber, I was suddenly aroused by a sound like that of
the rustling of a silken gown, and the tapping of a

pair of high-heeled shoes, as if a woman were walk-ing in the apartment. Ere I could draw the curtain to see what the matter was, the figure of a little woman passed between the bed and the fire. The back of this form was turned to me, and I could observe, from the shoulders and neck, it was that of an old woman, whose dress was an old-fashioned gown, which, I think, ladies call a sacque—that is, a sort of robe, completely loose in the body, but gath-ered into broad plaits upon the neck and shoulders, which fall down to the ground, and terminate in a species of train.

"I thought the intrusion singular enough, but never harboured for a moment the idea that what I saw was anything more than the mortal form of some old woman about the establishment, who had a fancy to dress like her grandmother, and who, hav-ing perhaps (as your lordship mentioned that you were rather straitened for room) been dislodged from her chamber for my accommodation, had forgotten the circumstance, and returned by twelve to her old haunt. Under this persuasion I moved myself in bed and coughed a little, to make the intruder sensi-ble of my being in possession of the premises. She turned slowly round, but gracious Heaven! My lord, what a countenance did she display to me!

"There was no longer any question what she was, or any thought of her being a living being. Upon a face which wore the fixed features of a corpse, were imprinted the traces of the vilest and most hideous passions which had animated her while she lived. The body of some atrocious criminal seemed to have been given up from the grave, and the soul restored from the penal fire, in order to form, for a space, a union with the ancient accomplice of its guilt. I started up in bed, and sat upright, supporting my-self on my palms, as I gazed on this horrible spectre. The hag made, as it seemed, a single and swift stride to the bed where I lay, and squatted herself down upon it, in precisely the same attitude which I had assumed in the extremity of horror, advancing her diabolical countenance within half a yard of mine, with a grin which seemed to intimate the malice and the derision of an incarnate fiend."

Here General Browne stopped, and wiped from his brow the cold perspiration with which the recollection of his horrible vision had covered it.

"My lord," he said, "I am no coward. I have been in all the mortal dangers incidental to my profession, and I may truly boast that no man ever knew Richard Browne dishonour the sword he wears; but in these horrible circumstances, under the eyes, and as it seemed, almost in the grasp of an incarnation of an evil spirit, all firmness forsook me, all manhood melted from me like wax in the furnace, and I felt my hair individually bristle. The current of my life-blood ceased to flow, and I sank back in a swoon, as very a victim to panic terror as ever was a village girl or a child of ten years old. How long I lay in this condition I cannot pretend to guess.

"But I was roused by the castle clock striking one, so loud that it seemed as if it were in the very room. It was some time before I dared open my eyes, lest they should again encounter the horrible spectacle. When, however, I summoned courage to look up, she was no longer visible. My first idea was to pull my bell, wake the servants, and remove to a garret or a hay-loft, to be ensured against a second visitation. Nay, I will confess the truth, that my resolution was altered, not by the shame of exposing myself, but by the very fear that, as the bell-cord hung by the chimney, I might, in making my way to it, be again crossed by the fiendish hag, who, I figured to myself, might be still lurking about some corner of the apartment.

"I will not pretend to describe what hot and cold fever-fits tormented me for the rest of the night, through broken sleep, weary vigils, and that dubious state which forms the neutral ground between them. An hundred terrible objects appeared to haunt me; but there was the great difference betwixt the vision which I have described, and those which followed, that I knew the last to be deceptions of my own fancy and overexcited nerves.

"Day at last appeared, and I rose from my bed ill in health, and humiliated in mind. I was ashamed of myself as a man and a soldier, and still more so,

at feeling my own extreme desire to escape from
the haunted apartment, which, however, conquered
all other considerations; so that, huddling on my
clothes with the most careless haste, I made my
escape from your lordship's mansion, to seek in the
open air some relief to my nervous system, shaken
as it was by this horrible rencountre with a visitant,
for such I must believe her, from the other world.
Your lordship has now heard the cause of my dis-
composure, and of my sudden desire to leave your
hospitable castle. In other places I trust we may
often meet; but God protect me from ever spending
a second night under that roof!"

Strange as the General's tale was, he spoke with
such a deep air of conviction, that it cut short all the
usual commentaries which are made on such stories.
Lord Woodville never once asked him if he was sure
he did not dream of the apparition, or suggested any
of the possibilities by which it is fashionable to explain supernatural appearances, as wild vagaries of
the fancy or deceptions of the optic nerves. On the
contrary, he seemed deeply impressed with the truth
and reality of what he had heard; and, after a considerable pause, regretted, with much appearance of
sincerity, that his early friend should in his house
have suffered so severely.

"I am the more sorry for your pain, my dear
Browne," he continued, "that it is the unhappy,
though most unexpected, result of an experiment

of my own. You must know that, for my father and grandfather's time, at least, the apartment which was assigned to you last night had been shut on account of reports that it was disturbed by supernatural sights and noises. When I came, a few weeks since, into possession of the estate, I thought the accommodation which the castle afforded for my friends was not extensive enough to permit the inhabitants of the invisible world to retain possession of a comfortable sleeping-apartment. I therefore caused the Tapestried Chamber, as we call it, to be opened; and without destroying its air of antiquity, I had such new articles of furniture placed in it as became the modern times.

"Yet, as the opinion that the room was haunted very strongly prevailed among the domestics, and was also known in the neighbourhood and to many of my friends, I feared some prejudice might be entertained by the first occupant of the Tapestried Chamber, which might tend to revive the evil report which it had laboured under, and so disappoint my purpose of rendering it a useful part of the house. I must confess, my dear Browne, that your arrival yesterday, agreeable to me for a thousand reasons besides, seemed the most favourable opportunity of removing the unpleasant rumours which attached to the room, since your courage was indubitable, and your mind free of any preoccupation on the subject. I could not, therefore, have chosen a more fitting subject for my experiment."

"Upon my life," said General Browne, somewhat hastily, "I am infinitely obliged to your lordship—very particularly indebted indeed. I am likely to remember for some time the consequences of the experiment, as your lordship is pleased to call it."

"Nay, now you are unjust, my dear friend," said Lord Woodville. "You have only to reflect for a single moment, in order to be convinced that I could not augur the possibility of the pain to which you have been so unhappily exposed. I was yesterday morning a complete sceptic on the subject of supernatural appearances. Nay, I am sure that, had I told you what was said about that room, those very reports would have induced you, by your own choice, to select it for your accommodation. It was my misfortune, perhaps my error, but really cannot be termed my fault, that you have been afflicted so strangely."

"Strangely indeed!" said the General, resuming his good temper; "and I acknowledge that I have no right to be offended with your lordship for treating me like what I used to think myself, a man of some firmness and courage. But I see my post-horses are arrived, and I must not detain your lordship from your amusement."

"Nay, my old friend," said Lord Woodville, "since you cannot stay with us another day, which, indeed, I can no longer urge, give me at least half an hour more. You used to love pictures, and I have a gallery of portraits, some of them by Vandyke, representing ancestry to whom this property and castle formerly belonged. I think that several of them will strike you as possessing merit."

General Browne accepted the invitation, though somewhat unwillingly. It was evident he was not to breathe freely or at ease until he left Woodville Castle far behind him. He could not refuse his friend's invitation, however; and the less so, that he was a little ashamed of the peevishness which he had displayed towards his well-meaning entertainer.

The general, therefore, followed Lord Woodville through several rooms, into a long gallery hung with pictures, which the latter pointed out to his guest, telling the names, and giving some account, of the personages whose portraits presented themselves in progression. General Browne was but little interested in the details which these accounts conveyed to him. They were, indeed, of the kind which are usually found in an old family gallery. Here was a cavalier who had ruined the estate in the royal cause; there, a fine lady who had reinstated it by contracting a match with a wealthy Roundhead. There hung a gallant who had been in danger for corresponding with the exiled court at St. Germain's; here, one who had taken arms for William at the Revolution; and there, a third that had thrown his weight alternately into the scale of Whig and Tory.

While Lord Woodville was cramming these words into his guest's ear, "against the stomach of his sense," they gained the middle of the gallery, when he beheld General Browne suddenly start, and assume an attitude of the utmost surprise, not unmixed with fear, as his eyes were caught and suddenly riveted by a portrait of an old lady in a sacque, the fashionable dress of the end of the 17th century.

"There she is!" he exclaimed—"there she is, in form and features, though inferior in demoniac expression to the accursed hag who visited me last night!"

"If that be the case," said the young nobleman, "there can remain no longer any doubt of the horrible reality of your apparition. That is the picture of a wretched ancestress of mine, of whose crimes a black and fearful catalogue is recorded in a family history in my charter-chest. The recital of them would be too horrible; it is enough to say, that in yon fatal apartment incest and unnatural murder were committed. I will restore it to the solitude to which the better judgement of those who preceded me had consigned it; and never shall any one, so long as I can prevent it, be exposed to a repetition of the supernatural horrors which could shake such courage as yours."

Thus the friends, who had met with such glee, parted in a very different mood—Lord Woodville to command the Tapestried Chamber to be unmantled and the door built up; and General Browne to seek in some less beautiful country, and with some less dignified friend, forgetfulness of the painful night which he had passed in Woodville Castle.

THE HAUNTED MANOR-HOUSE
OF PADDINGTON

CHARLES OLLIER
(1842)

The old manor-house was now a gloomy ruin. It was surrounded by an old-fashioned, spacious garden, overgrown with weeds; but, in the drowsy and half-veiled light of an April dawn, looking almost as beautiful as if it had been kept in trim order. The gravel walks were green with moss and grass, and the fruit-trees, trained against the wall, shot out a plenteous overgrowth of wild branches which hung unprofitably over the borders. A rank crop of thistles, bind-weed and groundsel, choked the beds, over which the slimy trace of slugs and snails shone in the horizontal gleam of the uprising sun. The noble elms, which stood about the lawn in groups, were the only objects that did not hear the melancholy evidence of neglect. These giants of the wood thrive best when not interfered with by man.

Scarcely a single window-pane was unbroken in the old house; the roof was untiled; the brick-work at the lower part of the building was without mortar, and seethed crumbling with damp; and many of the shutters, which in the dwellings of that date were fixed outside the windows, hung dangling upon one rusty hinge. The entrance-door, of which the lintel had either dropped from its socket or been forced away, was fastened to the side frame by a padlock.

All was silent, deserted, desolate; nor did the aspect of the tenement tend to dissipate, by any exhibition of beauty, either in outline, colour, or detached parts, the heavy, unimaginative melancholy which the view of it inspired. It was a square, red brick house, large enough indeed to contain many rooms, and were it in good repair, to accommodate even a wealthy family; but it was utterly destitute of external interest. It had no pointed roof, no fantastic gables, no grotesque projections, no pleasant porch, in the angles of which the rose and the honeysuckle could ascend, or the ivy cling, nor any twisted and spiral chimneys, like those which surmounted the truly English and picturesque homes built in the Elizabethan era, and which, together with the rich and glorious poetry of that time, gave way to the smooth neatness cultivated during the reign of William and Mary, to which epoch the Paddington Manor-House might be referred.

Two men stood, in the silence of an April morning, contemplating the deserted scene. One of them appeared to know something of its history, and, yielding to the entreaty of his companion, related the following story:

"Ten years ago," said he, "there dwelt in this house a man of high repute for virtue and piety. He had no wife nor children, but he lived with much liberality, and kept many servants. He was constant in his attendance at church, and gladdened the hearts of the neighbouring poor by the frequency of his almsgiving.

"His fame among his neighbours was increased by his great hospitality. Scarcely a day passed without his entertaining some of them with feasts at his house, when his conversation was admired, his judgment appealed to as something more than ordinarily wise, his decisions considered final, and his jokes received with hearty laughter; according to the time-hallowed and dutiful practice of guests at the tables of rich men.

"Nothing could exceed the costliness and rack of this man's wines, the lavish profusion of his plate nor the splendour of his rooms—*these very rooms!*—which were decorated with the richest furniture, the most costly specimens of the Italian and Flemish schools of painting, and resounded nightly with the harmony of dainty madrigals.

"One summer evening, after a sumptuous dinner had been enjoyed by himself and a numerous party, the weather being very sultry, a proposal was made by the host that the wine and dessert should be taken to the lawn, and that the revelry should be prolonged under the shade of the leafy elms which stood about the garden in groups, as now you see them. The company accordingly adjourned thither, and great was the merriment beneath the green boughs which hung over the table in heavy masses, and loud the songs in the sweet air of evening.

"Twilight came on; but still the happy revellers were loth to leave the spot, which seemed sacred to wine and music, and indolent enjoyment. The leaves which canopied them were motionless; even those which hung on the extreme point of the tenderest sprays, quivered not. One shining star, poised in the clear ether, seemed to look down with curious gaze on the jocund scene; and the soft west wind had breathed its last drowsy evening hymn. The calm, indeed, was so perfect that the master of the house ordered lights to be brought there where they sat, that the out-of-door carouse might be still enjoyed.

"'Hang care!' exclaimed he. 'This is a delicious evening; the wine has a finer relish here than in the house, and the song is more exciting and melodious under the tranquil sky than in the close room, where the sound is stifled. Come, let us have a bacchanalian chant—let us, with old Sir Toby, make the welkin dance and rouse the night-owl with a catch! I am right merry. Pass the bottle, and tune your voices—a catch, a catch! The lights will be here anon.'

"Thus he spoke; but his merriment seemed forced and unnatural. A grievous change awaited him.

"As one of the servants was proceeding from the house with a flambeau in his hand, to light the tapers already placed on the table, he saw in the walk leading from the outer gate, a matron of lofty bearing, in widow's weeds, whose skin, as the rays of the torch fell on it, looked white as the monumental effigy, and made a ghastly contrast with her black robe. Her face was like that of the grisly phantom, Death-in-life; it was rigid and sunken; but her eyes glanced about from their hollow sockets with a restless motion, and her brow was knit as if in anger. A corpse-like infant was in her arms; and she paced with proud and stately tread towards the spot where the master of the house, apparently

'Merry in heart and filled with swelling wine,'

was sitting among his jovial friends.

"The servant shuddered as he beheld the strange intruder; but he, too, had partaken of the good cheer, and felt bolder than usual. Mustering up his courage, he faced the awful woman, and demanded her errand.

"'I seek your master,' said she.

"'He is engaged, and cannot be interrupted,' replied the man. 'Ugh! turn your face from me—I like not your looks. You are enough to freeze one's very blood.'

"'Fool!' returned the woman. Your master *must* see me.' And she pushed the servant aside.

"The menial shivered at the touch of her hand, which was heavy and cold, like marble. He felt as if rooted to the spot; he could not move to follow her as she walked on to the scene of the banquet.

"On arriving at the spot, she drew herself up beside the host, and stood there without uttering a word! He saw her, and shook in every joint. The song ceased; the guests were speechless with amazement, and sat like petrifactions, bending their gaze one way towards the strange and solemn figure which confronted them.

"'Why comest thou here?' at length demanded the rich man, in low and gasping accents. 'Vanish! Who opened the vault to let thee forth? Thou shouldst be a hundred miles away. Sink again into the earth! Hence, horrible thing! Delusion of hell! Dead creature! Ghost! Hence! What seekest thou? What can I do to keep thee in the grave? I will resign thy lands: to whom shall they be given? Thy child is dead. Who is now thy heir? Speak, and be invisible!'

"The pale woman stooped with unseemly effort, as if an image of stone were to bend, and whispered something in the ear of her questioner, which made him tremble still more violently. Then beckoning him, she passed through the deepening twilight towards the house, while he, with bristling hair and faltering gait, followed her. The terror-stricken man, the gaunt woman, and white child, looked like three corpses moving in the heavy and uncertain shades of evening, against the order of nature.

"After waiting an hour for their friend's return, the guests, who had now recovered from their first panic, became impatient to solve the mystery, and determined to seek the owner of the house, and offer such comfort as his evident trepidation required. They accordingly directed their steps towards the room into which they were informed the woman and child, and their host, had entered.

"On approaching the door, piteous groans, and incoherent exclamations were heard; above which these words were plainly audible in a female voice: 'Remember what I have said! Think of my slaughtered husband! A more terrible intruder will some night come to thy house! Thou shalt perish here and hereafter!'

"Hearing these groans and these menaces, the party instantly burst into the room, followed by a servant with a light. The man, whose face was buried in his hands, was standing alone. But, as his friends gazed around in amazement, a shadow of the woman with the infant in her arms was seen to flicker on the wall, as if moved about uncouthly by a faint wind. By degrees it faded entirely away. No one knew how the stately widow herself had disappeared, nor by what means she had obtained admittance through the outer gate.

"To the earnest inquiries of his friends the host would give no answer; and the party left the place perplexed with fearful thoughts. From that time no feasts were given in the Manor House. The apartment where the secret interview took place, and which is, to this day, called 'THE ROOM OF THE SHADOW,' was closed, and, it is said, has never since been opened. It is the chamber immediately above this, and is now the haunt of bats, and other night-birds.

"After having lived here several years in comparative solitude, a mortal sickness came upon the owner of the house. But, if his bodily sufferings were grievous to behold, the agony of his mind seemed tenfold greater, so that the friends who called to cheer him in his malady were amazed to see one of so pure a life (as they thought) given over to remorse. He felt that he must shortly appear before the Supreme Judge; and the anticipated terrors of the judgment were already upon his spirit. His countenance underwent many ghastly changes, and the sweat of dismal suffering poured in heavy beads from his face and breast.

"The throes of his conscience were too strong to be any longer endured and hidden; and, summoning one or two of his neighbours to his bedside, he confessed many sins of which he had been guilty in another part of England; he had, he said, enriched himself by the ruin of widows and orphans; and, he added, that the accursed lust for gold had made him a murderer.

"It was in vain that the pastor of the parish, who saw his bitter agony, strove to absolve him of his manifold crimes. He could not be comforted. His works, and alms, and all the good endeavours of the latter years of his life were of no avail. They were as chaff, and flew off from the weight of his transgressions. The vengeance of eternal fire haunted him while living, and he did not dare even to pray. 'Alas! my friends,' said he, to those who besought him to lift up his voice in supplication to the Most High, 'I have no heart to pray, for I am already condemned! Hell is even now in my soul, there to burn for ever. Resign me, I pray you, to my lost condition, and to the fiends hovering around to seize me.'

"The menace of the strange woman was now about to be fulfilled.

"On the last night of this person's miserable life, one of his neighbours, a benevolent and pious man, sat up with the expiring wretch by his bed-side. He had for some time fallen into a state of stupor, being afraid to look any human being in the face, or even to open his eyes. He slept, or seemed to sleep for a while; then suddenly arousing himself, he appeared to be in intolerable agitation of body and mind, and with an indescribable expression of countenance, shrieked out, 'Oh the intolerable horrors of damnation!'

"Midnight had now arrived. The servants were in bed, and no one was stirring in the house but the old nurse, and the friend who watched the last moments of the sufferer. All was in quiet profound as that of the sepulchre; when suddenly the sound of loud and impatient footsteps was heard in the room adjoining the forlorn man's bed-chamber.

"'What can that be?' said the nurse under her breath, and with an expression of ghastly alarm. 'Hark! the noise continues!'

"'Is any one up in the house?' inquired the friend.

"'No: besides, would a servant dare to tramp with such violence about the next room to that of his dying master?'

"The gentleman snatched up a lamp, and went forth into the next chamber. It was empty! but still the footsteps sounded loudly as those of a person waiting in angry impatience.

"Bewildered and aghast, the friend returned to the bedside of the wretch, and could not find utterance to tell the nurse what had been the result of his examination of the adjoining room.

"'For the love of heaven!' exclaimed the woman, 'speak! tell me what you have seen in the next chamber. Who is there? Why do you look so pale? What has made you dumb? Hark! The noise of the footsteps grows louder and louder. Oh! how I wish I had never entered this accursed house—this house abhorred of God and man!'

"Meanwhile, the sound of the horrid footsteps grew not only louder, but quicker and more impatient.

"The scene of their trampling was, after a time, changed. They approached the sick man's room, and were heard—plainly heard—lose by the bedside of the dying wretch, whose nurse and friend stared with speechless terror upon the floor, which sounded and shook as the invisible foot-falls passed over it.

"'Something is here—something terrible—in this very room, and close to us, though we cannot see it!' whispered the gentleman in panting accents to his companion. 'Go up stairs and call the servants, and let all in the house assemble here.'

"'I dare not move,' exclaimed the trembling woman. 'My brain—my brain! I am faint—I shall go mad! Let us fly from this place—the fiend is here. Help! Help! in the name of the Almighty.'

"'Be composed, I beseech you,' said the gentleman, in a voice scarcely audible. 'Recall your scattered senses. I too should be scared to death, did I not with a strong effort keep down the mad throbbing that torment me. Recollect our duty. We are Christians, and must not abandon the expiring man. God will protect us. Merciful Heaven!' he continued, with a frenzied glance into the shadowy recesses of the chamber, 'Listen! the noise is stronger than ever—those iron footsteps!—and still we cannot discern the cause! Go and bring some companions—some human faces—our own are transformed!'

"The nurse, thus adjured, left the demon-haunted apartment with a visage white as snow; and the

benevolent friend, whose spirits had been subdued
by long watching in the chamber of death, and by
witnessing the sick man's agony and remorse, became, now that he was left alone, wild and frantic.
Assuming a courage from the very intensity of fear,
he shrieked out in a voice which scarcely sounded
like his own, 'What art thou, execrable thing! that
comest at this dead hour? Speak, if thou canst; show
thyself, if thou darest!'

"These cries roused the dying man from the miserable slumber into which he had fallen. He opened
his glassy eyes—gasped for utterance, and seemed
as though he would now have prayed—prayed in
mortal anguish; but the words died in his throat.
His lips quivered and seemed parched, as if by fire;
they stood apart, and his clenched teeth grinned
horribly. It was evident that he heard the footsteps;
for an agony, fearful to behold, came over him. He
arose in his bed—held out his arms, as if to keep off
the approach of some hateful thing; and, having sat
thus for a few moments, fell back, and with a dismal
groan expired!

"From that very instant the sound of the footsteps was heard no more! Silence fell upon the room:
when the nurse re-entered, followed by the servants,
they found the sick man dead, with a face of horrible contortion—and his friend stretched on the
floor in a swoon.

"The mortal part of the wretch was soon buried; and, after that time (the dismal story becoming generally known) no one would dare to inhabit the house, which gradually fell into decay, and got the fatal reputation of being haunted."

(From *Ferrers: A Romance of the Reign of George II*)

THE HAUNTED AND THE HAUNTERS; OR, THE HOUSE AND THE BRAIN

Edward Bulwer-Lytton

(1859)

A friend of mine, who is a man of letters and a philosopher, said to me one day, as if between jest and earnest, "Fancy! since we last met I have discovered a haunted house in the midst of London."

"Really haunted—and by what?—ghosts?"

"Well, I can't answer that question; all I know is this: six weeks ago my wife and I were in search of a furnished apartment. Passing a quiet street, we saw on the window of one of the houses a bill, 'Apartments, Furnished.' The situation suited us; we entered the house, liked the rooms, engaged them by the week—and left them the third day. No power on earth could have reconciled my wife to stay longer; and I don't wonder at it."

"What did you see?"

"Excuse me; I have no desire to be ridiculed as a superstitious dreamer—nor, on the other hand, could I ask you to accept on my affirmation what you would hold to be incredible without the evidence of your own senses. Let me only say this, it

was not so much what we saw or heard (in which
you might fairly suppose that we were the dupes of
our own excited fancy, or the victims of imposture
in others) that drove us away, as it was an undefinable terror which seized both of us whenever we
passed by the door of a certain unfurnished room, in
which we neither saw nor heard anything. And the
strangest marvel of all was, that for once in my life
I agreed with my wife, silly woman though she be—
and allowed, after the third night, that it was impossible to stay a fourth in that house. Accordingly,
on the fourth morning I summoned the woman who
kept the house and attended on us, and told her that
the rooms did not quite suit us, and we would not
stay out our week." She said dryly, "I know why; you
have stayed longer than any other lodger. Few ever
stayed a second night; none before you a third. But
I take it they have been very kind to you."

"'They—who?' I asked, affecting to smile.

"'Why, they who haunt the house, whoever they
are. I don't mind them. I remember them many years
ago, when I lived in this house, not as a servant; but
I know they will be the death of me some day. I don't
care—I'm old, and must die soon anyhow; and then
I shall be with them, and in this house still.' The
woman spoke with so dreary a calmness that really it
was a sort of awe that prevented my conversing with
her further. I paid for my week, and too happy were
my wife and I to get off so cheaply."

"You excite my curiosity," said I; "nothing I should like better than to sleep in a haunted house. Pray give me the address of the one which you left so ignominiously."

My friend gave me the address; and when we parted, I walked straight towards the house thus indicated.

It is situated on the north side of Oxford Street, in a dull but respectable thoroughfare. I found the house shut up—no bill at the window, and no response to my knock. As I was turning away, a beer-boy, collecting pewter pots at the neighboring areas, said to me, "Do you want any one at that house, sir?"

"Yes, I heard it was to be let."

"Let!—why, the woman who kept it is dead—has been dead these three weeks, and no one can be found to stay there, though Mr. J— offered ever so much. He offered mother, who chars for him, £1 a week just to open and shut the windows, and she would not."

"Would not!—and why?"

"The house is haunted; and the old woman who kept it was found dead in her bed, with her eyes wide open. They say the devil strangled her."

"Pooh! You speak of Mr. J—. Is he the owner of the house?"

"Yes."

"Where does he live?"

"In G— Street, No. —."

"What is he? In any business?"

"No, sir—nothing particular; a single gentle-man."

I gave the pot-boy the gratuity earned by his liberal information, and proceeded to Mr. J— in G— Street, which was close by the street that boasted the haunted house. I was lucky enough to find Mr. J— at home—an elderly man with intelligent countenance and prepossessing manners.

I communicated my name and my business frankly. I said I heard the house was considered to be haunted—that I had a strong desire to examine a house with so equivocal a reputation; that I should be greatly obliged if he would allow me to hire it, though only for a night. I was willing to pay for that privilege whatever he might be inclined to ask. "Sir," said Mr. J— with great courtesy, "the house is at your service, for as short or as long a time as you please. Rent is out of the question—the obligation will be on my side should you be able to discover the cause of the strange phenomena which at present deprive it of all value. I cannot let it, for I cannot even get a servant to keep it in order or answer the door. Unluckily the house is haunted, if I may use that expression, not only by night, but by day; though at night the disturbances are of a more unpleasant and sometimes of a more alarming character. The poor old woman who died in it three weeks ago was a pauper whom I took out of a workhouse; for in her childhood she had been known to some of my family, and had once been in such good circumstances that she had rented that house of my uncle. She was a woman of superior education and strong mind, and was the only person I could ever induce to remain in the house. Indeed, since her death, which was sudden, and the coroner's inquest, which gave it a notoriety in the neighborhood, I have so despaired of finding any person to take charge of the house, much more a tenant, that I would willingly let it rent free for a year to any one who would pay its rates and taxes."

"How long is it since the house acquired this sinister character?"

"That I can scarcely tell you, but very many years since. The old woman I spoke of, said it was haunted when she rented it between thirty and forty years ago. The fact is, that my life has been spent in the East Indies, and in the civil service of the Company. I returned to England last year, on inheriting the fortune of an uncle, among whose possessions was the house in question. I found it shut up and uninhabited. I was told that it was haunted, that no one would inhabit it. I smiled at what seemed to me so idle a story. I spent some money in repairing it, added to its old-fashioned furniture a few modern articles—advertised it, and obtained a lodger for a year. He was a colonel on half-pay. He came in with his family, a son and a daughter, and four or five servants: they all left the house the next day; and, although each of them declared that he had seen something different from that which had scared the others, that something was equally terrible to all. I really could not in conscience sue, nor even blame, the colonel for breach of agreement. Then I put in the old woman I have spoken of, and she was empowered to let the house in apartments. I never had one lodger who stayed more than three days. I do not tell you their stories—to no two lodgers have there been exactly the same phenomena repeated. It is better that you should judge for yourself, than enter the house with an imagination influenced by previous narratives; only be prepared to see and to hear something or other, and take whatever precautions you yourself please."

"Have you never had a curiosity yourself to pass a night in that house?"

"Yes. I passed not a night, but three hours in broad daylight alone in that house. My curiosity is not satisfied, but it is quenched. I have no desire to renew the experiment. You cannot complain, you see, sir, that I am not sufficiently candid; and unless your interest be exceedingly eager and your nerves unusually strong, I honestly add, that I advise you *not* to pass a night in that house."

"My interest *is* exceedingly keen," said I; "and though only a coward will boast of his nerves in situations wholly unfamiliar to him, yet my nerves have been seasoned in such variety of danger that I have the right to rely on them—even in a haunted house."

Mr. J— said very little more; he took the keys of the house out of his bureau, gave them to me—and, thanking him cordially for his frankness, and his urbane concession to my wish, I carried off my prize.

Impatient for the experiment, as soon as I reached home, I summoned my confidential servant—a young man of gay spirits, fearless temper, and as free from superstitious prejudice as any one I could think of.

"F—" said I, "you remember in Germany how disappointed we were at not finding a ghost in that old castle, which was said to be haunted by a headless apparition? Well, I have heard of a house in London which, I have reason to hope, is decidedly haunted. I mean to sleep there to-night. From what I hear, there is no doubt that something will allow itself to be seen or to be heard—something, perhaps, excessively horrible. Do you think if I take you with me, I may rely on your presence of mind, whatever may happen?"

"Oh, sir, pray trust me," answered F— grinning with delight.

"Very well; then here are the keys of the house— this is the address. Go now—select for me any bedroom you please; and since the house has not been inhabited for weeks, make up a good fire, air the bed well—see, of course, that there are candles as well as fuel. Take with you my revolver and my dagger—so much for my weapons; arm yourself equally well; and if we are not a match for a dozen ghosts, we shall be but a sorry couple of Englishmen."

I was engaged for the rest of the day on business so urgent that I had not leisure to think much on the nocturnal adventure to which I had plighted my honor. I dined alone, and very late, and while dining, read, as is my habit. I selected one of the volumes of Macaulay's *Essays*. I thought to myself that I would take the book with me; there was so much of healthfulness in the style, and practical life in the subjects, that it would serve as an antidote against the influences of superstitious fancy.

Accordingly, about half-past nine, I put the book into my pocket, and strolled leisurely towards the haunted house. I took with me a favorite dog: an exceedingly sharp, bold, and vigilant bull-terrier—a dog fond of prowling about strange, ghostly corners and passages at night in search of rats; a dog of dogs for a ghost.

It was a summer night but chilly, the sky somewhat gloomy and overcast. Still there was a moon, faint and sickly but still a moon, and if the clouds permitted, after midnight it would be brighter.

I reached the house, knocked, and my servant opened with a cheerful smile.

"All right, sir, and very comfortable."

"Oh!" said I, rather disappointed; "have you not seen nor heard anything remarkable?"

"Well, sir, I must own I have heard something queer."

"What?—what?"

"The sound of feet pattering behind me; and once or twice small noises like whispers close at my ear—nothing more."

"You are not at all frightened?"

"I! not a bit of it, sir;" and the man's bold look reassured me on one point—namely, that happen what might, he would not desert me.

We were in the hall, the street-door closed, and my attention was now drawn to my dog. He had at first run in eagerly enough, but had sneaked back to the door, and was scratching and whining to get out. After patting him on the head, and encouraging him gently, the dog seemed to reconcile himself to the situation, and followed me and F— through the house, but keeping close at my heels instead of hurrying inquisitively in advance, which was his usual and normal habit in all strange places. We first visited the subterranean apartments—the kitchen and other offices, and especially the cellars, in which last there were two or three bottles of wine still left in a bin, covered with cobwebs, and evidently, by their appearance, undisturbed for many years. It was clear that the ghosts were not winebibbers. For the rest we discovered nothing of interest. There was a gloomy

little backyard, with very high walls. The stones of
this yard were very damp; and what with the damp,
and what with the dust and smoke-grime on the
pavement, our feet left a slight impression where
we passed. And now appeared the first strange phenomenon witnessed by myself in this strange abode.
I saw, just before me, the print of a foot suddenly
form itself, as it were. I stopped, caught hold of my
servant, and pointed to it. In advance of that footprint as suddenly dropped another. We both saw it.
I advanced quickly to the place; the footprint kept
advancing before me, a small footprint—the foot of
a child: the impression was too faint thoroughly to
distinguish the shape, but it seemed to us both that
it was the print of a naked foot. This phenomenon
ceased when we arrived at the opposite wall, nor
did it repeat itself on returning. We remounted the
stairs, and entered the rooms on the ground-floor, a
dining parlor, a small back-parlor, and a still smaller
third room that had been probably appropriated
to a footman—all still as death. We then visited
the drawing-rooms, which seemed fresh and new.
In the front room I seated myself in an arm-chair.
F— placed on the table the candlestick with which
he had lighted us. I told him to shut the door. As
he turned to do so a chair opposite to me moved
from the wall quickly and noiselessly, and dropped
itself about a yard from my own chair, immediately
fronting it.

"Why, this is better than the turning-tables," said I, with a half-laugh; and as I laughed, my dog put back his head and howled.

F— coming back, had not observed the movement of the chair. He employed himself now in stilling the dog. I continued to gaze on the chair, and fancied I saw on it a pale, blue, misty outline of a human figure, but an outline so indistinct that I could only distrust my own vision. The dog now was quiet.

"Put back that chair opposite to me," said I to F—; "put it back to the wall."

F— obeyed. "Was that you, sir?" said he, turning abruptly.

"I— what?"

"Why, something struck me. I felt it sharply on the shoulder—just here."

"No," said I. "But we have jugglers present, and though we may not discover their tricks, we shall catch *them* before they frighten *us*."

We did not stay long in the drawing-rooms—in fact, they felt so damp and so chilly that I was glad to get to the fire upstairs. We locked the doors of the drawing-rooms—a precaution which, I should observe, we had taken with all the rooms we had searched below. The bedroom my servant had selected for me was the best on the floor—a large one, with two windows fronting the street. The four-posted bed, which took up no inconsiderable space, was

opposite to the fire, which burned clear and bright;
a door in the wall to the left, between the bed and
the window, communicated with the room which
my servant appropriated to himself. This last was a
small room with a sofa-bed, and had no communication with the landing-place—no other door but
that which conducted to the bedroom I was to occupy. On either side of my fireplace was a cupboard
without locks, flush with the wall, and covered
with the same dull-brown paper. We examined these
cupboards—only hooks to suspend female dresses,
nothing else; we sounded the walls—evidently solid,
the outer walls of the building. Having finished the
survey of these apartments, warmed myself a few
moments, and lighted my cigar, I then, still accompanied by F— went forth to complete my reconnoi-
tre. In the landing-place there was another door; it
was closed firmly. "Sir," said my servant, in surprise,
"I unlocked this door with all the others when I first
came; it cannot have got locked from the inside,
for—"

Before he had finished his sentence, the door,
which neither of us then was touching, opened quietly of itself. We looked at each other a single instant. The same thought seized both—some human
agency might be detected here. I rushed in first,
my servant followed. A small, blank, dreary room
without furniture; a few empty boxes and hampers
in a corner; a small window; the shutters closed; not

even a fireplace; no other door but that by which we had entered; no carpet on the floor, and the floor seemed very old, uneven, worm-eaten, mended here and there, as was shown by the whiter patches on the wood; but no living being, and no visible place in which a living being could have hidden. As we stood gazing round, the door by which we had entered closed as quietly as it had before opened; we were imprisoned.

For the first time I felt a creep of undefinable horror. Not so my servant. "Why, they don't think to trap us, sir; I could break that trumpery door with a kick of my foot."

"Try first if it will open to your hand," said I, shaking off the vague apprehension that had seized me, "while I open the shutters and see what is without."

I unbarred the shutters—the window looked on the little backyard I have before described; there was no ledge without—nothing to break the sheer descent of the wall. No man getting out of that window would have found any footing till he had fallen on the stones below.

F— meanwhile, was vainly attempting to open the door. He now turned round to me and asked my permission to use force. And I should here state, in justice to the servant, that, far from evincing any superstitious terrors, his nerve, composure, and even gayety amidst circumstances so extraordinary,

compelled my admiration, and made me congratu-
late myself on having secured a companion in every
way fitted to the occasion. I willingly gave him the
permission he required. But though he was a remarkably strong man, his force was as idle as his milder
efforts; the door did not even shake to his stout-
est kick. Breathless and panting, he desisted. I then
tried the door myself, equally in vain. As I ceased
from the effort, again that creep of horror came over
me; but this time it was more cold and stubborn. I
felt as if some strange and ghastly exhalation were
rising up from the chinks of that rugged floor, and
filling the atmosphere with a venomous influence
hostile to human life. The door now very slowly and
quietly opened as of its own accord. We precipitat-
ed ourselves into the landing-place. We both saw a
large, pale light—as large as the human figure, but
shapeless and unsubstantial—move before us, and
ascend the stairs that led from the landing into the
attics. I followed the light, and my servant followed
me. It entered, to the right of the landing, a small
garret, of which the door stood open. I entered in
the same instant. The light then collapsed into a
small globule, exceedingly brilliant and vivid, rested
a moment on a bed in the corner, quivered, and vanished. We approached the bed and examined it—a
half-tester, such as is commonly found in attics devoted to servants. On the drawers that stood near
it we perceived an old faded silk kerchief, with the

needle still left in a rent half repaired. The kerchief was covered with dust; probably it had belonged to the old woman who had last died in that house, and this might have been her sleeping-room. I had sufficient curiosity to open the drawers: there were a few odds and ends of female dress, and two letters tied round with a narrow ribbon of faded yellow. I took the liberty to possess myself of the letters. We found nothing else in the room worth noticing— nor did the light reappear; but we distinctly heard, as we turned to go, a pattering footfall on the floor, just before us. We went through the other attics (in all four), the footfall still preceding us. Nothing to be seen—nothing but the footfall heard. I had the letters in my hand; just as I was descending the stairs I distinctly felt my wrist seized, and a faint, soft effort made to draw the letters from my clasp. I only held them the more tightly, and the effort ceased.

We regained the bedchamber appropriated to myself, and I then remarked that my dog had not followed us when we had left it. He was thrusting himself close to the fire, and trembling. I was impatient to examine the letters; and while I read them, my servant opened a little box in which he had deposited the weapons I had ordered him to bring, took them out, placed them on a table close at my bedhead, and then occupied himself in soothing the dog, who, however, seemed to heed him very little.

The letters were short—they were dated; the dates exactly thirty-five years ago. They were evidently from a lover to his mistress, or a husband to some young wife. Not only the terms of expression, but a distinct reference to a former voyage, indicated the writer to have been a seafarer. The spelling and handwriting were those of a man imperfectly educated, but still the language itself was forcible. In the expressions of endearment there was a kind of rough, wild love; but here and there were dark unintelligible hints at some secret not of love— some secret that seemed of crime. "We ought to love each other," was one of the sentences I remember, "for how every one else would execrate us if all was known." Again: "Don't let any one be in the same room with you at night—you talk in your sleep." And again: "What's done can't be undone; and I tell you there's nothing against us unless the dead could come to life." Here there was underlined in a better handwriting (a female's), "They do!" At the end of the letter latest in date the same female hand had written these words: "Lost at sea the 4th of June, the same day as —"

I put down the letters, and began to muse over their contents.

Fearing, however, that the train of thought into which I fell might unsteady my nerves, I fully determined to keep my mind in a fit state to cope with whatever of marvellous the advancing night might bring forth. I roused myself; laid the letters on the table; stirred up the fire, which was still bright and cheering; and opened my volume of Macaulay. I read quietly enough till about half-past eleven. I then threw myself dressed upon the bed, and told my servant he might retire to his own room, but must keep himself awake. I bade him leave open the door between the two rooms. Thus alone, I kept two candles burning on the table by my bed-head. I placed my watch beside the weapons, and calmly resumed my Macaulay. Opposite to me the fire burned clear; and on the hearthrug, seemingly asleep, lay the dog. In about twenty minutes I felt an exceedingly cold air pass by my cheek, like a sudden draught. I fancied the door to my right, communicating with the landing-place, must have got open; but no—it was closed. I then turned my glance to my left, and saw the flame of the candles violently swayed as by a wind. At the same moment the watch beside the revolver softly slid from the table—softly, softly; no visible hand—it was gone. I sprang up, seizing the revolver with the one hand, the dagger with the other; I was not willing that my weapons should share the fate of the watch. Thus armed, I looked round the floor—no sign of the watch. Three slow, loud, distinct knocks were now heard at the bed-head; my servant called out, "Is that you, sir?"

"No; be on your guard."

The dog now roused himself and sat on his haunches, his ears moving quickly backwards and forwards. He kept his eyes fixed on me with a look so strange that he concentrated all my attention on himself. Slowly he rose up, all his hair bristling, and stood perfectly rigid, and with the same wild stare. I had no time, however, to examine the dog. Presently my servant emerged from his room; and if ever I saw horror in the human face, it was then. I should not have recognized him had we met in the street, so altered was every lineament. He passed by me quickly, saying, in a whisper that seemed scarcely to come from his lips, "Run, run! it is after me!" He gained the door to the landing, pulled it open, and rushed forth. I followed him into the landing involuntarily, calling him to stop; but, without heeding me, he bounded down the stairs, clinging to the balusters, and taking several steps at a time. I heard, where I stood, the street-door open—heard it again clap to. I was left alone in the haunted house.

It was but for a moment that I remained undecided whether or not to follow my servant; pride and curiosity alike forbade so dastardly a flight. I re-entered my room, closing the door after me, and proceeded cautiously into the interior chamber. I encountered nothing to justify my servant's terror. I again carefully examined the walls, to see if there were any concealed door. I could find no trace of one—not even a seam in the dull-brown paper with which the room was hung. How, then, had the THING, whatever it was, which had so scared him, obtained ingress except through my own chamber?

I returned to my room, shut and locked the door that opened upon the interior one, and stood on the hearth, expectant and prepared. I now perceived that the dog had slunk into an angle of the wall, and was pressing himself close against it, as if literally striving to force his way into it. I approached the animal and spoke to it; the poor brute was evidently beside itself with terror. It showed all its teeth, the slaver dropping from its jaws, and would certainly have bitten me if I had touched it. It did not seem to recognize me. Whoever has seen at the Zoological Gardens a rabbit, fascinated by a serpent, cowering in a corner, may form some idea of the anguish which the dog exhibited. Finding all efforts to soothe the animal in vain, and fearing that his bite might be as venomous in that state as in the madness of hydrophobia, I left him alone, placed my weapons on the table beside the fire, seated myself, and recommenced my Macaulay.

Perhaps, in order not to appear seeking credit for a courage, or rather a coolness, which the reader may conceive I exaggerate, I may be pardoned if I pause to indulge in one or two egotistical remarks.

As I hold presence of mind, or what is called courage, to be precisely proportioned to familiarity with the circumstances that lead to it, so I should say that I had been long sufficiently familiar with all experiments that appertain to the marvellous. I had witnessed many very extraordinary phenomena in various parts of the world—phenomena that would be either totally disbelieved if I stated them, or ascribed to supernatural agencies. Now, my theory is that the supernatural is the impossible, and that what is called supernatural is only a something in the laws of Nature of which we have been hitherto ignorant. Therefore, if a ghost rise before me, I have not the right to say, "So, then, the supernatural is possible;" but rather, "So, then, the apparition of a ghost, is, contrary to received opinion, within the laws of Nature—that is, not supernatural."

Now, in all that I had hitherto witnessed, and indeed in all the wonders which the amateurs of mystery in our age record as facts, a material living agency is always required. On the Continent you will find still magicians who assert that they can raise spirits. Assume for the moment that they assert truly, still the living material form of the magician is present; and he is the material agency by which, from some constitutional peculiarities, certain strange phenomena are represented to your natural senses.

Accept, again, as truthful, the tales of spirit-manifestation in America—musical or other sounds; writings on paper, produced by no discernible hand;

articles of furniture moved without apparent human agency; or the actual sight and touch of hands, to which no bodies seem to belong—still there must be found the MEDIUM, or living being, with constitutional peculiarities capable of obtaining these signs. In fine, in all such marvels, supposing even that there is no imposture, there must be a human being like ourselves by whom, or through whom, the effects presented to human beings are produced. It is so with the now familiar phenomena of mesmerism or electro-biology; the mind of the person operated on is affected through a material living agent. Nor, supposing it true that a mesmerized patient can respond to the will or passes of a mesmerizer a hundred miles distant, is the response less occasioned by a material being; it may be through a material fluid—call it Electric, call it Odic, call it what you will—which has the power of traversing space and passing obstacles, that the material effect is communicated from one to the other. Hence, all that I had hitherto witnessed, or expected to witness, in this strange house, I believed to be occasioned through some agency or medium as mortal as myself; and this idea necessarily prevented the awe with which those who regard as supernatural things that are not within the ordinary operations of Nature, might have been impressed by the adventures of that memorable night.

As, then, it was my conjecture that all that was presented, or would be presented to my senses, must originate in some human being gifted by constitution with the power so to present them, and having some motive so to do, I felt an interest in my theory which, in its way, was rather philosophical than superstitious. And I can sincerely say that I was in as tranquil a temper for observation as any practical experimentalist could be in awaiting the effects of some rare, though perhaps perilous, chemical combination. Of course, the more I kept my mind detached from fancy, the more the temper fitted for observation would be obtained; and I therefore riveted eye and thought on the strong daylight sense in the page of my Macaulay.

I now became aware that something interposed between the page and the light—the page was over-shadowed. I looked up, and I saw what I shall find it very difficult, perhaps impossible, to describe.

It was a Darkness shaping itself forth from the air in very undefined outline. I cannot say it was of a human form, and yet it had more resemblance to a human form, or rather shadow, than to anything else. As it stood, wholly apart and distinct from the air and the light around it, its dimensions seemed gigantic, the summit nearly touching the ceiling. While I gazed, a feeling of intense cold seized me. An iceberg before me could not more have chilled me; nor could the cold of an iceberg have been more purely physical. I feel convinced that it was not the cold caused by fear. As I continued to gaze, I thought—but this I cannot say with precision—that I distinguished two eyes looking down on me from the height. One moment I fancied that I distinguished them clearly, the next they seemed gone; but still two rays of a pale-blue light frequently shot through the darkness, as from the height on which I half believed, half doubted, that I had encountered the eyes.

I strove to speak—my voice utterly failed me; I could only think to myself, "Is this fear? It is *not* fear!" I strove to rise—in vain; I felt as if weighed down by an irresistible force. Indeed, my impression was that of an immense and overwhelming Power opposed to my volition—that sense of utter inadequacy to cope with a force beyond man's, which one may feel *physically* in a storm at sea, in a conflagration, or when confronting some terrible wild beast, or rather, perhaps, the shark of the ocean, I felt *morally*. Opposed to my will was another will, as far superior to its strength as storm, fire, and shark are superior in material force to the force of man.

And now, as this impression grew on me—now came, at last, horror, horror to a degree that no words can convey. Still I retained pride, if not courage; and in my own mind I said, "This is horror, but it is not fear; unless I fear I cannot be harmed; my reason rejects this thing; it is an illusion—I do not fear." With a violent effort I succeeded at last in stretching out my hand towards the weapon on the table; as I did so, on the arm and shoulder I received a strange shock, and my arm fell to my side powerless. And now, to add to my horror, the light began slowly to wane from the candles—they were not, as it were, extinguished, but their flame seemed very gradually withdrawn; it was the same with the fire—the light was extracted from the fuel; in a few minutes the room was in utter darkness. The dread that came over me, to be thus in the dark with that dark Thing, whose power was so intensely felt, brought a reaction of nerve. In fact, terror had reached that climax, that either my senses must have deserted me, or I must have burst through the spell. I did burst through it. I found voice, though the voice was a shriek. I remember that I broke forth with words like these, "I do not fear, my soul does not fear;" and at the same time I found strength to rise. Still in that profound gloom I rushed to one of the windows; tore aside the curtain; flung open the shutters; my first thought was—LIGHT. And when I saw the moon high, clear, and calm, I felt a joy that almost compensated for the previous terror. There was the moon, there was also the light from the gas-lamps in the deserted slumberous street. I turned to look back into the room; the moon penetrated its shadow very palely and partially—but still there was light. The dark Thing, whatever it might be, was gone—except that I could yet see a dim shadow, which seemed the shadow of that shade, against the opposite wall.

My eye now rested on the table, and from under the table (which was without cloth or cover—an old mahogany round-table) there rose a hand, visible as far as the wrist. It was a hand, seemingly, as much of flesh and blood as my own, but the hand of an aged person, lean, wrinkled, small too—a woman's hand. That hand very softly closed on the two letters that lay on the table; hand and letters both vanished. There then came the same three loud, measured knocks I had heard at the bedhead before this extraordinary drama had commenced.

As those sounds slowly ceased, I felt the whole room vibrate sensibly; and at the far end there rose, as from the floor, sparks or globules like bubbles of light, many colored—green, yellow, fire-red, azure. Up and down, to and fro, hither, thither, as tiny Will-o'-the-Wisps, the sparks moved, slow or swift, each at its own caprice. A chair (as in the drawing-room below) was now advanced from the wall without apparent agency, and placed at the opposite side of the table. Suddenly, as forth from the chair, there grew a shape—a woman's shape. It was distinct as a shape of life—ghastly as a shape of death. The face was that of youth, with a strange, mournful beauty; the throat and shoulders were bare, the rest of the form in a loose robe of cloudy white. It began sleeking its long, yellow hair, which fell over its shoulders; its eyes were not turned towards me, but to the door; it seemed listening, watching, waiting. The shadow of the shade in the background grew darker; and again I thought I beheld the eyes gleaming out from the summit of the shadow—eyes fixed upon that shape.

As if from the door, though it did not open, there grew out another shape, equally distinct, equally ghastly—a man's shape, a young man's. It was in the dress of the last century, or rather in a likeness of such dress (for both the male shape and the female, though defined, were evidently unsubstantial, impalpable—simulacra, phantasms); and there was something incongruous, grotesque, yet fearful, in the contrast between the elaborate finery, the courtly precision of that old-fashioned garb, with its ruffles and lace and buckles, and the corpse-like aspect and ghost-like stillness of the flitting wearer. Just as the male shape approached the female, the dark Shadow started from the wall, all three for a moment wrapped in darkness. When the pale light returned, the two phantoms were as if in the grasp of the Shadow that towered between them; and there was a blood-stain on the breast of the female; and the phantom male was leaning on its phantom sword, and blood seemed trickling fast from the ruffles, from the lace; and the darkness of the intermediate Shadow swallowed them up—they were gone. And again the bubbles of light shot, and sailed, and undulated, growing thicker and thicker and more wildly confused in their movements.

The closet door to the right of the fireplace now opened, and from the aperture there came the form of an aged woman. In her hand she held letters—the very letters over which I had seen *the* Hand close; and behind her I heard a footstep. She turned round as if to listen, and then she opened the letters and seemed to read; and over her shoulder I saw a livid face, the face as of a man long drowned—bloated, bleached, seaweed tangled in its dripping hair; and at her feet lay a form as of a corpse; and beside the corpse there cowered a child, a miserable, squalid child, with famine in its cheeks and fear in its eyes. And as I looked in the old woman's face, the wrinkles and lines vanished, and it became a face of youth—hard-eyed, stony, but still youth; and the Shadow darted forth, and darkened over these phantoms as it had darkened over the last.

Nothing now was left but the Shadow, and on that my eyes were intently fixed, till again eyes grew out of the Shadow—malignant, serpent eyes. And the bubbles of light again rose and fell, and in their disordered, irregular, turbulent maze, mingled with the wan moonlight. And now from these globules themselves, as from the shell of an egg, monstrous things burst out; the air grew filled with them: larvae so bloodless and so hideous that I can in no way describe them except to remind the reader of the swarming life which the solar microscope brings before his eyes in a drop of water—things transparent, supple, agile, chasing each other, devouring each, other; forms like nought ever beheld by the naked eye. As the shapes were without symmetry, so their movements were without order. In their very vagrancies there was no sport; they came round me and round, thicker and faster and swifter, swarming over my head, crawling over my right arm, which was outstretched in involuntary command against all evil beings. Sometimes I felt myself touched, but not by them; invisible hands touched me. Once I felt the clutch as of cold, soft fingers at my throat. I was still equally conscious that if I gave way to fear I should be in bodily peril; and I concentrated all my faculties in the single focus of resisting stubborn will. And I turned my sight from the Shadow; above all, from those strange serpent eyes—eyes that had now become distinctly visible. For there, though in nought else around me, I was aware that there was a WILL, and a will of intense, creative, working evil, which might crush down my own.

The pale atmosphere in the room began now to redden as if in the air of some near conflagration. The larvæ grew lurid as things that live in fire. Again the room vibrated; again were heard the three measured knocks; and again all things were swallowed up in the darkness of the dark Shadow, as if out of that darkness all had come, into that darkness all returned.

As the gloom receded, the Shadow was wholly gone. Slowly, as it had been withdrawn, the flame grew again into the candles on the table, again into the fuel in the grate. The whole room came once more calmly, healthfully into sight.

The two doors were still closed, the door communicating with the servant's room still locked. In the corner of the wall, into which he had so convulsively niched himself, lay the dog. I called to him—no movement; I approached—the animal was dead: his eyes protruded; his tongue out of his mouth; the froth gathered round his jaws. I took him in my arms; I brought him to the fire. I felt acute grief for the loss of my poor favorite—acute self-reproach; I accused myself of his death; I imagined he had died of fright. But what was my surprise on finding that his neck was actually broken. Had this been done in the dark? Must it not have been by a hand human as mine; must there not have been a human agency all the while in that room? Good cause to suspect it. I cannot tell. I cannot do more than state the fact fairly; the reader may draw his own inference.

Another surprising circumstance—my watch was restored to the table from which it had been so mysteriously withdrawn; but it had stopped at the very moment it was so withdrawn, nor, despite all the skill of the watchmaker, has it ever gone since— that is, it will go in a strange, erratic way for a few hours, and then come to a dead stop; it is worthless.

Nothing more chanced for the rest of the night. Nor, indeed, had I long to wait before the dawn broke. Nor till it was broad daylight did I quit the haunted house. Before I did so, I revisited the little blind room in which my servant and myself had been for a time imprisoned. I had a strong impression— for which I could not account—that from that room had originated the mechanism of the phenomena, if I may use the term, which had been experienced in my chamber. And though I entered it now in the clear day, with the sun peering through the filmy window, I still felt, as I stood on its floors, the creep of the horror which I had first there experienced the night before, and which had been so aggravated by what had passed in my own chamber. I could not, indeed, bear to stay more than half a minute within those walls. I descended the stairs, and again I heard the footfall before me; and when I opened the street door, I thought I could distinguish a very low laugh. I gained my own home, expecting to find my run-away servant there; but he had not presented himself, nor did I hear more of him for three days, when I received a letter from him, dated from Liverpool to this effect:—

"HONORED SIR—I humbly entreat your pardon, though I can scarcely hope that you will think that I deserve it, unless—which Heaven forbid!—you saw what I did. I feel that it will be years before I can recover myself; and as to being fit for service, it is out of the question. I am therefore going to my brother-in-law at Melbourne. The ship sails tomorrow. Perhaps the long voyage may set me up. I do nothing now but start and tremble, and fancy It is behind me. I humbly beg you, honored sir, to order my clothes, and whatever wages are due to me, to be sent to my mother's, at Walworth—John knows her address."

The letter ended with additional apologies, somewhat incoherent, and explanatory details as to effects that had been under the writer's charge. This flight may perhaps warrant a suspicion that the man wished to go to Australia, and had been somehow or other fraudulently mixed up with the events of the night. I say nothing in refutation of that conjecture; rather, I suggest it as one that would seem to many persons the most probable solution of improbable occurrences. My belief in my own theory remained unshaken. I returned in the evening to the house, to bring away in a hack cab the things I had left there, with my poor dog's body. In this task I was not disturbed, nor did any incident worth note befall me, except that still, on ascending and descending the stairs, I heard the same footfall in advance. On leaving the house, I went to Mr. J—'s. He was at home. I returned him the keys, told him that my curiosity was sufficiently gratified, and was about to relate quickly what had passed, when he stopped me, and said, though with much politeness, that he had no

longer any interest in a mystery which none had
ever solved.

I determined at least to tell him of the two letters
I had read, as well as of the extraordinary manner in
which they had disappeared; and I then inquired if
he thought they had been addressed to the woman
who had died in the house, and if there were anything in her early history which could possibly confirm the dark suspicions to which the letters gave
rise. Mr. J— seemed startled, and, after musing a
few moments, answered, "I am but little acquainted
with the woman's earlier history, except as I before
told you, that her family were known to mine. But
you revive some vague reminiscences to her prejudice.
I will make inquiries, and inform you of their result.
Still, even if we could admit the popular superstition
that a person who had been either the perpetrator
or the victim of dark crimes in life could revisit, as
a restless spirit, the scene in which those crimes had
been committed, I should observe that the house was
infested by strange sights and sounds before the old
woman died—you smile—what would you say?"

"I would say this, that I am convinced, if we could
get to the bottom of these mysteries, we should find
a living human agency."

"What! you believe it is all an imposture? For
what object?"

"Not an imposture in the ordinary sense of the
word. If suddenly I were to sink into a deep sleep,

from which you could not awake me, but in that sleep could answer questions with an accuracy which I could not pretend to when awake—tell you what money you had in your pocket, nay, describe your very thoughts—it is not necessarily an imposture, any more than it is necessarily supernatural. I should be, unconsciously to myself, under a mesmeric influence, conveyed to me from a distance by a human being who had acquired power over me by previous *rapport*!"

"Granting mesmerism, so far carried, to be a fact, you are right. And you would infer from this that a mesmerizer might produce the extraordinary effects you and others have witnessed over inanimate objects—fill the air with sights and sounds?"

"Or impress our senses with the belief in such effects—we never having been *en rapport* with the person acting on us? No. What is commonly called mesmerism could not do this; but there may be a power akin to mesmerism, and superior to it—the power that in the old days was called Magic. That such a power may extend to all inanimate objects of matter, I do not say; but if so, it would not be against Nature—it would be only a rare power in Nature which might be given to constitutions with certain peculiarities, and cultivated by practice to an extraordinary degree. That such a power might extend over the dead—that is, over certain thoughts and memories that the dead may still retain—and

compel, not that which ought properly to be called
the SOUL, and which is far beyond human reach,
but rather a phantom of what has been most earth-
stained on earth, to make itself apparent to our
senses, is a very ancient though obsolete theory
upon which I will hazard no opinion. But I do not
conceive the power would be supernatural. Let me
illustrate what I mean from an experiment which
Paracelsus describes as not difficult, and which the
author of the *Curiosities of Literature* cites as credible: A flower perishes; you burn it. Whatever were
the elements of that flower while it lived are gone,
dispersed, you know not whither; you can never discover nor re-collect them. But you can, by chemistry, out of the burned dust of that flower, raise a
spectrum of the flower, just as it seemed in life. It
may be the same with the human being. The soul has
as much escaped you as the essence or elements of
the flower. Still you may make a spectrum of it. And
this phantom, though in the popular superstition it
is held to be the soul of the departed, must not be
confounded with the true soul; it is but the eidolon
of the dead form. Hence, like the best attested stories of ghosts or spirits, the thing that most strikes
us is the absence of what we hold to be soul—that
is, of superior emancipated intelligence. These ap-
paritions come for little or no object—they seldom
speak when they do come; if they speak, they utter no ideas above those of an ordinary person on

earth. American spirit-seers have published volumes of communications, in prose and verse, which they assert to be given in the names of the most illustrious dead: Shakespeare, Bacon—Heaven knows whom. Those communications, taking the best, are certainly not a whit of higher order than would be communications from living persons of fair talent and education; they are wondrously inferior to what Bacon, Shakespeare, and Plato said and wrote when on earth. Nor, what is more noticeable, do they ever contain an idea that was not on the earth before. Wonderful, therefore, as such phenomena may be (granting them to be truthful), I see much that philosophy may question, nothing that it is incumbent on philosophy to deny—namely, nothing supernatural. They are but ideas conveyed somehow or other (we have not yet discovered the means) from one mortal brain to another. Whether, in so doing, tables walk of their own accord, or fiendlike shapes appear in a magic circle, or bodiless hands rise and remove material objects, or a Thing of Darkness, such as presented itself to me, freeze our blood—still am I persuaded that these are but agencies conveyed, as by electric wires, to my own brain from the brain of another. In some constitutions there is a natural chemistry, and those constitutions may produce chemic wonders—in others a natural fluid, call it electricity, and these may produce electric wonders. But the wonders differ from Normal Science

in this—they are alike objectless, purposeless, puerile, frivolous. They lead on to no grand results; and
therefore the world does not heed, and true sages
have not cultivated them. But sure I am, that of all
I saw or heard, a man, human as myself, was the
remote originator; and I believe unconsciously to
himself as to the exact effects produced, for this
reason: no two persons, you say, have ever told you
that they experienced exactly the same thing. Well,
observe, no two persons ever experience exactly the
same dream. If this were an ordinary imposture, the
machinery would be arranged for results that would
but little vary; if it were a supernatural agency permitted by the Almighty, it would surely be for some
definite end. These phenomena belong to neither
class; my persuasion is, that they originate in some
brain now far distant; that that brain had no distinct
volition in anything that occurred; that what does
occur reflects but its devious, motley, ever-shifting,
half-formed thoughts; in short, that it has been but
the dreams of such a brain put into action and in-
vested with a semi-substance. That this brain is of
immense power, that it can set matter into movement, that it is malignant and destructive, I believe;
some material force must have killed my dog; the
same force might, for aught I know, have sufficed
to kill myself, had I been as subjugated by terror as
the dog—had my intellect or my spirit given me no
countervailing resistance in my will."

"It killed your dog—that is fearful! Indeed it is strange that no animal can be induced to stay in that house; not even a cat. Rats and mice are never found in it."

"The instincts of the brute creation detect influences deadly to their existence. Man's reason has a sense less subtle, because it has a resisting power more supreme. But enough; do you comprehend my theory?"

"Yes, though imperfectly—and I accept any crotchet (pardon the word), however odd, rather than embrace at once the notion of ghosts and hobgoblins we imbibed in our nurseries. Still, to my unfortunate house, the evil is the same. What on earth can I do with the house?"

"I will tell you what I would do. I am convinced from my own internal feelings that the small, unfurnished room at right angles to the door of the bed-room which I occupied, forms a starting-point or receptacle for the influences which haunt the house; and I strongly advise you to have the walls opened, the floor removed—nay, the whole room pulled down. I observe that it is detached from the body of the house, built over the small backyard, and could be removed without injury to the rest of the building."

"And you think, if I did that—"

"You would cut off the telegraph wires. Try it. I am so persuaded that I am right, that I will pay half

the expense if you will allow me to direct the operations."

"Nay, I am well able to afford the cost; for the
rest allow me to write to you."

About ten days after I received a letter from
Mr. J— telling me that he had visited the house
since I had seen him; that he had found the two letters
I had described, replaced in the drawer from which
I had taken them; that he had read them with mis-
givings like my own; that he had instituted a cautious inquiry about the woman to whom I rightly
conjectured they had been written. It seemed that
thirty-six years ago (a year before the date of the
letters) she had married, against the wish of her relations, an American of very suspicious character;
in fact, he was generally believed to have been a
pirate. She herself was the daughter of very respectable tradespeople, and had served in the capacity of
a nursery governess before her marriage. She had a
brother, a widower, who was considered wealthy, and
who had one child of about six years old. A month
after the marriage the body of this brother was found
in the Thames, near London Bridge; there seemed
some marks of violence about his throat, but they
were not deemed sufficient to warrant the inquest
in any other verdict than that of "found drowned."

The American and his wife took charge of the
little boy, the deceased brother having by his will
left his sister the guardian of his only child—and in

event of the child's death the sister inherited. The child died about six months afterwards—it was supposed to have been neglected and ill-treated. The neighbors deposed to have heard it shriek at night. The surgeon who had examined it after death said that it was emaciated as if from want of nourishment, and the body was covered with livid bruises. It seemed that one winter night the child had sought to escape; crept out into the backyard; tried to scale the wall; fallen back exhausted; and been found at morning on the stones in a dying state. But though there was some evidence of cruelty, there was none of murder; and the aunt and her husband had sought to palliate cruelty by alleging the exceeding stubbornness and perversity of the child, who was declared to be half-witted. Be that as it may, at the orphan's death the aunt inherited her brother's fortune. Before the first wedded year was out, the American quitted England abruptly, and never returned to it. He obtained a cruising vessel, which was lost in the Atlantic two years afterwards. The widow was left in affluence, but reverses of various kinds had befallen her: a bank broke; an investment failed; she went into a small business and became insolvent; then she entered into service, sinking lower and lower, from housekeeper down to maid-of-all-work—never long retaining a place, though nothing decided against her character was ever alleged. She was considered sober, honest, and peculiarly quiet in her ways; still nothing prospered with her. And so she had dropped into the workhouse, from which Mr. J— had taken her, to be placed in charge of the very house which she had rented as mistress in the first year of her wedded life.

Mr. J— added that he had passed an hour alone in the unfurnished room which I had urged him to destroy, and that his impressions of dread while there were so great, though he had neither heard nor seen anything, that he was eager to have the walls bared and the floors removed as I had suggested. He had engaged persons for the work, and would commence any day I would name.

The day was accordingly fixed. I repaired to the haunted house—we went into the blind, dreary room, took up the skirting, and then the floors. Under the rafters, covered with rubbish, was found a trap-door, quite large enough to admit a man. It was closely nailed down, with clamps and rivets of iron. On removing these we descended into a room below, the existence of which had never been suspected. In this room there had been a window and a flue, but they had been bricked over, evidently for many years. By the help of candles we examined this place; it still retained some mouldering furniture—three chairs, an oak settle, a table—all of the fashion of about eighty years ago. There was a chest of drawers against the wall, in which we found, half-rotted away, old-fashioned articles of a man's dress, such as might have been worn eighty or a hundred years ago by a gentleman of some rank; costly steel buckles and buttons, like those yet worn in court-dresses, a handsome court sword; in a waistcoat which had once been rich with gold-lace, but which was now blackened and foul with damp, we found five guineas, a few silver coins, and an ivory ticket, probably for some place of entertainment long since passed away. But our main discovery was in a kind of iron safe fixed to the wall, the lock of which it cost us much trouble to get picked.

In this safe were three shelves and two small drawers. Ranged on the shelves were several small bottles of crystal, hermetically stopped. They contained colorless, volatile essences, of the nature of which I shall only say that they were not poisons—phosphor and ammonia entered into some of them. There were also some very curious glass tubes, and a small pointed rod of iron, with a large lump of rock-crystal, and another of amber—also a loadstone of great power.

In one of the drawers we found a miniature portrait set in gold, and retaining the freshness of its colors most remarkably, considering the length of time it had probably been there. The portrait was that of a man who might be somewhat advanced in middle life, perhaps forty-seven or forty-eight. It was a remarkable face—a most impressive face. If you could fancy some mighty serpent transformed

into man, preserving in the human lineaments the
old serpent type, you would have a better idea of that
countenance than long descriptions can convey: the
width and flatness of frontal; the tapering elegance
of contour disguising the strength of the deadly jaw;
the long, large, terrible eye, glittering and green as
the emerald—and withal a certain ruthless calm, as
if from the consciousness of an immense power. The
strange thing was this—the instant I saw the miniature I recognized a startling likeness to one of the
rarest portraits in the world—the portrait of a man
of rank only below that of royalty, who in his own
day had made a considerable noise. History says
little or nothing of him; but search the correspondence of his contemporaries, and you find reference
to his wild daring, his bold profligacy, his restless
spirit, his taste for the occult sciences. While still in
the meridian of life he died and was buried, so say
the chronicles, in a foreign land. He died in time
to escape the grasp of the law, for he was accused of
crimes which would have given him to the heads-
man. After his death, the portraits of him, which
had been numerous, for he had been a munificent
encourager of art, were bought up and destroyed—
it was supposed by his heirs, who might have been
glad could they have razed his very name from their
splendid line. He had enjoyed a vast wealth; a large
portion of this was believed to have been embez-
zled by a favourite astrologer or soothsayer—at all

events, it had unaccountably vanished at the time of his death. One portrait alone of him was supposed to have escaped the general destruction; I had seen it in the house of a collector some months before. It had made on me a wonderful impression, as it does on all who behold it—a face never to be forgotten; and there was that face in the miniature that lay within my hand. True, that in the miniature the man was a few years older than in the portrait I had seen, or than the original was even at the time of his death. But a few years!—why, between the date in which flourished that direful noble and the date in which the miniature was evidently painted, there was an interval of more than two centuries. While I was thus gazing, silent and wondering, Mr. J— said,

"But is it possible! I have known this man."

"How—where!" cried I.

"In India. He was high in the confidence of the Rajah of —, and well-nigh drew him into a revolt which would have lost the Rajah his dominions. The man was a Frenchman— his name de V—, clever, bold, lawless. We insisted on his dismissal and banishment: it must be the same man—no two faces like his—yet this miniature seems nearly a hundred years old."

Mechanically I turned round the miniature to examine the back of it, and on the back was engraved a pentacle; in the middle of the pentacle a ladder, and the third step of the ladder was formed by the

date 1765. Examining still more minutely, I detected a spring; this, on being pressed, opened the back
of the miniature as a lid. Within-side the lid were
engraved, "Marianna to thee—Be faithful in life and
in death to —." Here follows a name that I will not
mention, but it was not unfamiliar to me. I had
heard it spoken of by old men in my childhood as
the name borne by a dazzling charlatan who had
made a great sensation in London for a year or so,
and had fled the country on the charge of a double
murder within his own house—that of his mistress
and his rival. I said nothing of this to Mr. J— to
whom reluctantly I resigned the miniature.

We had found no difficulty in opening the first
drawer within the iron safe; we found great difficulty in opening the second: it was not locked, but
it resisted all efforts, till we inserted in the chinks
the edge of a chisel. When we had thus drawn it
forth, we found a very singular apparatus in the nic-
est order. Upon a small, thin book, or rather tablet,
was placed a saucer of crystal; this saucer was filled
with a clear liquid—on that liquid floated a kind of
compass, with a needle shifting rapidly round; but
instead of the usual points of a compass were seven
strange characters, not very unlike those used by
astrologers to denote the planets. A peculiar but not
strong nor displeasing odor came from this drawer, which was lined with a wood that we afterwards
discovered to be hazel. Whatever the cause of this

odor, it produced a material effect on the nerves. We all felt it, even the two workmen who were in the room—a creeping, tingling sensation from the tips of the fingers to the roots of the hair. Impatient to examine the tablet, I removed the saucer. As I did so the needle of the compass went round and round with exceeding swiftness, and I felt a shock that ran through my whole frame, so that I dropped the saucer on the floor. The liquid was spilled; the saucer was broken; the compass rolled to the end of the room, and at that instant the walls shook to and fro, as if a giant had swayed and rocked them.

The two workmen were so frightened that they ran up the ladder by which we had descended from the trapdoor; but seeing that nothing more happened, they were easily induced to return.

Meanwhile I had opened the tablet: it was bound in plain red leather, with a silver clasp; it contained but one sheet of thick vellum, and on that sheet were inscribed, within a double pentacle, words in old monkish Latin, which are literally to be translated thus: "On all that it can reach within these walls, sentient or inanimate, living or dead, as moves the needle, so work my will! Accursed be the house, and restless be the dwellers therein."

We found no more. Mr. J— burned the tablet and its anathema. He razed to the foundations the part of the building containing the secret room with the chamber over it. He had then the courage to inhabit the house himself for a month, and a quieter, better-conditioned house could not be found in all London. Subsequently he let it to advantage, and his tenant has made no complaints.

But my story is not yet done. A few days after Mr. J— had removed into the house, I paid him a visit. We were standing by the open window and conversing. A van containing some articles of furniture which he was moving from his former house was at the door.

I had just urged on him my theory that all those phenomena regarded as supermundane had emanated from a human brain; adducing the charm, or rather curse we had found and destroyed, in support of my theory. Mr. J— was observing in reply, "That even if mesmerism, or whatever analogous power it might be called, could really thus work in the absence of the operator, and produce effects so extraordinary, still could those effects continue when the operator himself was dead? and if the spell had been wrought, and, indeed, the room walled up, more than seventy years ago, the probability was that the operator had long since departed this life;" Mr. J—, I say, was thus answering, when I caught hold of his arm and pointed to the street below.

A well-dressed man had crossed from the opposite side, and was accosting the carrier in charge of the van. His face, as he stood, was exactly fronting our window. It was the face of the miniature we had discovered; it was the face of the portrait of the noble three centuries ago.

"Good heavens!" cried Mr. J—; "that is the face of de V—, and scarcely a day older than when I saw it in the Rajah's court in my youth!"

Seized by the same thought, we both hastened down-stairs; I was first in the street, but the man had already gone. I caught sight of him, however, not many yards in advance, and in another moment I was by his side.

I had resolved to speak to him, but when I looked into his face I felt as if it were impossible to do so. That eye—the eye of the serpent—fixed and held me spellbound. And withal, about the man's whole person there was a dignity, an air of pride and station and superiority that would have made any one, habituated to the usages of the world, hesitate long before venturing upon a liberty or impertinence. And what could I say? What was it I could ask? Thus ashamed of my first impulse, I fell a few paces back, still, however, following the stranger, undecided what else to do. Meanwhile he turned the corner of the street; a plain carriage was in waiting with a servant out of livery, dressed like a *valet de place,* at the carriage door. In another moment he had stepped into the carriage, and it drove off. I returned to the house. Mr. J— was still at the street-door. He had asked the carrier what the stranger had said to him.

"Merely asked whom that house now belonged to."

The same evening I happened to go with a friend to a place in town called the Cosmopolitan Club, a place open to men of all countries, all opinions, all degrees. One orders one's coffee, smokes one's cigar. One is always sure to meet agreeable, sometimes remarkable persons.

I had not been two minutes in the room before I beheld at table, conversing with an acquaintance of mine, whom I will designate by the initial G— the man, the original of the miniature. He was now without his hat, and the likeness was yet more startling, only I observed that while he was conversing there was less severity in the countenance; there was even a smile, though a very quiet and very cold one. The dignity of mien I had acknowledged in the street was also more striking; a dignity akin to that which invests some prince of the East, conveying the idea of supreme indifference and habitual, indisputable, indolent but resistless power.

G— soon after left the stranger, who then took up a scientific journal, which seemed to absorb his attention.

I drew G— aside. "Who and what is that gentleman?"

"That? Oh, a very remarkable man indeed! I met him last year amid the caves of Petra, the scriptural Edom. He is the best Oriental scholar I know. We joined company, had an adventure with robbers, in which he showed a coolness that saved our lives; afterward he invited me to spend a day with him in a house he had bought at Damascus, buried among almond-blossoms and roses—the most beautiful thing! He had lived there for some time, quite as an Oriental, in grand style. I half suspect he is a renegade, immensely rich, very odd; by the by, a great mesmerizer. I have seen him with my own eyes produce an effect on inanimate things. If you take a letter from your pocket and throw it to the other end of the room, he will order it to come to his feet, and you will see the letter wriggle itself along the floor till it has obeyed his command. 'Pon my honor 'tis true; I have seen him affect even the weather, disperse or collect clouds by means of a glass tube or wand. But he does not like talking of these matters to strangers. He has only just arrived in England; says he has not been here for a great many years; let me introduce him to you."

"Certainly! He is English, then? What is his name?"

"Oh! a very homely one—Richards."

"And what is his birth—his family?"

"How do I know? What does it signify? No doubt some *parvenuc;* but rich, so infernally rich!"

G— drew me up to the stranger, and the introduction was effected. The manners of Mr. Richards were not those of an adventurous traveler. Travelers

are in general gifted with high animal spirits; they
are talkative, eager, imperious. Mr. Richards was
calm and subdued in tone, with manners which were
made distant by the loftiness of punctilious courtesy, the manners of a former age. I observed that
the English he spoke was not exactly of our day. I
should even have said that the accent was slightly
foreign. But then Mr. Richards remarked that he
had been little in the habit for years of speaking
in his native tongue. The conversation fell upon
the changes in the aspect of London since he had
last visited our metropolis. G— then glanced off to
the moral changes—literary, social, political—the
great men who were removed from the stage within the last twenty years; the new great men who
were coming on. In all this Mr. Richards evinced no
interest. He had evidently read none of our living
authors, and seemed scarcely acquainted by name
with our younger statesmen. Once, and only once,
he laughed; it was when G— asked him whether he
had any thoughts of getting into Parliament; and the
laugh was inward, sarcastic, sinister—a sneer raised
into a laugh. After a few minutes, G— left us to talk
to some other acquaintances who had just lounged
into the room, and I then said, quietly:

"I have seen a miniature of you, Mr. Richards, in
the house you once inhabited, and perhaps built—if
not wholly, at least in part, in — Street. You passed
by that house this morning."

Not till I had finished did I raise my eyes to his, and then he fixed my gaze so steadfastly that I could not withdraw it—those fascinating serpent-eyes. But involuntarily, and as if the words that translated my thought were dragged from me, I added, in a low whisper, "I have been a student in the mysteries of life and nature; of those mysteries I have known the occult professors. I have the right to speak to you thus." And I uttered a certain password.

"Well, I concede the right. What would you ask?"

"To what extent human will in certain temperaments can extend?"

"To what extent can thought extend? Think, and before you draw breath you are in China!"

"True; but my thought has no power in China."

"Give It expression, and it may have. You may write down a thought which, sooner or later, may alter the whole condition of China. What is a law but a thought? Therefore thought is infinite. Therefore thought has power; not in proportion to its value—a bad thought may make a bad law as potent as a good thought can make a good one."

"Yes; what you say confirms my own theory. Through invisible currents one human brain may transmit its ideas to other human brains, with the same rapidity as a thought promulgated by visible means. And as thought is imperishable, as it leaves its stamp behind it in the natural world, even when the thinker has passed out of this world, so the thought of the living may have power to rouse up and revive the thoughts of the dead, such as those thoughts *were in life,* though the thought of the living cannot reach the thoughts which the dead *now* may entertain. Is it not so?"

"I decline to answer, if, in my judgment thought has the limit you would fix to it. But proceed; you have a special question you wish to put."

"Intense malignity in an intense will, engendered in a peculiar temperament, and aided by natural means within the reach of science, may produce effects like those ascribed of old to evil magic. It might thus haunt the walls of a human habitation with spectral revivals of all guilty thoughts and guilty deeds once conceived and done within those walls; all, in short, with which the evil will claims *rapport* and affinity—imperfect, incoherent, fragmentary snatches at the old dramas acted therein years ago. Thoughts thus crossing each other haphazard, as in the nightmare of a vision, growing up into phantom sights and sounds, and all serving to create horror; not because those sights and sounds are really visitations from a world without, but that they are ghastly, monstrous renewals of what have been in this world itself, set into malignant play by a malignant mortal. And it is through the material agency of that human brain that these things would acquire even a human power; would strike as with the shock of electricity, and might kill, if the thought of the person assailed did not rise superior to the dignity of the original assailer; might kill the most powerful animal, if unnerved by fear, but not injure the feeblest man, if, while his flesh crept, his mind stood out fearless. Thus when in old stories we read of a magician rent to pieces by the fiends he had invoked, or still more, in Eastern legends, that one magician succeeds by arts in destroying another, there may be so far truth, that a material being has clothed, from his own evil propensities, certain elements and fluids, usually quiescent or harmless, with awful shapes and terrific force; just as the lightning, that had lain hidden and innocent in the cloud, becomes by natural law suddenly visible, takes a distinct shape to the eye, and can strike destruction on the object to which it is attracted."

"You are not without glimpses of a mighty secret," said Mr. Richards, composedly. "According to your view, could a mortal obtain the power you speak of, he would necessarily be a malignant and evil being."

"If the power were exercised, as I have said, most malignant and most evil; though I believe in the ancient traditions that he could not injure the good. His will could only injure those with whom it has established an affinity, or over whom it forces unresisted sway. I will now imagine an example that may be within the laws of nature, yet seem wild as the fables of a bewildered monk.

"You will remember that Albertus Magnus, after describing minutely the process by which the spirits may be invoked and commanded, adds emphatically that the process will instruct and avail only to the few; that *a man must be born a magician!*— that is, born with a peculiar physical temperament, as a man is born a poet. Rarely are men in whose constitutions lurks this occult power of the highest order of Intellect; usually in the intellect there is some twist, perversity, or disease. But, on the other hand, they must possess, to an astonishing degree, the faculty to concentrate thought on a single object—the energic faculty that we call WILL. Therefore, though their intellect be not sound, it is exceedingly forcible for the attainment of what it desires. I will imagine such a person, preeminently gifted with this constitution and its concomitant forces. I will place him in the loftier grades of society. I will suppose his desires emphatically those of the sensualist; he has, therefore, a strong love of life. He is an absolute egotist; his will is concentered in himself; he has fierce passions; he knows no enduring, no holy affections, but he can covet eagerly what for the moment he desires; he can hate implacably what opposes itself to his objects; he can commit fearful crimes, yet feel small remorse; he resorts rather to curses upon others than to penitence for his misdeeds. Circumstances, to which his constitution guides him, lead him to a rare knowledge of the natural secrets which may serve his egotism. He is a close observer where his passions encourage observation; he is a minute calculator, not from love of truth, but where love of self sharpens his faculties; therefore he can be a man of science. I suppose such a being, having by experience learned the power of his arts over others, trying what may be the power of will over his own frame, and studying all that in natural philosophy may increase that power. He loves life, he dreads death; *he wills to live on.* He cannot restore himself to youth; he cannot entirely stay the progress of death; he cannot make himself immortal in the flesh and blood. But he may arrest, for a time so long as to appear incredible if I said it, that hardening of the parts which constitutes old age. A year may age him no more than an hour ages another. His intense will, scientifically trained into system, operates, in short, over the wear and tear of his own frame. He lives on. That he may not seem a portent and a miracle, he *dies* from time to time, seemingly, to certain persons. Having schemed the transfer of a wealth that suffices to his wants, he disappears from one corner of the world, and contrives that his obsequies shall be celebrated. He reappears at another corner of the world, where he resides undetected, and does not visit the scenes of his former career till all who could remember his features are no more. He would be profoundly miserable if he had affections; he has none but for himself.

No good man would accept his longevity; and to no man, good or bad, would he or could he communicate its true secret. Such a man might exist; such a man as I have described I see now before me!—Duke of —, in the court of —, dividing time between lust and brawl, alchemists and wizards; again, in the last century, charlatan and criminal, with name less noble, domiciled in the house at which you gazed to-day, and flying from the law you had outraged, none knew whither; traveler once more revisiting London with the same earthly passion which filled your heart when races now no more walked through yonder streets; outlaw from the school of all the nobler and diviner mysteries. Execrable image of life in death and death in life, I warn you back from the cities and homes of healthful men! back to the ruins of departed empires! back to the deserts of nature unredeemed!"

There answered me a whisper so musical, so potently musical, that it seemed to enter into my whole being and subdue me despite myself. Thus it said:

"I have sought one like you for the last hundred years. Now I have found you, we part not till I know what I desire. The vision that sees through the past and cleaves through the veil of the future is in you at this hour—never before, never to come again. The vision of no puling, fantastic girl, of no sick-bed somnambule, but of a strong man with a vigorous brain. Soar, and look forth!"

As he spoke, I felt as if I rose out of myself upon eagle wings. All the weight seemed gone from air, roofless the room, roofless the dome of space. I was not in the body—where, I knew not; but aloft over time, over earth.

Again I heard the melodious whisper:

"You say right. I have mastered great secrets by the power of will. True, by will and by science I can retard the process of years, but death comes not by age alone. Can I frustrate the accidents which bring death upon the young?"

"No; every accident is a providence. Before a providence snaps every human will."

"Shall I die at last, ages and ages hence, by the slow though inevitable growth of time, or by the cause that I call accident?"

"By a cause you call accident."

"Is not the end still remote?" asked the whisper, with a slight tremor.

"Regarded as my life regards time, it is still remote."

"And shall I, before then, mix with the world of men as I did ere I learned these secrets; resume eager interest in their strife and their trouble; battle with ambition, and use the power of the sage to win the power that belongs to kings?"

"You will yet play a part on the earth that will fill earth with commotion and amaze. For wondrous designs have you, a wonder yourself, been permitted

to live on through the centuries. All the secrets you
have stored will then have their uses; all that now
makes you a stranger amid the generations will con-
tribute then to make you their lord. As the trees and
the straws are drawn into a whirlpool, as they spin
round, are sucked to the deep, and again tossed aloft
by the eddies, so shall races and thrones be drawn
into your vortex. Awful destroyer! but in destroying,
made, against your own will, a constructor."

"And that date, too, is far off?"

"Far off; when it comes, think your end in this
world is at hand!"

"How and what is the end? Look east, west, south,
and north."

"In the north, where you never yet trod, toward
the point whence your instincts have warned you,
there a specter will seize you. 'Tis Death! I see a
ship; it is haunted; 'tis chased! it sails on. Baffled
navies sail after that ship. It enters the region of
ice. It passes a sky red with meteors. Two moons
stand on high, over ice-reefs. I see the ship locked
between white defiles; they are ice-rocks. I see the
dead strew the decks, stark and livid, green mold
on their limbs. All are dead but one man—it is you!
But years, though so slowly they come, have then
scathed you. There is the coming of age on your
brow, and the will is relaxed in the cells of the brain.
Still that will, though enfeebled, exceeds all that
man knew before you; through the will you live on,

gnawed with famine. And nature no longer obeys you in that death-spreading region; the sky is a sky of iron, and the air has iron clamps, and the ice-rocks wedge in the ship. Hark how it cracks and groans! Ice will imbed it as amber imbeds a straw. And a man has gone forth, living yet, from the ship and its dead; and he has clambered up the spikes of an iceberg, and the two moons gaze down on his form. That man is yourself, and terror is on you—terror; and terror has swallowed up your will.

"And I see, swarming up the steep ice-rock, gray, grizzly things. The bears of the North have scented their quarry; they come nearer and nearer, shambling, and rolling their bulk. In that day every moment shall seem to you longer than the centuries through which you have passed. Heed this: after life, moments continued make the bliss or the hell of eternity."

"Hush!" said the whisper. "But the day, you assure me, is far off, very far! I go back to the almond and rose of Damascus! Sleep!"

The room swam before my eyes. I became insensible. When I recovered, I found G— holding my hand and smiling. He said, "You, who have always declared yourself proof against mesmerism, have succumbed at last to my friend Richards."

"Where is Mr. Richards?"

"Gone, when you passed into a trance, saying quietly to me, 'Your friend will not wake for an hour.'"

I asked, as collectedly as I could, where Mr. Richards lodged.

"At the Trafalgar Hotel."

"Give me your arm," said I to G—. "Let us call on him; I have something to say."

When we arrived at the hotel we were told that Mr. Richards had returned twenty minutes before, paid his bill, left directions with his servant (a Greek) to pack his effects, and proceed to Malta by the steamer that should leave Southampton the next day. Mr. Richards had merely said of his own movements that he had visits to pay in the neighborhood of London, and it was uncertain whether he should be able to reach Southampton in time for that steamer; if not, he should follow in the next one.

The waiter asked me my name. On my informing him, he gave me a note that Mr. Richards had left for me in case I called.

The note was as follows:

> I wished you to utter what was in your mind. You obeyed. I have therefore established power over you. For three months from this day you can communicate to no living man what has passed between us. You cannot even show this note to the friend by your side. During three months, silence complete as to me and mine. Do you doubt my power to lay on

you this command? Try to disobey me.
At the end of the third month the spell
is raised. For the rest, I spare you. I shall
visit your grave a year and a day after it
has received you.

So ends this strange story, which I ask no one to
believe. I write it down exactly three months after I
received the above note. I could not write it before,
nor could I show to G—, in spite of his urgent request, the note which I read under the gas-lamp by
his side.

AN AUTHENTIC NARRATIVE
OF A HAUNTED HOUSE

Sheridan Le Fanu
(1862)

[The Editor of the University Magazine submits the following very remarkable statement, with every detail of which he has been for some years acquainted, upon the ground that it affords the most authentic and ample relation of a series of marvellous phenoma, in nowise connected with what is technically termed "spiritualism," which he has anywhere met with. All the persons—and there are many of them living—upon whose separate evidence some parts, and upon whose united testimony others, of this most singular recital depend, are, in their several walks of life, respectable, and such as would in any matter of judicial investigation be deemed wholly unexceptionable witnesses. There is not an incident here recorded which would not have been distinctly deposed to on oath had any necessity existed, by the persons who severally, and some of them in great fear, related their own distinct experiences. The Editor begs most pointedly to meet in limine *the suspicion, that he is elaborating a trick, or vouching for another ghost of Mrs. Veal. As a mere*

story the narrative is valueless: its sole claim to attention is its absolute truth. For the good faith of its relator he pledges his own and the character of this Magazine. With the Editor's concurrence, the name of the watering-place, and some special circumstances in no essential way bearing upon the peculiar character of the story, but which might have indicated the locality, and possibly annoyed persons interested in house property there, have been suppressed by the narrator. Not the slightest liberty has been taken with the narrative, which is presented precisely in the terms in which the writer of it, who employs throughout the first person, would, if need were, fix it in the form of an affidavit.]

Within the last eight years—the precise date I purposely omit—I was ordered by my physician, my health being in an unsatisfactory state, to change my residence to one upon the sea-coast; and accordingly, I took a house for a year in a fashionable watering-place, at a moderate distance from the city in which I had previously resided, and connected with it by a railway.

Winter was setting in when my removal thither was decided upon; but there was nothing whatever dismal or depressing in the change. The house I had taken was to all appearance, and in point of convenience, too, quite a modern one. It formed one in a cheerful row, with small gardens in front, facing the sea, and commanding sea air and sea views in perfection. In the rear it had coach-house and stable, and between them and the house a considerable grass-plot, with some flower-beds, interposed.

Our family consisted of my wife and myself, with three children, the eldest about nine years old, she and the next in age being girls; and the youngest, between six and seven, a boy. To these were added six servants, whom, although for certain reasons I decline giving their real names, I shall indicate, for the sake of clearness, by arbitrary ones. There was a nurse, Mrs. Southerland; a nursery-maid, Ellen Page; the cook, Mrs. Greenwood; and the house-maid, Ellen Faith; a butler, whom I shall call Smith, and his son, James, about two-and-twenty.

We came out to take possession at about seven o'clock in the evening; every thing was comfortable and cheery; good fires lighted, the rooms neat and airy, and a general air of preparation and comfort, highly conducive to good spirits and pleasant anticipations.

The sitting-rooms were large and cheerful, and they and the bed-rooms more than ordinarily lofty, the kitchen and servants' rooms, on the same level, were well and comfortably furnished, and had, like the rest of the house, an air of recent painting and fitting up, and a completely modern character, which imparted a very cheerful air of cleanliness and convenience.

There had been just enough of the fuss of settling agreeably to occupy us, and to give a pleasant turn to our thoughts after we had retired to our rooms. Being an invalid, I had a small bed to myself—re-signing the four-poster to my wife. The candle was extinguished, but a night-light was burning. I was coming up stairs, and she, already in bed, had just dismissed her maid, when we were both startled by a wild scream from her room; I found her in a state of the extremest agitation and terror. She insisted that she had seen an unnaturally tall figure come beside her bed and stand there. The light was too faint to enable her to define any thing respecting this appa-rition, beyond the fact of her having most distinctly seen such a shape, colourless from the insufficiency of the light to disclose more than its dark outline.

We both endeavoured to re-assure her. The room once more looked so cheerful in the candlelight, that we were quite uninfluenced by the contagion of her terrors. The movements and voices of the servants down stairs still getting things into their places and completing our comfortable arrangements, had also their effect in steeling us against any such influ-ence, and we set the whole thing down as a dream, or an imperfectly-seen outline of the bed-curtains. When, however, we were alone, my wife reiterated, still in great agitation, her clear assertion that she had most positively seen, being at the time as com-pletely awake as ever she was, precisely what she had described to us. And in this conviction she contin-ued perfectly firm.

A day or two after this, it came out that our servants were under an apprehension that, somehow or other, thieves had established a secret mode of access to the lower part of the house. The butler, Smith, had seen an ill-looking woman in his room on the first night of our arrival; and he and other servants constantly saw, for many days subsequently, glimpses of a retreating figure, which corresponded with that so seen by him, passing through a passage which led to a back area in which were some coal-vaults.

This figure was seen always in the act of retreating, its back turned, generally getting round the corner of the passage into the area, in a stealthy and hurried way, and, when closely followed, imperfectly seen again entering one of the coal-vaults, and when pursued into it, nowhere to be found.

The idea of any thing supernatural in the matter had, strange to say, not yet entered the mind of any one of the servants. They had heard some stories of smugglers having secret passages into houses, and using their means of access for purposes of pillage, or with a view to frighten superstitious people out of houses which they needed for their own objects, and a suspicion of similar practices here, caused them extreme uneasiness. The apparent anxiety also manifested by this retreating figure to escape observation, and her always appearing to make her egress at the same point, favoured this romantic hypothesis.

The men, however, made a most careful examination of the back area, and of the coal-vaults, with a view to discover some mode of egress, but entirely without success. On the contrary, the result was, so far as it went, subversive of the theory; solid masonry met them on every hand.

I called the man, Smith, up, to hear from his own lips the particulars of what he had seen; and certainly his report was very curious. I give it as literally as my memory enables me:—

His son slept in the same room, and was sound asleep; but he lay awake, as men sometimes will on a change of bed, and having many things on his mind. He was lying with his face towards the wall, but observing a light and some little stir in the room, he turned round in his bed, and saw the figure of a woman, squalid, and ragged in dress; her figure rather low and broad; as well as I recollect, she had something—either a cloak or shawl—on, and wore a bonnet. Her back was turned, and she appeared to be searching or rummaging for something on the floor, and, without appearing to observe him, she turned in doing so towards him. The light, which was more like the intense glow of a coal, as he described it, being of a deep red colour, proceeded from the hollow of her hand, which she held beside her head, and he saw her perfectly distinctly. She appeared middle-aged, was deeply pitted with the smallpox, and blind of one eye. His phrase in describing her general appearance was, that she was "a miserable, poor-looking creature."

He was under the impression that she must be the woman who had been left by the proprietor in charge of the house, and who had that evening, after having given up the keys, remained for some little time with the female servants. He coughed, therefore, to apprize her of his presence, and turned again towards the wall. When he again looked round she and the light were gone; and odd as was her method of lighting herself in her search, the circumstances excited neither uneasiness nor curiosity in his mind, until he discovered next morning that the woman in question had left the house long before he had gone to his bed.

I examined the man very closely as to the appearance of the person who had visited him, and the result was what I have described. It struck me as an odd thing, that even then, considering how prone to superstition persons in his rank of life usually are, he did not seem to suspect any thing supernatural in the occurrence; and, on the contrary, was thoroughly persuaded that his visitant was a living person, who had got into the house by some hidden entrance.

On Sunday, on his return from his place of worship, he told me that, when the service was ended, and the congregation making their way slowly out, he saw the very woman in the crowd, and kept his

eye upon her for several minutes, but such was the
crush, that all his efforts to reach her were unavail-
ing, and when he got into the open street she was
gone. He was quite positive as to his having distinctly seen her, however, for several minutes, and
scouted the possibility of any mistake as to identity;
and fully impressed with the substantial and living
reality of his visitant, he was very much provoked at
her having escaped him. He made inquiries also in
the neighbourhood, but could procure no information, nor hear of any other persons having seen any
woman corresponding with his visitant.

The cook and the housemaid occupied a bed-room
on the kitchen floor. It had whitewashed walls, and
they were actually terrified by the appearance of the
shadow of a woman passing and repassing across the
side wall opposite to their beds. They suspected that
this had been going on much longer than they were
aware, for its presence was discovered by a sort of
accident, its movements happening to take a direction in distinct contrariety to theirs.

This shadow always moved upon one particular
wall, returning after short intervals, and causing
them extreme terror. They placed the candle, as the
most obvious specific, so close to the infested wall,
that the flame all but touched it; and believed for
some time that they had effectually got rid of this
annoyance; but one night, notwithstanding this
arrangement of the light, the shadow returned,

passing and repassing, as heretofore, upon the same wall, although their only candle was burning within an inch of it, and it was obvious that no substance capable of casting such a shadow could have interposed; and, indeed, as they described it, the shadow seemed to have no sort of relation to the position of the light, and appeared, as I have said, in manifest defiance of the laws of optics.

I ought to mention that the housemaid was a particularly fearless sort of person, as well as a very honest one; and her companion, the cook, a scrupulously religious woman, and both agreed in every particular in their relation of what occurred.

Meanwhile, the nursery was not without its annoyances, though as yet of a comparatively trivial kind. Sometimes, at night, the handle of the door was turned hurriedly as if by a person trying to come in, and at others a knocking was made at it. These sounds occurred after the children had settled to sleep, and while the nurse still remained awake. Whenever she called to know "who is there," the sounds ceased; but several times, and particularly at first, she was under the impression that they were caused by her mistress, who had come to see the children, and thus impressed she had got up and opened the door, expecting to see her, but discovering only darkness, and receiving no answer to her inquiries.

With respect to this nurse, I must mention that I believe no more perfectly trustworthy servant was ever employed in her capacity; and, in addition to her integrity, she was remarkably gifted with sound common sense.

One morning, I think about three or four weeks after our arrival, I was sitting at the parlour window which looked to the front, when I saw the little iron door which admitted into the small garden that lay between the window where I was sitting and the public road, pushed open by a woman who so exactly answered the description given by Smith of the woman who had visited his room on the night of his arrival as instantaneously to impress me with the conviction that she must be the identical person. She was a square, short woman, dressed in soiled and tattered clothes, scarred and pitted with small-pox, and blind of an eye. She stepped hurriedly into the little enclosure, and peered from a distance of a few yards into the room where I was sitting. I felt that now was the moment to clear the matter up; but there was something stealthy in the manner and look of the woman which convinced me that I must not appear to notice her until her retreat was fairly cut off. Unfortunately, I was suffering from a lame foot, and could not reach the bell as quickly as I wished. I made all the haste I could, and rang violently to bring up the servant Smith. In the short interval that intervened, I observed the woman from the window, who having in a leisurely way, and with a kind of scrutiny, looked along the front windows of the house, passed quickly out again, closing the gate after her, and followed a lady who was walking along the footpath at a quick pace, as if with the intention of begging from her. The moment the man entered I told him—"the blind woman you described to me has this instant followed a lady in that direction, try to overtake her." He was, if possible, more eager than I in the chase, but returned in a short time after a vain pursuit, very hot, and utterly disappointed. And, thereafter, we saw her face no more.

All this time, and up to the period of our leaving the house, which was not for two or three months later, there occurred at intervals the only phenomenon in the entire series having any resemblance to what we hear described of "Spiritualism." This was a knocking, like a soft hammering with a wooden mallet, as it seemed in the timbers between the bedroom ceilings and the roof. It had this special peculiarity, that it was always rhythmical, and, I think, invariably, the emphasis upon the last stroke. It would sound rapidly "one, two, three, *four*—one, two, three, *four*;" or "one, two, *three*—one, two, *three*," and sometimes "one, *two*—one, *two*," &c., and this, with intervals and resumptions, monotonously for hours at a time.

At first this caused my wife, who was a good deal confined to her bed, much annoyance; and we sent to our neighbours to inquire if any hammering or carpentering was going on in their houses but were informed that nothing of the sort was taking place. I have myself heard it frequently, always in the same inaccessible part of the house, and with the same monotonous emphasis. One odd thing about it was, that on my wife's calling out, as she used to do when it became more than usually troublesome, "stop that noise," it was invariably arrested for a longer or shorter time.

Of course none of these occurrences were ever mentioned in hearing of the children. They would have been, no doubt, like most children, greatly terrified had they heard any thing of the matter, and known that their elders were unable to account for what was passing; and their fears would have made them wretched and troublesome.

They used to play for some hours every day in the back garden—the house forming one end of this oblong inclosure, the stable and coach-house the other, and two parallel walls of considerable height the sides. Here, as it afforded a perfectly safe playground, they were frequently left quite to themselves; and in talking over their days' adventures, as children will, they happened to mention a woman, or rather the woman, for they had long grown familiar with her appearance, whom they used to see in the garden while they were at play. They assumed that she came in and went out at the stable door, but they never actually saw her enter or depart. They merely saw a figure—that of a very poor woman, soiled and ragged—near the stable wall, stooping over the ground, and apparently grubbing in the loose clay in search of something. She did not disturb, or appear to observe them; and they left her in undisturbed possession of her nook of ground. When seen it was always in the same spot, and similarly occupied; and the description they gave of her general appearance—for they never saw her face—corresponded with that of the one-eyed woman whom Smith, and subsequently as it seemed, I had seen.

The other man, James, who looked after a mare which I had purchased for the purpose of riding exercise, had, like every one else in the house, his little trouble to report, though it was not much. The stall in which, as the most comfortable, it was decided to place her, she peremptorily declined to enter. Though a very docile and gentle little animal, there was no getting her into it. She would snort and rear, and, in fact, do or suffer any thing rather than set her hoof in it. He was fain, therefore, to place her in another. And on several occasions he found her there, exhibiting all the equine symptoms of extreme fear. Like the rest of us, however, this man was not troubled in the particular case with any superstitious qualms. The mare had evidently been frightened; and he was puzzled to find out how, or by whom, for the stable was well-secured, and had, I am nearly certain, a lock-up yard outside.

One morning I was greeted with the intelligence that robbers had certainly got into the house in the night; and that one of them had actually been seen in the nursery. The witness, I found, was my eldest child, then, as I have said, about nine years of age. Having awoke in the night, and lain awake for some time in her bed, she heard the handle of the door turn, and a person whom she distinctly saw—for it was a light night, and the window-shutters unclosed—but whom she had never seen before, stepped in on tiptoe, and with an appearance of great caution. He was a rather small man, with a very red face; he wore an oddly cut frock coat, the collar of which stood up, and trousers, rough and wide, like those of a sailor, turned up at the ankles, and either short boots or clumsy shoes, covered with mud. This man listened beside the nurse's bed, which stood next the door, as if to satisfy himself that she was sleeping soundly; and having done so for some seconds, he began to move cautiously in a diagonal line, across the room to the chimney-piece, where he stood for a while, and so resumed his tiptoe walk, skirting the wall, until he reached a chest of drawers, some of which were open, and into which he looked, and began to rummage in a hurried way, as the child supposed, making search for something worth taking away. He then passed on to the window, where was a dressing-table, at which he also stopped, turning over the things upon it, and standing for some time at the window as if looking out, and then resuming his walk by the side wall opposite to that by which he had moved up to the window, he returned in the same way toward the nurse's bed, so as to reach it at the foot. With its side to the end wall, in which was the door, was placed the little bed in which lay my eldest child, who watched his proceedings with the extremest terror. As he drew near she instinctively moved herself in the bed, with her head and shoulders to the wall, drawing up her feet; but he passed by without appearing to observe, or, at least, to care for her presence. Immediately after the nurse turned in her bed as if about to waken; and when the child, who had drawn the clothes about her head, again ventured to peep out, the man was gone.

The child had no idea of her having seen any thing more formidable than a thief. With the prowling, cautious, and noiseless manner of proceeding common to such marauders, the air and movements of the man whom she had seen entirely corresponded. And on hearing her perfectly distinct and consistent account, I could myself arrive at no other conclusion than that a stranger had actually got into the house. I had, therefore, in the first instance, a most careful examination made to discover any traces of an entrance having been made by any window into the house. The doors had been found barred and locked as usual; but no sign of any thing of the sort was discernible. I then had the various

articles—plate, wearing apparel, books, &c., counted; and after having conned over and reckoned
up every thing, it became quite clear that nothing
whatever had been removed from the house, nor was
there the slightest indication of any thing having
been so much as disturbed there. I must here state
that this child was remarkably clear, intelligent, and
observant; and that her description of the man, and
of all that had occurred, was most exact, and as detailed as the want of perfect light rendered possible.

I felt assured that an entrance had actually been
effected into the house, though for what purpose
was not easily to be conjectured. The man, Smith,
was equally confident upon this point; and his
theory was that the object was simply to frighten
us out of the house by making us believe it haunted; and he was more than ever anxious and on the
alert to discover the conspirators. It often since
appeared to me odd. Every year, indeed, more odd,
as this cumulative case of the marvellous becomes
to my mind more and more inexplicable—that un-
derlying my sense of mystery and puzzle, was all
along the quiet assumption that all these occurrences
were one way or another referable to natural causes.
I could not account for them, indeed, myself; but
during the whole period I inhabited that house, I
never once felt, though much alone, and often up
very late at night, any of those tremors and thrills
which every one has at times experienced when

situation and the hour are favourable. Except the cook and housemaid, who were plagued with the shadow I mentioned crossing and recrossing upon the bedroom wall, we all, without exception, experienced the same strange sense of security, and regarded these phenomena rather with a perplexed sort of interest and curiosity, than with any more unpleasant sensations.

The knockings which I have mentioned at the nursery door, preceded generally by the sound of a step on the lobby, meanwhile continued. At that time (for my wife, like myself, was an invalid) two eminent physicians, who came out occasionally by rail, were attending us. These gentlemen were at first only amused, but ultimately interested, and very much puzzled by the occurrences which we described. One of them, at last, recommended that a candle should be kept burning upon the lobby. It was in fact a recurrence to an old woman's recipe against ghosts—of course it might be serviceable, too, against impostors; at all events, seeming, as I have said, very much interested and puzzled, he advised it, and it was tried. We fancied that it was successful; for there was an interval of quiet for, I think, three or four nights. But after that, the noises —the footsteps on the lobby—the knocking at the door, and the turning of the handle recommenced in full force, notwithstanding the light upon the table outside; and these particular phenomena became only more perplexing than ever.

The alarm of robbers and smugglers gradually subsided after a week or two; but we were again to hear news from the nursery. Our second little girl, then between seven and eight years of age, saw in the night time—she alone being awake—a young woman, with black, or very dark hair, which hung loose, and with a black cloak on, standing near the middle of the floor, opposite the hearthstone, and fronting the foot of her bed. She appeared quite unobservant of the children and nurse sleeping in the room. She was very pale, and looked, the child said, both "sorry and frightened," and with something very peculiar and terrible about her eyes, which made the child conclude that she was dead. She was looking, not at, but in the direction of the child's bed, and there was a dark streak across her throat, like a scar with blood upon it. This figure was not motionless; but once or twice turned slowly, and without appearing to be conscious of the presence of the child, or the other occupants of the room, like a person in vacancy or abstraction. There was on this occasion a night-light burning in the chamber; and the child saw, or thought she saw, all these particulars with the most perfect distinctness. She got her head under the bed-clothes; and although a good many years have passed since then, she cannot recall the spectacle without feelings of peculiar horror.

One day, when the children were playing in the back garden, I asked them to point out to me the

spot where they were accustomed to see the woman
who occasionally showed herself as I have described,
near the stable wall. There was no division of opinion as to this precise point, which they indicated
in the most distinct and confident way. I suggested
that, perhaps, something might be hidden there in
the ground; and advised them digging a hole there
with their little spades, to try for it. Accordingly,
to work they went, and by my return in the evening
they had grubbed up a piece of a jawbone, with several teeth in it. The bone was very much decayed,
and ready to crumble to pieces, but the teeth were
quite sound. I could not tell whether they were human grinders; but I showed the fossil to one of the
physicians I have mentioned, who came out the next
evening, and he pronounced them human teeth. The
same conclusion was come to a day or two later by
the other medical man. It appears to me now, on
reviewing the whole matter, almost unaccountable
that, with such evidence before me, I should not
have got in a labourer, and had the spot effectually
dug and searched. I can only say, that so it was. I was
quite satisfied of the moral truth of every word that
had been related to me, and which I have here set
down with scrupulous accuracy. But I experienced
an apathy, for which neither then nor afterwards
did I quite know how to account. I had a vague,
but immovable impression that the whole affair was
referable to natural agencies. It was not until some

time after we had left the house, which, by-the-by,
we afterwards found had had the reputation of being haunted before we had come to live in it, that on
reconsideration I discovered the serious difficulty of
accounting satisfactorily for all that had occurred
upon ordinary principles. A great deal we might ar-
bitrarily set down to imagination. But even in so
doing there was, *in limine*, the oddity, not to say
improbability, of so many different persons having
nearly simultaneously suffered from different spectral and other illusions during the short period for
which we had occupied that house, who never before, nor so far as we learned, afterwards were troubled by any fears or fancies of the sort. There were
other things, too, not to be so accounted for. The
odd knockings in the roof I frequently heard myself.

There were also, which I before forgot to mention, in the daytime, rappings at the doors of the
sitting-rooms, which constantly deceived us; and it
was not till our "come in" was unanswered, and the
hall or passage outside the door was discovered to
be empty, that we learned that whatever else caused
them, human hands did not. All the persons who reported having seen the different persons or appearances here described by me, were just as confident
of having literally and distinctly seen them, as I was
of having seen the hard-featured woman with the
blind eye, so remarkably corresponding with Smith's
description.

About a week after the discovery of the teeth, which were found, I think, about two feet under the ground, a friend, much advanced in years, and who remembered the town in which we had now taken up our abode, for a very long time, happened to pay us a visit. He good-humouredly pooh-poohed the whole thing; but at the same time was evidently curious about it. "We might construct a sort of story," said I (I am giving, of course, the substance and purport, not the exact words, of our dialogue), "and assign to each of the three figures who appeared their respective parts in some dreadful tragedy enacted in this house. The male figure represents the murderer; the ill-looking, one-eyed woman his accomplice, who, we will suppose, buried the body where she is now so often seen grubbing in the earth, and where the human teeth and jawbone have so lately been disinterred; and the young woman with dishevelled tresses, and black cloak, and the bloody scar across her throat, their victim. A difficulty, however, which I cannot get over, exists in the cheerfulness, the great publicity, and the evident very recent date of the house." "Why, as to that," said he, "the house is *not* modern; it and those beside it formed an old government store, altered and fitted up recently as you see. I remember it well in my young days, fifty years ago, before the town had grown out in this direction, and a more entirely lonely spot, or one more fitted for the commission of a secret crime, could not have been imagined."

I have nothing to add, for very soon after this my physician pronounced a longer stay unnecessary for my health, and we took our departure for another place of abode. I may add, that although I have resided for considerable periods in many other houses, I never experienced any annoyances of a similar kind elsewhere; neither have I made (stupid dog! you will say), any inquiries respecting either the antecedents or subsequent history of the house in which we made so disturbed a sojourn. I was content with what I knew, and have here related as clearly as I could, and I think it a very pretty puzzle as it stands.

[*Thus ends the statement, which we abandon to the ingenuity of our readers, having ourselves no satisfactory explanation to suggest; and simply repeating the assurance with which we prefaced it, namely, that we can vouch for the perfect good faith and the accuracy of the narrator.—E.D.U.M.*]

THE GHOST AT LABURNUM VILLA

ANONYMOUS

(1870)

There can be no doubt that Mr. Paul Withers is con-
stitutionally nervous. Mrs. Withers says so; and as
a man's wife ought to know something about his
weak points, the fact may be considered indisputable. Not that Withers himself seeks to conceal or
deny this peculiarity; on the contrary, he makes
rather a parade of it; just as some people do with
their cynicism, their bad temper, or any other feature which they think gives them distinctiveness of
character. Withers, being an author, is in the habit
of declaring that he considers his nervousness an
advantage; but when he tries to define this position,
he gets too misty to follow very closely. Mrs. W., it
need scarcely be said, takes the opposite view, and
invariably clinches the discussion by declaring, that
if Paul hadn't been so absurdly nervous he would
never have seen the ghost at Laburnum Villa. As
Paul believes devoutly in the one spectral experience of his life, he does not find the illustration

convincing; but out of respect for his wife's strength
of scepticism, changes the subject.

Was there a ghost at Laburnum Villa, or was it
merely a creation of Withers' over-excited brain?
Our readers shall judge for themselves.

The 'neat detached villa-residence' in question
was situated in a semi-rural suburb of London.
The agent's advertisement, just quoted, farther described it as being 'elegantly furnished,' and 'within
five minutes of a railway-station.' If anything more
antagonistic to the supernatural than this can be
imagined, we shall be glad to hear of it. The advertisement attracted the attention of Mrs. Withers
while seated at breakfast with her family in a remote Welsh watering-place; and in the evening of
the same day, just as the heavy twilight of a dull
September was changing into night, Withers stood
at the gate of Laburnum Villa with a small travelling-bag in his hand, and the key of that residence
in his pocket.

It had been a miserable day. In the first place, his
breakfast had been spoiled by the 'impetuosity' of
Mrs. Withers. That worthy lady had been for some
time bringing a legitimate pressure to bear to secure
a month or two's stay in London. When she saw the
advertisement, she became immediately and completely possessed by the idea that the neighbourhood in question combined every advantage attain-
able in this necessarily imperfect state of existence.

To resolve and act being with her one and the same impulse, she began at once to pack Withers' travelling-bag in spite of his almost pathetic remonstrances. Finding pathos of no use he tried argument, and from that drifted into what he called 'firmness' and Mrs. W. 'stupidity.' At this point, when there was just ten minutes to catch the mail-train from Holyhead, Mrs. W. asked in a tone of assumed calmness, if he intended to go to London in his slippers. His only reply was to put on his boots with a gloomy frown, snatch up his bag, and depart without even a 'good-morning.' That circumstance, however, did not in the least affect the appetite with which Mrs. Withers continued her interrupted breakfast. Withers meantime speeding Londonwards, and suffering as only nervous men can suffer from the irritating strain of an express journey, was brooding over a terrible scheme of vengeance. He would take the house—O yes, *he* would take it at any risk; if it was steaming with damp, infested with the most formidable rats, overrun with specimens of natural history, with a leaky cistern and defective drains, broken-windowed, dilapidated, ay, even roofless! 'His great revenge had stomach for them all!' But he never for a moment contemplated the possibility of its being 'haunted.'

Arrived in London, shattered in body and mind, but with his gloomy purpose strong upon him, he enlisted the obstructiveness of a maddening cabman

to place as many difficulties as possible in the way
of his finding the house-agent. After this slave of the
rank had shut him in a rickety and strong-smelling
box on wheels, he displayed an amount of obtuseness
about the required address that nearly made Withers
jump through the window with rage. Then, when
he had acquired some dim notion of where his fare
wanted to go, he proceeded with great deliberation
in an entirely wrong direction. After two or three
false starts of this sort, and the consequent dissipa-
tion of a good deal of valuable time, the right office
was found at last; and the agent himself discovered
in the act of closing his labours for the day, in order
to retire to the 'bosom of his family.' This is never
a good time to meet a man who hates doing things
in a hurry. Therefore Withers had expended some
energy against the impassible composure of Mr. Leese
in vain, until he happened to mention the name of
the house he wished to occupy. The words 'Laburnum Villa' seemed to act like a spell; and in ten
minutes more Withers found himself in possession
of the key of that 'neat detached villa-residence.'
Confiding himself once more to the care of cabby,
he soon forgot the temporary gleam of elation produced by this small success in gloomy reflections
on the probability of his being obliged to spend the
night wandering aimlessly about the suburbs in that
strong-smelling cab. Then he remembered a newspaper controversy about conveying hospital-patients

in public vehicles. Unpleasant impressions began to
crowd upon him, and he was on the point of stopping the cab and jumping out, when it was pulled-
up with a violent jerk, and he was informed that he
was 'there.'

When he found himself alone in a front garden of
tolerable size, he began to find the situation singular. Then a lurking suspicion that it might prove disagreeable obtruded itself. He glanced up at the front
of the house, which was of the usual commonplace
bow-windowed pattern, and was struck by the fact
that there was no appearance of occupation. To resolve this doubt at once he knocked at the door. The
sound seemed to raise a dozen melancholy echoes in
the neighbourhood; but after these had died away in
a low-spirited style, there was no response from the
interior of Laburnum Villa. At this point a servant,
in full evening dress of light cotton print, fluttered
across from one of the nearest villas for the purpose
of informing him that, "Please, sir, no one lives in
that 'ouse."

"No one! Is it left to take care of itself?"

"O no, sir. There's a person—leastways an old
woman—comes in the daytime, but she don't live
there regular. No one has lived there regular since
Miss Steel died."

After imparting these agreeable facts, the servant fluttered genteelly away again, leaving Withers standing on the door-step with an awkward

consciousness that, from the drawing-room window
of the nearest villa, eyes were bent upon him through
the laths of the venetians. It would be absurd to retreat. He took the key from his pocket and entered.

Falling over a pail, happily empty, which had
been carelessly left in the little hall, did not tend to
put him in a good temper, or to decrease the nervousness that had been growing upon him all day.
He sat down on the pail, rubbed his shins, and tried
to realise the situation. Alone in a strange house,
with nothing to eat, and with that faint sickness
upon him which comes of the fatigue and semi-star-
vation of express travelling. Obviously the thing
to do was to look for the kitchen. There might be
something to eat: at any rate the chance was worth
trying. Fortunately the kitchen was not far off, on
the ground-floor, and he groped his way there without much difficulty. Here he was rejoiced by discovering the remains of a good fire, and received a
momentary shock from a woman's dress, which was
hanging from a hook in a way suggestive, in the dim
light from the grate, of the person—'leastways the
old woman'—having made a violent end of herself.
A box of matches was the next fortunate discovery
made by Withers, who began to feel himself a sort
of Crusoe; but after burning two or three in a vain
attempt to light the gas, he was forced to the unpleasant conclusion that it was either turned off at
the meter, or 'cut off' by the gas company. Deferring

farther experiments in this direction for the present, he began, with the aid of a candle, to search for provisions. The prosecution of this laudable object naturally took him into the pantry. He was standing here, holding the candle above his head, and peering anxiously about the shelves, when he heard close to him, as it seemed, the shrill treble shout in which boyhood proclaims its eternal war with mankind. "Yah ! yah! the post!" the cry sounded like. What did they mean by "post"? Withers opened the window a little way, and listened more intently. The juvenile destroyers of peace were some distance across the field by this time, so he couldn't be sure whether his ears deceived him or not; but he certainly thought he heard "Yah! yah! the ghost!" It was very absurd, of course; but still Withers felt 'queer' as he closed the window again and continued his search. He was rewarded by a magnificent 'find'—a half-consumed meat-pie in prime condition, doubtless the personal property of the 'person' before mentioned. It was evident that *she,* at least, was no ghost, which was so far satisfactory. With the help of the brandy in his travelling-flask, Withers made a hearty supper off the meat-pie; and, strange to say, never bestowed a thought on the probability of its 'disagreeing' with him—a subject upon which, on ordinary occasions, he was wont to be discreetly but pathetically eloquent.

"Now for the meter," thought Withers, after finishing supper by the light of his solitary candle. He had always entertained rather a high opinion of himself, had Withers, in a modest self-contained way; but now, under the combined influence of meat-pie, brandy, and a pipe of cavendish, he began to think he had done himself scanty justice. "Strange," he mused over his pipe, "how a novel situation, strange conditions, bring out what is self-reliant in a man. How soon a fellow with any stuff in him grasps and subdues unfamiliar surroundings! The curled and scented military darling of drawing-rooms becomes a hero in war and a Spartan in the camp. The refined son of metropolitan civilisation, the polished cynic of club smoking-rooms, goes to the diggings, and straightway becomes 'hail fellow well met' with navvies, and a thoroughgoing advocate of Lynch law." And then Withers began to think pleasantly of his own fertility of resource, though he had, after all, only gone into an unoccupied house, and consumed another person's provisions. Rousing himself from such meditations with a gentle melancholy upon him, as became a person never destined to be thoroughly appreciated, he went to look for the meter. He found the place where the meter *had* been, but that was all. This being an emergency to which his resources were by no means equal, he began to doubt the absolute sufficiency of self-reliance under all circumstances. At any rate, no tolerably efficient substitute for the missing meter suggested itself to him, so he determined to distinguish himself in another unfamiliar direction. Returning upstairs, he occupied an hour or so very pleasantly, blacking his face and hands to an impossible extent, in the attempt to light a fire in the dining-room. He had chosen the dining-room to pass the night in in preference to running the risk of damp beds, because it was compact, not to say diminutive, in its proportions, and therefore more easily warmed and lighted by a fire and a couple of candles. Here, then, after the completion of his arrangements, he will be left to continue the story in his own words.

I do not know what the general experience in such cases may be, but I never can feel on thoroughly good terms with other people's furniture; there is a sense of antagonism which I find it impossible to subdue. Even while lounging in the very comfortable easy-chair in the dining-room of Laburnum Villa, I felt as strongly as possible that I was being seated under protest. The companion easy-chair balancing mine on the opposite side of the fire-place had, to my sensitive mind, a distinctly disparaging expression in its arms, and a shrug, as of contempt, in its well-stuffed back. A fiercely-gilt warrior, who was careering at a terrible rate on the top of a clock (run down and silent) decorating the mantelpiece, seemed to point his weapon at me in an openly threatening manner, and challenge me to mortal combat. Even the engravings on the walls rejected me as an alien.

'Shakespeare and his Contemporaries' were evidently engaged in discussing me in an unfavourable spirit; and Frith's 'Merrymakers' ignored me so completely that I ought to have sunk terribly in my own
esteem. There was a portrait in oil, too, of a gentleman, which it was impossible to escape, because it
hung opposite the chimney-glass; so that whenever
I raised my head, I caught it apparently looking at
me over the mantelpiece with an unmistakable expression of indignant surprise. I could almost hear
it saying in an injured tone, "What the deuce is that
fellow doing in my dining-room!"

This state of feeling was becoming intensified to
a most disagreeable pitch, when a framed photograph 'caught my eye'—if I may be permitted to use
the phrase—and gave a new turn to my thoughts.
It was a full-length of a young lady with one of
the most singular faces I ever saw in my life; not
a pleasant face by any means, but full of decided
character, though the mouth and chin were weak
without being feminine. I thought, with something
like a shudder of repugnance, that Elsie Venner—
that curious creature with the reptile taint in her
blood—must have looked like this girl, who seemed
to have nothing of girlhood about her but its physical weakness. The small colourless face, with its
retreating chin, unsmiling mouth, and slightly prominent nose, its sloping narrow forehead and brilliant black eyes, had such a repellent unsympathetic

character, that it created the most disagreeable impressions. I returned to my seat, from which I had
risen to examine the portrait; but I found it impossible to shake-off the feeling it had produced. It was
as repugnant to me as if it had been some noxious
thing endowed with a sluggish vitality which found
expression in the glittering eyes alone: they seemed
to hold me with a triumphant consciousness of their
power, though they were looking in another direction, out of the picture, but not at the spectator. I
got up under an uncontrollable impulse, and turned
the face to the wall. In doing so, I discovered that
on the back of the frame there was pasted one of
those 'funeral cards' which some people are in the
habit of sending to their friends on the occasion
of a death in the family. That there might be no
mistake as to the identity of the 'Laura Steel' here
mentioned, a miniature photograph was affixed at
the top of the card. So Laura Steel was the name of
the unprepossessing young lady, and she was dead.
All the nameless fascination went out of those singular orbs at the thought, and I felt something like
remorse for my fancies about her.

I ought to have begun to feel fatigued by this
time; but though I lay back as comfortably as possible in the easy-chair, put my feet on the fender,
and stared at the fire, no drooping of the eyelids
hinted at an approaching doze. It was no use trying to persuade myself that I wanted to take 'forty

winks.' The fact was not to be disguised that I was
most distressingly wakeful, restless, and listening;
distinctly *listening*, for I caught myself in the act. It
was very plain that nature was revenging itself for
my ill-spent day in the abnormal activity of my nervous system. I got up, and going to a book-case in a
recess, took down a volume at random. It proved to
be a collection of German plays of the sanguinary
school: Lessing's *Emilia Galotti*, Schiller's *Robbers*,
and others of the same type. This proved a fortunate
speculation; and I soon found myself going through
the most harrowing and bloodthirsty scenes with
that luxurious sense of suspended attention which
is the first phase of an inevitable doze. Emilia was
about to stab herself, and I was just nodding my admiration of her courage and virtue, when suddenly
I started up broad awake, and let the book fall. I
glanced almost involuntarily at the photograph, and
saw, or fancied I saw, in the averted glittering eyes
the same indefinable expression revived that had
struck me so unpleasantly at first. What was it that
had startled me? I did not know. Still less could I
explain the intensity of a new sensation, possessing
me completely, which seemed to hold all my being
in the one act of *listening*.

A house does not need to be old and dilapidated in order to supply plenty of mysterious noises;
indeed, new houses are more prolific in this respect than old ones. I heard any quantity of the

usual creaking, straining, and flapping in Laburnum Villa, but nothing to which I felt inclined to give any special significance. After a few minutes, therefore, the acute tension of my nerves began to relax, and I turned once more to my book. Here I met with a disappointment; for I soon became sensible that the horrors of the German dramatist had lost their soporific effect, and, inexplicably enough, were acting as an irritant. I was reading with sharpened senses, and realising what I read. It was another disagreeable surprise to find that the late Miss Steel—or, at least, my idea of her—was getting involved in the scenes, identifying herself with the sanguinary interest as a pervading evil influence. The criminal personages seemed to gleam at me from the page with the snake-like brilliancy of her eyes, and the malignant bitterness of the wicked speeches to come from the same lax unsmiling lips. I threw down the book impatiently, and began to trim the candles; but though I smiled while doing so at the idea of being reduced to candles in this age of gas, I could not help noticing that my hands trembled violently. I was so awkward about my work that I nearly extinguished the light. I poked the fire into a blaze, and set myself resolutely to think.

Some considerable time passed in a vain attempt to resume the mastery of myself; but I gave up the struggle at last, and resigned myself passively to wait and listen. I was sensible of no alarm, or even anxiety; I was simply held down, physically and mentally, and kept quiet. An imperious expectation of something, I did not know what, absorbed every sense and faculty of my being. How long I half sat, half lay thus, I do not know. Nature seemed to stand still; there was no time, and everything came to a breathless pause.

Then over this dead peace there came stealing a subtle infection of terror. The air was charged with it as with a plague. This horror gathered and thickened, like the darkness before a storm, until it became a palpable oppression. My body was paralysed; only my soul struggled feebly against the threatenings of madness or death.

It came at last. With my quickened senses, I could hear the stir in the air that heralded its approach, as if the atmosphere of Nature recoiled from the awful thing. It was in the room, and I recognised the figure at once, though the face was turned from me: the girl of the portrait with the snake-like eyes. I felt that if those eyes met mine, I should go mad; and yet I was powerless to look away, or move, or cry out. My heart stood still, and life was slipping away from my paralysed grasp. It was kneeling before the drawers in the lower part of the book-case, and appeared to be searching anxiously in one of them. Suddenly it recoiled, and threw its arms wildly above its head. It arose swiftly, and in the instant it stood erect was confronted by another figure, that of an old man. It seemed to read a sentence of condemnation in the face of this second corner, for it sank into a kneeling position, and clasped the other despairingly by the knees. There were savagely-rapid blows rained upon the face of the petitioner, upturned in an agony of entreaty, and a furious thrusting away. With a long wailing scream, it rolled writhing almost at my feet, and the awful eyes glared full into mine. Merciful oblivion came upon me, and I fell into a death-like unconsciousness.

When I revived, it was to find myself in a state of physical prostration as great as if I had just been recovering from a severe illness. The nervous restlessness from which I had suffered in the early part of the night had completely disappeared. It seemed that I had exhausted my powers of endurance, and my capacity for receiving violent mental impressions. I could only lie still and try, in a feeble groping way, to renew my hold upon the familiar every-day life which had become so distant and indistinct. I endeavoured to remember the incidents that had preceded my arrival at the villa; but I could only do so in a confused wandering style, without sequence or coherency. Mr. Loose the house-agent got mixed up with the cabman, and both receded into some indefinite past, the duration of which it was impossible to calculate. And all the time I was thus trying to rearrange the history of the day, I was sensible of a shadowy horror in the background of my thoughts, which I knew, evade it as I might, I should be obliged to face by and by. That dreadful remembrance, I was conscious, would force itself upon me with returning physical strength, without any effort of mine to rouse it. Let it sleep now, like a coiled serpent; there were hours enough of depression in store in the future to be darkened by its malignant influence. Should I ever forget it? I could not help asking myself, even in my almost imbecile state of prostration. Would it be always, as it was now, a lurking horror, crouching for a spring when its victim was most helpless?

I must have sat for a long time in this state of mental suspension; for when I gained energy enough to take active note of external things, I found the candles burnt out, and the fire a black mass, with some faint red sparks here and there. My first act of vitality was to seize the brandy-bottle, and take a draught of raw spirit such as would have completely stupefied me under ordinary circumstances. As it was, it produced such an immediate effect, in my weak state, that I could just stagger to the sofa, where I fell into a heavy and dreamless sleep.

It was broad daylight when I wakened again, and found a singular-looking old woman standing by the side of my improvised couch. We stared at each other, with much bewilderment on my side, and apparently much solemn relish on hers, for several minutes. She was the first to break the awkward silence, by remarking in a husky tone, "Lor' a-mussy!" Then I sat up, and became aware that I had a very active collection of steam-hammers at work in my head. This indisposed me for conversation, especially with an old woman who seemed to breathe gin, and I lay down again. She wheezed interrogatively, and did not appear to have any intention of going away. I turned towards her, and she repeated the exclamation or observation before quoted. "What do you want?" I asked at last, feeling under an obligation to say something. This simple question confused her so much, that she could only wheeze louder than ever, and rub her hands aimlessly with a very dirty duster. "I suppose you are the person who takes care of the house?" I added, with the benevolent design of assisting her comprehension. "Yes, sir; Mrs. Panting, sir, as Mr. Leese allus 'as engaged, me bein', as 'e says, trustworthy, with the 'ighest of characters, as was wrote out most beautiful by Mr. Leese's young man; an' I 'ope, sir, if you've took the 'ouse, as your good lady'll keep me on, sir, bein' easy satisfied, with a pore appetite, through bein' a widow, sir, with a small fambly, as allus did the charin' and washin' for pore Mr. Steel, and giv' the 'ighest satisfaction." I had collapsed at first, under this sudden shower-bath of information; but the name of Steel roused me, and I determined to extract what information Mrs. Panting possessed about the family. She possessed a great deal, as it

proved, and no doubt invented whatever was necessary to fill-up the gaps in her knowledge; but in its
broad outlines the story was probable enough.

Miss Steel's was one of those histories, commonplace in appearance to the outside spectator, the external features of which may be summed-up in a few
lines, while an internal analysis would fill volumes.
Mrs. Panting's amplified, decorated, and very dis-
cursive history may be told in a few words. Laura
Steel had conceived a violent and unreasoning
passion for a man who was utterly and hopelessly
unworthy of the slightest public notice from any
woman who valued her reputation. There had been
a clandestine correspondence, and a regular series
of stolen meetings, before her father discovered the
state of affairs. Then came a sickening struggle for
supremacy between the father and daughter: she
bold, defiant, and reckless; he mad with passionate rage and the bare possibility of social disgrace.
There was a short and deceitful truce, but it was only
the sullen calm that precedes the fury of the storm.
It came to a sudden end one day, for he had been
searching among her papers during her absence, and
found a certificate of marriage dated about seven
months before. There was a terrible scene when she
returned home at night; a scene which even imaginative Mrs. Panting trembled at the mere recollection of. He cast his daughter off with such frightful
imprecations as raving demons might have uttered,

and swore a horrible oath of hatred even beyond the grave. A few days after, she died in giving birth to a still-born child. The terrible passion of the old man was too much for his enfeebled frame; and he too succumbed soon after to an attack of paralysis, which, though it deprived him of speech, could not quench the hatred that burned in his eyes to the last.

When Mrs. Panting had finished her story, she exhibited as corroborative evidence a manuscript volume, much burned on the outside, which she had picked up from under the grate the morning after the tragedy. As she could not read, however, she had no idea how irresistible that corroboration was. It was Miss Steel's diary, or at any rate all that was left of it. A more appalling production, for a woman's hand, I never met before, and devoutly hope never to meet again.

How is it that the worst women, if they have the power of expression, are always the most eager to make a morbid analysis of their wickedness on paper? Let philosophers answer, if they can. Miss Steel's diary was not one of incident; about her personal surroundings she wrote little beyond the facts that her mother had died while she was an infant, and that she had never loved her father. The 'sentiment,' as she considered it, of filial affection was the subject of her most caustic sarcasms. Her father, on the other hand, had reciprocated her indifference most thoroughly, and thus she had grown in a state of complete isolation. An intelligence so acute and observant that it only wanted a touch of human sympathy to produce the fruits of genius, had been perverted by indiscriminate and unwholesome reading into a field for the growth of the wildest and most unhealthy fancies. No question was too high, or too low, or too sacred for the effrontery of her amazing speculations. Themes that mankind have been accustomed to approach with reverent awe were treated with revolting flippancy, as almost unworthy of serious thought. But it was when she had passed under the dominion of a new passion that all the distorted strength of her character was put forth. It was simply raving, with few intervals of lucidity; and I was compelled to give up the task of reading it from sheer inability to bear the painful feeling of mental irritation it produced. I need only add, that I felt it a duty to superintend carefully the process of reducing it by fire to a harmless pile of feathery ashes.

Human nature, even nervous human nature, will bear a great deal, we know; and I must have got over the effects of my night's experience to some extent when I could feel a sort of grim satisfaction in despatching the following telegram to Mrs. Withers at Llanfairfechan: "Don't come. Laburnum Villa won't do."

THE SPOOK HOUSE

AMBROSE BIERCE

(1889)

On the road leading north from Manchester, in eastern Kentucky, to Booneville, twenty miles away, stood, in 1862, a wooden plantation house of a somewhat better quality than most of the dwellings in that region. The house was destroyed by fire in the year following—probably by some stragglers from the retreating column of General George W. Morgan, when he was driven from Cumberland Gap to the Ohio river by General Kirby Smith. At the time of its destruction, it had for four or five years been vacant. The fields about it were overgrown with brambles, the fences gone, even the few negro quarters, and out-houses generally, fallen partly into ruin by neglect and pillage; for the negroes and poor whites of the vicinity found in the building and fences an abundant supply of fuel, of which they availed themselves without hesitation, openly and by daylight. By daylight alone; after nightfall no human being except passing strangers ever went near the place.

It was known as the "Spook House." That it was
tenanted by evil spirits, visible, audible and active,
no one in all that region doubted any more than he
doubted what he was told of Sundays by the traveling
preacher. Its owner's opinion of the matter was unknown; he and his family had disappeared one night
and no trace of them had ever been found. They left
everything—household goods, clothing, provisions,
the horses in the stable, the cows in the field, the
negroes in the quarters—all as it stood; nothing was
missing—except a man, a woman, three girls, a boy
and a babe! It was not altogether surprising that a
plantation where seven human beings could be simultaneously effaced and nobody the wiser should
be under some suspicion.

One night in June, 1859, two citizens of Frankfort, Col. J. C. McArdle, a lawyer, and Judge My-
ron Veigh, of the State Militia, were driving from
Booneville to Manchester. Their business was so
important that they decided to push on, despite
the darkness and the mutterings of an approaching
storm, which eventually broke upon them just as
they arrived opposite the "Spook House." The lightning was so incessant that they easily found their
way through the gateway and into a shed, where
they hitched and unharnessed their team. They then
went to the house, through the rain, and knocked
at all the doors without getting any response.
Attributing this to the continuous uproar of the

thunder they pushed at one of the doors, which yielded. They entered without further ceremony and closed the door. That instant they were in darkness and silence. Not a gleam of the lightning's unceasing blaze penetrated the windows or crevices; not a whisper of the awful tumult without reached them there. It was as if they had suddenly been stricken blind and deaf, and McArdle afterward said that for a moment he believed himself to have been killed by a stroke of lightning as he crossed the threshold. The rest of this adventure can as well be related in his own words, from the Frankfort *Advocate* of August 6, 1876:

"When I had somewhat recovered from the dazing effect of the transition from uproar to silence, my first impulse was to reopen the door which I had closed, and from the knob of which I was not conscious of having removed my hand; I felt it distinctly, still in the clasp of my fingers. My notion was to ascertain by stepping again into the storm whether I had been deprived of sight and hearing. I turned the doorknob and pulled open the door. It led into another room!

"This apartment was suffused with a faint greenish light, the source of which I could not determine, making everything distinctly visible, though nothing was sharply defined. Everything, I say, but in truth the only objects within the blank stone walls of that room were human corpses. In number they were perhaps eight or ten—it may well be understood that I did not truly count them. They were of different ages, or rather sizes, from infancy up, and of both sexes. All were prostrate on the floor, excepting one, apparently a young woman, who sat up, her back supported by an angle of the wall. A babe was clasped in the arms of another and older woman. A half-grown lad lay face downward across the legs of a full-bearded man. One or two were nearly naked, and the hand of a young girl held the fragment of a gown which she had torn open at the breast. The bodies were in various stages of decay, all greatly shrunken in face and figure. Some were but little more than skeletons.

"While I stood stupefied with horror by this ghastly spectacle and still holding open the door, by some unaccountable perversity my attention was diverted from the shocking scene and concerned itself with trifles and details. Perhaps my mind, with an instinct of self-preservation, sought relief in matters which would relax its dangerous tension. Among other things, I observed that the door that I was holding open was of heavy iron plates, riveted. Equidistant from one another and from the top and bottom, three strong bolts protruded from the beveled edge. I turned the knob and they were retracted flush with the edge; released it, and they shot out. It was a spring lock. On the inside there was no knob, nor any kind of projection—a smooth surface of iron.

"While noting these things with an interest and attention which it now astonishes me to recall I felt myself thrust aside, and Judge Veigh, whom in the intensity and vicissitudes of my feelings I had altogether forgotten, pushed by me into the room. 'For God's sake,' I cried, 'do not go in there! Let us get out of this dreadful place!'

"He gave no heed to my entreaties, but (as fearless a gentleman as lived in all the South) walked quickly to the center of the room, knelt beside one of the bodies for a closer examination and tenderly raised its blackened and shriveled head in his hands. A strong disagreeable odor came through the doorway, completely overpowering me. My senses reeled; I felt myself falling, and in clutching at the edge of the door for support pushed it shut with a sharp click!

"I remember no more: six weeks later I recovered my reason in a hotel at Manchester, whither I had been taken by strangers the next day. For all these weeks I had suffered from a nervous fever, attended with constant delirium. I had been found lying in the road several miles away from the house; but how I had escaped from it to get there I never knew. On recovery, or as soon as my physicians permitted me to talk, I inquired the fate of Judge Veigh, whom (to quiet me, as I now know) they represented as well and at home.

"No one believed a word of my story, and who can wonder? And who can imagine my grief when, arriving at my home in Frankfort two months later, I learned that Judge Veigh had never been heard of since that night? I then regretted bitterly the pride which since the first few days after the recovery of my reason had forbidden me to repeat my discredited story and insist upon its truth.

"With all that afterward occurred—the examination of the house; the failure to find any room corresponding to that which I have described; the attempt to have me adjudged insane, and my triumph over my accusers—the readers of the *Advocate* are familiar. After all these years I am still confident that excavations which I have neither the legal right to undertake nor the wealth to make would disclose the secret of the disappearance of my unhappy friend, and possibly of the former occupants and owners of the deserted and now destroyed house. I do not despair of yet bringing about such a search, and it is a source of deep grief to me that it has been delayed by the undeserved hostility and unwise incredulity of the family and friends of the late Judge Veigh."

Colonel McArdle died in Frankfort on the thirteenth day of December, in the year 1879.

THE LITTLE ROOM

Madeline Yale Wynne

(1895)

"How would it do for a smoking-room?"

"Just the very place! only, you know, Roger, you must not think of smoking in the house. I am almost afraid that having just a plain, common man around, let alone a smoking man, will upset Aunt Hannah. She is New England—Vermont New England—boiled down."

"You leave Aunt Hannah to me; I'll find her tender side. I'm going to ask her about the old sea-captain and the yellow calico."

"Not yellow calico—blue chintz."

"Well, yellow *shell* then."

"No, no! don't mix it up so; you won't know yourself what to expect, and that's half the fun."

"Now you tell me again exactly what to expect; to tell the truth, I didn't half hear about it the other day; I was wool-gathering. It was something queer that happened when you were a child, wasn't it?"

"Something that began to happen long before that, and kept happening, and may happen again; but I hope not."

"What was it?"

"I wonder if the other people in the car can hear us?"

"I fancy not; we don't hear them—not consecutively, at least."

"Well, mother was born in Vermont, you know; she was the only child by a second marriage. Aunt Hannah and Aunt Maria are only half-aunts to me, you know."

"I hope they are half as nice as you are."

"Roger, be still; they certainly will hear us."

"Well, don't you want them to know we are married?"

"Yes, but not just married. There's all the difference in the world."

"You are afraid we look too happy!"

"No; only I want my happiness all to myself."

"Well, the little room?"

"My aunts brought mother up; they were nearly twenty years older than she. I might say Hiram and they brought her up. You see, Hiram was bound out to my grandfather when he was a boy, and when grandfather died Hiram said he 's'posed he went with the farm, 'long o' the critters,' and he has been there ever since. He was my mother's only refuge from the decorum of my aunts. They are simply workers. They make me think of the Maine woman who wanted her epitaph to be: 'She was a *hard* working woman.'"

"They must be almost beyond their working-days. How old are they?"

"Seventy, or thereabouts; but they will die standing; or, at least, on a Saturday night, after all the house-work is done up. They were rather strict with mother, and I think she had a lonely childhood. The house is almost a mile away from any neighbors, and off on top of what they call Stony Hill. It is bleak enough up there, even in summer.

"When mamma was about ten years old they sent her to cousins in Brooklyn, who had children of their own, and knew more about bringing them up. She staid there till she was married; she didn't go to Vermont in all that time, and of course hadn't seen her sisters, for they never would leave home for a day. They couldn't even be induced to go to Brooklyn to her wedding, so she and father took their wedding trip up there."

"And that's why we are going up there on our own?"

"Don't, Roger; you have no idea how loud you speak."

"You never say so except when I am going to say that one little word."

"Well, don't say it, then, or say it very, very quietly."

"Well, what was the queer thing?"

"When they got to the house, mother wanted to take father right off into the little room; she had been telling him about it, just as I am going to tell you, and she had said that of all the rooms, that one was the only one that seemed pleasant to her. She described the furniture and the books and paper and everything, and said it was on the north side, between the front and back room. Well, when they went to look for it, there was no little room there; there was only a shallow china-closet. She asked her sisters when the house had been altered and a closet made of the room that used to be there. They both said the house was exactly as it had been built—that they had never made any changes, except to tear down the old wood-shed and build a smaller one.

"Father and mother laughed a good deal over it, and when anything was lost they would always say it must be in the little room, and any exaggerated statement was called 'little-roomy.' When I was a child I thought that was a regular English phrase, I heard it so often.

"Well, they talked it over, and finally they concluded that my mother had been a very imaginative sort of a child, and had read in some book about such a little room, or perhaps even dreamed it, and then had 'made believe,' as children do, till she herself had really thought the room was there."

"Why, of course, that might easily happen."

"Yes, but you haven't heard the queer part yet; you wait and see if you can explain the rest as easily.

"They stayed at the farm two weeks, and then went to New York to live. When I was eight years old my father was killed in the war, and mother was broken-hearted. She never was quite strong afterwards, and that summer we decided to go up to the farm for three months.

"I was a restless sort of a child, and the journey seemed very long to me; and finally, to pass the time, mamma told me the story of the little room, and how it was all in her own imagination, and how there really was only a china-closet there.

"She told it with all the particulars; and even to me, who knew beforehand that the room wasn't there, it seemed just as real as could be. She said it was on the north side, between the front and back rooms; that it was very small, and they sometimes called it an entry. There was a door also that opened out-of-doors, and that one was painted green, and was cut in the middle like the old Dutch doors, so that it could be used for a window by opening the top part only. Directly opposite the door was a lounge or couch; it was covered with blue chintz— India chintz—some that had been brought over by an old Salem sea-captain as a 'venture.' He had given it to Hannah when she was a young girl. She was sent to Salem for two years to school. Grandfather originally came from Salem."

"I thought there wasn't any room or chintz."

"*That is just it.* They had decided that mother had imagined it all, and yet you see how exactly everything was painted in her mind, for she had even remembered that Hiram had told her that Hannah could have married the sea-captain if she had wanted to!

"The India cotton was the regular blue stamped chintz, with the peacock figure on it. The head and body of the bird were in profile, while the tail was full front view behind it. It had seemed to take mamma's fancy, and she drew it for me on a piece of paper as she talked. Doesn't it seem strange to you that she could have made all that up, or even dreamed it?

"At the foot of the lounge were some hanging shelves with some old books on them. All the books were leather-colored except one; that was bright red, and was called the *Ladies' Album*. It made a bright break between the other thicker books.

"On the lower shelf was a beautiful pink sea-shell, lying on a mat made of balls of red shaded worsted. This shell was greatly coveted by mother, but she was only allowed to play with it when she had been particularly good. Hiram had shown her how to hold it close to her ear and hear the roar of the sea in it.

"I know you will like Hiram, Roger; he is quite a character in his way.

"Mamma said she remembered, or *thought* she remembered, having been sick once, and she had to

lie quietly for some days on the lounge; then was
the time she had become so familiar with everything
in the room, and she had been allowed to have the
shell to play with all the time. She had had her toast
brought to her in there, with make-believe tea. It
was one of her pleasant memories of her childhood;
it was the first time she had been of any importance
to anybody, even herself.

"Right at the head of the lounge was a light-stand,
as they called it, and on it was a very brightly polished brass candlestick and a brass tray, with snuff-
ers. That is all I remember of her describing, except
that there was a braided rag rug on the floor, and on
the wall was a beautiful flowered paper—roses and
morning-glories in a wreath on a light blue ground.
The same paper was in the front room."

"And all this never existed except in her imagination?"

"She said that when she and father went up there,
there wasn't any little room at all like it anywhere
in the house; there was a china-closet where she had
believed the room to be."

"And your aunts said there had never been any
such room."

"That is what they said."

"Wasn't there any blue chintz in the house with a
peacock figure?"

"Not a scrap, and Aunt Hannah said there had
never been any that she could remember; and Aunt

Maria just echoed her—she always does that. You
see, Aunt Hannah is an up-and-down New England
woman. She looks just like herself; I mean, just
like her character. Her joints move up and down or
backward and forward in a plain square fashion. I
don't believe she ever leaned on anything in her life,
or sat in an easy-chair. But Maria is different; she is
rounder and softer; she hasn't any ideas of her own;
she never had any. I don't believe she would think
it right or becoming to have one that differed from
Aunt Hannah's, so what would be the use of having
any? She is an echo, that's all.

"When mamma and I got there, of course I was
all excitement to see the china-closet, and I had a
sort of feeling that it would be the little room after
all. So I ran ahead and threw open the door, crying,
'Come and see the little room.'

"And Roger," said Mrs. Grant, laying her hand in
his, "there really was a little room there, exactly as
mother had remembered it. There was the lounge,
the peacock chintz, the green door, the shell, the
morning-glory, and rose paper, *everything exactly as
she had described it to me.*"

"What in the world did the sisters say about it?"

"Wait a minute and I will tell you. My mother
was in the front hall still talking with Aunt Hannah.
She didn't hear me at first, but I ran out there and
dragged her through the front room, saying, 'The
room *is* here—it is all right.'

"It seemed for a minute as if my mother would faint. She clung to me in terror. I can remember now how strained her eyes looked and how pale she was.

"I called out to Aunt Hannah and asked her when they had had the closet taken away and the little room built; for in my excitement I thought that that was what had been done.

"'That little room has always been there,' said Aunt Hannah, 'ever since the house was built.'

"'But mamma said there wasn't any little room here, only a china-closet, when she was here with papa,' said I.

"'No, there has never been any china-closet there; it has always been just as it is now,' said Aunt Hannah.

"Then mother spoke; her voice sounded weak and far off. She said, slowly, and with an effort, 'Maria, don't you remember that you told me that there had *never been any little room here*? and Hannah said so too, and then I said I must have dreamed it?'

"'No, I don't remember anything of the kind,' said Maria, without the slightest emotion. 'I don't remember you ever said anything about any china-closet. The house has never been altered; you used to play in this room when you were a child, don't you remember?'

"'I know it,' said mother, in that queer slow voice that made me feel frightened. 'Hannah, don't you remember my finding the china-closet here, with

the gilt-edged china on the shelves, and then *you*
said that the *china-closet* had always been here?'

"'No,' said Hannah, pleasantly but unemotionally—'no, I don't think you ever asked me about any
china-closet, and we haven't any gilt-edged china
that I know of.'

"And that was the strangest thing about it. We
never could make them remember that there had ever
been any question about it. You would think they
could remember how surprised mother had been before, unless she had imagined the whole thing. Oh,
it was so queer! They were always pleasant about it,
but they didn't seem to feel any interest or curiosity.
It was always this answer: 'The house is just as it
was built; there have never been any changes, so far
as we know.'

"And my mother was in an agony of perplexity.
How cold their gray eyes looked to me! There was
no reading anything in them. It just seemed to break
my mother down, this queer thing. Many times that
summer, in the middle of the night, I have seen her
get up and take a candle and creep softly downstairs. I could hear the steps creak under her weight.
Then she would go through the front room and peer
into the darkness, holding her thin hand between
the candle and her eyes. She seemed to think the little room might vanish. Then she would come back
to bed and toss about all night, or lie still and shiver; it used to frighten me.

"She grew pale and thin, and she had a little cough; then she did not like to be left alone. Sometimes she would make errands in order to send me to the little room for something—a book, or her fan, or her handkerchief; but she would never sit there or let me stay in there long, and sometimes she wouldn't let me go in there for days together. Oh, it was pitiful!"

"Well, don't talk any more about it, Margaret, if it makes you feel so," said Mr. Grant.

"Oh yes, I want you to know all about it, and there isn't much more—no more about the room.

"Mother never got well, and she died that autumn. She used often to sigh, and say, with a wan little laugh, 'There is one thing I am glad of, Margaret: your father knows now all about the little room.' I think she was afraid I distrusted her. Of course, in a child's way, I thought there was something queer about it, but I did not brood over it. I was too young then, and took it as a part of her illness. But, Roger, do you know, it really did affect me. I almost hate to go there after talking about it; I somehow feel as if it might, you know, be a china-closet again."

"That's an absurd idea."

"I know it; of course it can't be. I saw the room, and there isn't any china-closet there, and no gilt-edged china in the house, either."

And then she whispered: "But, Roger, you may hold my hand as you do now, if you will, when we go to look for the little room."

"And you won't mind Aunt Hannah's gray eyes?"

"I won't mind *anything*."

It was dusk when Mr. and Mrs. Grant went into the gate under the two old Lombardy poplars and walked up the narrow path to the door, where they were met by the two aunts.

Hannah gave Mrs. Grant a frigid but not un-friendly kiss; and Maria seemed for a moment to tremble on the verge of an emotion, but she glanced at Hannah, and then gave her greeting in exactly the same repressed and non-committal way.

Supper was waiting for them. On the table was the *gilt-edged china*. Mrs. Grant didn't notice it im-mediately, till she saw her husband smiling at her over his teacup; then she felt fidgety, and couldn't eat. She was nervous, and kept wondering what was behind her, whether it would be a little room or a closet.

After supper she offered to help about the dishes, but, mercy! she might as well have offered to help bring the seasons round; Maria and Hannah couldn't be helped.

So she and her husband went to find the little room, or closet, or whatever was to be there.

Aunt Maria followed them, carrying the lamp, which she set down, and then went back to the dish-washing.

Margaret looked at her husband. He kissed her, for she seemed troubled; and then, hand in hand, they opened the door. It opened into a *china-closet*. The shelves were neatly draped with scalloped paper; on them was the gilt-edged china, with the dishes missing that had been used at the supper, and which at that moment were being carefully washed and wiped by the two aunts.

Margaret's husband dropped her hand and looked at her. She was trembling a little, and turned to him for help, for some explanation, but in an instant she knew that something was wrong. A cloud had come between them; he was hurt; he was antagonized.

He paused for an appreciable instant, and then said, kindly enough, but in a voice that cut her deeply:

"I am glad this ridiculous thing is ended; don't let us speak of it again."

"Ended!" said she. "How ended?" And somehow her voice sounded to her as her mother's voice had when she stood there and questioned her sisters about the little room. She seemed to have to drag her words out. She spoke slowly: "It seems to me to have only just begun in my case. It was just so with mother when she—"

"I really wish, Margaret, you would let it drop. I don't like to hear you speak of your mother in connection with it. It—" He hesitated, for was not this their wedding-day? "It doesn't seem quite the thing, quite delicate, you know, to use her name in the matter."

She saw it all now: *he didn't believe her*. She felt a chill sense of withering under his glance.

"Come," he added, "let us go out, or into the dining-room, somewhere, anywhere, only drop this nonsense."

He went out; he did not take her hand now—he was vexed, baffled, hurt. Had he not given her his sympathy, his attention, his belief—and his hand?—and she was fooling him. What did it mean?—she so truthful, so free from morbidness—a thing he hated. He walked up and down under the poplars, trying to get into the mood to go and join her in the house.

Margaret heard him go out; then she turned and shook the shelves; she reached her hand behind them and tried to push the boards away; she ran out of the house on to the north side and tried to find in the darkness, with her hands, a door, or some steps leading to one. She tore her dress on the old rose-trees, she fell and rose and stumbled, then she sat down on the ground and tried to think. What could she think—was she dreaming?

She went into the house and out into the kitchen, and begged Aunt Maria to tell her about the little room—what had become of it, when had they built the closet, when had they bought the gilt-edged china?

They went on washing dishes and drying them on the spotless towels with methodical exactness; and as they worked they said that there had never been any little room, so far as they knew; the china-closet had always been there, and the gilt-edged china had belonged to their mother, it had always been in the house.

"No, I don't remember that your mother ever asked about any little room," said Hannah. "She didn't seem very well that summer, but she never asked about any changes in the house; there hadn't ever been any changes."

There it was again: not a sign of interest, curiosity, or annoyance, not a spark of memory.

She went out to Hiram. He was telling Mr. Grant about the farm. She had meant to ask him about the room, but her lips were sealed before her husband.

Months afterwards, when time had lessened the sharpness of their feelings, they learned to speculate reasonably about the phenomenon, which Mr. Grant had accepted as something not to be scoffed away, not to be treated as a poor joke, but to be put aside as something inexplicable on any ordinary theory.

Margaret alone in her heart knew that her mother's words carried a deeper significance than she had dreamed of at the time. "One thing I am glad of, your father knows now," and she wondered if Roger or she would ever know.

Five years later they were going to Europe. The packing was done; the children were lying asleep, with their travelling things ready to be slipped on for an early start.

Roger had a foreign appointment. They were not to be back in America for some years. She had meant to go up to say good-by to her aunts; but a mother of three children intends to do a great many things that never get done. One thing she had done that very day, and as she paused for a moment between the writing of two notes that must be posted before she went to bed, she said:

"Roger, you remember Rita Lash? Well, she and Cousin Nan go up to the Adirondacks every autumn. They are clever girls, and I have intrusted to them something I want done very much."

"They are the girls to do it, then, every inch of them."

"I know it, and they are going to."

"Well?"

"Why, you see, Roger, that little room—"

"Oh—"

"Yes, I was a coward not to go myself, but I didn't find time, because I hadn't the courage."

"Oh! *that* was it, was it?"

"Yes, just that. They are going, and they will write us about it."

"Want to bet?"

"No; I only want to know."

Rita Lash and Cousin Nan planned to go to Vermont on their way to the Adirondacks. They found they would have three hours between trains, which would give them time to drive up to the Keys farm, and they could still get to the camp that night. But, at the last minute, Rita was prevented from going. Nan had to go to meet the Adirondack party, and she promised to telegraph her when she arrived at the camp. Imagine Rita's amusement when she received this message: "Safely arrived; went to the Keys farm; it is a little room."

Rita was amused, because she did not in the least think Nan had been there. She thought it was a hoax; but it put it into her mind to carry the joke further by really stopping herself when she went up, as she meant to do the next week.

She did stop over. She introduced herself to the two maiden ladies, who seemed familiar, as they had been described by Mrs. Grant.

They were, if not cordial, at least not disconcerted at her visit, and willingly showed her over the house. As they did not speak of any other stranger's having been to see them lately, she became confirmed in her belief that Nan had not been there.

In the north room she saw the roses and morning-glory paper on the wall, and also the door that should open into—what?

She asked if she might open it.

"Certainly," said Hannah; and Maria echoed, "Certainly."

She opened it, and found the china-closet. She experienced a certain relief; she at least was not under any spell. Mrs. Grant left it a china-closet; she found it the same. Good.

But she tried to induce the old sisters to remember that there had at various times been certain questions relating to a confusion as to whether the closet had always been a closet. It was no use; their stony eyes gave no sign.

Then she thought of the story of the sea-captain, and said, "Miss Keys, did you ever have a lounge covered with India chintz, with a figure of a peacock on it, given to you in Salem by a sea-captain, who brought it from India?"

"I dun'no' as I ever did," said Hannah. That was all. She thought Maria's cheeks were a little flushed, but her eyes were like a stone wall.

She went on that night to the Adirondacks. When Nan and she were alone in their room she said, "By-the-way, Nan, what did you see at the farm-house? and how did you like Maria and Hannah?"

Nan didn't mistrust that Rita had been there, and she began excitedly to tell her all about her visit. Rita could almost have believed Nan had been there if she hadn't known it was not so. She let her go on for some time, enjoying her enthusiasm, and the impressive way in which she described her opening the door and finding the 'little room.' Then Rita said: "Now, Nan, that is enough fibbing. I went to the farm myself on my way up yesterday, and there is *no* little room, and there *never* has been any; it is a china-closet, just as Mrs. Grant saw it last."

She was pretending to be busy unpacking her trunk, and did not look up for a moment; but as Nan did not say anything, she glanced at her over her shoulder. Nan was actually pale, and it was hard to say whether she was most angry or frightened. There was something of both in her look. And then Rita began to explain how her telegram had put her in the spirit of going up there alone. She hadn't meant to cut Nan out. She only thought— Then Nan broke in: "It isn't that; I am sure you can't think it is that. But I went myself, and you did not go; you can't have been there, for *it is a little room*."

Oh, what a night they had! They couldn't sleep. They talked and argued, and then kept still for a while, only to break out again, it was so absurd. They both maintained that they had been there, but both felt sure the other one was either crazy or obstinate beyond reason. They were wretched; it was perfectly ridiculous, two friends at odds over such a thing; but there it was—"little room," "china-closet,"—"china-closet," "little room."

The next morning Nan was tacking up some tarlatan at a window to keep the midges out. Rita offered to help her, as she had done for the past ten years. Nan's "No, thanks," cut her to the heart.

"Nan," said she, "come right down from that step-ladder and pack your satchel. The stage leaves in just twenty minutes. We can catch the afternoon express train, and we will go together to the farm. I am either going there or going home. You better go with me."

Nan didn't say a word. She gathered up the hammer and tacks, and was ready to start when the stage came round.

It meant for them thirty miles of staging and six hours of train, besides crossing the lake; but what of that, compared with having a lie lying round loose between them! Europe would have seemed easy to accomplish, if it would settle the question.

At the little junction in Vermont they found a farmer with a wagon full of meal-bags. They asked him if he could not take them up to the old Keys farm and bring them back in time for the return train, due in two hours.

They had planned to call it a sketching trip, so they said, "We have been there before, we are artists, and we might find some views worth taking; and we want also to make a short call upon the Misses Keys."

"Did ye calculate to paint the old *house* in the picture?"

They said it was possible they might do so. They wanted to see it, anyway.

"Waal, I guess you are too late. The *house* burnt down last night, and everything in it."

THE RED ROOM

H. G. WELLS

(1896)

"I can assure you," said I, "that it will take a very tangible ghost to frighten me." And I stood up before the fire with my glass in my hand.

"It is your own choosing," said the man with the withered arm, and glanced at me askance.

"Eight-and-twenty years," said I, "I have lived, and never a ghost have I seen as yet."

The old woman sat staring hard into the fire, her pale eyes wide open. "Ay," she broke in; "and eight-and-twenty years you have lived and never seen the likes of this house, I reckon. There's a many things to see, when one's still but eight-and-twenty." She swayed her head slowly from side to side. "A many things to see and sorrow for."

I half suspected the old people were trying to enhance the spiritual terrors of their house by their droning insistence. I put down my empty glass on the table and looked about the room, and caught a glimpse of myself, abbreviated and broadened to an impossible sturdiness, in the queer old mirror at the

end of the room. "Well," I said, "if I see anything
to-night, I shall be so much the wiser. For I come to
the business with an open mind."

"It's your own choosing," said the man with the
withered arm once more.

I heard the faint sound of a stick and a shambling
step on the flags in the passage outside. The door
creaked on its hinges as a second old man entered,
more bent, more wrinkled, more aged even than the
first. He supported himself by the help of a crutch,
his eyes were covered by a shade, and his lower lip,
half averted, hung pale and pink from his decaying yellow teeth. He made straight for an armchair
on the opposite side of the table, sat down clumsily, and began to cough. The man with the withered
hand gave the newcomer a short glance of positive
dislike; the old woman took no notice of his arrival,
but remained with her eyes fixed steadily on the fire.

"I said—it's your own choosing," said the man
with the withered hand, when the coughing had
ceased for a while.

"It's my own choosing," I answered.

The man with the shade became aware of my presence for the first time, and threw his head back for
a moment, and sidewise, to see me. I caught a momentary glimpse of his eyes, small and bright and
inflamed. Then he began to cough and splutter again.

"Why don't you drink?" said the man with the
withered arm, pushing the beer toward him. The

man with the shade poured out a glassful with a
shaking hand, that splashed half as much again on
the deal table. A monstrous shadow of him crouched
upon the wall, and mocked his action as he poured
and drank. I must confess I had scarcely expected
these grotesque custodians. There is, to my mind,
something inhuman in senility, something crouching and atavistic; the human qualities seem to drop
from old people insensibly day by day. The three of
them made me feel uncomfortable with their gaunt
silences, their bent carriage, their evident unfriend-
liness to me and to one another. And that night,
perhaps, I was in the mood for uncomfortable impressions. I resolved to get away from their vague
foreshadowings of the evil things upstairs.

"If," said I, "you will show me to this haunted
room of yours, I will make myself comfortable there."

The old man with the cough jerked his head back
so suddenly that it startled me, and shot another
glance of his red eyes at me from out of the darkness
under the shade, but no one answered me. I waited
a minute, glancing from one to the other. The old
woman stared like a dead body, glaring into the fire
with lack-lustre eyes.

"If," I said, a little louder, "if you will show me
to this haunted room of yours, I will relieve you
from the task of entertaining me."

"There's a candle on the slab outside the door,"
said the man with the withered hand, looking at my

feet as he addressed me. "But if you go to the Red
Room to-night—"

("This night of all nights!" said the old woman,
softly.)

"You go alone."

"Very well," I answered, shortly, "and which way
do I go?"

"You go along the passage for a bit," said he, nodding his head on his shoulder at the door, "until you
come to a spiral staircase; and on the second landing
is a door covered with green baize. Go through that,
and down the long corridor to the end, and the Red
Room is on your left up the steps."

"Have I got that right?" I said, and repeated his
directions.

He corrected me in one particular.

"And you are really going?" said the man with the
shade, looking at me again for the third time with
that queer, unnatural tilting of the face.

("This night of all nights!" whispered the old
woman.)

"It is what I came for," I said, and moved toward
the door. As I did so, the old man with the shade
rose and staggered round the table, so as to be closer
to the others and to the fire. At the door I turned
and looked at them, and saw they were all close together, dark against the firelight, staring at me over
their shoulders, with an intent expression on their
ancient faces.

"Good-night," I said, setting the door open. "It's your own choosing," said the man with the withered arm.

I left the door wide open until the candle was well alight, and then I shut them in, and walked down the chilly, echoing passage.

I must confess that the oddness of these three old pensioners in whose charge her ladyship had left the castle, and the deep-toned, old-fashioned furniture of the housekeeper's room, in which they foregathered, had affected me curiously in spite of my effort to keep myself at a matter-of-fact phase. They seemed to belong to another age, an older age, an age when things spiritual were indeed to be feared, when common sense was uncommon, an age when omens and witches were credible, and ghosts beyond denying. Their very existence, thought I, is spectral; the cut of their clothing, fashions born in dead brains; the ornaments and conveniences in the room about them even are ghostly—the thoughts of vanished men, which still haunt rather than participate in the world of to-day. And the passage I was in, long and shadowy, with a film of moisture glistening on the wall, was as gaunt and cold as a thing that is dead and rigid. But with an effort I sent such thoughts to the right-about. The long, drafty subterranean passage was chilly and dusty, and my candle flared and made the shadows cower and quiver. The echoes rang up and down the spiral staircase, and a shadow came sweeping up after me, and another fled before me into the darkness overhead. I came to the wide landing and stopped there for a moment listening to a rustling that I fancied I heard creeping behind me, and then, satisfied of the absolute silence, pushed open the unwilling baize-covered door and stood in the silent corridor.

The effect was scarcely what I expected, for the moonlight, coming in by the great window on the grand staircase, picked out everything in vivid black shadow or reticulated silvery illumination. Everything seemed in its proper position; the house might have been deserted on the yesterday instead of twelve months ago. There were candles in the sockets of the sconces, and whatever dust had gathered on the carpets or upon the polished flooring was distributed so evenly as to be invisible in my candlelight. A waiting stillness was over everything. I was about to advance, and stopped abruptly. A bronze group stood upon the landing hidden from me by a corner of the wall; but its shadow fell with marvelous distinctness upon the white paneling, and gave me the impression of some one crouching to waylay me. The thing jumped upon my attention suddenly. I stood rigid for half a moment, perhaps. Then, with my hand in the pocket that held the revolver, I advanced, only to discover a Ganymede and Eagle, glistening in the moonlight. That incident for a time restored my nerve, and a dim porcelain Chinaman on a buhl table, whose head rocked as I passed, scarcely startled me.

The door of the Red Room and the steps up to it were in a shadowy corner. I moved my candle from side to side in order to see clearly the nature of the recess in which I stood, before opening the door. Here it was, thought I, that my predecessor was found, and the memory of that story gave me a sudden twinge of apprehension. I glanced over my shoulder at the black Ganymede in the moonlight, and opened the door of the Red Room rather hastily, with my face half turned to the pallid silence of the corridor.

I entered, closed the door behind me at once, turned the key I found in the lock within, and stood with the candle held aloft surveying the scene of my vigil, the great Red Room of Lorraine Castle, in which the young Duke had died; or rather in which he had begun his dying, for he had opened the door and fallen headlong down the steps I had just ascended. That had been the end of *his* vigil, of his gallant attempt to conquer the ghostly tradition of the place, and never, I thought, had apoplexy better served the ends of superstition. There were other and older stories that clung to the room, back to the half-incredible beginning of it all, the tale of a timid wife and the tragic end that came to her husband's jest of frightening her. And looking round that huge shadowy room with its black window bays, its recesses and alcoves, its dusty brown-red hangings and dark gigantic furniture, one could well understand the legends that had sprouted in its black corners, its germinating darknesses. My candle was a little tongue of light in the vastness of the chamber; its rays failed to pierce to the opposite end of the room, and left an ocean of dull red mystery and suggestion, sentinel shadows and watching darknesses beyond its island of light. And the stillness of desolation brooded over it all.

I must confess some impalpable quality of that ancient room disturbed me. I tried to fight the feeling down. I resolved to make a systematic examination of the place, and so, by leaving nothing to the imagination, dispel the fanciful suggestions of the obscurity before they obtained a hold upon me. After satisfying myself of the fastening of the door, I began to walk round the room, peering round each article of furniture, tucking up the valances of the bed and opening its curtains wide. In one place there was a distinct echo to my footsteps, the noises I made seemed so little that they enhanced rather than broke the silence of the place. I pulled up the blinds and examined the fastenings of the several windows. Attracted by the fall of a particle of dust, I leaned forward and looked up the blackness of the wide chimney. Then, trying to preserve my scientific attitude of mind, I walked round and began tapping the oak paneling for any secret opening, but I desisted before reaching the alcove. I saw my face in a mirror—white.

There were two big mirrors in the room, each with a pair of sconces bearing candles, and on the mantelshelf, too, were candles in china candle-sticks. All these I lit one after the other. The fire was laid—an unexpected consideration from the old housekeeper—and I lit it, to keep down any disposition to shiver, and when it was burning well I stood round with my back to it and regarded the room again. I had pulled up a chintz-covered armchair and a table to form a kind of barricade before me. On this lay my revolver, ready to hand. My precise examination had done me a little good, but I still found the remoter darkness of the place and its perfect stillness too stimulating for the imagination. The echoing of the stir and crackling of the fire was no sort of comfort to me. The shadow in the alcove at the end of the room began to display that undefinable quality of a presence, that odd suggestion of a lurking living thing that comes so easily in silence and solitude. And to reassure myself, I walked with a candle into it and satisfied myself that there was nothing tangible there. I stood that candle upon the floor of the alcove and left it in that position.

By this time I was in a state of considerable nervous tension, although to my reason there was no ad-

equate cause for my condition. My mind, however,
was perfectly clear. I postulated quite unreservedly
that nothing supernatural could happen, and to pass
the time I began stringing some rhymes together,
Ingoldsby fashion, concerning the original legend of
the place. A few I spoke aloud, but the echoes were
not pleasant* For the same reason I also abandoned,
after a time, a conversation with myself upon the
impossibility of ghosts and haunting. My mind re-
verted to the three old and distorted people downstairs, and I tried to keep it upon that topic.

The sombre reds and grays of the room troubled
me; even with its seven candles the place was merely
dim. The light in the alcove flaring in a draft, and
the fire flickering, kept the shadows and penum-
bra perpetually shifting and stirring in a noiseless
flighty dance. Casting about for a remedy, I recalled
the wax candles I had seen in the corridor, and,
with a slight effort, carrying a candle and leaving
the door open, I walked out into the moonlight, and
presently returned with as many as ten. These I put
in the various knick-knacks of china with which the
room was sparsely adorned, and lit and placed them
where the shadows had lain deepest, some on the
floor, some in the window recesses, arranging and
rearranging them until at last my seventeen candles
were so placed that not an inch of the room but had
the direct light of at least one of them. It occurred to
me that when the ghost came I could warn him not

to trip over them. The room was now quite brightly illuminated. There was something very cheering and reassuring in these little silent streaming flames, and to notice their steady diminution of length offered me an occupation and gave me a reassuring sense of the passage of time.

Even with that, however, the brooding expectation of the vigil weighed heavily enough upon me. I stood watching the minute hand of my watch creep towards midnight.

Then something happened in the alcove. I did not see the candle go out, I simply turned and saw that the darkness was there, as one might start and see the unexpected presence of a stranger. The black shadow had sprung back to its place. "By Jove," said I aloud, recovering from my surprise, "that draft's a strong one;" and taking the matchbox from the table, I walked across the room in a leisurely manner to relight the corner again. My first match would not strike, and as I succeeded with the second, something seemed to blink on the wall before me. I turned my head involuntarily and saw that the two candles on the little table by the fireplace were extinguished. I rose at once to my feet.

"Odd," I said. "Did I do that myself in a flash of absent-mindedness?"

I walked back, relit one, and as I did so I saw the candle in the right sconce of one of the mirrors wink and go right out, and almost immediately its companion followed it. The flames vanished as if the wick had been suddenly nipped between a finger and thumb, leaving the wick neither glowing nor smoking, but black. While I stood gaping the candle at the foot of the bed went out, and the shadows seemed to take another step toward me.

"This won't do!" said I, and first one and then another candle on the mantelshelf followed.

"What's up?" I cried, with a queer high note getting into my voice somehow. At that the candle on the corner of the wardrobe went out, and the one I had relit in the alcove followed.

"Steady on!" I said, "those candles are wanted," speaking with a half-hysterical facetiousness, and scratching away at a match the while, "for the mantel candlesticks." My hands trembled so much that twice I missed the rough paper of the matchbox. As the mantel emerged from darkness again, two candles in the remoter end of the room were eclipsed. But with the same match I also relit the larger mirror candles, and those on the floor near the doorway, so that for the moment I seemed to gain on the extinctions. But then in a noiseless volley there vanished four lights at once in different corners of the room, and I struck another match in quivering haste, and stood hesitating whither to take it.

As I stood undecided, an invisible hand seemed to sweep out the two candles on the table. With a cry of terror I dashed at the alcove, then into the

corner and then into the window, relighting three as
two more vanished by the fireplace, and then, perceiving a better way, I dropped matches on the iron-
bound deedbox in the corner, and caught up the
bedroom candlestick. With this I avoided the delay
of striking matches, but for all that the steady process of extinction went on, and the shadows I feared
and fought against returned, and crept in upon me,
first a step gained on this side of me, then on that. I
was now almost frantic with the horror of the coming darkness, and my self-possession deserted me.
I leaped panting from candle to candle in a vain
struggle against that remorseless advance.

I bruised myself in the thigh against the table,
I sent a chair headlong, I stumbled and fell and
whisked the cloth from the table in my fall. My candle rolled away from me and I snatched another as I
rose. Abruptly this was blown out as I swung it off
the table by the wind of my sudden movement, and
immediately the two remaining candles followed.
But there was light still in the room, a red light,
that streamed across the ceiling and staved off the
shadows from me. The fire! Of course I could still
thrust my candle between the bars and relight it.

I turned to where the flames were still dancing
between the glowing coals and splashing red reflections upon the furniture; made two steps toward the
grate, and incontinently the flames dwindled and
vanished, the glow vanished, the reflections rushed

together and disappeared, and as I thrust the candle between the bars darkness closed upon me like the shutting of an eye, wrapped about me in a stifling embrace, sealed my vision, and crushed the last vestiges of self-possession from my brain. And it was not only palpable darkness, but intolerable terror. The candle fell from my hands. I flung out my arms in a vain effort to thrust that ponderous blackness away from me, and lifting up my voice, screamed with all my might, once, twice, thrice. Then I think I must have staggered to my feet. I know I thought suddenly of the moonlit corridor, and with my head bowed and my arms over my face, made a stumbling run for the door.

But I had forgotten the exact position of the door, and I struck myself heavily against the corner of the bed. I staggered back, turned, and was either struck or struck myself against some other bulky furnishing. I have a vague memory of battering myself thus to and fro in the darkness, of a heavy blow at last upon my forehead, of a horrible sensation of falling that lasted an age, of my last frantic effort to keep my footing, and then I remember no more.

I opened my eyes in daylight. My head was roughly bandaged, and the man with the withered hand was watching my face. I looked about me trying to remember what had happened, and for a space I could not recollect. I rolled my eyes into the corner and saw the old woman, no longer abstracted, no longer terrible, pouring out some drops of medicine from a little blue phial into a glass. "Where am I?" I said. "I seem to remember you, and yet I can not remember who you are."

They told me then, and I heard of the haunted Red Room as one who hears a tale. "We found you at dawn," said he, "and there was blood on your forehead and lips."

I wondered that I had ever disliked him. The three of them in the daylight seemed commonplace old folk enough. The man with the green shade had his head bent as one who sleeps.

It was very slowly I recovered the memory of my experience. "You believe now," said the old man with the withered hand, "that the room is haunted?" He spoke no longer as one who greets an intruder, but as one who condoles with a friend.

"Yes," said I, "the room is haunted."

"And you have seen it. And we who have been here all our lives have never set eyes upon it. Because we have never dared. Tell us, is it truly the old earl who—"

"No," said I, "it is not."

"I told you so," said the old lady, with the glass in her hand. "It is his poor young countess who was frightened—"

"It is not," I said. "There is neither ghost of earl nor ghost of countess in that room; there is no ghost there at all, but worse, far worse, something impalpable—"

"Well?" they said.

"The worst of all the things that haunt poor mortal men," said I; "and that is, in all its nakedness— *Fear!* Fear that will not have light nor sound, that will not bear with reason, that deafens and darkens and overwhelms. It followed me through the corridor, it fought against me in the room—"

I stopped abruptly. There was an interval of silence. My hand went up to my bandages. "The candles went out one after another, and I fled—"

Then the man with the shade lifted his face sideways to see me and spoke.

"That is it," said he. "I knew that was it. A Power of Darkness. To put such a curse upon a home! It lurks there always. You can feel it even in the daytime, even of a bright summer's day, in the hangings, in the curtains, keeping behind you however you face about. In the dusk it creeps in the corridor and follows you, so that you dare not turn. It is even as you say. Fear itself is in that room. Black Fear. . . . And there it will be . . . so long as this house of sin endures."

THE HOUSE THAT WAS NOT

ELIA WILKINSON PEATTIE
(1898)

Bart Fleming took his bride out to his ranch on the
plains when she was but seventeen years old, and the
two set up housekeeping in three hundred and twenty acres of corn and rye. Off toward the west there
was an unbroken sea of tossing corn at that time of
the year when the bride came out, and as her sewing
window was on the side of the house which faced
the sunset, she passed a good part of each day looking into that great rustling mass, breathing in its
succulent odors and listening to its sibilant melody.
It was her picture gallery, her opera, her spectacle,
and, being sensible,—or perhaps, being merely happy,—she made the most of it.

When harvesting time came and the corn was cut,
she had much entertainment in discovering what lay
beyond. The town was east, and it chanced that she
had never ridden west. So, when the rolling hills of
this newly beholden land lifted themselves for her
contemplation, and the harvest sun, all in an angry and sanguinary glow sank in the veiled horizon,

and at noon a scarf of golden vapor wavered up and down along the earth line, it was as if a new world had been made for her. Sometimes, at the coming of a storm, a whip-lash of purple cloud, full of electric agility, snapped along the western horizon.

"Oh, you'll see a lot of queer things on these here plains," her husband said when she spoke to him of these phenomena. "I guess what you see is the wind."

"The wind!" cried Flora. "You can't see the wind, Bart."

"Now look here, Flora," returned Bart, with benevolent emphasis, "you're a smart one, but you don't know all I know about this here country. I've lived here three mortal years, waitin' for you to git up out of your mother's arms and come out to keep me company, and I know what there is to know. Some things out here is queer—so queer folks wouldn't believe 'em unless they saw. An' some's so pig-headed they don't believe their own eyes. As for th' wind, if you lay down flat and squint toward th' west, you can see it blowin' along near th' ground, like a big ribbon; an' sometimes it's th' color of air, an' sometimes it's silver an' gold, an' sometimes, when a storm is comin', it's purple."

"If you got so tired looking at the wind, why didn't you marry some other girl, Bart, instead of waiting for me?"

Flora was more interested in the first part of Bart's speech than in the last.

"Oh, come on!" protested Bart, and he picked her up in his arms and jumped her toward the ceiling of the low shack as if she were a little girl—but then, to be sure, she wasn't much more.

Of all the things Flora saw when the corn was cut down, nothing interested her so much as a low cottage, something like her own, which lay away in the distance. She could not guess how far it might be, because distances are deceiving out there, where the altitude is high and the air is as clear as one of those mystic balls of glass in which the sallow mystics of India see the moving shadows of the future.

She had not known there were neighbors so near, and she wondered for several days about them before she ventured to say anything to Bart on the subject. Indeed, for some reason which she did not attempt to explain to herself, she felt shy about broaching the matter. Perhaps Bart did not want her to know the people. The thought came to her, as naughty thoughts will come, even to the best of persons, that some handsome young men might be "baching" it out there by themselves, and Bart didn't wish her to make their acquaintance. Bart had flattered her so much that she had actually begun to think herself beautiful, though as a matter of fact she was only a nice little girl with a lot of reddish-brown hair, and a bright pair of reddish-brown eyes in a white face.

"Bart," she ventured one evening, as the sun, at its fiercest, rushed toward the great black hollow of the west, "who lives over there in that shack?"

She turned away from the window where she had been looking at the incarnadined disk, and she thought she saw Bart turn pale. But then, her eyes were so blurred with the glory she had been gazing at, that she might easily have been mistaken.

"I say, Bart, why don't you speak? If there's any one around to associate with, I should think you'd let me have the benefit of their company. It isn't as funny as you think, staying here alone days and days."

"You ain't gettin' homesick, be you, sweetheart?" cried Bart, putting his arms around her. "You ain't gettin' tired of my society, be yeh?"

It took some time to answer this question in a satisfactory manner, but at length Flora was able to return to her original topic.

"But the shack, Bart! Who lives there, anyway?"

"I'm not acquainted with 'em," said Bart, sharply. "Ain't them biscuits done, Flora?"

Then, of course, she grew obstinate.

"Those biscuits will never be done, Bart, till I know about that house, and why you never spoke of it, and why nobody ever comes down the road from there. Some one lives there I know, for in the mornings and at night I see the smoke coming out of the chimney."

"Do you now?" cried Bart, opening his eyes and looking at her with unfeigned interest. "Well, do you know, sometimes I've fancied I seen that too?"

"Well, why not," cried Flora, in half anger. "Why shouldn't you?"

"See here, Flora, take them biscuits out an' listen to me. There ain't no house there. Hello! I didn't know you'd go for to drop the biscuits. Wait, I'll help you pick 'em up. By cracky, they're hot, ain't they? What you puttin' a towel over 'em for? Well, you set down here on my knee, so. Now you look over at that there house. You see it, don't yeh? Well, it ain't there! No! I saw it the first week I was out here. I was jus' half dyin', thinkin' of you an' wonderin' why you didn't write. That was the time you was mad at me. So I rode over there one day—lookin' up company, so t' speak—and there wa'n't no house there. I spent all one Sunday lookin' for it. Then I spoke to Jim Geary about it. He laughed an' got a little white about th' gills, an' he said he guessed I'd have to look a good while before I found it. He said that there shack was an ole joke."

"Why—what—"

"Well, this here is th' story he tol' me. He said a man an' his wife come out here t' live an' put up that there little place. An' she was young, you know, an' kind o' skeery, and she got lonesome. It worked on her an' worked on her, an' one day she up an' killed the baby an' her husband an' herself. Th' folks found 'em and buried 'em right there on their own ground. Well, about two weeks after that, th' house was burned down. Don't know how. Tramps, maybe. Anyhow, it burned. At least, I guess it burned!"

"You guess it burned!"

"Well, it ain't there, you know."

"But if it burned the ashes are there."

"All right, girlie, they're there then. Now let's have tea."

This they proceeded to do, and were happy and cheerful all evening, but that didn't keep Flora from rising at the first flush of dawn and stealing out of the house. She looked away over west as she went to the barn and there, dark and firm against the horizon, stood the little house against the pellucid sky of morning. She got on Ginger's back—Ginger being her own yellow broncho—and set off at a hard pace for the house. It didn't appear to come any nearer, but the objects which had seemed to be beside it came closer into view, and Flora pressed on, with her mind steeled for anything. But as she approached the poplar windbreak which stood to the north of the house, the little shack waned like a shadow before her. It faded and dimmed before her eyes.

She slapped Ginger's flanks and kept him going, and she at last got him up to the spot. But there was nothing there. The bunch grass grew tall and rank and in the midst of it lay a baby's shoe. Flora thought of picking it up, but something cold in her veins withheld her. Then she grew angry, and set

Ginger's head toward the place and tried to drive him over it. But the yellow broncho gave one snort of fear, gathered himself in a bunch, and then, all tense, leaping muscles, made for home as only a broncho can.

A CASE OF EAVESDROPPING

ALGERNON BLACKWOOD

(1900)

Jim Shorthouse was the sort of fellow who always made a mess of things. Everything with which his hands or mind came into contact issued from such contact in an unqualified and irremediable state of mess. His college days were a mess: he was twice rusticated. His schooldays were a mess: he went to half a dozen, each passing him on to the next with a worse character and in a more developed state of mess. His early boyhood was the sort of mess that copy-books and dictionaries spell with a big "M," and his babyhood—ugh! was the embodiment of howling, yowling, screaming mess.

At the age of forty, however, there came a change in his troubled life, when he met a girl with half a million in her own right, who consented to marry him, and who very soon succeeded in reducing his most messy existence into a state of comparative order and system.

Certain incidents, important and otherwise, of Jim's life would never have come to be told here but for the fact that in getting into his "messes" and out of them again he succeeded in drawing himself into the atmosphere of peculiar circumstances and strange happenings. He attracted to his path the curious adventures of life as unfailingly as meat attracts flies, and jam wasps. It is to the meat and jam of his life, so to speak, that he owes his experiences; his after-life was all pudding, which attracts nothing but greedy children. With marriage the interest of his life ceased for all but one person, and his path became regular as the sun's instead of erratic as a comet's.

The first experience in order of time that he related to me shows that somewhere latent behind his disarranged nervous system there lay psychic perceptions of an uncommon order. About the age of twenty-two—I think after his second rustication—his father's purse and patience had equally given out, and Jim found himself stranded high and dry in a large American city. High and dry! And the only clothes that had no holes in them safely in the keeping of his uncle's wardrobe.

Careful reflection on a bench in one of the city parks led him to the conclusion that the only thing to do was to persuade the city editor of one of the daily journals that he possessed an observant mind and a ready pen, and that he could "do good work for your paper, sir, as a reporter." This, then, he did, standing at a most unnatural angle between the editor and the window to conceal the whereabouts of the holes.

"Guess we'll have to give you a week's trial," said the editor, who, ever on the lookout for good chance material, took on shoals of men in that way and retained on the average one man per shoal. Anyhow it gave Jim Shorthouse the wherewithal to sew up the holes and relieve his uncle's wardrobe of its burden.

Then he went to find living quarters; and in this proceeding his unique characteristics already referred to—what theosophists would call his Karma—began unmistakably to assert themselves, for it was in the house he eventually selected that this sad tale took place.

There are no "diggings" in American cities. The alternatives for small incomes are grim enough—rooms in a boarding-house where meals are served, or in a room-house where no meals are served—not even breakfast. Rich people live in palaces, of course, but Jim had nothing to do with "sich-like." His horizon was bounded by boarding-houses and room-houses; and, owing to the necessary irregularity of his meals and hours, he took the latter.

It was a large, gaunt-looking place in a side street, with dirty windows and a creaking iron gate, but the rooms were large, and the one he selected and paid for in advance was on the top floor. The landlady looked gaunt and dusty as the house, and quite as old. Her eyes were green and faded, and her features large.

"Waal," she twanged, with her electrifying Western drawl, "that's the room, if you like it, and that's the price I said. Now, if you want it, why, just say so; and if you don't, why, it don't hurt me any."

Jim wanted to shake her, but he feared the clouds of long-accumulated dust in her clothes, and as the price and size of the room suited him, he decided to take it.

"Anyone else on this floor?" he asked.

She looked at him queerly out of her faded eyes before she answered.

"None of my guests ever put such questions to me before," she said; "but I guess you're different. Why, there's no one at all but an old gent that's stayed here every bit of five years. He's over thar," pointing to the end of the passage.

"Ah! I see," said Shorthouse feebly. "So I'm alone up here?"

"Reckon you are, pretty near," she twanged out, ending the conversation abruptly by turning her back on her new "guest," and going slowly and deliberately downstairs.

The newspaper work kept Shorthouse out most of the night. Three times a week he got home at 1 a.m., and three times at 3 a.m. The room proved comfortable enough, and he paid for a second week. His unusual hours had so far prevented his meeting any inmates of the house, and not a sound had been heard from the "old gent" who shared the floor with him. It seemed a very quiet house.

One night, about the middle of the second week, he came home tired after a long day's work. The lamp that usually stood all night in the hall had burned itself out, and he had to stumble upstairs in the dark. He made considerable noise in doing so, but nobody seemed to be disturbed. The whole house was utterly quiet, and probably everybody was asleep. There were no lights under any of the doors. All was in darkness. It was after two o'clock.

After reading some English letters that had come during the day, and dipping for a few minutes into a book, he became drowsy and got ready for bed. Just as he was about to get in between the sheets, he stopped for a moment and listened. There rose in the night, as he did so, the sound of steps somewhere in the house below. Listening attentively, he heard that it was somebody coming upstairs—a heavy tread, and the owner taking no pains to step quietly. On it came up the stairs, tramp, tramp, tramp—evidently the tread of a big man, and one in something of a hurry.

At once thoughts connected somehow with fire and police flashed through Jim's brain, but there were no sounds of voices with the steps, and he reflected in the same moment that it could only be the old gentleman keeping late hours and tumbling

upstairs in the darkness. He was in the act of turning out the gas and stepping into bed, when the
house resumed its former stillness by the footsteps
suddenly coming to a dead stop immediately outside
his own room.

With his hand on the gas, Shorthouse paused
a moment before turning it out to see if the steps
would go on again, when he was startled by a loud
knocking on his door. Instantly, in obedience to a
curious and unexplained instinct, he turned out the
light, leaving himself and the room in total darkness.

He had scarcely taken a step across the room to
open the door, when a voice from the other side of
the wall, so close it almost sounded in his ear, exclaimed in German, "Is that you, father? Come in."

The speaker was a man in the next room, and the
knocking, after all, had not been on his own door,
but on that of the adjoining chamber, which he had
supposed to be vacant.

Almost before the man in the passage had time to
answer in German, "Let me in at once," Jim heard
someone cross the floor and unlock the door. Then
it was slammed to with a bang, and there was audible the sound of footsteps about the room, and
of chairs being drawn up to a table and knocking
against furniture on the way. The men seemed wholly regardless of their neighbour's comfort, for they
made noise enough to waken the dead.

"Serves me right for taking a room in such a cheap hole," reflected Jim in the darkness. "I wonder whom she's let the room to!"

The two rooms, the landlady had told him, were originally one. She had put up a thin partition—just a row of boards—to increase her income. The doors were adjacent, and only separated by the massive upright beam between them. When one was opened or shut the other rattled.

With utter indifference to the comfort of the other sleepers in the house, the two Germans had meanwhile commenced to talk both at once and at the top of their voices. They talked emphatically, even angrily. The words "Father" and "Otto" were freely used. Shorthouse understood German, but as he stood listening for the first minute or two, an eavesdropper in spite of himself, it was difficult to make head or tail of the talk, for neither would give way to the other, and the jumble of guttural sounds and unfinished sentences was wholly unintelligible. Then, very suddenly, both voices dropped together; and, after a moment's pause, the deep tones of one of them, who seemed to be the "father," said, with the utmost distinctness—

"You mean, Otto, that you refuse to get it?"

There was a sound of someone shuffling in the chair before the answer came. "I mean that I don't know how to get it. It is so much, father. It is *too* much. A part of it—"

"A part of it!" cried the other, with an angry oath, "a part of it, when ruin and disgrace are already in the house, is worse than useless. If you can get half you can get all, you wretched fool. Half-measures only damn all concerned."

"You told me last time—" began the other firmly, but was not allowed to finish. A succession of horrible oaths drowned his sentence, and the father went on, in a voice vibrating with anger—

"You know she will give you anything. You have only been married a few months. If you ask and give a plausible reason you can get all we want and more. You can ask it temporarily. All will be paid back. It will re-establish the firm, and she will never know what was done with it. With that amount, Otto, you know I can recoup all these terrible losses, and in less than a year all will be repaid. But without it. . . . You must get it, Otto. Hear me, you must. Am I to be arrested for the misuse of trust moneys? Is our honoured name to be cursed and spat on?" The old man choked and stammered in his anger and desperation.

Shorthouse stood shivering in the darkness and listening in spite of himself. The conversation had carried him along with it, and he had been for some reason afraid to let his neighbourhood be known. But at this point he realised that he had listened too long and that he must inform the two men that they could be overheard to every single syllable. So he coughed loudly, and at the same time rattled the handle of his door. It seemed to have no effect, for the voices continued just as loudly as before, the son protesting and the father growing more and more angry. He coughed again persistently, and also contrived purposely in the darkness to tumble against the partition, feeling the thin boards yield easily under his weight, and making a considerable noise in so doing. But the voices went on unconcernedly, and louder than ever. Could it be possible they had not heard?

By this time Jim was more concerned about his own sleep than the morality of overhearing the private scandals of his neighbours, and he went out into the passage and knocked smartly at their door. Instantly, as if by magic, the sounds ceased. Everything dropped into utter silence. There was no light under the door and not a whisper could be heard within. He knocked again, but received no answer.

"Gentlemen," he began at length, with his lips close to the keyhole and in German, "please do not talk so loud. I can overhear all you say in the next room. Besides, it is very late, and I wish to sleep."

He paused and listened, but no answer was forthcoming. He turned the handle and found the door was locked. Not a sound broke the stillness of the night except the faint swish of the wind over the skylight and the creaking of a board here and there in the house below. The cold air of a very early morning crept down the passage, and made him shiver. The silence of the house began to impress him disagreeably. He looked behind him and about him, hoping, and yet fearing, that something would break the stillness. The voices still seemed to ring on in his ears; but that sudden silence, when he knocked at the door, affected him far more unpleasantly than the voices, and put strange thoughts in his brain—thoughts he did not like or approve.

Moving stealthily from the door, he peered over the banisters into the space below. It was like a deep vault that might conceal in its shadows anything that was not good. It was not difficult to fancy he saw an indistinct moving to-and-fro below him. Was that a figure sitting on the stairs peering up obliquely at him out of hideous eyes? Was that a sound of whispering and shuffling down there in the dark halls and forsaken landings? Was it something more than the inarticulate murmur of the night?

The wind made an effort overhead, singing over the skylight, and the door behind him rattled and made him start. He turned to go back to his room, and the draught closed the door slowly in his face as if there were someone pressing against it from the other side. When he pushed it open and went in, a hundred shadowy forms seemed to dart swiftly and silently back to their corners and hiding-places. But in the adjoining room the sounds had entirely ceased, and Shorthouse soon crept into bed, and left the house with its inmates, waking or sleeping, to take care of themselves, while he entered the region of dreams and silence.

Next day, strong in the common sense that the sunlight brings, he determined to lodge a complaint against the noisy occupants of the next room and make the landlady request them to modify their voices at such late hours of the night and morning. But it so happened that she was not to be seen that day, and when he returned from the office at midnight it was, of course, too late.

Looking under the door as he came up to bed he noticed that there was no light, and concluded that the Germans were not in. So much the better. He went to sleep about one o'clock, fully decided that if they came up later and woke him with their horrible noises he would not rest till he had roused the landlady and made her reprove them with that authoritative twang, in which every word was like the lash of a metallic whip.

However, there proved to be no need for such drastic measures, for Shorthouse slumbered peacefully all night, and his dreams—chiefly of the fields of grain and flocks of sheep on the far-away farms of his father's estate—were permitted to run their fanciful course unbroken.

Two nights later, however, when he came home tired out, after a difficult day, and wet and blown about by one of the wickedest storms he had ever

A HOUSE A-HAUNT

seen, his dreams—always of the fields and sheep—
were not destined to be so undisturbed.

He had already dozed off in that delicious glow
that follows the removal of wet clothes and the immediate snuggling under warm blankets, when his
consciousness, hovering on the borderland between
sleep and waking, was vaguely troubled by a sound
that rose indistinctly from the depths of the house,
and, between the gusts of wind and rain, reached
his ears with an accompanying sense of uneasiness
and discomfort. It rose on the night air with some
pretence of regularity, dying away again in the roar
of the wind to reassert itself distantly in the deep,
brief hushes of the storm.

For a few minutes Jim's dreams were coloured
only—tinged, as it were, by this impression of fear
approaching from somewhere insensibly upon him.
His consciousness, at first, refused to be drawn back
from that enchanted region where it had wandered,
and he did not immediately awaken. But the nature of his dreams changed unpleasantly. He saw
the sheep suddenly run huddled together, as though
frightened by the neighbourhood of an enemy, while
the fields of waving corn became agitated as though
some monster were moving uncouthly among the
crowded stalks. The sky grew dark, and in his dream
an awful sound came somewhere from the clouds. It
was in reality the sound downstairs growing more
distinct.

Shorthouse shifted uneasily across the bed with something like a groan of distress. The next minute he awoke, and found himself sitting straight up in bed—listening. Was it a nightmare? Had he been dreaming evil dreams, that his flesh crawled and the hair stirred on his head?

The room was dark and silent, but outside the wind howled dismally and drove the rain with repeated assaults against the rattling windows. How nice it would be—the thought flashed through his mind—if all winds, like the west wind, went down with the sun! They made such fiendish noises at night, like the crying of angry voices. In the daytime they had such a different sound. If only—

Hark! It was no dream after all, for the sound was momentarily growing louder, and its *cause* was coming up the stairs. He found himself speculating feebly what this cause might be, but the sound was still too indistinct to enable him to arrive at any definite conclusion.

The voice of a church clock striking two made itself heard above the wind. It was just about the hour when the Germans had commenced their performance three nights before. Shorthouse made up his mind that if they began it again he would not put up with it for very long. Yet he was already horribly conscious of the difficulty he would have of getting out of bed. The clothes were so warm and comforting against his back. The sound, still steadily

coming nearer, had by this time become differen-
tiated from the confused clamour of the elements,
and had resolved itself into the footsteps of one or
more persons.

"The Germans, hang 'em!" thought Jim. "But
what on earth is the matter with me? I never felt so
queer in all my life."

He was trembling all over, and felt as cold as
though he were in a freezing atmosphere. His nerves
were steady enough, and he felt no diminution of
physical courage, but he was conscious of a curious
sense of malaise and trepidation, such as even the
most vigorous men have been known to experience
when in the first grip of some horrible and deadly
disease. As the footsteps approached this feeling
of weakness increased. He felt a strange lassitude
creeping over him, a sort of exhaustion, accompanied by a growing numbness in the extremities, and
a sensation of dreaminess in the head, as if perhaps
the consciousness were leaving its accustomed seat
in the brain and preparing to act on another plane.
Yet, strange to say, as the vitality was slowly withdrawn from his body, his senses seemed to grow
more acute.

Meanwhile the steps were already on the landing
at the top of the stairs, and Shorthouse, still sitting
upright in bed, heard a heavy body brush past his
door and along the wall outside, almost immediately

afterwards the loud knocking of someone's knuckles on the door of the adjoining room.

Instantly, though so far not a sound had proceeded from within, he heard, through the thin partition, a chair pushed back and a man quickly cross the floor and open the door.

"Ah! it's you," he heard in the son's voice. Had the fellow, then, been sitting silently in there all this time, waiting for his father's arrival? To Shorthouse it came not as a pleasant reflection by any means.

There was no answer to this dubious greeting, but the door was closed quickly, and then there was a sound as if a bag or parcel had been thrown on a wooden table and had slid some distance across it before stopping.

"What's that?" asked the son, with anxiety in his tone.

"You may know before I go," returned the other gruffly. Indeed his voice was more than gruff: it betrayed ill-suppressed passion.

Shorthouse was conscious of a strong desire to stop the conversation before it proceeded any further, but somehow or other his will was not equal to the task, and he could not get out of bed. The conversation went on, every tone and inflexion distinctly audible above the noise of the storm.

In a low voice the father continued. Jim missed some of the words at the beginning of the sentence.

It ended with: " . . . but now they've all left, and I've managed to get up to you. You know what I've come for." There was distinct menace in his tone.

"Yes," returned the other; "I have been waiting."

"And the money?" asked the father impatiently.

No answer.

"You've had three days to get it in, and I've contrived to stave off the worst so far—but to-morrow is the end."

No answer.

"Speak, Otto! What have you got for me? Speak, my son; for God's sake, tell me."

There was a moment's silence, during which the old man's vibrating accents seemed to echo through the rooms. Then came in a low voice the answer—

"I have nothing."

"Otto!" cried the other with passion, "nothing!"

"I can get nothing," came almost in a whisper.

"You lie!" cried the other, in a half-stifled voice. "I swear you lie. Give me the money."

A chair was heard scraping along the floor. Evidently the men had been sitting over the table, and one of them had risen. Shorthouse heard the bag or parcel drawn across the table, and then a step as if one of the men was crossing to the door.

"Father, what's in that? I must know," said Otto, with the first signs of determination in his voice. There must have been an effort on the son's part to gain possession of the parcel in question, and on the father's to retain it, for between them it fell to the ground. A curious rattle followed its contact with the floor. Instantly there were sounds of a scuffle. The men were struggling for the possession of the box. The elder man with oaths, and blasphemous imprecations, the other with short gasps that betokened the strength of his efforts. It was of short duration, and the younger man had evidently won, for a minute later was heard his angry exclamation.

"I knew it. Her jewels! You scoundrel, you shall never have them. It is a crime."

The elder man uttered a short, guttural laugh, which froze Jim's blood and made his skin creep. No word was spoken, and for the space of ten seconds there was a living silence. Then the air trembled with the sound of a thud, followed immediately by a groan and the crash of a heavy body falling over on to the table. A second later there was a lurching from the table on to the floor and against the partition that separated the rooms. The bed quivered an instant at the shock, but the unholy spell was lifted from his soul and Jim Shorthouse sprang out of bed and across the floor in a single bound. He knew that ghastly murder had been done—the murder by a father of his son.

With shaking fingers but a determined heart he lit the gas, and the first thing in which his eyes corroborated the evidence of his ears was the horrifying detail that the lower portion of the partition bulged unnaturally into his own room. The glaring paper with which it was covered had cracked under the tension and the boards beneath it bent inwards towards him. What hideous load was behind them, he shuddered to think.

All this he saw in less than a second. Since the final lurch against the wall not a sound had proceeded from the room, not even a groan or a footstep. All was still but the howl of the wind, which to his ears had in it a note of triumphant horror.

Shorthouse was in the act of leaving the room to rouse the house and send for the police—in fact his hand was already on the door-knob—when something in the room arrested his attention. Out of the corner of his eyes he thought he caught sight of something moving. He was sure of it, and turning his eyes in the direction, he found he was not mistaken.

Something was creeping slowly towards him along the floor. It was something dark and serpentine in shape, and it came from the place where the partition bulged. He stooped down to examine it with feelings of intense horror and repugnance, and he discovered that it was moving toward him from the *other side* of the wall. His eyes were fascinated, and for the moment he was unable to move. Silently, slowly, from side to side like a thick worm, it crawled forward into the room beneath his frightened eyes, until at length he could stand it no longer and stretched out his arm to touch it. But at the instant of contact he withdrew his hand with a suppressed scream. It was sluggish—and it was warm! and he saw that his fingers were stained with living crimson.

A second more, and Shorthouse was out in the passage with his hand on the door of the next room. It was locked. He plunged forward with all his weight against it, and, the lock giving way, he fell headlong into a room that was pitch dark and very cold. In a moment he was on his feet again and trying to penetrate the blackness. Not a sound, not a movement. Not even the sense of a presence. It was empty, miserably empty!

Across the room he could trace the outline of a window with rain streaming down the outside, and the blurred lights of the city beyond. But the room was empty, appallingly empty; and so still. He stood there, cold as ice, staring, shivering listening. Suddenly there was a step behind him and a light flashed into the room, and when he turned quickly with his arm up as if to ward off a terrific blow he found himself face to face with the landlady. Instantly the reaction began to set in.

It was nearly three o'clock in the morning, and he was standing there with bare feet and striped pyjamas in a small room, which in the merciful light he perceived to be absolutely empty, carpetless, and without a stick of furniture, or even a window-blind. There he stood staring at the disagreeable landlady.

And there she stood too, staring and silent, in a black wrapper, her head almost bald, her face white as chalk, shading a sputtering candle with one bony hand and peering over it at him with her blinking green eyes. She looked positively hideous.

"Waal?" she drawled at length, "I heard yer right enough. Guess you couldn't sleep! Or just prowlin' round a bit—is that it?"

The empty room, the absence of all traces of the recent tragedy, the silence, the hour, his striped py-jamas and bare feet—everything together combined to deprive him momentarily of speech. He stared at her blankly without a word.

"Waal?" clanked the awful voice.

"My dear woman," he burst out finally, "there's been something awful—" So far his desperation took him, but no farther. He positively stuck at the substantive.

"Oh! there hasn't been nothin'," she said slowly still peering at him. "I reckon you've only seen and heard what the others did. I never can keep folks on this floor long. Most of 'em catch on soon-er or later—that is, the ones that's kind of quick and sensitive. Only you being an Englishman I thought you wouldn't mind. Nothin' really happens; it's only thinkin' like."

Shorthouse was beside himself. He felt ready to pick her up and drop her over the banisters, candle and all.

"Look there," he said, pointing at her within an inch of her blinking eyes with the fingers that had touched the oozing blood; "look there, my good woman. Is that only thinking?"

She stared a minute, as if not knowing what he meant.

"I guess so," she said at length.

He followed her eyes, and to his amazement saw that his fingers were as white as usual, and quite free from the awful stain that had been there ten minutes before. There was no sign of blood. No amount of staring could bring it back. Had he gone out of his mind? Had his eyes and ears played such tricks with him? Had his senses become false and perverted? He dashed past the landlady, out into the passage, and gained his own room in a couple of strides. Whew! . . . the partition no longer bulged. The paper was not torn. There was no creeping, crawling thing on the faded old carpet.

"It's all over now," drawled the metallic voice behind him. "I'm going to bed again."

He turned and saw the landlady slowly going downstairs again, still shading the candle with her hand and peering up at him from time to time as she moved. A black, ugly, unwholesome object, he thought, as she disappeared into the darkness below, and the last flicker of her candle threw a queer-shaped shadow along the wall and over the ceiling.

Without hesitating a moment, Shorthouse threw himself into his clothes and went out of the house. He preferred the storm to the horrors of that top floor, and he walked the streets till daylight. In the evening he told the landlady he would leave next day, in spite of her assurances that nothing more would happen.

"It never comes back," she said—"that is, not after he's killed."

Shorthouse gasped.

"You gave me a lot for my money," he growled.

"Waal, it aren't my show," she drawled. "I'm no spirit medium. You take chances. Some'll sleep right along and never hear nothin'. Others, like yourself, are different and get the whole thing."

"Who's the old gentleman?—does he hear it?" asked Jim.

"There's no old gentleman at all," she answered coolly. "I just told you that to make you feel easy like in case you did hear anythin'. You were all alone on the floor."

"Say now," she went on, after a pause in which Shorthouse could think of nothing to say but un-publishable things, "say now, do tell, did you feel sort of cold when the show was on, sort of tired and weak, I mean, as if you might be going to die?"

"How can I say?" he answered savagely; "what I felt God only knows."

"Waal, but He won't tell," she drawled out. "Only I was wonderin' how you really did feel, because the man who had that room last was found one morning in bed—"

"In bed?"

"He was dead. He was the one before you. Oh! You don't need to get rattled so. You're all right. And it all really happened, they do say. This house used to be a private residence some twenty-five years ago, and a German family of the name of Steinhardt lived here. They had a big business in Wall Street, and stood 'way up in things."

"Ah!" said her listener.

"Oh yes, they did, right at the top, till one fine day it all bust and the old man skipped with the boodle—"

"Skipped with the boodle?"

"That's so," she said; "got clear away with all the money, and the son was found dead in his house, committed soocide it was thought. Though there was some as said he couldn't have stabbed himself and fallen in that position. They said he was murdered. The father died in prison. They tried to fasten the murder on him, but there was no motive, or no evidence, or no somethin'. I forget now."

"Very pretty," said Shorthouse.

"I'll show you somethin' mighty queer anyways," she drawled, "if you'll come upstairs a minute. I've heard the steps and voices lots of times; they don't pheaze me any. I'd just as lief hear so many dogs barkin'. You'll find the whole story in the newspapers if you look it up—not what goes on here, but the story of the Germans. My house would be ruined if they told all, and I'd sue for damages."

They reached the bedroom, and the woman went in and pulled up the edge of the carpet where Shorthouse had seen the blood soaking in the previous night.

"Look thar, if you feel like it," said the old hag. Stooping down, he saw a dark, dull stain in the boards that corresponded exactly to the shape and position of the blood as he had seen it.

That night he slept in a hotel, and the following day sought new quarters. In the newspapers on file in his office after a long search he found twenty years back the detailed story, substantially as the woman had said, of Steinhardt & Co.'s failure, the absconding and subsequent arrest of the senior partner, and the suicide, or murder, of his son Otto. The landlady's room-house had formerly been their private residence.

THE SOUTHWEST CHAMBER

MARY E. WILKINS FREEMAN

(1903)

"That school-teacher from Acton is coming to-day," said the elder Miss Gill, Sophia.

"So she is," assented the younger Miss Gill, Amanda.

"I have decided to put her in the southwest chamber," said Sophia.

Amanda looked at her sister with an expression of mingled doubt and terror. "You don't suppose she would—" she began hesitatingly.

"Would what?" demanded Sophia, sharply.

She was more incisive than her sister. Both were below the medium height, and stout, but Sophia was firm where Amanda was flabby. Amanda wore a baggy old muslin (it was a hot day), and Sophia was uncompromisingly hooked up in a starched and boned cambric over her high shelving figure.

"I didn't know but she would object to sleeping in that room, as long as Aunt Harriet died there such a little time ago," faltered Amanda.

"Well!" said Sophia, "of all the silly notions! If you are going to pick out rooms in this house where nobody has died, for the boarders, you'll have your hands full. Grandfather Ackley had seven children; four of them died here to my certain knowledge, besides grandfather and grandmother. I think Great-grandmother Ackley, grandfather's mother, died here, too; she must have; and Great-grandfather Ackley, and grandfather's unmarried sister, Great-aunt Fanny Ackley. I don't believe there's a room nor a bed in this house that somebody hasn't passed away in."

"Well, I suppose I am silly to think of it, and she had better go in there," said Amanda.

"I know she had. The northeast room is small and hot, and she's stout and likely to feel the heat, and she's saved money and is able to board out summers, and maybe she'll come here another year if she's well accommodated," said Sophia. "Now I guess you'd better go in there and see if any dust has settled on anything since it was cleaned, and open the west windows and let the sun in, while I see to that cake."

Amanda went to her task in the southwest chamber while her sister stepped heavily down the back stairs on her way to the kitchen.

"It seems to me you had better open the bed while you air and dust, then make it up again," she called back.

"Yes, sister," Amanda answered, shudderingly.

Nobody knew how this elderly woman with the untrammeled imagination of a child dreaded to enter the southwest chamber, and yet she could not have told why she had the dread. She had entered and occupied rooms which had been once tenanted by persons now dead. The room which had been hers in the little house in which she and her sister had lived before coming here had been her dead mother's. She had never reflected upon the fact with anything but loving awe and reverence. There had never been any fear. But this was different. She entered and her heart beat thickly in her ears. Her hands were cold. The room was a very large one. The four windows, two facing south, two west, were closed, the blinds also. The room was in a film of green gloom. The furniture loomed out vaguely. The gilt frame of a blurred old engraving on the wall caught a little light. The white counterpane on the bed showed like a blank page.

Amanda crossed the room, opened with a straining motion of her thin back and shoulders one of the west windows, and threw back the blind. Then the room revealed itself an apartment full of an aged and worn but no less valid state. Pieces of old mahogany swelled forth; a peacock-patterned chintz draped the bedstead. This chintz also covered a great easy chair which had been the favourite seat of the former occupant of the room. The closet door stood ajar. Amanda noticed that with wonder. There was

a glimpse of purple drapery floating from a peg inside the closet. Amanda went across and took down
the garment hanging there. She wondered how her
sister had happened to leave it when she cleaned
the room. It was an old loose gown which had belonged to her aunt. She took it down, shuddering,
and closed the closet door after a fearful glance into
its dark depths. It was a long closet with a strong
odour of lovage. The Aunt Harriet had had a habit
of eating lovage and had carried it constantly in her
pocket. There was very likely some of the pleasant
root in the pocket of the musty purple gown which
Amanda threw over the easy chair.

Amanda perceived the odour with a start as if
before an actual presence. Odour seems in a sense a
vital part of a personality. It can survive the flesh to
which it has clung like a persistent shadow, seeming
to have in itself something of the substance of that
to which it pertained. Amanda was always conscious
of this fragrance of lovage as she tidied the room.
She dusted the heavy mahogany pieces punctiliously
after she had opened the bed as her sister had directed. She spread fresh towels over the wash-stand and
the bureau; she made the bed. Then she thought to
take the purple gown from the easy chair and carry
it to the garret and put it in the trunk with the other
articles of the dead woman's wardrobe which had
been packed away there; *but the purple gown was not
on the chair!*

Amanda Gill was not a woman of strong convictions even as to her own actions. She directly thought that possibly she had been mistaken and had not removed it from the closet. She glanced at the closet door and saw with surprise that it was open, and she had thought she had closed it, but she instantly was not sure of that. So she entered the closet and looked for the purple gown. *It was not there!*

Amanda Gill went feebly out of the closet and looked at the easy chair again. The purple gown was not there! She looked wildly around the room. She went down on her trembling knees and peered under the bed, she opened the bureau drawers, she looked again in the closet. Then she stood in the middle of the floor and fairly wrung her hands.

"What does it mean?" she said in a shocked whisper.

She had certainly seen that loose purple gown of her dead Aunt Harriet's.

There is a limit at which self-refutation must stop in any sane person. Amanda Gill had reached it. She knew that she had seen that purple gown in that closet; she knew that she had removed it and put it on the easy chair. She also knew that she had not taken it out of the room. She felt a curious sense of being inverted mentally. It was as if all her traditions and laws of life were on their heads. Never in her simple record had any garment not remained

where she had placed it unless removed by some palpable human agency.

Then the thought occurred to her that possibly
her sister Sophia might have entered the room un-
observed while her back was turned and removed
the dress. A sensation of relief came over her. Her
blood seemed to flow back into its usual channels;
the tension of her nerves relaxed.

"How silly I am," she said aloud.

She hurried out and downstairs into the kitchen
where Sophia was making cake, stirring with splendid circular sweeps of a wooden spoon a creamy
yellow mass. She looked up as her sister entered.

"Have you got it done?" said she.

"Yes," replied Amanda. Then she hesitated. A
sudden terror overcame her. It did not seem as if it
were at all probable that Sophia had left that foamy
cake mixture a second to go to Aunt Harriet's chamber and remove that purple gown.

"Well," said Sophia, "if you have got that done
I wish you would take hold and string those beans.
The first thing we know there won't be time to boil
them for dinner."

Amanda moved toward the pan of beans on the
table, then she looked at her sister.

"Did you come up in Aunt Harriet's room while
I was there?" she asked weakly.

She knew while she asked what the answer would
be.

"Up in Aunt Harriet's room? Of course I didn't. I couldn't leave this cake without having it fall. You know that well enough. Why?"

"Nothing," replied Amanda.

Suddenly she realized that she could not tell her sister what had happened, for before the utter absurdity of the whole thing her belief in her own reason quailed. She knew what Sophia would say if she told her. She could hear her.

"Amanda Gill, have you gone stark staring mad?"

She resolved that she would never tell Sophia. She dropped into a chair and begun shelling the beans with nerveless fingers. Sophia looked at her curiously.

"Amanda Gill, what on earth ails you?" she asked.

"Nothing," replied Amanda. She bent her head very low over the green pods.

"Yes, there is, too! You are as white as a sheet, and your hands are shaking so you can hardly string those beans. I did think you had more sense, Amanda Gill."

"I don't know what you mean, Sophia."

"Yes, you do know what I mean, too; you needn't pretend you don't. Why did you ask me if I had been in that room, and why do you act so queer?"

Amanda hesitated. She had been trained to truth. Then she lied.

"I wondered if you'd noticed how it had leaked in on the paper over by the bureau, that last rain," said she.

"What makes you look so pale then?"

"I don't know. I guess the heat sort of overcame me."

"I shouldn't think it could have been very hot in that room when it had been shut up so long," said Sophia.

She was evidently not satisfied, but then the grocer came to the door and the matter dropped.

For the next hour the two women were very busy. They kept no servant. When they had come into possession of this fine old place by the death of their aunt it had seemed a doubtful blessing. There was not a cent with which to pay for repairs and taxes and insurance, except the twelve hundred dollars which they had obtained from the sale of the little house in which they had been born and lived all their lives. There had been a division in the old Ackley family years before. One of the daughters had married against her mother's wish and had been disinherited. She had married a poor man by the name of Gill, and shared his humble lot in sight of her former home and her sister and mother living in prosperity, until she had borne three daughters; then she died, worn out with overwork and worry.

The mother and the elder sister had been pitiless to the last. Neither had ever spoken to her since she left her home the night of her marriage. They were hard women.

The three daughters of the disinherited sister had lived quiet and poor, but not actually needy lives.

Jane, the middle daughter, had married, and died in less than a year. Amanda and Sophia had taken the girl baby she left when the father married again. Sophia had taught a primary school for many years; she had saved enough to buy the little house in which they lived. Amanda had crocheted lace, and embroidered flannel, and made tidies and pincushions, and had earned enough for her clothes and the child's, little Flora Scott.

Their father, William Gill, had died before they were thirty, and now in their late middle life had come the death of the aunt to whom they had never spoken, although they had often seen her, who had lived in solitary state in the old Ackley mansion until she was more than eighty. There had been no will, and they were the only heirs with the exception of young Flora Scott, the daughter of the dead sister.

Sophia and Amanda thought directly of Flora when they knew of the inheritance.

"It will be a splendid thing for her; she will have enough to live on when we are gone," Sophia said.

She had promptly decided what was to be done. The small house was to be sold, and they were to move into the old Ackley house and take boarders to pay for its keeping. She scouted the idea of selling it. She had an enormous family pride. She had always held her head high when she had walked past that fine old mansion, the cradle of her race, which she was forbidden to enter. She was unmoved when the lawyer who was advising her disclosed to her the fact that Harriet Ackley had used every cent of the Ackley money.

"I realize that we have to work," said she, "but my sister and I have determined to keep the place."

That was the end of the discussion. Sophia and Amanda Gill had been living in the old Ackley house a fortnight, and they had three boarders: an elderly widow with a comfortable income, a young congregationalist clergyman, and the middle-aged single woman who had charge of the village library. Now the school-teacher from Acton, Miss Louisa Stark, was expected for the summer, and would make four.

Sophia considered that they were comfortably provided for. Her wants and her sister's were very few, and even the niece, although a young girl, had small expenses, since her wardrobe was supplied for years to come from that of the deceased aunt. There were stored away in the garret of the Ackley house enough voluminous black silks and satins and bombazines to keep her clad in somber richness for years to come.

Flora was a very gentle girl, with large, serious blue eyes, a seldom-smiling, pretty mouth, and smooth flaxen hair. She was delicate and very young—sixteen on her next birthday.

She came home soon now with her parcels of sugar and tea from the grocer's. She entered the kitchen gravely and deposited them on the table by which

her Aunt Amanda was seated stringing beans. Flora
wore an obsolete turban-shaped hat of black straw
which had belonged to the dead aunt; it set high
like a crown, revealing her forehead. Her dress was
an ancient purple-and-white print, too long and too
large except over the chest, where it held her like a
straight waistcoat.

"You had better take off your hat, Flora," said
Sophia. She turned suddenly to Amanda. "Did you
fill the water-pitcher in that chamber for the school-
teacher?" she asked severely. She was quite sure that
Amanda had not filled the water-pitcher.

Amanda blushed and started guiltily. "I declare, I
don't believe I did," said she.

"I didn't think you had," said her sister with sarcastic emphasis.

"Flora, you go up to the room that was your
Great-aunt Harriet's, and take the water-pitcher off
the wash-stand and fill it with water. Be real careful, and don't break the pitcher, and don't spill the
water."

"In *that* chamber?" asked Flora. She spoke very
quietly, but her face changed a little.

"Yes, in that chamber," returned her Aunt Sophia
sharply. "Go right along."

Flora went, and her light footstep was heard on
the stairs. Very soon she returned with the blue-
and-white water-pitcher and filled it carefully at the
kitchen sink.

"Now be careful and not spill it," said Sophia as she went out of the room carrying it gingerly.

Amanda gave a timidly curious glance at her; she wondered if she had seen the purple gown.

Then she started, for the village stagecoach was seen driving around to the front of the house. The house stood on a corner.

"Here, Amanda, you look better than I do; you go and meet her," said Sophia. "I'll just put the cake in the pan and get it in the oven and I'll come. Show her right up to her room."

Amanda removed her apron hastily and obeyed. Sophia hurried with her cake, pouring it into the baking-tins. She had just put it in the oven, when the door opened and Flora entered carrying the blue water-pitcher.

"What are you bringing down that pitcher again for?" asked Sophia.

"She wants some water, and Aunt Amanda sent me," replied Flora.

Her pretty pale face had a bewildered expression.

"For the land sake, she hasn't used all that great pitcherful of water so quick?"

"There wasn't any water in it," replied Flora.

Her high, childish forehead was contracted slightly with a puzzled frown as she looked at her aunt.

"Wasn't any water in it?"

"No, ma'am."

"Didn't I see you filling the pitcher with water not ten minutes ago, I want to know?"

"Yes, ma'am."

"What did you do with that water?"

"Nothing."

"Did you carry that pitcherful of water up to that room and set it on the washstand?"

"Yes, ma'am."

"Didn't you spill it?"

"No, ma'am."

"Now, Flora Scott, I want the truth! Did you fill that pitcher with water and carry it up there, and wasn't there any there when she came to use it?"

"Yes, ma'am."

"Let me see that pitcher." Sophia examined the pitcher. It was not only perfectly dry from top to bottom, but even a little dusty. She turned severely on the young girl. "That shows," said she, "you did not fill the pitcher at all. You let the water run at the side because you didn't want to carry it upstairs. I am ashamed of you. It's bad enough to be so lazy, but when it comes to not telling the truth—"

The young girl's face broke up suddenly into piteous confusion, and her blue eyes became filmy with tears.

"I did fill the pitcher, honest," she faltered, "I did, Aunt Sophia. You ask Aunt Amanda."

"I'll ask nobody. This pitcher is proof enough. Water don't go off and leave the pitcher dusty on the inside if it was put in ten minutes ago. Now you fill that pitcher full quick, and you carry it upstairs, and if you spill a drop there'll be something besides talk."

Flora filled the pitcher, with the tears falling over her cheeks. She sniveled softly as she went out, balancing it carefully against her slender hip. Sophia followed her.

"Stop crying," said she sharply; "you ought to be ashamed of yourself. What do you suppose Miss Louisa Stark will think. No water in her pitcher in the first place, and then you come back crying as if you didn't want to get it."

In spite of herself, Sophia's voice was soothing. She was very fond of the girl. She followed her up the stairs to the chamber where Miss Louisa Stark was waiting for the water to remove the soil of travel. She had removed her bonnet, and its tuft of red geraniums lightened the obscurity of the mahogany dresser. She had placed her little beaded cape carefully on the bed. She was replying to a tremulous remark of Amanda's, who was nearly fainting from the new mystery of the water-pitcher, that it was warm and she suffered a good deal in warm weather.

Louisa Stark was stout and solidly built. She was much larger than either of the Gill sisters. She was a masterly woman inured to command from years of school-teaching. She carried her swelling bulk with majesty; even her face, moist and red with the heat, lost nothing of its dignity of expression.

She was standing in the middle of the floor with an air which gave the effect of her standing upon an elevation. She turned when Sophia and Flora, carrying the water-pitcher, entered.

"This is my sister Sophia," said Amanda tremulously.

Sophia advanced, shook hands with Miss Louisa Stark and bade her welcome and hoped she would like her room. Then she moved toward the closet. "There is a nice large closet in this room—the best closet in the house. You might have your trunk—" she said, then she stopped short.

The closet door was ajar, and a purple garment seemed suddenly to swing into view as if impelled by some wind.

"Why, here is something left in this closet," Sophia said in a mortified tone. "I thought all those things had been taken away."

She pulled down the garment with a jerk, and as she did so Amanda passed her in a weak rush for the door.

"I am afraid your sister is not well," said the school-teacher from Acton. "She looked very pale when you took that dress down. I noticed it at once. Hadn't you better go and see what the matter is? She may be going to faint."

"She is not subject to fainting spells," replied Sophia, but she followed Amanda.

She found her in the room which they occupied together, lying on the bed, very pale and gasping. She leaned over her.

"Amanda, what is the matter; don't you feel well?" she asked.

"I feel a little faint."

Sophia got a camphor bottle and began rubbing her sister's forehead.

"Do you feel better?" she said.

Amanda nodded.

"I guess it was that green apple pie you ate this noon," said Sophia. "I declare, what did I do with that dress of Aunt Harriet's? I guess if you feel better I'll just run and get it and take it up garret. I'll stop in here again when I come down. You'd better lay still. Flora can bring you up a cup of tea. I wouldn't try to eat any supper."

Sophia's tone as she left the room was full of loving concern. Presently she returned; she looked disturbed, but angrily so. There was not the slightest hint of any fear in her expression.

"I want to know," said she, looking sharply and quickly around, "if I brought that purple dress in here, after all?"

"I didn't see you," replied Amanda.

"I must have. It isn't in that chamber, nor the closet. You aren't lying on it, are you?"

"I lay down before you came in," replied Amanda.

"So you did. Well, I'll go and look again."

Presently Amanda heard her sister's heavy step on the garret stairs. Then she returned with a queer defiant expression on her face.

"I carried it up garret, after all, and put it in the trunk," said, she. "I declare, I forgot it. I suppose your being faint sort of put it out of my head. There it was, folded up just as nice, right where I put it."

Sophia's mouth was set; her eyes upon her sister's scared, agitated face were full of hard challenge.

"Yes," murmured Amanda.

"I must go right down and see to that cake," said Sophia, going out of the room. "If you don't feel well, you pound on the floor with the umbrella."

Amanda looked after her. She knew that Sophia had not put that purple dress of her dead Aunt Harriet in the trunk in the garret.

Meantime Miss Louisa Stark was settling herself in the southwest chamber. She unpacked her trunk and hung her dresses carefully in the closet. She filled the bureau drawers with nicely folded linen and small articles of dress. She was a very punctilious woman. She put on a black India silk dress with purple flowers. She combed her grayish-blond hair in smooth ridges back from her broad forehead. She pinned her lace at her throat with a brooch, very handsome, although somewhat obsolete—a bunch of pearl grapes on black onyx, set in gold filagree. She had purchased it several years ago with a considerable portion of the stipend from her spring term of school-teaching.

As she surveyed herself in the little swing mirror surmounting the old-fashioned mahogany bureau she suddenly bent forward and looked closely at the brooch. It seemed to her that something was wrong with it. As she looked she became sure. Instead of the familiar bunch of pearl grapes on the black onyx, she saw a knot of blonde and black hair under glass surrounded by a border of twisted gold. She felt a thrill of horror, though she could not tell why. She unpinned the brooch, and it was her own familiar one, the pearl grapes and the onyx. "How very foolish I am," she thought. She thrust the pin in the laces at her throat and again looked at herself in the glass, and there it was again—the knot of blond and black hair and the twisted gold.

Louisa Stark looked at her own large, firm face above the brooch and it was full of terror and dismay which were new to it. She straightway began to wonder if there could be anything wrong with her mind. She remembered that an aunt of her mother's had been insane. A sort of fury with herself possessed her. She stared at the brooch in the glass with eyes at once angry and terrified. Then she removed it again and there was her own old brooch. Finally she thrust the gold pin through the lace again, fastened it and turning a defiant back on the glass, went down to supper.

At the supper table she met the other boarders— the elderly widow, the young clergyman and the middle-aged librarian. She viewed the elderly widow with reserve, the clergyman with respect, the middle-aged librarian with suspicion. The latter wore a very

youthful shirt-waist, and her hair in a girlish fashion
which the school-teacher, who twisted hers severely from the straining roots at the nape of her neck
to the small, smooth coil at the top, condemned as
straining after effects no longer hers by right.

The librarian, who had a quick acridness of manner, addressed her, asking what room she had, and
asked the second time in spite of the school-teacher's evident reluctance to hear her. She even, since
she sat next to her, nudged her familiarly in her rigid black silk side.

"What room are you in, Miss Stark?" said she.

"I am at a loss how to designate the room," replied Miss Stark stiffly.

"Is it the big southwest room?"

"It evidently faces in that direction," said Miss
Stark.

The librarian, whose name was Eliza Lippincott,
turned abruptly to Miss Amanda Gill, over whose
delicate face a curious colour compounded of flush
and pallour was stealing.

"What room did your aunt die in, Miss Amanda?" asked she abruptly.

Amanda cast a terrified glance at her sister, who
was serving a second plate of pudding for the minister.

"That room," she replied feebly.

"That's what I thought," said the librarian with
a certain triumph. "I calculated that must be the

room she died in, for it's the best room in the house,
and you haven't put anybody in it before. Somehow
the room that anybody has died in lately is generally
the last room that anybody is put in. I suppose *you*
are so strong-minded you don't object to sleeping in
a room where anybody died a few weeks ago?" she
inquired of Louisa Stark with sharp eyes on her face.

"No, I do not," replied Miss stark with emphasis.

"Nor in the same bed?" persisted Eliza Lippincott
with a kittenish reflection.

The young minister looked up from his pudding.
He was very spiritual, but he had had poor pickings
in his previous boarding place, and he could not
help a certain abstract enjoyment over Miss Gill's
cooking.

"You would certainly not be afraid, Miss Lippincott?" he remarked, with his gentle, almost caressing
inflection of tone. "You do not for a minute believe
that a higher power would allow any manifestation
on the part of a disembodied spirit—who we trust is
in her heavenly home—to harm one of His servants?"

"Oh, Mr. Dunn, of course not," replied Eliza Lippincott with a blush. "Of course not. I never meant
to imply—"

"I could not believe you did," said the minister gently. He was very young, but he already had
a wrinkle of permanent anxiety between his eyes
and a smile of permanent ingratiation on his lips.

The lines of the smile were as deeply marked as the wrinkle.

"Of course dear Miss Harriet Gill was a professing Christian," remarked the widow, "and I don't suppose a professing Christian would come back and scare folks if she could. I wouldn't be a mite afraid to sleep in that room; I'd rather have it than the one I've got. If I was afraid to sleep in a room where a good woman died, I wouldn't tell of it. If I saw things or heard things I'd think the fault must be with my own guilty conscience." Then she turned to Miss Stark. "Any time you feel timid in that room I'm ready and willing to change with you," said she.

"Thank you; I have no desire to change. I am perfectly satisfied with my room," replied Miss Stark with freezing dignity, which was thrown away upon the widow.

"Well," said she, "any time, if you should feel timid, you know what to do. I've got a real nice room; it faces east and gets the morning sun, but it isn't so nice as yours, according to my way of thinking. I'd rather take my chances any day in a room anybody had died in than in one that was hot in summer. I'm more afraid of a sunstroke than of spooks, for my part."

Miss Sophia Gill, who had not spoken one word, but whose mouth had become more and more rigidly compressed, suddenly rose from the table, forcing

the minister to leave a little pudding, at which he
glanced regretfully.

Miss Louisa Stark did not sit down in the parlour
with the other boarders. She went straight to her
room. She felt tired after her journey, and meditated
a loose wrapper and writing a few letters quietly before she went to bed. Then, too, she was conscious
of a feeling that if she delayed, the going there at all
might assume more terrifying proportions. She was
full of defiance against herself and her own lurking
weakness.

So she went resolutely and entered the southwest
chamber. There was through the room a soft twilight. She could dimly discern everything, the white
satin scroll-work on the wall paper and the white
counterpane on the bed being most evident. Con-
sequently both arrested her attention first. She saw
against the wall-paper directly facing the door the
waist of her best black satin dress hung over a picture.

"That is very strange," she said to herself, and
again a thrill of vague horror came over her.

She knew, or thought she knew, that she had put
that black satin dress waist away nicely folded between towels in her trunk. She was very choice of
her black satin dress.

She took down the black waist and laid it on the
bed preparatory to folding it, but when she attempted to do so she discovered that the two sleeves were

firmly sewed together. Louisa Stark stared at the sewed sleeves. "What does this mean?" she asked herself. She examined the sewing carefully; the stitches were small, and even, and firm, of black silk.

She looked around the room. On the stand beside the bed was something which she had not noticed before: a little old-fashioned work-box with a picture of a little boy in a pinafore on the top. Beside this work-box lay, as if just laid down by the user, a spool of black silk, a pair of scissors, and a large steel thimble with a hole in the top, after an old style. Louisa stared at these, then at the sleeves of her dress. She moved toward the door. For a moment she thought that this was something legitimate about which she might demand information; then she became doubtful. Suppose that work-box had been there all the time; suppose she had forgotten; suppose she herself had done this absurd thing, or suppose that she had not, what was to hinder the others from thinking so; what was to hinder a doubt being cast upon her own memory and reasoning powers?

Louisa Stark had been on the verge of a nervous breakdown in spite of her iron constitution and her great will power. No woman can teach school for forty years with absolute impunity. She was more credulous as to her own possible failings than she had ever been in her whole life. She was cold with horror and terror, and yet not so much horror and

terror of the supernatural as of her own self. The
weakness of belief in the supernatural was nearly
impossible for this strong nature. She could more
easily believe in her own failing powers.

"I don't know but I'm going to be like Aunt Mar-
cia," she said to herself, and her fat face took on a
long rigidity of fear.

She started toward the mirror to unfasten her
dress, then she remembered the strange circumstance
of the brooch and stopped short. Then she straightened herself defiantly and marched up to the bureau
and looked in the glass. She saw reflected therein,
fastening the lace at her throat, the old-fashioned
thing of a large oval, a knot of fair and black hair
under glass, set in a rim of twisted gold. She unfastened it with trembling fingers and looked at it. It
was her own brooch, the cluster of pearl grapes on
black onyx. Louisa Stark placed the trinket in its
little box on the nest of pink cotton and put it away
in the bureau drawer. Only death could disturb her
habit of order.

Her fingers were so cold they felt fairly numb as
she unfastened her dress; she staggered when she
slipped it over her head. She went to the closet to
hang it up and recoiled. A strong smell of lovage
came in her nostrils; a purple gown near the door
swung softly against her face as if impelled by some
wind from within. All the pegs were filled with garments not her own, mostly of somber black, but

there were some strange-patterned silk things and satins.

Suddenly Louisa Stark recovered her nerve. This, she told herself, was something distinctly tangible. Somebody had been taking liberties with her wardrobe. Somebody had been hanging some one else's clothes in her closet. She hastily slipped on her dress again and marched straight down to the parlour. The people were seated there; the widow and the minister were playing backgammon. The librarian was watching them. Miss Amanda Gill was mending beside the large lamp on the centre table. They all looked up with amazement as Louisa Stark entered. There was something strange in her expression. She noticed none of them except Amanda.

"Where is your sister?" she asked peremptorily of her.

"She's in the kitchen mixing up bread," Amanda quavered; "is there anything—" But the school-teacher was gone.

She found Sophia Gill standing by the kitchen table kneading dough with dignity. The young girl Flora was bringing some flour from the pantry. She stopped and stared at Miss Stark, and her pretty, delicate young face took on an expression of alarm.

Miss Stark opened at once upon the subject in her mind.

"Miss Gill," said she, with her utmost school-teacher manner, "I wish to inquire why you have had my

own clothes removed from the closet in my room
and others substituted?"

Sophia Gill stood with her hands fast in the
dough, regarding her. Her own face paled slowly
and reluctantly, her mouth stiffened.

"What? I don't quite understand what you mean,
Miss Stark," said she.

"My clothes are not in the closet in my room and
it is full of things which do not belong to me," said
Louisa Stark.

"Bring me that flour," said Sophia sharply to
the young girl, who obeyed, casting timid, startled glances at Miss Stark as she passed her. Sophia
Gill began rubbing her hands clear of the dough. "I
am sure I know nothing about it," she said with a
certain tempered asperity. "Do you know anything
about it, Flora?"

"Oh, no, I don't know anything about it, Aunt
Sophia," answered the young girl, fluttering.

Then Sophia turned to Miss Stark. "I'll go upstairs with you, Miss Stark," said she, "and see what
the trouble is. There must be some mistake." She
spoke stiffly with constrained civility.

"Very well," said Miss Stark with dignity. Then
she and Miss Sophia went upstairs. Flora stood staring after them.

Sophia and Louisa Stark went up to the southwest
chamber. The closet door was shut. Sophia threw it

open, then she looked at Miss Stark. On the pegs hung the schoolteacher's own garments in ordinary array.

"I can't see that there is anything wrong," remarked Sophia grimly.

Miss Stark strove to speak but she could not. She sank down on the nearest chair. She did not even attempt to defend herself. She saw her own clothes in the closet. She knew there had been no time for any human being to remove those which she thought she had seen and put hers in their places. She knew it was impossible. Again the awful horror of herself overwhelmed her.

"You must have been mistaken," she heard Sophia say.

She muttered something, she scarcely knew what. Sophia then went out of the room. Presently she undressed and went to bed. In the morning she did not go down to breakfast, and when Sophia came to inquire, requested that the stage be ordered for the noon train. She said that she was sorry, but was ill, and feared lest she might be worse, and she felt that she must return home at once. She looked ill, and could not take even the toast and tea which Sophia had prepared for her. Sophia felt a certain pity for her, but it was largely mixed with indignation. She felt that she knew the true reason for the school-teacher's illness and sudden departure, and it incensed her.

"If folks are going to act like fools we shall never be able to keep this house," she said to Amanda after Miss Stark had gone; and Amanda knew what she meant.

Directly the widow, Mrs. Elvira Simmons, knew that the school-teacher had gone and the southwest room was vacant, she begged to have it in exchange for her own. Sophia hesitated a moment; she eyed the widow sharply. There was something about the large, roseate face worn in firm lines of humour and decision which reassured her.

"I have no objection, Mrs. Simmons," said she, "if—"

"If what?" asked the widow.

"If you have common sense enough not to keep fussing because the room happens to be the one my aunt died in," said Sophia bluntly.

"Fiddlesticks!" said the widow, Mrs. Elvira Simmons.

That very afternoon she moved into the southwest chamber. The young girl Flora assisted her, though much against her will.

"Now I want you to carry Mrs. Simmons' dresses into the closet in that room and hang them up nicely, and see that she has everything she wants," said Sophia Gill. "And you can change the bed and put on fresh sheets. What are you looking at me that way for?"

"Oh, Aunt Sophia, can't I do something else?"

"What do you want to do something else for?"

"I am afraid."

"Afraid of what? I should think you'd hang your head. No; you go right in there and do what I tell you."

Pretty soon Flora came running into the sitting-room where Sophia was, as pale as death, and in her hand she held a queer, old-fashioned frilled nightcap.

"What's that?" demanded Sophia.

"I found it under the pillow."

"What pillow?"

"In the southwest room."

Sophia took it and looked at it sternly.

"It's Great-aunt Harriet's," said Flora faintly.

"You run down street and do that errand at the grocer's for me and I'll see that room," said Sophia with dignity. She carried the nightcap away and put it in the trunk in the garret where she had supposed it stored with the rest of the dead woman's belongings. Then she went into the southwest chamber and made the bed and assisted Mrs. Simmons to move, and there was no further incident.

The widow was openly triumphant over her new room. She talked a deal about it at the dinner-table.

"It is the best room in the house, and I expect you all to be envious of me," said she.

"And you are sure you don't feel afraid of ghosts?" said the librarian.

"Ghosts!" repeated the widow with scorn. "If a ghost comes I'll send her over to you. You are just across the hall from the southwest room."

"You needn't," returned Eliza Lippincott with a shudder. "I wouldn't sleep in that room, after—" she checked herself with an eye on the minister.

"After what?" asked the widow.

"Nothing," replied Eliza Lippincott in an embarrassed fashion.

"I trust Miss Lippincott has too good sense and too great faith to believe in anything of that sort," said the minister.

"I trust so, too," replied Eliza hurriedly.

"You did see or hear something—now what was it, I want to know?" said the widow that evening when they were alone in the parlour. The minister had gone to make a call.

Eliza hesitated.

"What was it?" insisted the widow.

"Well," said Eliza hesitatingly, "if you'll promise not to tell."

"Yes, I promise; what was it?"

"Well, one day last week, just before the school-teacher came, I went in that room to see if there were any clouds. I wanted to wear my gray dress, and I was afraid it was going to rain, so I wanted to look at the sky at all points, so I went in there, and—"

"And what?"

"Well, you know that chintz over the bed, and the valance, and the easy chair; what pattern should you say it was?"

"Why, peacocks on a blue ground. Good land, I shouldn't think any one who had ever seen that would forget it."

"Peacocks on a blue ground, you are sure?"

"Of course I am. Why?"

"Only when I went in there that afternoon it was not peacocks on a blue ground; it was great red roses on a yellow ground."

"Why, what do you mean?"

"What I say."

"Did Miss Sophia have it changed?"

"No. I went in there again an hour later and the peacocks were there."

"You didn't see straight the first time."

"I expected you would say that."

"The peacocks are there now; I saw them just now."

"Yes, I suppose so; I suppose they flew back."

"But they couldn't."

"Looks as if they did."

"Why, how could such a thing be? It couldn't be."

"Well, all I know is those peacocks were gone for an hour that afternoon and the red roses on the yellow ground were there instead."

The widow stared at her a moment, then she began to laugh rather hysterically.

"Well," said she, "I guess I sha'n't give up my nice room for any such tomfoolery as that. I guess I would just as soon have red roses on a yellow ground as peacocks on a blue; but there's no use talking, you couldn't have seen straight. How could such a thing have happened?"

"I don't know," said Eliza Lippincott; "but I know I wouldn't sleep in that room if you'd give me a thousand dollars."

"Well, I would," said the widow, "and I'm going to."

When Mrs. Simmons went to the southwest chamber that night she cast a glance at the bed-hanging and the easy chair. There were the peacocks on the blue ground. She gave a contemptuous thought to Eliza Lippincott.

"I don't believe but she's getting nervous," she thought. "I wonder if any of her family have been out at all."

But just before Mrs. Simmons was ready to get into bed she looked again at the hangings and the easy chair, and there were the red roses on the yellow ground instead of the peacocks on the blue. She looked long and sharply. Then she shut her eyes, and then opened them and looked. She still saw the red roses. Then she crossed the room, turned her back to the bed, and looked out at the night from the south window. It was clear and the full moon was shining. She watched it a moment sailing over the dark blue in its nimbus of gold. Then she looked around at the bed hangings. She still saw the red roses on the yellow ground.

Mrs. Simmons was struck in her most vulnerable point. This apparent contradiction of the reasonable as manifested in such a commonplace thing as chintz of a bed-hanging affected this ordinarily unimaginative woman as no ghostly appearance could have done. Those red roses on the yellow ground were to her much more ghostly than any strange figure clad in the white robes of the grave entering the room.

She took a step toward the door, then she turned with a resolute air. "As for going downstairs and owning up I'm scared and having that Lippincott girl crowing over me, I won't for any red roses instead of peacocks. I guess they can't hurt me, and as long as we've both of us seen 'em I guess we can't both be getting loony," she said.

Mrs. Elvira Simmons blew out her light and got into bed and lay staring out between the chintz hangings at the moonlit room. She said her prayers in bed always as being more comfortable, and presumably just as acceptable in the case of a faithful servant with a stout habit of body. Then after a little she fell asleep; she was of too practical a nature to be kept long awake by anything which had no power of actual bodily effect upon her. No stress of the spirit had ever disturbed her slumbers. So she slumbered between the red roses, or the peacocks, she did not know which.

But she was awakened about midnight by a strange sensation in her throat. She had dreamed that some one with long white fingers was strangling her, and she saw bending over her the face of an old woman in a white cap. When she waked there was no old woman, the room was almost as light as day in the full moonlight, and looked very peaceful; but the strangling sensation at her throat continued, and besides that, her face and ears felt muffled. She put up her hand and felt that her head was covered with a ruffled nightcap tied under her chin so tightly that it was exceedingly uncomfortable. A great qualm of horror shot over her. She tore the thing off frantically and flung it from her with a convulsive effort as if it had been a spider. She gave, as she did so, a quick, short scream of terror. She sprang out of bed and was going toward the door, when she stopped.

It had suddenly occurred to her that Eliza Lippincott might have entered the room and tied on the cap while she was asleep. She had not locked her door. She looked in the closet, under the bed; there was no one there. Then she tried to open the door, but to her astonishment found that it was locked—bolted on the inside. "I must have locked it, after all," she reflected with wonder, for she never locked her door. Then she could scarcely conceal from herself that there was something out of the usual about it all. Certainly no one could have entered the room and departed locking the door on the inside. She could not control the long shiver of horror that crept over her, but she was still resolute. She resolved that she would throw the cap out of the window. "I'll see if I have tricks like that played on me, I don't care who does it," said she quite aloud. She was still unable to believe wholly in the supernatural. The idea of some human agency was still in her mind, filling her with anger.

She went toward the spot where she had thrown the cap—she had stepped over it on her way to the door—but it was not there. She searched the whole room, lighting her lamp, but she could not find the cap. Finally she gave it up. She extinguished her lamp and went back to bed. She fell asleep again, to be again awakened in the same fashion. That time she tore off the cap as before, but she did not fling it on the floor as before. Instead she held to it with a fierce grip. Her blood was up.

Holding fast to the white flimsy thing, she sprang out of bed, ran to the window which was open, slipped the screen, and flung it out; but a sudden gust of wind, though the night was calm, arose and it floated back in her face. She brushed it aside like a cobweb and she clutched at it. She was actually furious. It eluded her clutching fingers. Then she did not see it at all. She examined the floor, she lighted her lamp again and searched, but there was no sign of it.

Mrs. Simmons was then in such a rage that all terror had disappeared for the time. She did not know with what she was angry, but she had a sense of some mocking presence which was silently proving too strong against her weakness, and she was aroused to the utmost power of resistance. To be baffled like this and resisted by something which was as nothing to her straining senses filled her with intensest resentment.

Finally she got back into bed again; she did not go to sleep. She felt strangely drowsy, but she fought against it. She was wide awake, staring at the moonlight, when she suddenly felt the soft white strings of the thing tighten around her throat and realized that her enemy was again upon her. She seized the strings, untied them, twitched off the cap, ran with it to the table where her scissors lay and furiously cut it into small bits. She cut and tore, feeling an insane fury of gratification.

"There!" said she quite aloud. "I guess I sha'n't have any more trouble with this old cap."

She tossed the bits of muslin into a basket and went back to bed. Almost immediately she felt the soft strings tighten around her throat. Then at last she yielded, vanquished. This new refutal of all laws of reason by which she had learned, as it were, to spell her theory of life, was too much for her equilibrium. She pulled off the clinging strings feebly, drew the thing from her head, slid weakly out of bed, caught up her wrapper and hastened out of the room. She went noiselessly along the hall to her own old room: she entered, got into her familiar bed, and lay there the rest of the night shuddering and listening, and if she dozed, waking with a start at the feeling of the pressure upon her throat to find that it was not there, yet still to be unable to shake off entirely the horror.

When daylight came she crept back to the south-west chamber and hurriedly got some clothes in which to dress herself. It took all her resolution to enter the room, but nothing unusual happened while she was there. She hastened back to her old chamber, dressed herself and went down to break-fast with an imperturbable face. Her colour had not faded. When asked by Eliza Lippincott how she had slept, she replied with an appearance of calmness which was bewildering that she had not slept very well. She never did sleep very well in a new bed, and she thought she would go back to her old room.

Eliza Lippincott was not deceived, however, nei-ther were the Gill sisters, nor the young girl, Flora. Eliza Lippincott spoke out bluntly.

"You needn't talk to me about sleeping well," said she. "I know something queer happened in that room last night by the way you act."

They all looked at Mrs. Simmons, inquiringly— the librarian with malicious curiosity and triumph, the minister with sad incredulity, Sophia Gill with fear and indignation, Amanda and the young girl with unmixed terror. The widow bore herself with dignity.

"I saw nothing nor heard nothing which I trust could not have been accounted for in some rational manner," said she.

"What was it?" persisted Eliza Lippincott.

"I do not wish to discuss the matter any further," replied Mrs. Simmons shortly. Then she passed her plate for more creamed potato. She felt that she would die before she confessed to the ghastly absurdity of that nightcap, or to having been disturbed by the flight of peacocks off a blue field of chintz after she had scoffed at the possibility of such a thing. She left the whole matter so vague that in a fashion she came off the mistress of the situation. She at all events impressed everybody by her coolness in the face of no one knew what nightly terror.

After breakfast, with the assistance of Amanda and Flora, she moved back into her old room. Scarcely a word was spoken during the process of moving, but they all worked with trembling haste and looked guilty when they met one another's eyes, as if conscious of betraying a common fear.

That afternoon the young minister, John Dunn, went to Sophia Gill and requested permission to occupy the southwest chamber that night.

"I don't ask to have my effects moved there," said he, "for I could scarcely afford a room so much superior to the one I now occupy, but I would like, if you please, to sleep there to-night for the purpose of refuting in my own person any unfortunate superstition which may have obtained root here."

Sophia Gill thanked the minister gratefully and eagerly accepted his offer.

"How anybody with common sense can believe for a minute in any such nonsense passes my comprehension," said she.

"It certainly passes mine how anybody with Christian faith can believe in ghosts," said the minister gently, and Sophia Gill felt a certain feminine contentment in hearing him. The minister was a child to her; she regarded him with no tincture of sentiment, and yet she loved to hear two other women covertly condemned by him and she herself thereby exalted.

That night about twelve o'clock the Reverend John Dunn essayed to go to his nightly slumber in the southwest chamber. He had been sitting up until that hour preparing his sermon.

He traversed the hall with a little night-lamp in his hand, opened the door of the southwest chamber, and essayed to enter. He might as well have essayed to enter the solid side of a house. He could not believe his senses. The door was certainly open; he could look into the room full of soft lights and shadows under the moonlight which streamed into the windows. He could see the bed in which he had expected to pass the night, but he could not enter. Whenever he strove to do so he had a curious sensation as if he were trying to press against an invisible person who met him with a force of opposition impossible to overcome. The minister was not an athletic man, yet he had considerable strength. He squared his elbows, set his mouth hard, and strove to push his way through into the room. The opposition which he met was as sternly and mutely terrible as the rocky fastness of a mountain in his way.

For a half hour John Dunn, doubting, raging, overwhelmed with spiritual agony as to the state of his own soul rather than fear, strove to enter that southwest chamber. He was simply powerless against this uncanny obstacle. Finally a great horror as of evil itself came over him. He was a nervous man and very young. He fairly fled to his own chamber and locked himself in like a terror-stricken girl.

The next morning he went to Miss Gill and told her frankly what had happened, and begged her to say nothing about it lest he should have injured the cause by the betrayal of such weakness, for he actually had come to believe that there was something wrong with the room.

"What it is I know not, Miss Sophia," said he, "but I firmly believe, against my will, that there is in that room some accursed evil power at work, of which modern faith and modern science know nothing."

Miss Sophia Gill listened with grimly lowering face. She had an inborn respect for the clergy, but she was bound to hold that southwest chamber in the dearly beloved old house of her fathers free of blame.

"I think I will sleep in that room myself to-night," she said, when the minister had finished.

He looked at her in doubt and dismay.

"I have great admiration for your faith and courage, Miss Sophia," he said, "but are you wise?"

"I am fully resolved to sleep in that room to-night," said she conclusively. There were occasions when Miss Sophia Gill could put on a manner of majesty, and she did now.

It was ten o'clock that night when Sophia Gill entered the southwest chamber. She had told her sister what she intended doing and had been proof against her tearful entreaties. Amanda was charged not to tell the young girl, Flora.

"There is no use in frightening that child over nothing," said Sophia.

Sophia, when she entered the southwest chamber, set the lamp which she carried on the bureau, and began moving about the rooms pulling down the curtains, taking off the nice white counterpane of the bed, and preparing generally for the night.

As she did so, moving with great coolness and deliberation, she became conscious that she was thinking some thoughts that were foreign to her.

She began remembering what she could not have remembered, since she was not then born: the trouble over her mother's marriage, the bitter opposition, the shutting the door upon her, the ostracizing her from heart and home. She became aware of a most singular sensation as of bitter resentment herself, and not against the mother and sister who had so treated her own mother, but against her own mother, and then she became aware of a like bitterness extended to her own self. She felt malignant toward her mother as a young girl whom she remembered, though she could not have remembered, and she felt malignant toward her own self, and her sister Amanda, and Flora. Evil suggestions surged in her brain—suggestions which turned her heart to stone and which still fascinated her. And all the time by a sort of double consciousness she knew that what she thought was strange and not due to her own volition. She knew that she was thinking the thoughts of some other person, and she knew who. She felt herself possessed.

But there was tremendous strength in the woman's nature. She had inherited strength for good and righteous self-assertion, from the evil strength of her ancestors. They had turned their own weapons against themselves. She made an effort which seemed almost mortal, but was conscious that the hideous thing was gone from her. She thought her own thoughts. Then she scouted to herself the idea

of anything supernatural about the terrific experience. "I am imagining everything," she told herself.
She went on with her preparations; she went to the
bureau to take down her hair. She looked in the glass
and saw, instead of her softly parted waves of hair,
harsh lines of iron-gray under the black borders of
an old-fashioned head-dress. She saw instead of her
smooth, broad forehead, a high one wrinkled with
the intensest concentration of selfish reflections of
a long life; she saw instead of her steady blue eyes,
black ones with depths of malignant reserve, behind a broad meaning of ill will; she saw instead of
her firm, benevolent mouth one with a hard, thin
line, a network of melancholic wrinkles. She saw instead of her own face, middle-aged and good to see,
the expression of a life of honesty and good will to
others and patience under trials, the face of a very
old woman scowling forever with unceasing hatred
and misery at herself and all others, at life, and
death, at that which had been and that which was to
come. She saw instead of her own face in the glass,
the face of her dead Aunt Harriet, topping her own
shoulders in her own well-known dress!

Sophia Gill left the room. She went into the one
which she shared with her sister Amanda. Amanda
looked up and saw her standing there. She had set
the lamp on a table, and she stood holding a handkerchief over her face. Amanda looked at her with
terror.

"What is it? What is it, Sophia?" she gasped.

Sophia still stood with the handkerchief pressed to her face.

"Oh, Sophia, let me call somebody. Is your face hurt? Sophia, what is the matter with your face?" fairly shrieked Amanda.

Suddenly Sophia took the handkerchief from her face.

"Look at me, Amanda Gill," she said in an awful voice.

Amanda looked, shrinking.

"What is it? Oh, what is it? You don't look hurt. What is it, Sophia?"

"What do you see?"

"Why, I see you."

"Me?"

"Yes, you. What did you think I would see?"

Sophia Gill looked at her sister. "Never as long as I live will I tell you what I thought you would see, and you must never ask me," said she.

"Well, I never will, Sophia," replied Amanda, half weeping with terror.

"You won't try to sleep in that room again, Sophia?"

"No," said Sophia; "and I am going to sell this house."

THE EMPTY HOUSE

ALGERNON BLACKWOOD
(1906)

Certain houses, like certain persons, manage somehow to proclaim at once their character for evil. In
the case of the latter, no particular feature need betray them; they may boast an open countenance and
an ingenuous smile; and yet a little of their company leaves the unalterable conviction that there
is something radically amiss with their being: that
they are evil. Willy nilly, they seem to communicate an atmosphere of secret and wicked thoughts
which makes those in their immediate neighbourhood shrink from them as from a thing diseased.

And, perhaps, with houses the same principle is
operative, and it is the aroma of evil deeds committed under a particular roof, long after the actual
doers have passed away, that makes the gooseflesh
come and the hair rise. Something of the original
passion of the evil-doer, and of the horror felt by
his victim, enters the heart of the innocent watcher,
and he becomes suddenly conscious of tingling

nerves, creeping skin, and a chilling of the blood. He is terror-stricken without apparent cause.

There was manifestly nothing in the external appearance of this particular house to bear out the tales of the horror that was said to reign within. It was neither lonely nor unkempt. It stood, crowded into a corner of the square, and looked exactly like the houses on either side of it. It had the same number of windows as its neighbours; the same balcony overlooking the gardens; the same white steps leading up to the heavy black front door; and, in the rear, there was the same narrow strip of green, with neat box borders, running up to the wall that divided it from the backs of the adjoining houses. Apparently, too, the number of chimney pots on the roof was the same; the breadth and angle of the eaves; and even the height of the dirty area railings.

And yet this house in the square, that seemed precisely similar to its fifty ugly neighbours, was as a matter of fact entirely different—horribly different.

Wherein lay this marked, invisible difference is impossible to say. It cannot be ascribed wholly to the imagination, because persons who had spent some time in the house, knowing nothing of the facts, had declared positively that certain rooms were so disagreeable they would rather die than enter them again, and that the atmosphere of the whole house produced in them symptoms of a genuine terror; while the series of innocent tenants who had tried to live in it and been forced to decamp at the shortest possible notice, was indeed little less than a scandal in the town.

When Shorthouse arrived to pay a "week-end" visit to his Aunt Julia in her little house on the sea-front at the other end of the town, he found her charged to the brim with mystery and excitement. He had only received her telegram that morning, and he had come anticipating boredom; but the moment he touched her hand and kissed her apple-skin wrinkled cheek, he caught the first wave of her electrical condition. The impression deepened when he learned that there were to be no other visitors, and that he had been telegraphed for with a very special object.

Something was in the wind, and the "something" would doubtless bear fruit; for this elderly spinster aunt, with a mania for psychical research, had brains as well as will power, and by hook or by crook she usually managed to accomplish her ends. The revelation was made soon after tea, when she sidled close up to him as they paced slowly along the sea-front in the dusk.

"I've got the keys," she announced in a delighted, yet half awesome voice. "Got them till Monday!"

"The keys of the bathing-machine, or—?" he asked innocently, looking from the sea to the town. Nothing brought her so quickly to the point as feigning stupidity.

"Neither," she whispered. "I've got the keys of the haunted house in the square—and I'm going there to-night."

Shorthouse was conscious of the slightest possible tremor down his back. He dropped his teasing tone. Something in her voice and manner thrilled him. She was in earnest.

"But you can't go alone—" he began.

"That's why I wired for you," she said with decision.

He turned to look at her. The ugly, lined, enigmatical face was alive with excitement. There was the glow of genuine enthusiasm round it like a halo. The eyes shone. He caught another wave of her excitement, and a second tremor, more marked than the first, accompanied it.

"Thanks, Aunt Julia," he said politely; "thanks awfully."

"I should not dare to go quite alone," she went on, raising her voice; "but with you I should enjoy it immensely. You're afraid of nothing, I know."

"Thanks *so* much," he said again. "Er—is anything likely to happen?"

"A great deal *has* happened," she whispered, "though it's been most cleverly hushed up. Three tenants have come and gone in the last few months, and the house is said to be empty for good now."

In spite of himself Shorthouse became interested. His aunt was so very much in earnest.

"The house is very old indeed," she went on, "and the story—an unpleasant one—dates a long way back. It has to do with a murder committed by a jealous stableman who had some affair with a servant in the house. One night he managed to secrete himself in the cellar, and when everyone was asleep, he crept upstairs to the servants' quarters, chased the girl down to the next landing, and before anyone could come to the rescue threw her bodily over the banisters into the hall below."

"And the stableman—?"

"Was caught, I believe, and hanged for murder; but it all happened a century ago, and I've not been able to get more details of the story."

Shorthouse now felt his interest thoroughly aroused; but, though he was not particularly nervous for himself, he hesitated a little on his aunt's account.

"On one condition," he said at length.

"Nothing will prevent my going," she said firmly; "but I may as well hear your condition."

"That you guarantee your power of self-control if anything really horrible happens. I mean—that you are sure you won't get too frightened."

"Jim," she said scornfully, "I'm not young, I know, nor are my nerves; but *with you* I should be afraid of nothing in the world!"

This, of course, settled it, for Shorthouse had no pretensions to being other than a very ordinary

young man, and an appeal to his vanity was irresistible. He agreed to go.

Instinctively, by a sort of sub-conscious preparation, he kept himself and his forces well in hand
the whole evening, compelling an accumulative reserve of control by that nameless inward process of
gradually putting all the emotions away and turning
the key upon them—a process difficult to describe,
but wonderfully effective, as all men who have lived
through severe trials of the inner man well understand. Later, it stood him in good stead.

But it was not until half-past ten, when they
stood in the hall, well in the glare of friendly lamps
and still surrounded by comforting human influences, that he had to make the first call upon this
store of collected strength. For, once the door was
closed, and he saw the deserted silent street stretching away white in the moonlight before them, it came
to him clearly that the real test that night would be
in dealing with *two fears* instead of one. He would
have to carry his aunt's fear as well as his own. And,
as he glanced down at her sphinx-like countenance
and realised that it might assume no pleasant aspect
in a rush of real terror, he felt satisfied with only
one thing in the whole adventure—that he had confidence in his own will and power to stand against
any shock that might come.

Slowly they walked along the empty streets of
the town; a bright autumn moon silvered the roofs,

casting deep shadows; there was no breath of wind;
and the trees in the formal gardens by the sea-front
watched them silently as they passed along. To his
aunt's occasional remarks Shorthouse made no reply, realising that she was simply surrounding herself with mental buffers—saying ordinary things to
prevent herself thinking of extra-ordinary things.
Few windows showed lights, and from scarcely a
single chimney came smoke or sparks. Shorthouse
had already begun to notice everything, even the
smallest details. Presently they stopped at the street
corner and looked up at the name on the side of
the house full in the moonlight, and with one accord, but without remark, turned into the square
and crossed over to the side of it that lay in shadow.

"The number of the house is thirteen," whispered
a voice at his side; and neither of them made the
obvious reference, but passed across the broad sheet
of moonlight and began to march up the pavement
in silence.

It was about half-way up the square that Shorthouse felt an arm slipped quietly but significantly
into his own, and knew then that their adventure
had begun in earnest, and that his companion was
already yielding imperceptibly to the influences
against them. She needed support.

A few minutes later they stopped before a tall,
narrow house that rose before them into the night,
ugly in shape and painted a dingy white. Shutterless

windows, without blinds, stared down upon them,
shining here and there in the moonlight. There were
weather streaks in the wall and cracks in the paint,
and the balcony bulged out from the first floor a
little unnaturally. But, beyond this generally forlorn appearance of an unoccupied house, there was
nothing at first sight to single out this particular
mansion for the evil character it had most certainly
acquired.

Taking a look over their shoulders to make sure
they had not been followed, they went boldly up
the steps and stood against the huge black door that
fronted them forbiddingly. But the first wave of
nervousness was now upon them, and Shorthouse
fumbled a long time with the key before he could
fit it into the lock at all. For a moment, if truth
were told, they both hoped it would not open, for
they were a prey to various unpleasant emotions as
they stood there on the threshold of their ghostly
adventure. Shorthouse, shuffling with the key and
hampered by the steady weight on his arm, certainly
felt the solemnity of the moment. It was as if the
whole world—for all experience seemed at that instant concentrated in his own consciousness—were
listening to the grating noise of that key. A stray
puff of wind wandering down the empty street woke
a momentary rustling in the trees behind them, but
otherwise this rattling of the key was the only sound
audible; and at last it turned in the lock and the

heavy door swung open and revealed a yawning gulf of darkness beyond.

With a last glance at the moonlit square, they passed quickly in, and the door slammed behind them with a roar that echoed prodigiously through empty halls and passages. But, instantly, with the echoes, another sound made itself heard, and Aunt Julia leaned suddenly so heavily upon him that he had to take a step backwards to save himself from falling.

A man had coughed close beside them—so close that it seemed they must have been actually by his side in the darkness.

With the possibility of practical jokes in his mind, Shorthouse at once swung his heavy stick in the direction of the sound; but it met nothing more solid than air. He heard his aunt give a little gasp beside him.

"There's someone here," she whispered; "I heard him."

"Be quiet!" he said sternly. "It was nothing but the noise of the front door."

"Oh! get a light—quick!" she added, as her nephew, fumbling with a box of matches, opened it upside down and let them all fall with a rattle on to the stone floor.

The sound, however, was not repeated; and there was no evidence of retreating footsteps. In another minute they had a candle burning, using an empty

end of a cigar case as a holder; and when the first
flare had died down he held the impromptu lamp
aloft and surveyed the scene. And it was dreary
enough in all conscience, for there is nothing more
desolate in all the abodes of men than an unfurnished house dimly lit, silent, and forsaken, and yet
tenanted by rumour with the memories of evil and
violent histories.

They were standing in a wide hall-way; on their
left was the open door of a spacious dining-room,
and in front the hall ran, ever narrowing, into a
long, dark passage that led apparently to the top of
the kitchen stairs. The broad uncarpeted staircase
rose in a sweep before them, everywhere draped in
shadows, except for a single spot about half-way up
where the moonlight came in through the window
and fell on a bright patch on the boards. This shaft
of light shed a faint radiance above and below it,
lending to the objects within its reach a misty outline that was infinitely more suggestive and ghostly
than complete darkness. Filtered moonlight always
seems to paint faces on the surrounding gloom, and
as Shorthouse peered up into the well of darkness
and thought of the countless empty rooms and passages in the upper part of the old house, he caught
himself longing again for the safety of the moonlit square, or the cosy, bright drawing-room they
had left an hour before. Then realising that these
thoughts were dangerous, he thrust them away again

and summoned all his energy for concentration on the present.

"Aunt Julia," he said aloud, severely, "we must now go through the house from top to bottom and make a thorough search."

The echoes of his voice died away slowly all over the building, and in the intense silence that followed he turned to look at her. In the candle-light he saw that her face was already ghastly pale; but she dropped his arm for a moment and said in a whisper, stepping close in front of him—

"I agree. We must be sure there's no one hiding. That's the first thing."

She spoke with evident effort, and he looked at her with admiration.

"You feel quite sure of yourself? It's not too late—"

"I think so," she whispered, her eyes shifting nervously toward the shadows behind. "Quite sure, only one thing—"

"What's that?"

"You must never leave me alone for an instant."

"As long as you understand that any sound or appearance must be investigated at once, for to hesitate means to admit fear. That is fatal."

"Agreed," she said, a little shakily, after a moment's hesitation. "I'll try—"

Arm in arm, Shorthouse holding the dripping candle and the stick, while his aunt carried the

cloak over her shoulders, figures of utter comedy to
all but themselves, they began a systematic search.

Stealthily, walking on tip-toe and shading the
candle lest it should betray their presence through
the shutterless windows, they went first into the big
dining-room. There was not a stick of furniture to
be seen. Bare walls, ugly mantel-pieces and empty
grates stared at them. Everything, they felt, resented their intrusion, watching them, as it were, with
veiled eyes; whispers followed them; shadows flitted
noiselessly to right and left; something seemed ever
at their back, watching, waiting an opportunity to
do them injury. There was the inevitable sense that
operations which went on when the room was empty
had been temporarily suspended till they were well
out of the way again. The whole dark interior of the
old building seemed to become a malignant Presence that rose up, warning them to desist and mind
their own business; every moment the strain on the
nerves increased.

Out of the gloomy dining-room they passed
through large folding doors into a sort of library or
smoking-room, wrapt equally in silence, darkness,
and dust; and from this they regained the hall near
the top of the back stairs.

Here a pitch black tunnel opened before them into
the lower regions, and—it must be confessed—they
hesitated. But only for a minute. With the worst of
the night still to come it was essential to turn from

nothing. Aunt Julia stumbled at the top step of the dark descent, ill lit by the flickering candle, and even Shorthouse felt at least half the decision go out of his legs.

"Come on!" he said peremptorily, and his voice ran on and lost itself in the dark, empty spaces below.

"I'm coming," she faltered, catching his arm with unnecessary violence.

They went a little unsteadily down the stone steps, a cold, damp air meeting them in the face, close and mal-odorous. The kitchen, into which the stairs led along a narrow passage, was large, with a lofty ceiling. Several doors opened out of it—some into cupboards with empty jars still standing on the shelves, and others into horrible little ghostly back offices, each colder and less inviting than the last. Black beetles scurried over the floor, and once, when they knocked against a deal table standing in a corner, something about the size of a cat jumped down with a rush and fled, scampering across the stone floor into the darkness. Everywhere there was a sense of recent occupation, an impression of sadness and gloom.

Leaving the main kitchen, they next went towards the scullery. The door was standing ajar, and as they pushed it open to its full extent Aunt Julia uttered a piercing scream, which she instantly tried to stifle by placing her hand over her mouth. For a second

Shorthouse stood stock-still, catching his breath. He felt as if his spine had suddenly become hollow and someone had filled it with particles of ice.

Facing them, directly in their way between the doorposts, stood the figure of a woman. She had dishevelled hair and wildly staring eyes, and her face was terrified and white as death.

She stood there motionless for the space of a single second. Then the candle flickered and she was gone—gone utterly—and the door framed nothing but empty darkness.

"Only the beastly jumping candle-light," he said quickly, in a voice that sounded like someone else's and was only half under control. "Come on, aunt. There's nothing there."

He dragged her forward. With a clattering of feet and a great appearance of boldness they went on, but over his body the skin moved as if crawling ants covered it, and he knew by the weight on his arm that he was supplying the force of locomotion for two. The scullery was cold, bare, and empty; more like a large prison cell than anything else. They went round it, tried the door into the yard, and the windows, but found them all fastened securely. His aunt moved beside him like a person in a dream. Her eyes were tightly shut, and she seemed merely to follow the pressure of his arm. Her courage filled him with amazement. At the same time he noticed that a certain odd change had come over her face, a change which somehow evaded his power of analysis.

"There's nothing here, aunty," he repeated aloud quickly. "Let's go upstairs and see the rest of the house. Then we'll choose a room to wait up in."

She followed him obediently, keeping close to his side, and they locked the kitchen door behind them. It was a relief to get up again. In the hall there was more light than before, for the moon had travelled a little further down the stairs. Cautiously they began to go up into the dark vault of the upper house, the boards creaking under their weight.

On the first floor they found the large double drawing-rooms, a search of which revealed nothing. Here also was no sign of furniture or recent occupancy; nothing but dust and neglect and shadows. They opened the big folding doors between front and back drawing-rooms and then came out again to the landing and went on upstairs.

They had not gone up more than a dozen steps when they both simultaneously stopped to listen, looking into each other's eyes with a new apprehension across the flickering candle flame. From the room they had left hardly ten seconds before came the sound of doors quietly closing. It was beyond all question; they heard the booming noise that accompanies the shutting of heavy doors, followed by the sharp catching of the latch.

"We must go back and see," said Shorthouse briefly, in a low tone, and turning to go downstairs again.

Somehow she managed to drag after him, her feet catching in her dress, her face livid.

When they entered the front drawing-room it was plain that the folding doors had been closed—half a minute before. Without hesitation Shorthouse opened them. He almost expected to see someone facing him in the back room; but only darkness and cold air met him. They went through both rooms, finding nothing unusual. They tried in every way to make the doors close of themselves, but there was not wind enough even to set the candle flame flickering. The doors would not move without strong pressure. All was silent as the grave. Undeniably the rooms were utterly empty, and the house utterly still.

"It's beginning," whispered a voice at his elbow which he hardly recognised as his aunt's.

He nodded acquiescence, taking out his watch to note the time. It was fifteen minutes before midnight; he made the entry of exactly what had occurred in his notebook, setting the candle in its case upon the floor in order to do so. It took a moment or two to balance it safely against the wall.

Aunt Julia always declared that at this moment she was not actually watching him, but had turned her head towards the inner room, where she fancied she heard something moving; but, at any rate, both positively agreed that there came a sound of rushing feet, heavy and very swift—and the next instant the candle was out!

But to Shorthouse himself had come more than this, and he has always thanked his fortunate stars that it came to him alone and not to his aunt too. For, as he rose from the stooping position of balancing the candle, and before it was actually extinguished, a face thrust itself forward so close to his own that he could almost have touched it with his lips. It was a face working with passion; a man's face, dark, with thick features, and angry, savage eyes. It belonged to a common man, and it was evil in its ordinary normal expression, no doubt, but as he saw it, alive with intense, aggressive emotion, it was a malignant and terrible human countenance.

There was no movement of the air; nothing but the sound of rushing feet—stockinged or muffled feet; the apparition of the face; and the almost simultaneous extinguishing of the candle.

In spite of himself, Shorthouse uttered a little cry, nearly losing his balance as his aunt clung to him with her whole weight in one moment of real, uncontrollable terror. She made no sound, but simply seized him bodily. Fortunately, however, she had seen nothing, but had only heard the rushing feet, for her control returned almost at once, and he was able to disentangle himself and strike a match.

The shadows ran away on all sides before the glare, and his aunt stooped down and groped for the cigar case with the precious candle. Then they discovered that the candle had not been blown out at all; it had been crushed out. The wick was pressed down into the wax, which was flattened as if by some smooth, heavy instrument.

How his companion so quickly overcame her terror, Shorthouse never properly understood; but his admiration for her self-control increased tenfold, and at the same time served to feed his own dying flame—for which he was undeniably grateful. Equally inexplicable to him was the evidence of physical force they had just witnessed. He at once suppressed the memory of stories he had heard of "physical mediums" and their dangerous phenomena; for if these were true, and either his aunt or himself was unwittingly a physical medium, it meant that they were simply aiding to focus the forces of a haunted house already charged to the brim. It was like walking with unprotected lamps among uncovered stores of gunpowder.

So, with as little reflection as possible, he simply relit the candle and went up to the next floor. The arm in his trembled, it is true, and his own tread was often uncertain, but they went on with thoroughness, and after a search revealing nothing they climbed the last flight of stairs to the top floor of all.

Here they found a perfect nest of small servants' rooms, with broken pieces of furniture, dirty cane-bottomed chairs, chests of drawers, cracked mirrors, and decrepit bedsteads. The rooms had low sloping ceilings already hung here and there with cobwebs, small windows, and badly plastered walls—a depressing and dismal region which they were glad to leave behind.

It was on the stroke of midnight when they entered a small room on the third floor, close to the top of the stairs, and arranged to make themselves comfortable for the remainder of their adventure. It was absolutely bare, and was said to be the room— then used as a clothes closet—into which the infuriated groom had chased his victim and finally caught her. Outside, across the narrow landing, began the stairs leading up to the floor above, and the servants' quarters where they had just searched.

In spite of the chilliness of the night there was something in the air of this room that cried for an open window. But there was more than this. Shorthouse could only describe it by saying that he felt less master of himself here than in any other part of the house. There was something that acted directly on the nerves, tiring the resolution, enfeebling the will. He was conscious of this result before he had been in the room five minutes, and it was in the short time they stayed there that he suffered the wholesale depletion of his vital forces, which was,

for himself, the chief horror of the whole experience.

They put the candle on the floor of the cupboard,
leaving the door a few inches ajar, so that there was
no glare to confuse the eyes, and no shadow to shift
about on walls and ceiling. Then they spread the
cloak on the floor and sat down to wait, with their
backs against the wall.

Shorthouse was within two feet of the door on to
the landing; his position commanded a good view
of the main staircase leading down into the darkness, and also of the beginning of the servants' stairs
going to the floor above; the heavy stick lay beside
him within easy reach.

The moon was now high above the house. Through
the open window they could see the comforting stars
like friendly eyes watching in the sky. One by one
the clocks of the town struck midnight, and when
the sounds died away the deep silence of a windless
night fell again over everything. Only the boom of
the sea, far away and lugubrious, filled the air with
hollow murmurs.

Inside the house the silence became awful; awful,
he thought, because any minute now it might be
broken by sounds portending terror. The strain of
waiting told more and more severely on the nerves;
they talked in whispers when they talked at all, for
their voices aloud sounded queer and unnatural. A

chilliness, not altogether due to the night air, invad-
ed the room, and made them cold. The influences
against them, whatever these might be, were slowly
robbing them of self-confidence, and the power of
decisive action; their forces were on the wane, and
the possibility of real fear took on a new and terrible meaning. He began to tremble for the elderly
woman by his side, whose pluck could hardly save
her beyond a certain extent.

He heard the blood singing in his veins. It sometimes seemed so loud that he fancied it prevented
his hearing properly certain other sounds that were
beginning very faintly to make themselves audible
in the depths of the house. Every time he fastened
his attention on these sounds, they instantly ceased.
They certainly came no nearer. Yet he could not
rid himself of the idea that movement was going
on somewhere in the lower regions of the house.
The drawing-room floor, where the doors had been
so strangely closed, seemed too near; the sounds
were further off than that. He thought of the great
kitchen, with the scurrying black-beetles, and of the
dismal little scullery; but, somehow or other, they
did not seem to come from there either. Surely they
were not *outside* the house!

Then, suddenly, the truth flashed into his mind,
and for the space of a minute he felt as if his blood
had stopped flowing and turned to ice.

The sounds were not downstairs at all; they were *upstairs*—upstairs, somewhere among those horrid gloomy little servants' rooms with their bits of broken furniture, low ceilings, and cramped windows—upstairs where the victim had first been disturbed and stalked to her death.

And the moment he discovered where the sounds were, he began to hear them more clearly. It was the sound of feet, moving stealthily along the passage overhead, in and out among the rooms, and past the furniture.

He turned quickly to steal a glance at the motionless figure seated beside him, to note whether she had shared his discovery. The faint candle-light coming through the crack in the cupboard door, threw her strongly-marked face into vivid relief against the white of the wall. But it was something else that made him catch his breath and stare again. An extraordinary something had come into her face and seemed to spread over her features like a mask; it smoothed out the deep lines and drew the skin everywhere a little tighter so that the wrinkles disappeared; it brought into the face—with the sole exception of the old eyes—an appearance of youth and almost of childhood.

He stared in speechless amazement—amazement that was dangerously near to horror. It was his aunt's face indeed, but it was her face of forty years ago, the vacant innocent face of a girl. He had heard stories

of that strange effect of terror which could wipe a
human countenance clean of other emotions, oblit-
erating all previous expressions; but he had never
realised that it could be literally true, or could mean
anything so simply horrible as what he now saw.
For the dreadful signature of overmastering fear was
written plainly in that utter vacancy of the girlish
face beside him; and when, feeling his intense gaze,
she turned to look at him, he instinctively closed his
eyes tightly to shut out the sight.

Yet, when he turned a minute later, his feelings
well in hand, he saw to his intense relief another
expression; his aunt was smiling, and though the
face was deathly white, the awful veil had lifted and
the normal look was returning.

"Anything wrong?" was all he could think of to
say at the moment. And the answer was eloquent,
coming from such a woman.

"I feel cold—and a little frightened," she whispered.

He offered to close the window, but she seized
hold of him and begged him not to leave her side
even for an instant.

"It's upstairs, I know," she whispered, with an
odd half laugh; "but I can't possibly go up."

But Shorthouse thought otherwise, knowing that
in action lay their best hope of self-control.

He took the brandy flask and poured out a glass
of neat spirit, stiff enough to help anybody over

anything. She swallowed it with a little shiver. His only idea now was to get out of the house before her collapse became inevitable; but this could not safely be done by turning tail and running from the enemy. Inaction was no longer possible; every minute he was growing less master of himself, and desperate, aggressive measures were imperative without further delay. Moreover, the action must be taken *towards* the enemy, not away from it; the climax, if necessary and unavoidable, would have to be faced boldly. He could do it now; but in ten minutes he might not have the force left to act for himself, much less for both!

Upstairs, the sounds were meanwhile becoming louder and closer, accompanied by occasional creaking of the boards. Someone was moving stealthily about, stumbling now and then awkwardly against the furniture.

Waiting a few moments to allow the tremendous dose of spirits to produce its effect, and knowing this would last but a short time under the circumstances, Shorthouse then quietly got on his feet, saying in a determined voice—

"Now, Aunt Julia, we'll go upstairs and find out what all this noise is about. You must come too. It's what we agreed."

He picked up his stick and went to the cupboard for the candle. A limp form rose shakily beside him breathing hard, and he heard a voice say very faintly something about being "ready to come." The woman's courage amazed him; it was so much greater than his own; and, as they advanced, holding aloft the dripping candle, some subtle force exhaled from this trembling, white-faced old woman at his side that was the true source of his inspiration. It held something really great that shamed him and gave him the support without which he would have proved far less equal to the occasion.

They crossed the dark landing, avoiding with their eyes the deep black space over the banisters. Then they began to mount the narrow staircase to meet the sounds which, minute by minute, grew louder and nearer. About half-way up the stairs Aunt Julia stumbled and Shorthouse turned to catch her by the arm, and just at that moment there came a terrific crash in the servants' corridor overhead. It was instantly followed by a shrill, agonised scream that was a cry of terror and a cry for help melted into one.

Before they could move aside, or go down a single step, someone came rushing along the passage overhead, blundering horribly, racing madly, at full speed, three steps at a time, down the very staircase where they stood. The steps were light and uncertain; but close behind them sounded the heavier tread of another person, and the staircase seemed to shake.

Shorthouse and his companion just had time to flatten themselves against the wall when the jumble

of flying steps was upon them, and two persons,
with the slightest possible interval between them,
dashed past at full speed. It was a perfect whirlwind
of sound breaking in upon the midnight silence of
the empty building.

The two runners, pursuer and pursued, had passed
clean through them where they stood, and already
with a thud the boards below had received first one,
then the other. Yet they had seen absolutely nothing—not a hand, or arm, or face, or even a shred of
flying clothing.

There came a second's pause. Then the first one,
the lighter of the two, obviously the pursued one,
ran with uncertain footsteps into the little room
which Shorthouse and his aunt had just left. The
heavier one followed. There was a sound of scuffling, gasping, and smothered screaming; and then
out on to the landing came the step—of a single
person *treading weightily.*

A dead silence followed for the space of half a
minute, and then was heard a rushing sound through
the air. It was followed by a dull, crashing thud in
the depths of the house below—on the stone floor
of the hall.

Utter silence reigned after. Nothing moved. The
flame of the candle was steady. It had been steady
the whole time, and the air had been undisturbed
by any movement whatsoever. Palsied with terror,
Aunt Julia, without waiting for her companion,

began fumbling her way downstairs; she was crying gently to herself, and when Shorthouse put his arm round her and half carried her he felt that she was trembling like a leaf. He went into the little room and picked up the cloak from the floor, and, arm in arm, walking very slowly, without speaking a word or looking once behind them, they marched down the three flights into the hall.

In the hall they saw nothing, but the whole way down the stairs they were conscious that someone followed them; step by step; when they went faster IT was left behind, and when they went more slowly IT caught them up. But never once did they look behind to see; and at each turning of the staircase they lowered their eyes for fear of the following horror they might see upon the stairs above.

With trembling hands Shorthouse opened the front door, and they walked out into the moonlight and drew a deep breath of the cool night air blowing in from the sea.

THE TOLL-HOUSE

W. W. JACOBS
(1909)

"It's all nonsense," said Jack Barnes. "Of course people have died in the house; people die in every house. As for the noises—wind in the chimney and rats in the wainscot are very convincing to a nervous man. Give me another cup of tea, Meagle."

"Lester and White are first," said Meagle, who was presiding at the tea-table of the Three Feathers Inn. "You've had two."

Lester and White finished their cups with irritating slowness, pausing between sips to sniff the aroma, and to discover the sex and dates of arrival of the "strangers" which floated in some numbers in the beverage. Mr. Meagle served them to the brim, and then, turning to the grimly expectant Mr. Barnes, blandly requested him to ring for hot water.

"We'll try and keep your nerves in their present healthy condition," he remarked. "For my part I have a sort of half-and-half belief in the supernatural."

"All sensible people have," said Lester. "An aunt of mine saw a ghost once."

White nodded.

"I had an uncle that saw one," he said.

"It always is somebody else that sees them," said Barnes.

"Well, there is a house," said Meagle, "a large house at an absurdly low rent, and nobody will take it. It has taken toll of at least one life of every family that has lived there—however short the time—and since it has stood empty caretaker after caretaker has died there. The last caretaker died fifteen years ago."

"Exactly," said Barnes. "Long enough ago for legends to accumulate."

"I'll bet you a sovereign you won't spend the night there alone, for all your talk," said White, suddenly.

"And I," said Lester.

"No," said Barnes slowly. "I don't believe in ghosts nor in any supernatural things whatever; all the same I admit that I should not care to pass a night there alone."

"But why not?" inquired White.

"Wind in the chimney," said Meagle with a grin.

"Rats in the wainscot," chimed in Lester.

"As you like," said Barnes coloring.

"Suppose we all go," said Meagle. "Start after supper, and get there about eleven. We have been walking for ten days now without an adventure—except Barnes's discovery that ditchwater smells longest. It will be a novelty, at any rate, and, if we break the spell by all surviving, the grateful owner ought to come down handsome."

"Let's see what the landlord has to say about it first," said Lester. "There is no fun in passing a night in an ordinary empty house. Let us make sure that it is haunted."

He rang the bell, and, sending for the landlord, appealed to him in the name of our common humanity not to let them waste a night watching in a house in which spectres and hobgoblins had no part. The reply was more than reassuring, and the landlord, after describing with considerable art the exact appearance of a head which had been seen hanging out of a window in the moonlight, wound up with a polite but urgent request that they would settle his bill before they went.

"It's all very well for you young gentlemen to have your fun," he said indulgently; "but supposing as how you are all found dead in the morning, what about me? It ain't called the Toll-House for nothing, you know."

"Who died there last?" inquired Barnes, with an air of polite derision.

"A tramp," was the reply. "He went there for the sake of half a crown, and they found him next morning hanging from the balusters, dead."

"Suicide," said Barnes. "Unsound mind."

The landlord nodded. "That's what the jury brought it in," he said slowly; "but his mind was sound enough when he went in there. I'd known him, off and on, for years. I'm a poor man, but I wouldn't spend the night in that house for a hundred pounds."

He repeated this remark as they started on their expedition a few hours later. They left as the inn was closing for the night; bolts shot noisily behind them, and, as the regular customers trudged slowly homewards, they set off at a brisk pace in the direction of the house. Most of the cottages were already in darkness, and lights in others went out as they passed.

"It seems rather hard that we have got to lose a night's rest in order to convince Barnes of the existence of ghosts," said White.

"It's in a good cause," said Meagle. "A most worthy object; and something seems to tell me that we shall succeed. You didn't forget the candles, Lester?"

"I have brought two," was the reply; "all the old man could spare."

There was but little moon, and the night was cloudy. The road between high hedges was dark, and in one place, where it ran through a wood, so black that they twice stumbled in the uneven ground at the side of it.

"Fancy leaving our comfortable beds for this!" said White again. "Let me see; this desirable residential sepulchre lies to the right, doesn't it?"

"Farther on," said Meagle.

They walked on for some time in silence, broken only by White's tribute to the softness, the cleanliness, and the comfort of the bed which was receding farther and farther into the distance. Under Meagle's guidance they turned off at last to the right, and, after a walk of a quarter of a mile, saw the gates of the house before them.

The lodge was almost hidden by overgrown shrubs and the drive was choked with rank growths. Meagle leading, they pushed through it until the dark pile of the house loomed above them.

"There is a window at the back where we can get in, so the landlord says," said Lester, as they stood before the hall door.

"Window?" said Meagle. "Nonsense. Let's do the thing properly. Where's the knocker?"

He felt for it in the darkness and gave a thundering rat-tat-tat at the door.

"Don't play the fool," said Barnes crossly.

"Ghostly servants are all asleep," said Meagle gravely, "but *I'll* wake them up before I've done with them. It's scandalous keeping us out here in the dark."

He plied the knocker again, and the noise volleyed in the emptiness beyond. Then with a sudden exclamation he put out his hands and stumbled forward.

"Why, it was open all the time," he said, with an odd catch in his voice. "Come on."

"I don't believe it was open," said Lester, hanging back. "Somebody is playing us a trick."

"Nonsense," said Meagle sharply. "Give me a candle. Thanks. Who's got a match?"

Barnes produced a box and struck one, and Meagle, shielding the candle with his hand, led the way forward to the foot of the stairs. "Shut the door, somebody," he said, "there's too much draught."

"It is shut," said White, glancing behind him.

Meagle fingered his chin. "Who shut it?" he inquired, looking from one to the other. "Who came in last?"

"I did," said Lester, "but I don't remember shutting it—perhaps I did, though."

Meagle, about to speak, thought better of it, and, still carefully guarding the flame, began to explore the house, with the others close behind. Shadows danced on the walls and lurked in the corners as they proceeded. At the end of the passage they found a second staircase, and ascending it slowly gained the first floor.

"Careful!" said Meagle, as they gained the landing.

He held the candle forward and showed where the balusters had broken away. Then he peered curiously into the void beneath.

"This is where the tramp hanged himself, I suppose," he said thoughtfully.

"You've got an unwholesome mind," said White, as they walked on. "This place is quite creepy enough without your remembering that. Now let's find a comfortable room and have a little nip of whiskey apiece and a pipe. How will this do?"

He opened a door at the end of the passage and revealed a small square room. Meagle led the way with the candle, and, first melting a drop or two of tallow, stuck it on the mantelpiece. The others seated themselves on the floor and watched pleasantly as White drew from his pocket a small bottle of whiskey and a tin cup.

"H'm! I've forgotten the water," he exclaimed.

"I'll soon get some," said Meagle.

He tugged violently at the bell-handle, and the rusty jangling of a bell sounded from a distant kitchen. He rang again.

"Don't play the fool," said Barnes roughly.

Meagle laughed. "I only wanted to convince you," he said kindly. "There ought to be, at any rate, one ghost in the servants' hall."

Barnes held up his hand for silence.

"Yes?" said Meagle with a grin at the other two. "Is anybody coming?"

"Suppose we drop this game and go back," said Barnes suddenly. "I don't believe in spirits, but nerves are outside anybody's command. You may laugh as you like, but it really seemed to me that I heard a door open below and steps on the stairs."

His voice was drowned in a roar of laughter.

"He is coming round," said Meagle with a smirk. "By the time I have done with him he will be a confirmed believer. Well, who will go and get some water? Will you, Barnes?"

"No," was the reply.

"If there is any it might not be safe to drink after all these years," said Lester. "We must do without it."

Meagle nodded, and taking a seat on the floor held out his hand for the cup. Pipes were lit and the clean, wholesome smell of tobacco filled the room. White produced a pack of cards; talk and laughter rang through the room and died away reluctantly in distant corridors.

"Empty rooms always delude me into the belief that I possess a deep voice," said Meagle. "To-morrow—"

He started up with a smothered exclamation as the light went out suddenly and something struck him on the head. The others sprang to their feet. Then Meagle laughed.

"It's the candle," he exclaimed. "I didn't stick it enough."

Barnes struck a match and relighting the candle stuck it on the mantelpiece, and sitting down took up his cards again.

"What was I going to say?" said Meagle. "Oh, I know; tomorrow I—"

"Listen!" said White, laying his hand on the other's sleeve. "Upon my word I really thought I heard a laugh."

"Look here!" said Barnes. "What do you say to going back? I've had enough of this. I keep fancying that I hear things too; sounds of something moving about in the passage outside. I know it's only fancy, but it's uncomfortable."

"You go if you want to," said Meagle, "and we will play dummy. Or you might ask the tramp to take your hand for you, as you go downstairs."

Barnes shivered and exclaimed angrily. He got up and, walking to the half-closed door, listened.

"Go outside," said Meagle, winking at the other two. "I'll dare you to go down to the hall door and back by yourself."

Barnes came back and, bending forward, lit his pipe at the candle.

"I am nervous but rational," he said, blowing out a thin cloud of smoke. "My nerves tell me that there is something prowling up and down the long passage outside; my reason tells me that it is all nonsense. Where are my cards?"

He sat down again, and taking up his hand, looked through it carefully and led.

"Your play, White," he said after a pause. White made no sign.

"Why, he is asleep," said Meagle. "Wake up, old man. Wake up and play."

Lester, who was sitting next to him, took the sleeping man by the arm and shook him, gently at first and then with some roughness; but White, with his back against the wall and his head bowed, made no sign. Meagle bawled in his ear and then turned a puzzled face to the others.

"He sleeps like the dead," he said, grimacing. "Well, there are still three of us to keep each other company."

"Yes," said Lester, nodding. "Unless— Good Lord! suppose—"

He broke off and eyed them trembling.

"Suppose what?" inquired Meagle.

"Nothing," stammered Lester. "Let's wake him. Try him again. *White! White!*"

"It's no good," said Meagle seriously; "there's something wrong about that sleep."

"That's what I meant," said Lester; "and if *he* goes to sleep like that, why shouldn't—"

Meagle sprang to his feet. "Nonsense," he said roughly. "He's tired out; that's all. Still, let's take him up and clear out. You take his legs and Barnes will lead the way with the candle. *Yes? Who's that?*"

He looked up quickly towards the door. "Thought I heard somebody tap," he said with a shamefaced laugh. "Now, Lester, up with him. One, two— Lester! Lester!"

He sprang forward too late; Lester, with his face buried in his arms, had rolled over on the floor fast asleep, and his utmost efforts failed to awaken him.

"He—is—asleep," he stammered. "'Asleep!'"

Barnes, who had taken the candle from the mantel-piece, stood peering at the sleepers in silence and dropping tallow over the floor.

"We must get out of this," said Meagle. "Quick!"

Barnes hesitated. "We can't leave them here—" he began.

"We must," said Meagle in strident tones. "If you go to sleep I shall go— Quick! Come."

He seized the other by the arm and strove to drag him to the door. Barnes shook him off, and putting the candle back on the mantelpiece, tried again to arouse the sleepers.

"It's no good," he said at last, and, turning from them, watched Meagle. "Don't you go to sleep," he said anxiously.

Meagle shook his head, and they stood for some time in uneasy silence. "May as well shut the door," said Barnes at last.

He crossed over and closed it gently. Then at a scuffling noise behind him he turned and saw Meagle in a heap on the hearthstone.

With a sharp catch in his breath he stood motionless. Inside the room the candle, fluttering in the draught, showed dimly the grotesque attitudes of the sleepers. Beyond the door there seemed to his over-wrought imagination a strange and stealthy unrest. He tried to whistle, but his lips were parched, and in a mechanical fashion he stooped, and began to pick up the cards which littered the floor.

He stopped once or twice and stood with bent head listening. The unrest outside seemed to increase; a loud creaking sounded from the stairs.

"Who is there?" he cried loudly.

The creaking ceased. He crossed to the door and flinging it open, strode out into the corridor. As he walked his fears left him suddenly.

"Come on!" he cried with a low laugh. "All of you! All of you! Show your faces—your infernal ugly faces! Don't skulk!"

He laughed again and walked on; and the heap in the fireplace put out his head tortoise fashion and listened in horror to the retreating footsteps. Not until they had become inaudible in the distance did the listeners' features relax.

"Good Lord, Lester, we've driven him mad," he said in a frightened whisper. "We must go after him."

There was no reply. Meagle sprung to his feet. "Do you hear?" he cried. "Stop your fooling now; this is serious. White! Lester! Do you hear?"

He bent and surveyed them in angry bewilderment. "All right," he said in a trembling voice. "You won't frighten me, you know."

He turned away and walked with exaggerated carelessness in the direction of the door. He even went outside and peeped through the crack, but the sleepers did not stir. He glanced into the blackness behind, and then came hastily into the room again.

He stood for a few seconds regarding them. The stillness in the house was horrible; he could not even hear them breathe. With a sudden resolution he snatched the candle from the mantelpiece and held the flame to White's finger. Then as he reeled back stupefied the footsteps again became audible.

He stood with the candle in his shaking hand listening. He heard them ascending the farther staircase, but they stopped suddenly as he went to the door. He walked a little way along the passage, and they went scurrying down the stairs and then at a jog-trot along the corridor below. He went back to the main staircase, and they ceased again.

For a time he hung over the balusters, listening and trying to pierce the blackness below; then slowly, step by step, he made his way downstairs, and, holding the candle above his head, peered about him.

"Barnes!" he called. "Where are you?"

Shaking with fright, he made his way along the passage, and summoning up all his courage pushed open doors and gazed fearfully into empty rooms. Then, quite suddenly, he heard the footsteps in front of him.

He followed slowly for fear of extinguishing the candle, until they led him at last into a vast bare kitchen with damp walls and a broken floor. In front of him a door leading into an inside room had just closed. He ran towards it and flung it open, and a cold air blew out the candle. He stood aghast.

"Barnes!" he cried again. "Don't be afraid! It is I—Meagle!"

There was no answer. He stood gazing into the darkness, and all the time the idea of something close at hand watching was upon him. Then suddenly the steps broke out overhead again.

He drew back hastily, and passing through the kitchen groped his way along the narrow passages. He could now see better in the darkness, and finding himself at last at the foot of the staircase began to ascend it noiselessly. He reached the landing just in time to see a figure disappear round the angle of a wall. Still careful to make no noise, he followed the sound of the steps until they led him to the top floor, and he cornered the chase at the end of a short passage.

"Barnes!" he whispered. "Barnes!"

Something stirred in the darkness. A small circular window at the end of the passage just softened the blackness and revealed the dim outlines of a motionless figure. Meagle, in place of advancing, stood almost as still as a sudden horrible doubt took possession of him. With his eyes fixed on the shape in front he fell back slowly and, as it advanced upon him, burst into a terrible cry.

"Barnes! For God's sake! Is it *you?*"

The echoes of his voice left the air quivering, but the figure before him paid no heed. For a moment he tried to brace his courage up to endure its approach, then with a smothered cry he turned and fled.

The passages wound like a maze, and he threaded them blindly in a vain search for the stairs. If he could get down and open the hall door—

He caught his breath in a sob; the steps had begun again. At a lumbering trot they clattered up and down the bare passages, in and out, up and down, as though in search of him. He stood appalled, and then as they drew near entered a small room and stood behind the door as they rushed by. He came out and ran swiftly and noiselessly in the other direction, and in a moment the steps were after him. He found the long corridor and raced along it at top speed. The stairs he knew were at the end, and with the steps close behind he descended them in blind haste. The steps gained on him, and he shrank to the side to let them pass, still continuing his headlong flight. Then suddenly he seemed to slip off the earth into space.

Lester awoke in the morning to find the sunshine streaming into the room, and White sitting up and regarding with some perplexity a badly blistered finger.

"Where are the others?" inquired Lester.

"Gone, I suppose," said White. "We must have been asleep."

Lester arose, and stretching his stiffened limbs, dusted his clothes with his hands, and went out into the corridor. White followed. At the noise of their approach a figure which had been lying asleep at the other end sat up and revealed the face of Barnes. "Why, I've been asleep," he said in surprise. "I don't remember coming here. How did I get here?"

"Nice place to come for a nap," said Lester, severely, as he pointed to the gap in the balusters. "Look there! Another yard and where would you have been?"

He walked carelessly to the edge and looked over. In response to his startled cry the others drew near, and all three stood gazing at the dead man below.

AFTERWARD

EDITH WHARTON

(1910)

I

"Oh, there *is* one, of course, but you'll never know it."

The assertion, laughingly flung out six months earlier in a bright June garden, came back to Mary Boyne with a sharp perception of its latent significance as she stood, in the December dusk, waiting for the lamps to be brought into the library.

The words had been spoken by their friend Alida Stair, as they sat at tea on her lawn at Pangbourne, in reference to the very house of which the library in question was the central, the pivotal "feature." Mary Boyne and her husband, in quest of a country place in one of the southern or southwestern counties, had, on their arrival in England, carried their problem straight to Alida Stair, who had successfully solved it in her own case; but it was not until they had rejected, almost capriciously, several practical and judicious suggestions that she threw it out: "Well, there's Lyng, in Dorsetshire. It belongs to Hugo's cousins, and you can get it for a song."

The reasons she gave for its being obtainable on these terms—its remoteness from a station, its lack of electric light, hot-water pipes, and other vulgar necessities—were exactly those pleading in its favor with two romantic Americans perversely in search of the economic drawbacks which were associated, in their tradition, with unusual architectural felicities.

"I should never believe I was living in an old house unless I was thoroughly uncomfortable," Ned Boyne, the more extravagant of the two, had jocosely insisted; "the least hint of 'convenience' would make me think it had been bought out of an exhibition, with the pieces numbered, and set up again." And they had proceeded to enumerate, with humorous precision, their various suspicions and exactions, refusing to believe that the house their cousin recommended was *really* Tudor till they learned it had no heating system, or that the village church was literally in the grounds till she assured them of the deplorable uncertainty of the water-supply.

"It's too uncomfortable to be true!" Edward Boyne had continued to exult as the avowal of each disadvantage was successively wrung from her; but he had cut short his rhapsody to ask, with a sudden relapse to distrust: "And the ghost? You've been concealing from us the fact that there is no ghost!"

Mary, at the moment, had laughed with him, yet almost with her laugh, being possessed of several sets of independent perceptions, had noted a sudden flatness of tone in Alida's answering hilarity.

"Oh, Dorsetshire's full of ghosts, you know."

"Yes, yes; but that won't do. I don't want to have to drive ten miles to see somebody else's ghost. I want one of my own on the premises. *Is* there a ghost at Lyng?"

His rejoinder had made Alida laugh again, and it was then that she had flung back tantalizingly: "Oh, there *is* one, of course, but you'll never know it."

"Never know it?" Boyne pulled her up. "But what in the world constitutes a ghost except the fact of its being known for one?"

"I can't say. But that's the story."

"That there's a ghost, but that nobody knows it's a ghost?"

"Well—not till afterward, at any rate."

"Till afterward?"

"Not till long, long afterward."

"But if it's once been identified as an unearthly visitant, why hasn't its *signalement* been handed down in the family? How has it managed to preserve its incognito?"

Alida could only shake her head. "Don't ask me. But it has."

"And then suddenly—" Mary spoke up as if from some cavernous depth of divination—"suddenly, long afterward, one says to one's self, '*That was* it?'"

She was oddly startled at the sepulchral sound
with which her question fell on the banter of the
other two, and she saw the shadow of the same surprise flit across Alida's clear pupils. "I suppose so.
One just has to wait."

"Oh, hang waiting!" Ned broke in. "Life's too
short for a ghost who can only be enjoyed in retro-
spect. Can't we do better than that, Mary?"

But it turned out that in the event they were not
destined to, for within three months of their conversation with Mrs. Stair they were established at
Lyng, and the life they had yearned for to the point
of planning it out in all its daily details had actually
begun for them.

It was to sit, in the thick December dusk, by just
such a wide-hooded fireplace, under just such black
oak rafters, with the sense that beyond the mullioned panes the downs were darkening to a deeper
solitude: it was for the ultimate indulgence in such
sensations that Mary Boyne had endured for nearly
fourteen years the soul-deadening ugliness of the
Middle West, and that Boyne had ground on dog-
gedly at his engineering till, with a suddenness that
still made her blink, the prodigious windfall of the
Blue Star Mine had put them at a stroke in possession of life and the leisure to taste it. They had
never for a moment meant their new state to be
one of idleness; but they meant to give themselves
only to harmonious activities. She had her vision

of painting and gardening (against a background of gray walls), he dreamed of the production of his long-planned book on the "Economic Basis of Culture"; and with such absorbing work ahead no existence could be too sequestered; they could not get far enough from the world, or plunge deep enough into the past.

Dorsetshire had attracted them from the first by a semblance of remoteness out of all proportion to its geographical position. But to the Boynes it was one of the ever-recurring wonders of the whole incredibly compressed island—a nest of counties, as they put it—that for the production of its effects so little of a given quality went so far: that so few miles made a distance, and so short a distance a difference.

"It's that," Ned had once enthusiastically explained, "that gives such depth to their effects, such relief to their least contrasts. They've been able to lay the butter so thick on every exquisite mouthful."

The butter had certainly been laid on thick at Lyng: the old gray house, hidden under a shoulder of the downs, had almost all the finer marks of commerce with a protracted past. The mere fact that it was neither large nor exceptional made it, to the Boynes, abound the more richly in its special sense—the sense of having been for centuries a deep, dim reservoir of life. The life had probably not been of the most vivid order: for long periods, no doubt, it had fallen as noiselessly into the past as the quiet drizzle of autumn fell, hour after hour, into the green fish-pond between the yews; but these back-waters of existence sometimes breed, in their sluggish depths, strange acuities of emotion, and Mary Boyne had felt from the first the occasional brush of an intenser memory.

The feeling had never been stronger than on the December afternoon when, waiting in the library for the belated lamps, she rose from her seat and stood among the shadows of the hearth. Her husband had gone off, after luncheon, for one of his long tramps on the downs. She had noticed of late that he preferred to be unaccompanied on these occasions; and, in the tried security of their personal relations, had been driven to conclude that his book was bothering him, and that he needed the afternoons to turn over in solitude the problems left from the morning's work. Certainly the book was not going as smoothly as she had imagined it would, and the lines of perplexity between his eyes had never been there in his engineering days. Then he had often looked fagged to the verge of illness, but the native demon of "worry" had never branded his brow. Yet the few pages he had so far read to her—the introduction, and a synopsis of the opening chapter—gave evidences of a firm possession of his subject, and a deepening confidence in his powers.

The fact threw her into deeper perplexity, since, now that he had done with "business" and its disturbing contingencies, the one other possible element of anxiety was eliminated. Unless it were his health, then? But physically he had gained since they had come to Dorsetshire, grown robuster, ruddier, and fresher-eyed. It was only within a week that she had felt in him the undefinable change that made her restless in his absence, and as tongue-tied in his presence as though it were *she* who had a secret to keep from him!

The thought that there *was* a secret somewhere between them struck her with a sudden smart rap of wonder, and she looked about her down the dim, long room.

"Can it be the house?" she mused.

The room itself might have been full of secrets. They seemed to be piling themselves up, as evening fell, like the layers and layers of velvet shadow dropping from the low ceiling, the dusky walls of books, the smoke-blurred sculpture of the hooded hearth.

"Why, of course—the house is haunted!" she reflected.

The ghost—Alida's imperceptible ghost—after figuring largely in the banter of their first month or two at Lyng, had been gradually discarded as too ineffectual for imaginative use. Mary had, indeed, as became the tenant of a haunted house, made the customary inquiries among her few rural neighbors, but, beyond a vague, "They dü say so, Ma'am," the villagers had nothing to impart. The elusive specter had apparently never had sufficient identity for a legend to crystallize about it, and after a time the Boynes had laughingly set the matter down to their profit-and-loss account, agreeing that Lyng was one of the few houses good enough in itself to dispense with supernatural enhancements.

"And I suppose, poor, ineffectual demon, that's why it beats its beautiful wings in vain in the void," Mary had laughingly concluded.

"Or, rather," Ned answered, in the same strain, "why, amid so much that's ghostly, it can never affirm its separate existence as *the* ghost." And thereupon their invisible housemate had finally dropped out of their references, which were numerous enough to make them promptly unaware of the loss.

Now, as she stood on the hearth, the subject of their earlier curiosity revived in her with a new sense of its meaning—a sense gradually acquired through close daily contact with the scene of the lurking mystery. It was the house itself, of course, that possessed the ghost-seeing faculty, that communed visually but secretly with its own past; and if one could only get into close enough communion with the house, one might surprise its secret, and acquire the ghost-sight on one's own account. Perhaps, in his long solitary hours in this very room, where she never

trespassed till the afternoon, her husband *had* acquired it already, and was silently carrying the dread
weight of whatever it had revealed to him. Mary was
too well-versed in the code of the spectral world not
to know that one could not talk about the ghosts
one saw: to do so was almost as great a breach of
good-breeding as to name a lady in a club. But this
explanation did not really satisfy her. "What, after
all, except for the fun of the *frisson*," she reflected,
"would he really care for any of their old ghosts?"
And thence she was thrown back once more on the
fundamental dilemma: the fact that one's greater or
less susceptibility to spectral influences had no particular bearing on the case, since, when one *did* see
a ghost at Lyng, one did not know it.

"Not till long afterward," Alida Stair had said.
Well, supposing Ned *had* seen one when they first
came, and had known only within the last week
what had happened to him? More and more under
the spell of the hour, she threw back her searching
thoughts to the early days of their tenancy, but at
first only to recall a gay confusion of unpacking, settling, arranging of books, and calling to each other
from remote corners of the house as treasure after
treasure of their habitation revealed itself to them.
It was in this particular connection that she presently recalled a certain soft afternoon of the previous October, when, passing from the first rapturous
flurry of exploration to a detailed inspection of the

old house, she had pressed (like a novel heroine) a
panel that opened at her touch, on a narrow flight
of stairs leading to an unsuspected flat ledge of the
roof—the roof which, from below, seemed to slope
away on all sides too abruptly for any but practised
feet to scale.

The view from this hidden coign was enchanting,
and she had flown down to snatch Ned from his papers and give him the freedom of her discovery. She
remembered still how, standing on the narrow ledge,
he had passed his arm about her while their gaze
flew to the long, tossed horizon-line of the downs,
and then dropped contentedly back to trace the
arabesque of yew hedges about the fish-pond, and
the shadow of the cedar on the lawn.

"And now the other way," he had said, gently turning her about within his arm; and closely pressed to
him, she had absorbed, like some long, satisfying
draft, the picture of the gray-walled court, the squat
lions on the gates, and the lime-avenue reaching up
to the highroad under the downs.

It was just then, while they gazed and held each
other, that she had felt his arm relax, and heard a
sharp "Hullo!" that made her turn to glance at him.

Distinctly, yes, she now recalled she had seen,
as she glanced, a shadow of anxiety, of perplexity, rather, fall across his face; and, following his
eyes, had beheld the figure of a man—a man in
loose, grayish clothes, as it appeared to her—who

was sauntering down the lime-avenue to the court with the tentative gait of a stranger seeking his way. Her short-sighted eyes had given her but a blurred impression of slightness and grayness, with something foreign, or at least unlocal, in the cut of the figure or its garb; but her husband had apparently seen more—seen enough to make him push past her with a sharp "Wait!" and dash down the twisting stairs without pausing to give her a hand for the descent.

A slight tendency to dizziness obliged her, after a provisional clutch at the chimney against which they had been leaning, to follow him down more cautiously; and when she had reached the attic landing she paused again for a less definite reason, leaning over the oak banister to strain her eyes through the silence of the brown, sun-flecked depths below. She lingered there till, somewhere in those depths, she heard the closing of a door; then, mechanically impelled, she went down the shallow flights of steps till she reached the lower hall.

The front door stood open on the mild sunlight of the court, and hall and court were empty. The library door was open, too, and after listening in vain for any sound of voices within, she quickly crossed the threshold, and found her husband alone, vaguely fingering the papers on his desk.

He looked up, as if surprised at her precipitate entrance, but the shadow of anxiety had passed from his face, leaving it even, as she fancied, a little brighter and clearer than usual.

"What was it? Who was it?" she asked.

"Who?" he repeated, with the surprise still all on his side.

"The man we saw coming toward the house."

He seemed honestly to reflect. "The man? Why, I thought I saw Peters; I dashed after him to say a word about the stable-drains, but he had disappeared before I could get down."

"Disappeared? Why, he seemed to be walking so slowly when we saw him."

Boyne shrugged his shoulders. "So I thought; but he must have got up steam in the interval. What do you say to our trying a scramble up Meldon Steep before sunset?"

That was all. At the time the occurrence had been less than nothing, had, indeed, been immediately obliterated by the magic of their first vision from Meldon Steep, a height which they had dreamed of climbing ever since they had first seen its bare spine heaving itself above the low roof of Lyng. Doubtless it was the mere fact of the other incident's having occurred on the very day of their ascent to Meldon that had kept it stored away in the unconscious fold of association from which it now emerged; for in itself it had no mark of the portentous. At the moment there could have been nothing more natural than that Ned should dash himself from the roof in

the pursuit of dilatory tradesmen. It was the period
when they were always on the watch for one or the
other of the specialists employed about the place;
always lying in wait for them, and dashing out at
them with questions, reproaches, or reminders. And
certainly in the distance the gray figure had looked
like Peters.

Yet now, as she reviewed the rapid scene, she felt
her husband's explanation of it to have been inval-
idated by the look of anxiety on his face. Why had
the familiar appearance of Peters made him anxious?
Why, above all, if it was of such prime necessity
to confer with that authority on the subject of the
stable-drains, had the failure to find him produced
such a look of relief? Mary could not say that any
one of these considerations had occurred to her at
the time, yet, from the promptness with which they
now marshaled themselves at her summons, she had
a sudden sense that they must all along have been
there, waiting their hour.

II

Weary with her thoughts, she moved toward the
window. The library was now completely dark, and
she was surprised to see how much faint light the
outer world still held.

As she peered out into it across the court, a figure shaped itself in the tapering perspective of bare
lines: it looked a mere blot of deeper gray in the

grayness, and for an instant, as it moved toward her, her heart thumped to the thought, "It's the ghost!"

She had time, in that long instant, to feel suddenly that the man of whom, two months earlier, she had a brief distant vision from the roof was now, at his predestined hour, about to reveal himself as *not* having been Peters; and her spirit sank under the impending fear of the disclosure. But almost with the next tick of the clock the ambiguous figure, gaining substance and character, showed itself even to her weak sight as her husband's; and she turned away to meet him, as he entered, with the confession of her folly.

"It's really too absurd," she laughed out from the threshold, "but I never *can* remember!"

"Remember what?" Boyne questioned as they drew together.

"That when one sees the Lyng ghost one never knows it."

Her hand was on his sleeve, and he kept it there, but with no response in his gesture or in the lines of his fagged, preoccupied face.

"Did you think you'd seen it?" he asked, after an appreciable interval.

"Why, I actually took *you* for it, my dear, in my mad determination to spot it!"

"Me—just now?" His arm dropped away, and he turned from her with a faint echo of her laugh.

"Really, dearest, you'd better give it up, if that's the best you can do."

"Yes, I give it up—I give it up. Have *you?*" she asked, turning round on him abruptly.

The parlor-maid had entered with letters and a lamp, and the light struck up into Boyne's face as he bent above the tray she presented.

"Have *you?*" Mary perversely insisted, when the servant had disappeared on her errand of illumination.

"Have I what?" he rejoined absently, the light bringing out the sharp stamp of worry between his brows as he turned over the letters.

"Given up trying to see the ghost." Her heart beat a little at the experiment she was making.

Her husband, laying his letters aside, moved away into the shadow of the hearth.

"I never tried," he said, tearing open the wrapper of a newspaper.

"Well, of course," Mary persisted, "the exasperating thing is that there's no use trying, since one can't be sure till so long afterward."

He was unfolding the paper as if he had hardly heard her; but after a pause, during which the sheets rustled spasmodically between his hands, he lifted his head to say abruptly, "Have you any idea *how long?*"

Mary had sunk into a low chair beside the fireplace. From her seat she looked up, startled, at her husband's profile, which was darkly projected against the circle of lamplight.

"No; none. Have *you?*" she retorted, repeating her former phrase with an added keenness of intention.

Boyne crumpled the paper into a bunch, and then inconsequently turned back with it toward the lamp.

"Lord, no! I only meant," he explained, with a faint tinge of impatience, "is there any legend, any tradition, as to that?"

"Not that I know of," she answered; but the impulse to add, "What makes you ask?" was checked by the reappearance of the parlor-maid with tea and a second lamp.

With the dispersal of shadows, and the repetition of the daily domestic office, Mary Boyne felt herself less oppressed by that sense of something mutely imminent which had darkened her solitary afternoon. For a few moments she gave herself silently to the details of her task, and when she looked up from it she was struck to the point of bewilderment by the change in her husband's face. He had seated himself near the farther lamp, and was absorbed in the perusal of his letters; but was it something he had found in them, or merely the shifting of her own point of view, that had restored his features to their normal aspect? The longer she looked, the more definitely the change affirmed itself. The lines of painful tension had vanished, and such traces of fatigue as lingered were of the kind easily attributable to steady mental effort. He glanced up, as if drawn by her gaze, and met her eyes with a smile.

"I'm dying for my tea, you know; and here's a letter for you," he said.

She took the letter he held out in exchange for the cup she proffered him, and, returning to her seat, broke the seal with the languid gesture of the reader whose interests are all inclosed in the circle of one cherished presence.

Her next conscious motion was that of starting to her feet, the letter falling to them as she rose, while she held out to her husband a long newspaper clipping.

"Ned! What's this? What does it mean?"

He had risen at the same instant, almost as if hearing her cry before she uttered it; and for a perceptible space of time he and she studied each other, like adversaries watching for an advantage, across the space between her chair and his desk.

"What's what? You fairly made me jump!" Boyne said at length, moving toward her with a sudden, half-exasperated laugh. The shadow of apprehension was on his face again, not now a look of fixed foreboding, but a shifting vigilance of lips and eyes that gave her the sense of his feeling himself invisibly surrounded.

Her hand shook so that she could hardly give him the clipping.

"This article—from the 'Waukesha Sentinel'—
that a man named Elwell has brought suit against
you—that there was something wrong about the
Blue Star Mine. I can't understand more than half."

They continued to face each other as she spoke,
and to her astonishment, she saw that her words
had the almost immediate effect of dissipating the
strained watchfulness of his look.

"Oh, *that!*" He glanced down the printed slip,
and then folded it with the gesture of one who han-
dles something harmless and familiar. "What's the
matter with you this afternoon, Mary? I thought
you'd got bad news."

She stood before him with her undefinable terror
subsiding slowly under the reassuring touch of his
composure.

"You knew about this, then—it's all right?"

"Certainly I knew about it; and it's all right."

"But what *is* it? I don't understand. What does
this man accuse you of?"

"Oh, pretty nearly every crime in the calendar."
Boyne had tossed the clipping down, and thrown
himself comfortably into an arm-chair near the fire.
"Do you want to hear the story? It's not particularly
interesting—just a squabble over interests in the
Blue Star."

"But who is this Elwell? I don't know the name."

"Oh, he's a fellow I put into it—gave him a hand
up. I told you all about him at the time."

"I daresay. I must have forgotten." Vainly she strained back among her memories. "But if you helped him, why does he make this return?"

"Oh, probably some shyster lawyer got hold of him and talked him over. It's all rather technical and complicated. I thought that kind of thing bored you."

His wife felt a sting of compunction. Theoretically, she deprecated the American wife's detachment from her husband's professional interests, but in practice she had always found it difficult to fix her attention on Boyne's report of the transactions in which his varied interests involved him. Besides, she had felt from the first that, in a community where the amenities of living could be obtained only at the cost of efforts as arduous as her husband's professional labors, such brief leisure as they could command should be used as an escape from immediate preoccupations, a flight to the life they always dreamed of living. Once or twice, now that this new life had actually drawn its magic circle about them, she had asked herself if she had done right; but hitherto such conjectures had been no more than the retrospective excursions of an active fancy. Now, for the first time, it startled her a little to find how little she knew of the material foundation on which her happiness was built.

She glanced again at her husband, and was reassured by the composure of his face; yet she felt the need of more definite grounds for her reassurance.

"But doesn't this suit worry you? Why have you never spoken to me about it?"

He answered both questions at once: "I didn't speak of it at first because it *did* worry me—annoyed me, rather. But it's all ancient history now. Your correspondent must have got hold of a back number of the 'Sentinel.'"

She felt a quick thrill of relief. "You mean it's over? He's lost his case?"

There was a just perceptible delay in Boyne's reply. "The suit's been withdrawn—that's all."

But she persisted, as if to exonerate herself from the inward charge of being too easily put off. "Withdrawn because he saw he had no chance?"

"Oh, he had no chance," Boyne answered.

She was still struggling with a dimly felt perplexity at the back of her thoughts.

"How long ago was it withdrawn?"

He paused, as if with a slight return of his former uncertainty. "I've just had the news now; but I've been expecting it."

"Just now—in one of your letters?"

"Yes; in one of my letters."

She made no answer, and was aware only, after a short interval of waiting, that he had risen, and strolling across the room, had placed himself on the sofa at her side. She felt him, as he did so, pass an arm about her, she felt his hand seek hers and clasp it, and turning slowly, drawn by the warmth of his cheek, she met the smiling clearness of his eyes.

"It's all right—it's all right?" she questioned, through the flood of her dissolving doubts; and "I give you my word it never was righter!" he laughed back at her, holding her close.

III

One of the strangest things she was afterward to recall out of all the next day's incredible strangeness was the sudden and complete recovery of her sense of security.

It was in the air when she woke in her low-ceilinged, dusky room; it accompanied her down-stairs to the breakfast-table, flashed out at her from the fire, and re-duplicated itself brightly from the flanks of the urn and the sturdy flutings of the Georgian teapot. It was as if, in some roundabout way, all her diffused apprehensions of the previous day, with their moment of sharp concentration about the newspaper article,—as if this dim questioning of the future, and startled return upon the past,—had between them liquidated the arrears of some haunting moral obligation. If she had indeed been careless of her husband's affairs, it was, her new state seemed to prove, because her faith in him instinctively justified such carelessness; and his right to her faith had overwhelmingly affirmed itself in the very face

of menace and suspicion. She had never seen him
more untroubled, more naturally and unconsciously in possession of himself, than after the cross-
examination to which she had subjected him: it
was almost as if he had been aware of her lurking
doubts, and had wanted the air cleared as much as
she did.

It was as clear, thank Heaven! as the bright outer
light that surprised her almost with a touch of summer when she issued from the house for her daily
round of the gardens. She had left Boyne at his desk,
indulging herself, as she passed the library door, by
a last peep at his quiet face, where he bent, pipe
in his mouth, above his papers, and now she had
her own morning's task to perform. The task involved on such charmed winter days almost as much
delighted loitering about the different quarters of
her demesne as if spring were already at work on
shrubs and borders. There were such inexhaustible
possibilities still before her, such opportunities to
bring out the latent graces of the old place, without
a single irreverent touch of alteration, that the winter months were all too short to plan what spring
and autumn executed. And her recovered sense of
safety gave, on this particular morning, a peculiar
zest to her progress through the sweet, still place.
She went first to the kitchen-garden, where the
espaliered pear-trees drew complicated patterns on
the walls, and pigeons were fluttering and preening

about the silvery-slated roof of their cot. There was
something wrong about the piping of the hothouse,
and she was expecting an authority from Dorchester, who was to drive out between trains and make
a diagnosis of the boiler. But when she dipped into
the damp heat of the greenhouses, among the spiced
scents and waxy pinks and reds of old-fashioned
exotics,—even the flora of Lyng was in the note!—
she learned that the great man had not arrived, and
the day being too rare to waste in an artificial atmosphere, she came out again and paced slowly along
the springy turf of the bowling-green to the gardens
behind the house. At their farther end rose a grass
terrace, commanding, over the fish-pond and the
yew hedges, a view of the long house-front, with its
twisted chimney-stacks and the blue shadows of its
roof angles, all drenched in the pale gold moisture
of the air.

Seen thus, across the level tracery of the yews,
under the suffused, mild light, it sent her, from its
open windows and hospitably smoking chimneys,
the look of some warm human presence, of a mind
slowly ripened on a sunny wall of experience. She
had never before had so deep a sense of her intimacy
with it, such a conviction that its secrets were all
beneficent, kept, as they said to children, "for one's
good," so complete a trust in its power to gather up
her life and Ned's into the harmonious pattern of
the long, long story it sat there weaving in the sun.

She heard steps behind her, and turned, expecting to see the gardener, accompanied by the engineer from Dorchester. But only one figure was in sight, that of a youngish, slightly built man, who, for reasons she could not on the spot have specified, did not remotely resemble her preconceived notion of an authority on hot-house boilers. The new-comer, on seeing her, lifted his hat, and paused with the air of a gentleman—perhaps a traveler—desirous of having it immediately known that his intrusion is involuntary. The local fame of Lyng occasionally attracted the more intelligent sight-seer, and Mary half-expected to see the stranger dissemble a camera, or justify his presence by producing it. But he made no gesture of any sort, and after a moment she asked, in a tone responding to the courteous deprecation of his attitude: "Is there any one you wish to see?"

"I came to see Mr. Boyne," he replied. His intonation, rather than his accent, was faintly American, and Mary, at the familiar note, looked at him more closely. The brim of his soft felt hat cast a shade on his face, which, thus obscured, wore to her short-sighted gaze a look of seriousness, as of a person arriving "on business," and civilly but firmly aware of his rights.

Past experience had made Mary equally sensible to such claims; but she was jealous of her husband's morning hours, and doubtful of his having given any one the right to intrude on them.

"Have you an appointment with Mr. Boyne?" she asked.

He hesitated, as if unprepared for the question.

"Not exactly an appointment," he replied.

"Then I'm afraid, this being his working-time, that he can't receive you now. Will you give me a message, or come back later?"

The visitor, again lifting his hat, briefly replied that he would come back later, and walked away, as if to regain the front of the house. As his figure receded down the walk between the yew hedges, Mary saw him pause and look up an instant at the peaceful house-front bathed in faint winter sunshine; and it struck her, with a tardy touch of compunction, that it would have been more humane to ask if he had come from a distance, and to offer, in that case, to inquire if her husband could receive him. But as the thought occurred to her he passed out of sight behind a pyramidal yew, and at the same moment her attention was distracted by the approach of the gardener, attended by the bearded pepper-and-salt figure of the boiler-maker from Dorchester.

The encounter with this authority led to such far-reaching issues that they resulted in his finding it expedient to ignore his train, and beguiled Mary into spending the remainder of the morning in absorbed confabulation among the greenhouses. She was startled to find, when the colloquy ended, that it was nearly luncheon-time, and she half expected, as she hurried back to the house, to see her husband coming out to meet her. But she found no one in the court but an under-gardener raking the gravel, and the hall, when she entered it, was so silent that she guessed Boyne to be still at work behind the closed door of the library.

Not wishing to disturb him, she turned into the drawing-room, and there, at her writing-table, lost herself in renewed calculations of the outlay to which the morning's conference had committed her. The knowledge that she could permit herself such follies had not yet lost its novelty; and somehow, in contrast to the vague apprehensions of the previous days, it now seemed an element of her recovered security, of the sense that, as Ned had said, things in general had never been "righter."

She was still luxuriating in a lavish play of figures when the parlor-maid, from the threshold, roused her with a dubiously worded inquiry as to the expediency of serving luncheon. It was one of their jokes that Trimmle announced luncheon as if she were divulging a state secret, and Mary, intent upon her papers, merely murmured an absent-minded assent.

She felt Trimmle wavering expressively on the threshold as if in rebuke of such offhand acquiescence; then her retreating steps sounded down the passage, and Mary, pushing away her papers, crossed the hall, and went to the library door. It was still closed, and she wavered in her turn, disliking to disturb her husband, yet anxious that he should not exceed his normal measure of work. As she stood there, balancing her impulses, the esoteric Trimmle returned with the announcement of luncheon, and Mary, thus impelled, opened the door and went into the library.

Boyne was not at his desk, and she peered about her, expecting to discover him at the book-shelves, somewhere down the length of the room; but her call brought no response, and gradually it became clear to her that he was not in the library.

She turned back to the parlor-maid.

"Mr. Boyne must be up-stairs. Please tell him that luncheon is ready."

The parlor-maid appeared to hesitate between the obvious duty of obeying orders and an equally obvious conviction of the foolishness of the injunction laid upon her. The struggle resulted in her saying doubtfully, "If you please, Madam, Mr. Boyne's not up-stairs."

"Not in his room? Are you sure?"

"I'm sure, Madam."

Mary consulted the clock. "Where is he, then?"

"He's gone out," Trimmle announced, with the superior air of one who has respectfully waited for the question that a well-ordered mind would have first propounded.

Mary's previous conjecture had been right, then. Boyne must have gone to the gardens to meet her, and since she had missed him, it was clear that he had taken the shorter way by the south door, instead of going round to the court. She crossed the hall to the glass portal opening directly on the yew garden, but the parlor-maid, after another moment of inner conflict, decided to bring out recklessly, "Please, Madam, Mr. Boyne didn't go that way."

Mary turned back. "Where *did* he go? And when?"

"He went out of the front door, up the drive, Madam." It was a matter of principle with Trimmle never to answer more than one question at a time.

"Up the drive? At this hour?" Mary went to the door herself, and glanced across the court through the long tunnel of bare limes. But its perspective was as empty as when she had scanned it on entering the house.

"Did Mr. Boyne leave no message?" she asked.

Trimmle seemed to surrender herself to a last struggle with the forces of chaos.

"No, Madam. He just went out with the gentleman."

"The gentleman? What gentleman?" Mary wheeled about, as if to front this new factor.

"The gentleman who called, Madam," said Trimmle, resignedly.

"When did a gentleman call? Do explain yourself, Trimmle!"

Only the fact that Mary was very hungry, and that she wanted to consult her husband about the greenhouses, would have caused her to lay so unusual an injunction on her attendant; and even now she was detached enough to note in Trimmle's eye the dawning defiance of the respectful subordinate who has been pressed too hard.

"I couldn't exactly say the hour, Madam, because I didn't let the gentleman in," she replied, with the air of magnanimously ignoring the irregularity of her mistress's course.

"You didn't let him in?"

"No, Madam. When the bell rang I was dressing, and Agnes—"

"Go and ask Agnes, then," Mary interjected. Trimmle still wore her look of patient magnanimity. "Agnes would not know, Madam, for she had unfortunately burnt her hand in trying the wick of the new lamp from town—" Trimmle, as Mary was aware, had always been opposed to the new lamp—"and so Mrs. Dockett sent the kitchen-maid instead."

Mary looked again at the clock. "It's after two! Go and ask the kitchen-maid if Mr. Boyne left any word."

She went into luncheon without waiting, and Trimmle presently brought her there the kitchen-maid's statement that the gentleman had called about one o'clock, that Mr. Boyne had gone out with him without leaving any message. The kitchen-maid did not even know the caller's name, for he had written it on a slip of paper, which he had folded and handed to her, with the injunction to deliver it at once to Mr. Boyne.

Mary finished her luncheon, still wondering, and when it was over, and Trimmle had brought the coffee to the drawing-room, her wonder had deepened to a first faint tinge of disquietude. It was unlike Boyne to absent himself without explanation at so unwonted an hour, and the difficulty of identifying the visitor whose summons he had apparently obeyed made his disappearance the more unaccountable. Mary Boyne's experience as the wife of a busy engineer, subject to sudden calls and compelled to keep irregular hours, had trained her to the philosophic acceptance of surprises; but since Boyne's withdrawal from business he had adopted a Benedictine regularity of life. As if to make up for the dispersed and agitated years, with their "stand-up" lunches and dinners rattled down to the joltings of the dining-car, he cultivated the last refinements of punctuality and monotony, discouraging his wife's fancy for the unexpected; and declaring that to a delicate taste there were infinite gradations of pleasure in the fixed recurrences of habit.

Still, since no life can completely defend itself from the unforeseen, it was evident that all Boyne's precautions would sooner or later prove unavailable, and Mary concluded that he had cut short a tiresome visit by walking with his caller to the station, or at least accompanying him for part of the way.

This conclusion relieved her from farther preoccupation, and she went out herself to take up her conference with the gardener. Thence she walked to the village post-office, a mile or so away; and when she turned toward home, the early twilight was setting in.

She had taken a foot-path across the downs, and as Boyne, meanwhile, had probably returned from the station by the highroad, there was little likelihood of their meeting on the way. She felt sure, however, of his having reached the house before her; so sure that, when she entered it herself, without even pausing to inquire of Trimmle, she made directly for the library. But the library was still empty, and with an unwonted precision of visual memory she immediately observed that the papers on her husband's desk lay precisely as they had lain when she had gone in to call him to luncheon.

Then of a sudden she was seized by a vague dread of the unknown. She had closed the door behind her on entering, and as she stood alone in the long, silent, shadowy room, her dread seemed to take shape and sound, to be there audibly breathing and lurking among the shadows. Her short-sighted eyes strained through them, half-discerning an actual presence, something aloof, that watched and knew; and in the recoil from that intangible propinquity she threw herself suddenly on the bell-rope and gave it a desperate pull.

The long, quavering summons brought Trimmle in precipitately with a lamp, and Mary breathed again at this sobering reappearance of the usual.

"You may bring tea if Mr. Boyne is in," she said, to justify her ring.

"Very well, Madam. But Mr. Boyne is not in," said Trimmle, putting down the lamp.

"Not in? You mean he's come back and gone out again?"

"No, Madam. He's never been back."

The dread stirred again, and Mary knew that now it had her fast.

"Not since he went out with—the gentleman?"

"Not since he went out with the gentleman."

"But who *was* the gentleman?" Mary gasped out, with the sharp note of some one trying to be heard through a confusion of meaningless noises.

"That I couldn't say, Madam." Trimmle, standing there by the lamp, seemed suddenly to grow less round and rosy, as though eclipsed by the same creeping shade of apprehension.

"But the kitchen-maid knows—wasn't it the kitchen-maid who let him in?"

"She doesn't know either, Madam, for he wrote his name on a folded paper."

Mary, through her agitation, was aware that they were both designating the unknown visitor by a vague pronoun, instead of the conventional formula which, till then, had kept their allusions within the bounds of custom. And at the same moment her mind caught at the suggestion of the folded paper.

"But he must have a name! Where is the paper?"

She moved to the desk, and began to turn over the scattered documents that littered it. The first that caught her eye was an unfinished letter in her husband's hand, with his pen lying across it, as though dropped there at a sudden summons.

"My dear Parvis,"—who was Parvis?—"I have just received your letter announcing Elwell's death, and while I suppose there is now no farther risk of trouble, it might be safer—"

She tossed the sheet aside, and continued her search; but no folded paper was discoverable among the letters and pages of manuscript which had been swept together in a promiscuous heap, as if by a hurried or a startled gesture.

"But the kitchen-maid *saw* him. Send her here," she commanded, wondering at her dullness in not thinking sooner of so simple a solution.

Trimmle, at the behest, vanished in a flash, as if thankful to be out of the room, and when she reappeared, conducting the agitated underling, Mary had regained her self-possession, and had her questions pat.

The gentleman was a stranger, yes—that she understood. But what had he said? And, above all, what had he looked like? The first question was easily enough answered, for the disconcerting reason that he had said so little—had merely asked for Mr. Boyne, and, scribbling something on a bit of paper, had requested that it should at once be carried in to him.

"Then you don't know what he wrote? You're not sure it *was* his name?"

The kitchen-maid was not sure, but supposed it was, since he had written it in answer to her inquiry as to whom she should announce.

"And when you carried the paper in to Mr. Boyne, what did he say?"

The kitchen-maid did not think that Mr. Boyne had said anything, but she could not be sure, for just as she had handed him the paper and he was opening it, she had become aware that the visitor had followed her into the library, and she had slipped out, leaving the two gentlemen together.

"But then, if you left them in the library, how do you know that they went out of the house?"

This question plunged the witness into momentary inarticulateness, from which she was rescued by Trimmle, who, by means of ingenious circumlocutions, elicited the statement that before she could cross the hall to the back passage she had heard the gentlemen behind her, and had seen them go out of the front door together.

"Then, if you saw the gentleman twice, you must be able to tell me what he looked like."

But with this final challenge to her powers of expression it became clear that the limit of the kitchen-maid's endurance had been reached. The obligation of going to the front door to "show in" a visitor was in itself so subversive of the fundamental order of things that it had thrown her faculties into hopeless disarray, and she could only stammer out, after various panting efforts at evocation, "His hat, mum, was different-like, as you might say—"

"Different? How different?" Mary flashed out at her, her own mind, in the same instant, leaping back to an image left on it that morning, but temporarily lost under layers of subsequent impressions.

"His hat had a wide brim, you mean? and his face was pale—a youngish face?" Mary pressed her, with a white-lipped intensity of interrogation. But if the kitchen-maid found any adequate answer to this challenge, it was swept away for her listener down the rushing current of her own convictions. The stranger—the stranger in the garden! Why had Mary not thought of him before? She needed no one now to tell her that it was he who had called for her husband and gone away with him. But who was he, and why had Boyne obeyed his call?

IV

It leaped out at her suddenly, like a grin out of the dark, that they had often called England so little—"such a confoundedly hard place to get lost in."

A confoundedly hard place to get lost in! That had been her husband's phrase. And now, with the whole machinery of official investigation sweeping its flash-lights from shore to shore, and across the dividing straits; now, with Boyne's name blazing from the walls of every town and village, his portrait (how that wrung her!) hawked up and down the country like the image of a hunted criminal; now the little compact, populous island, so policed, surveyed, and administered, revealed itself as a Sphinx-like guardian of abysmal mysteries, staring back into his wife's anguished eyes as if with the malicious joy of knowing something they would never know!

In the fortnight since Boyne's disappearance there had been no word of him, no trace of his movements. Even the usual misleading reports that raise expectancy in tortured bosoms had been few and fleeting. No one but the bewildered kitchen-maid had seen him leave the house, and no one else had seen "the gentleman" who accompanied him. All inquiries in the neighborhood failed to elicit the memory of a stranger's presence that day in the neighborhood of Lyng. And no one had met Edward Boyne, either alone or in company, in any of the neighboring villages, or on the road across the downs, or at either of the local railway-stations. The sunny English noon had swallowed him as completely as if he had gone out into Cimmerian night.

Mary, while every external means of investigation was working at its highest pressure, had ransacked her husband's papers for any trace of antecedent complications, of entanglements or obligations unknown to her, that might throw a faint ray into the darkness. But if any such had existed in the background of Boyne's life, they had disappeared as completely as the slip of paper on which the visitor had written his name. There remained no possible thread of guidance except—if it were indeed an exception—the letter which Boyne had apparently been in the act of writing when he received his mysterious summons. That letter, read and reread by his wife, and submitted by her to the police, yielded little enough for conjecture to feed on.

"I have just heard of Elwell's death, and while I suppose there is now no farther risk of trouble, it might be safer—" That was all. The "risk of trouble" was easily explained by the newspaper clipping which had apprised Mary of the suit brought against her husband by one of his associates in the Blue Star enterprise. The only new information conveyed in the letter was the fact of its showing Boyne, when he wrote it, to be still apprehensive of the results of the suit, though he had assured his wife that it had been withdrawn, and though the letter itself

declared that the plaintiff was dead. It took several
weeks of exhaustive cabling to fix the identity of
the "Parvis" to whom the fragmentary communication was addressed, but even after these inquiries
had shown him to be a Waukesha lawyer, no new
facts concerning the Elwell suit were elicited. He
appeared to have had no direct concern in it, but
to have been conversant with the facts merely as
an acquaintance, and possible intermediary; and he
declared himself unable to divine with what object
Boyne intended to seek his assistance.

This negative information, sole fruit of the first
fortnight's feverish search, was not increased by a
jot during the slow weeks that followed. Mary knew
that the investigations were still being carried on,
but she had a vague sense of their gradually slack-
ening, as the actual march of time seemed to slack-
en. It was as though the days, flying horror-struck
from the shrouded image of the one inscrutable day,
gained assurance as the distance lengthened, till at
last they fell back into their normal gait. And so
with the human imaginations at work on the dark
event. No doubt it occupied them still, but week by
week and hour by hour it grew less absorbing, took
up less space, was slowly but inevitably crowded
out of the foreground of consciousness by the new
problems perpetually bubbling up from the vapor-
ous caldron of human experience.

Even Mary Boyne's consciousness gradually felt the same lowering of velocity. It still swayed with the incessant oscillations of conjecture; but they were slower, more rhythmical in their beat. There were moments of overwhelming lassitude when, like the victim of some poison which leaves the brain clear, but holds the body motionless, she saw herself domesticated with the Horror, accepting its perpetual presence as one of the fixed conditions of life.

These moments lengthened into hours and days, till she passed into a phase of stolid acquiescence. She watched the familiar routine of life with the incurious eye of a savage on whom the meaningless processes of civilization make but the faintest impression. She had come to regard herself as part of the routine, a spoke of the wheel, revolving with its motion; she felt almost like the furniture of the room in which she sat, an insensate object to be dusted and pushed about with the chairs and tables. And this deepening apathy held her fast at Lyng, in spite of the urgent entreaties of friends and the usual medical recommendation of "change." Her friends supposed that her refusal to move was inspired by the belief that her husband would one day return to the spot from which he had vanished, and a beautiful legend grew up about this imaginary state of waiting. But in reality she had no such belief: the depths of anguish inclosing her were no longer lighted by flashes of hope. She was sure that Boyne would never come back, that he had gone out of her sight as completely as if Death itself had waited that day on the threshold. She had even renounced, one by one, the various theories as to his disappearance which had been advanced by the press, the police, and her own agonized imagination. In sheer lassitude her mind turned from these alternatives of horror, and sank back into the blank fact that he was gone.

No, she would never know what had become of him—no one would ever know. But the house *knew*; the library in which she spent her long, lonely evenings knew. For it was here that the last scene had been enacted, here that the stranger had come, and spoken the word which had caused Boyne to rise and follow him. The floor she trod had felt his tread; the books on the shelves had seen his face; and there were moments when the intense consciousness of the old, dusky walls seemed about to break out into some audible revelation of their secret. But the revelation never came, and she knew it would never come. Lyng was not one of the garrulous old houses that betray the secrets intrusted to them. Its very legend proved that it had always been the mute accomplice, the incorruptible custodian of the mysteries it had surprised. And Mary Boyne, sitting face to face with its portentous silence, felt the futility of seeking to break it by any human means.

V

"I don't say it *wasn't* straight, yet don't say it *was* straight. It was business."

Mary, at the words, lifted her head with a start, and looked intently at the speaker.

When, half an hour before, a card with "Mr. Parvis" on it had been brought up to her, she had been immediately aware that the name had been a part of her consciousness ever since she had read it at the head of Boyne's unfinished letter. In the library she had found awaiting her a small neutral-tinted man with a bald head and gold eye-glasses, and it sent a strange tremor through her to know that this was the person to whom her husband's last known thought had been directed.

Parvis, civilly, but without vain preamble,—in the manner of a man who has his watch in his hand,—had set forth the object of his visit. He had "run over" to England on business, and finding himself in the neighborhood of Dorchester, had not wished to leave it without paying his respects to Mrs. Boyne; without asking her, if the occasion offered, what she meant to do about Bob Elwell's family.

The words touched the spring of some obscure dread in Mary's bosom. Did her visitor, after all, know what Boyne had meant by his unfinished phrase? She asked for an elucidation of his question, and noticed at once that he seemed surprised at her continued ignorance of the subject. Was it possible that she really knew as little as she said?

"I know nothing—you must tell me," she faltered out; and her visitor thereupon proceeded to unfold his story. It threw, even to her confused perceptions, and imperfectly initiated vision, a lurid glare on the whole hazy episode of the Blue Star Mine. Her husband had made his money in that brilliant speculation at the cost of "getting ahead" of some one less alert to seize the chance; the victim of his ingenuity was young Robert Elwell, who had "put him on" to the Blue Star scheme.

Parvis, at Mary's first startled cry, had thrown her a sobering glance through his impartial glasses.

"Bob Elwell wasn't smart enough, that's all; if he had been, he might have turned round and served Boyne the same way. It's the kind of thing that happens every day in business. I guess it's what the scientists call the survival of the fittest," said Mr. Parvis, evidently pleased with the aptness of his analogy.

Mary felt a physical shrinking from the next question she tried to frame; it was as though the words on her lips had a taste that nauseated her.

"But then—you accuse my husband of doing something dishonorable?"

Mr. Parvis surveyed the question dispassionately. "Oh, no, I don't. I don't even say it wasn't straight." He glanced up and down the long lines of books, as if one of them might have supplied him with the definition he sought. "I don't say it *wasn't* straight, and yet I don't say it *was* straight. It was business." After all, no definition in his category could be more comprehensive than that.

Mary sat staring at him with a look of terror. He seemed to her like the indifferent, implacable emissary of some dark, formless power.

"But Mr. Elwell's lawyers apparently did not take your view, since I suppose the suit was withdrawn by their advice."

"Oh, yes, they knew he hadn't a leg to stand on, technically. It was when they advised him to withdraw the suit that he got desperate. You see, he'd borrowed most of the money he lost in the Blue Star, and he was up a tree. That's why he shot himself when they told him he had no show."

The horror was sweeping over Mary in great, deafening waves.

"He shot himself? He killed himself because of *that?*"

"Well, he didn't kill himself, exactly. He dragged on two months before he died." Parvis emitted the statement as unemotionally as a gramophone grinding out its "record."

"You mean that he tried to kill himself, and failed? And tried again?"

"Oh, he didn't have to try again," said Parvis, grimly.

They sat opposite each other in silence, he swinging his eye-glass thoughtfully about his finger, she,
motionless, her arms stretched along her knees in an
attitude of rigid tension.

"But if you knew all this," she began at length,
hardly able to force her voice above a whisper, "how
is it that when I wrote you at the time of my husband's disappearance you said you didn't understand
his letter?"

Parvis received this without perceptible discomfiture. "Why, I didn't understand it—strictly speaking. And it wasn't the time to talk about it, if I had.
The Elwell business was settled when the suit was
withdrawn. Nothing I could have told you would
have helped you to find your husband."

Mary continued to scrutinize him. "Then why
are you telling me now?"

Still Parvis did not hesitate. "Well, to begin with,
I supposed you knew more than you appear to—I
mean about the circumstances of Elwell's death. And
then people are talking of it now; the whole matter's
been raked up again. And I thought, if you didn't
know, you ought to."

She remained silent, and he continued: "You see,
it's only come out lately what a bad state Elwell's
affairs were in. His wife's a proud woman, and she
fought on as long as she could, going out to work,
and taking sewing at home, when she got too sick—
something with the heart, I believe. But she had his

bedridden mother to look after, and the children, and she broke down under it, and finally had to ask for help. That attracted attention to the case, and the papers took it up, and a subscription was started. Everybody out there liked Bob Elwell, and most of the prominent names in the place are down on the list, and people began to wonder why—"

Parvis broke off to fumble in an inner pocket. "Here," he continued, "here's an account of the whole thing from the 'Sentinel'—a little sensational, of course. But I guess you'd better look it over."

He held out a newspaper to Mary, who unfolded it slowly, remembering, as she did so, the evening when, in that same room, the perusal of a clipping from the "Sentinel" had first shaken the depths of her security.

As she opened the paper, her eyes, shrinking from the glaring head-lines, "Widow of Boyne's Victim Forced to Appeal for Aid," ran down the column of text to two portraits inserted in it. The first was her husband's, taken from a photograph made the year they had come to England. It was the picture of him that she liked best, the one that stood on the writing-table up-stairs in her bedroom. As the eyes in the photograph met hers, she felt it would be impossible to read what was said of him, and closed her lids with the sharpness of the pain.

"I thought if you felt disposed to put your name down—" she heard Parvis continue.

She opened her eyes with an effort, and they fell on the other portrait. It was that of a youngish man, slightly built, in rough clothes, with features somewhat blurred by the shadow of a projecting hatbrim. Where had she seen that outline before? She stared at it confusedly, her heart hammering in her throat and ears. Then she gave a cry.

"This is the man—the man who came for my husband!"

She heard Parvis start to his feet, and was dimly aware that she had slipped backward into the corner of the sofa, and that he was bending above her in alarm. With an intense effort she straightened herself, and reached out for the paper, which she had dropped.

"It's the man! I should know him anywhere!" she cried in a voice that sounded in her own ears like a scream.

Parvis's voice seemed to come to her from far off, down endless, fog-muffled windings.

"Mrs. Boyne, you're not very well. Shall I call somebody? Shall I get a glass of water?"

"No, no, no!" She threw herself toward him, her hand frantically clenching the newspaper. "I tell you, it's the man! I *know* him! He spoke to me in the garden!"

Parvis took the journal from her, directing his glasses to the portrait. "It can't be, Mrs. Boyne. It's Robert Elwell."

"Robert Elwell?" Her white stare seemed to travel into space. "Then it was Robert Elwell who came for him."

"Came for Boyne? The day he went away?" Parvis's voice dropped as hers rose. He bent over, laying a fraternal hand on her, as if to coax her gently back into her seat. "Why, Elwell was dead! Don't you remember?"

Mary sat with her eyes fixed on the picture, unconscious of what he was saying.

"Don't you remember Boyne's unfinished letter to me—the one you found on his desk that day? It was written just after he'd heard of Elwell's death." She noticed an odd shake in Parvis's unemotional voice. "Surely you remember that!" he urged her.

Yes, she remembered: that was the profoundest horror of it. Elwell had died the day before her husband's disappearance; and this was Elwell's portrait; and it was the portrait of the man who had spoken to her in the garden. She lifted her head and looked slowly about the library. The library could have borne witness that it was also the portrait of the man who had come in that day to call Boyne from his unfinished letter. Through the misty surgings of her brain she heard the faint boom of half-forgotten words—words spoken by Alida Stair on the lawn at Pangbourne before Boyne and his wife had ever seen the house at Lyng, or had imagined that they might one day live there.

"This was the man who spoke to me," she repeated.

She looked again at Parvis. He was trying to conceal his disturbance under what he imagined to be an expression of indulgent commiseration; but the edges of his lips were blue. "He thinks me mad; but I'm not mad," she reflected; and suddenly there flashed upon her a way of justifying her strange affirmation.

She sat quiet, controlling the quiver of her lips, and waiting till she could trust her voice to keep its habitual level; then she said, looking straight at Parvis: "Will you answer me one question, please? When was it that Robert Elwell tried to kill himself?"

"When—when?" Parvis stammered.

"Yes; the date. Please try to remember."

She saw that he was growing still more afraid of her. "I have a reason," she insisted gently.

"Yes, yes. Only I can't remember. About two months before, I should say."

"I want the date," she repeated.

Parvis picked up the newspaper. "We might see here," he said, still humoring her. He ran his eyes down the page. "Here it is. Last October—the—"

She caught the words from him. "The 20th, wasn't it?" With a sharp look at her, he verified. "Yes, the 20th. Then you *did* know?"

"I know now." Her white stare continued to travel past him. "Sunday, the 20th—that was the day he came first."

Parvis's voice was almost inaudible. "Came *here* first?"

"Yes."

"You saw him twice, then?"

"Yes, twice." She breathed it at him with dilated eyes. "He came first on the 20th of October. I remember the date because it was the day we went up Meldon Steep for the first time." She felt a faint gasp of inward laughter at the thought that but for that she might have forgotten.

Parvis continued to scrutinize her, as if trying to intercept her gaze.

"We saw him from the roof," she went on. "He came down the lime-avenue toward the house. He was dressed just as he is in that picture. My husband saw him first. He was frightened, and ran down ahead of me; but there was no one there. He had vanished."

"Elwell had vanished?" Parvis faltered.

"Yes." Their two whispers seemed to grope for each other. "I couldn't think what had happened. I see now. He *tried* to come then; but he wasn't dead enough—he couldn't reach us. He had to wait for two months; and then he came back again—and Ned went with him."

She nodded at Parvis with the look of triumph of a child who has successfully worked out a difficult puzzle. But suddenly she lifted her hands with a desperate gesture, pressing them to her bursting temples.

"Oh, my God! I sent him to Ned—I told him where to go! I sent him to this room!" she screamed out.

She felt the walls of the room rush toward her, like inward falling ruins; and she heard Parvis, a long way off, as if through the ruins, crying to her, and struggling to get at her. But she was numb to his touch, she did not know what he was saying. Through the tumult she heard but one clear note, the voice of Alida Stair, speaking on the lawn at Pangbourne.

"You won't know till afterward," it said. "You won't know till long, long afterward."

THE BECKONING FAIR ONE

OLIVER ONIONS

(1911)

I

The three or four "To Let" boards had stood within the low paling as long as the inhabitants of the little triangular "Square" could remember, and if they had ever been vertical it was a very long time ago. They now overhung the palings each at its own angle, and resembled nothing so much as a row of wooden choppers, ever in the act of falling upon some passer-by, yet never cutting off a tenant for the old house from the stream of his fellows. Not that there was ever any great "stream" through the square; the stream passed a furlong and more away, beyond the intricacy of tenements and alleys and byways that had sprung up since the old house had been built, hemming it in completely; and probably the house itself was only suffered to stand pending the falling-in of a lease or two, when doubtless a clearance would be made of the whole neighbourhood.

It was of bloomy old red brick, and built into its walls were the crowns and clasped hands and other insignia of insurance companies long since defunct. The children of the secluded square had swung upon the low gate at the end of the entrance-alley until little more than the solid top bar of it remained, and the alley itself ran past boarded basement windows on which tramps had chalked their cryptic marks. The path was washed and worn uneven by the spilling of water from the eaves of the encroaching next house, and cats and dogs had made the approach their own. The chances of a tenant did not seem such as to warrant the keeping of the "To Let" boards in a state of legibility and repair, and as a matter of fact they were not so kept.

For six months Oleron had passed the old place twice a day or oftener, on his way from his lodgings to the room, ten minutes' walk away, he had taken to work in; and for six months no hatchet-like notice-board had fallen across his path. This might have been due to the fact that he usually took the other side of the square. But he chanced one morning to take the side that ran past the broken gate and the rain-worn entrance alley, and to pause before one of the inclined boards. The board bore, besides the agent's name, the announcement, written apparently about the time of Oleron's own early youth, that the key was to be had at Number Six.

Now Oleron was already paying, for his separate bedroom and workroom, more than an author who, without private means, habitually disregards his public, can afford; and he was paying in addition a small rent for the storage of the greater part of his grandmother's furniture. Moreover, it invariably happened that the book he wished to read in bed was at his working-quarters half a mile or more away, while the note or letter he had sudden need of during the day was as likely as not to be in the pocket of another coat hanging behind his bedroom door. And there were other inconveniences in having a divided domicile. Therefore Oleron, brought suddenly up by the hatchet-like notice board, looked first down through some scanty privet-bushes at the boarded basement windows, then up at the blank and grimy windows of the first floor, and so up to the second floor and the flat stone coping of the leads. He stood for a minute thumbing his lean and shaven jaw; then, with another glance at the board, he walked slowly across the square to Number Six.

He knocked, and waited for two or three minutes, but, although the door stood open, received no answer. He was knocking again when a long-nosed man in shirt-sleeves appeared.

"I was arsking a blessing on our food," he said in severe explanation.

Oleron asked if he might have the key of the old house; and the long-nosed man withdrew again.

Oleron waited for another five minutes on the step; then the man, appearing again and masticating some of the food of which he had spoken, announced that the key was lost.

"But you won't want it," he said. "The entrance door isn't closed, and a push 'll open any of the others. I'm a agent for it, if you're thinking of taking it—"

Oleron recrossed the square, descended the two steps at the broken gate, passed along the alley, and turned in at the old wide doorway. To the right, immediately within the door, steps descended to the roomy cellars, and the staircase before him had a carved rail, and was broad and handsome and filthy. Oleron ascended it, avoiding contact with the rail and wall, and stopped at the first landing. A door facing him had been boarded up, but he pushed at that on his right hand, and an insecure bolt or staple yielded. He entered the empty first floor.

He spent a quarter of an hour in the place, and then came out again. Without mounting higher, he descended and recrossed the square to the house of the man who had lost the key.

"Can you tell me how much the rent is?" he asked.

The man mentioned a figure, the comparative lowness of which seemed accounted for by the character of the neighbourhood and the abominable state of unrepair of the place.

"Would it be possible to rent a single floor?"

The long-nosed man did not know; they might. . . .

"Who are they?"

The man gave Oleron the name of a firm of lawyers in Lincoln's Inn.

"You might mention my name—Barrett," he added.

Pressure of work prevented Oleron from going down to Lincoln's Inn that afternoon, but he went on the morrow, and was instantly offered the whole house as a purchase for fifty pounds down, the remainder of the purchase-money to remain on mortgage. It took him half an hour to disabuse the lawyer's mind of the idea that he wished anything more of the place than to rent a single floor of it. This made certain hums and haws of a difference, and the lawyer was by no means certain that it lay within his power to do as Oleron suggested; but it was finally extracted from him that, provided the notice-boards were allowed to remain up, and that, provided it was agreed that in the event of the whole house letting, the arrangement should terminate automatically without further notice, something might be done. That the old place should suddenly let over his head seemed to Oleron the slightest of risks to take, and he promised a decision within a week. On the morrow he visited the house again, went through it from top to bottom, and then went home to his lodgings to take a bath.

He was immensely taken with that portion of the house he had already determined should be his own. Scraped clean and repainted, and with that old furniture of Oleron's grandmother's, it ought

to be entirely charming. He went to the storage
warehouse to refresh his memory of his half-forgotten belongings, and to take the measurements; and
thence he went to a decorator's. He was very busy
with his regular work, and could have wished that
the notice-board had caught his attention either a
few months earlier or else later in the year; but the
quickest way would be to suspend work entirely until after his removal. . . .

A fortnight later his first floor was painted
throughout in a tender, eider-flower white, the paint
was dry, and Oleron was in the middle of his installation. He was animated, delighted; and he rubbed
his hands as he polished and made disposals of his
grandmother's effects—the tall lattice-parted china
cupboard with its Derby and Mason and Spode, the
large folding Sheraton table, the long, low book-
shelves (he had had two of them "copied"), the
chairs, the Sheffield candlesticks, the riveted rose-
bowls. These things he set against his newly painted eider-white walls—walls of wood panelled in the
happiest proportions, and moulded and coffered to
the low-seated window-recesses. in a mood of gaiety
and rest that the builders of rooms no longer know.
The ceilings were lofty, and faintly painted with an
old pattern of stars; even the tapering mouldings
of his iron fireplace were as delicately designed as
jewellery; and Oleron walked about rubbing his

hands, frequently stopping for the mere pleasure of the glimpses from white room to white room. . . .

"Charming, charming!" he said to himself. "I wonder what Elsie Bengough will think of this!"

He bought a bolt and a Yale lock for his door, and shut off his quarters from the rest of the house. If he now wanted to read in bed, his book could be had for stepping into the next room. All the time, he thought how exceedingly lucky he was to get the place. He put up a hat-rack in the little square hall, and hung up his hats and caps and coats; and pass-ers through the small triangular square late at night, looking up over the little serried row of wooden "To Let" hatchets, could see the light within Oleron's red blinds, or else the sudden darkening of one blind and the illumination of another, as Oleron, candle-stick in hand, passed from room to room, making final settings of his furniture, or preparing to re-sume the work that his removal had interrupted.

II

As far as the chief business of his life—his writ-ing—was concerned, Paul Oleron treated the world a good deal better than he was treated by it; but he seldom took the trouble to strike a balance, or to compute how far, at forty-four years of age, he was behind his points on the handicap. To have done so wouldn't have altered matters, and it might have

depressed Oleron. He had chosen his path, and was
committed to it beyond possibility of withdrawal.
Perhaps he had chosen it in the days when he had
been easily swayed by something a little disinterest-
ed, a little generous, a little noble; and had he ever
thought of questioning himself he would still have
held to it that a life without nobility and generos-
ity and disinterestedness was no life for him. Only
quite recently, and rarely, had he even vaguely suspected that there was more in it than this; but it was
no good anticipating the day when, he supposed, he
would reach that maximum point of his powers beyond which he must inevitably decline, and be left
face to face with the question whether it would not
have profited him better to have ruled his life by
less exigent ideals.

In the meantime, his removal into the old house
with the insurance marks built into its brick merely
interrupted *Romilly Bishop* at the fifteenth chapter.

As this tall man with the lean, ascetic face moved
about his new abode, arranging, changing, altering,
hardly yet into his working-stride again, he gave
the impression of almost spinster-like precision and
nicety. For twenty years past, in a score of lodgings,
garrets, fiats, and rooms furnished and unfurnished,
he had been accustomed to do many things for himself, and he had discovered that it saves time and
temper to be methodical. He had arranged with the
wife of the long-nosed Barrett, a stout Welsh woman

with a falsetto voice, the Merionethshire accent of which long residence in London had not perceptibly modified, to come across the square each morning to prepare his breakfast, and also to "turn the place out" on Saturday mornings; and for the rest, he even welcomed a little housework as a relaxation from the strain of writing.

His kitchen, together with the adjoining strip of an apartment into which a modern bath had been fitted, overlooked the alley at the side of the house; and at one end of it was a large closet with a door, and a square sliding hatch in the upper part of the door. This had been a powder-closet and through the hatch the elaborately dressed head had been thrust to receive the click and puff of the powder-pistol. Oleron puzzled a little over this closet; then, as its use occurred to him, he smiled faintly, a little moved, he knew not by what. . . . He would have to put it to a very different purpose from its original one; it would probably have to serve as his larder. . . . It was in this closet that he made a discovery. The back of it was shelved, and, rummaging on an upper shelf that ran deeply into the wall, Oleron found a couple of mushroom-shaped old wooden wig-stands. He did not know how they had come to be there. Doubtless the painters had turned them up somewhere or other, and had put them there. But his five rooms, as a whole, were short of cupboard and closet-room; and it was only by the exercise of

some ingenuity that he was able to find places for
the bestowal of his household linen, his boxes, and
his seldom-used but not-to-be-destroyed accumula-
tion of papers.

It was in early spring that Oleron entered on his
tenancy, and he was anxious to have *Romilly* ready
for publication in the coming autumn. Nevertheless,
he did not intend to force its production. Should it
demand longer in the doing, so much the worse; he
realised its importance, its crucial importance, in
his artistic development, and it must have its own
length and time. In the workroom he had recently
left he had been making excellent progress; *Romilly*
had begun, as the saying is, to speak and act of herself; and he did not doubt she would continue to
do so the moment the distraction of his removal
was over. This distraction was almost over; he told
himself it was time he pulled himself together again;
and on a March morning he went out, returned again
with two great bunches of yellow daffodils, placed
one bunch on his mantelpiece between the Sheffield
sticks and the other on the table before him, and
took out the half-completed manuscript of *Romilly
Bishop*.

But before beginning work he went to a small
rosewood cabinet and took from a drawer his
cheque-book and pass book. He totted them up, and
his monk-like face grew thoughtful. His installation
had cost him more than he had intended it should,

and his balance was rather less than fifty pounds, with no immediate prospect of more.

"Hm! I'd forgotten rugs and chintz curtains and so forth mounted up so," said Oleron. "But it would have been a pity to spoil the place for the want of ten pounds or so. . . . Well, *Romilly* simply *must* be out for the autumn, that's all. So here goes—"

He drew his papers towards him.

But he worked badly; or, rather, he did not work at all. The square outside had its own noises, frequent and new, and Oleron could only hope that he would speedily become accustomed to these. First came hawkers, with their carts and cries; at midday the children, returning from school, trooped into the square and swung on Oleron's gate; and when the children had departed again for afternoon school, an itinerant musician with a mandoline posted himself beneath Oleron's window and began to strum. This was a not unpleasant distraction, and Oleron, pushing up his window, threw the man a penny. Then he returned to his table again. . . .

But it was no good. He came to himself, at long intervals, to find that he had been looking about his room and wondering how he had formerly been furnished—whether a settee in buttercup or petunia satin had stood under the farther window, whether from the centre moulding of the light lofty ceiling had depended a glimmering. crystal chandelier, or where the tambour-frame or the picquet-table had

stood. . . . No, it was no good; he had far better
be frankly doing nothing than getting fruitlessly
tired; and he decided that he would take a walk,
but, chancing to sit down for a moment, dozed in
his chair instead.

"This won't do," he yawned when he awoke at
half-past four in the afternoon; "I must do better
than this tomorrow—"

And he felt so deliciously lazy that for some minutes he even contemplated the breach of an appointment he had for the evening.

The next morning he sat down to work without
even permitting himself to answer one of his three
letters—two of them tradesmen's accounts, the third
a note from Miss Bengough, forwarded from his old
address. It was a jolly day of white and blue, with
a gay noisy wind and a subtle turn in the colour
of growing things; and over and over again, once
or twice a minute, his room became suddenly light
and then subdued again, as the shining white clouds
robed north-eastwards over the square. The soft fitful illumination was reflected in the polished surface of the table and even in the footworn old floor;
and the morning noises had begun again.

Oleron made a pattern of dots on the paper before him, and then broke off to move the jar of
daffodils exactly opposite the centre of a creamy
panel. Then he wrote a sentence that ran continu-
ously for a couple of lines, after which it broke off

into notes and jottings. For a time he succeeded in persuading himself that in making these memoranda he was really working; then he rose and began to pace his room. As he did so, he was struck by an idea. It was that the place might possibly be a little better for more positive colour. It was, perhaps, a thought *too* pale—mild and sweet as a kind old face, but a little devitalised, even wan. . . . Yes, decidedly it would bear a robuster note—more and richer flowers, and possibly some warm and gay stuff for cushions for the window-seats. . . .

"Of course, I really can't afford it," he muttered, as he went for a two-foot and began to measure the width of the window recesses. . . .

In stooping to measure a recess, his attitude suddenly changed to one of interest and attention. Presently he rose again, rubbing his hands with gentle glee.

"Oho, oho!" he said. "These look to me very much like window-boxes, nailed up. We must look into this! Yes, those are boxes, or I'm . . . oho, this is an adventure!"

On that wall of his sitting-room there were two windows (the third was in another corner), and, beyond the open bedroom door, on the same wall, was another. The seats of all had been painted, repainted, and painted again; and Oleron's investigating finger had barely detected the old nailheads beneath the paint. Under the ledge over which he stooped an old keyhole also had been puttied up. Oleron took out his penknife.

He worked carefully for five minutes, and then went into the kitchen for a hammer and chisel. Driving the chisel cautiously under the seat, he started the whole lid slightly. Again using the penknife, he cut along the hinged edge and outward along the ends; and then he fetched a wedge and a wooden mallet.

"Now for our little mystery—" he said.

The sound of the mallet on the wedge seemed, in that sweet and pale apartment, somehow a little brutal—nay, even shocking. The panelling rang and rattled and vibrated to the blows like a sounding-board. The whole house seemed to echo; from the roomy cellarage to the garrets above a flock of echoes seemed to awake; and the sound got a little on Oleron's nerves. All at once he paused, fetched a duster, and muffled the mallet. . . . When the edge was sufficiently raised he put his fingers under it and lifted. The paint flaked and starred a little; the rusty old nails squeaked and grunted; and the lid came up, laying open the box beneath. Oleron looked into it. Save for a couple of inches of scurf and mould and old cobwebs it was empty.

"No treasure there," said Oleron, a little amused that he should have fancied there might have been. "*Romilly* will still have to be out by the autumn. Let's have a look at the others."

He turned to the second window.

The raising of the two remaining seats occupied him until well into the afternoon. That of the bed-room like the first, was empty; but from the second seat of his sitting-room he drew out something yielding and folded and furred over an inch thick with dust. He carried the object into the kitchen, and having swept it over a bucket, took a duster to it.

It was some sort of a large bag, of an ancient frieze-like material, and when unfolded it occupied the greater part of the small kitchen floor. In shape it was an irregular, a very irregular, triangle, and it had a couple of wide flaps, with the remains of straps and buckles. The patch that had been upper-most in the folding was of a faded yellowish brown; but the rest of it was of shades of crimson that var-ied according to the exposure of the parts of it.

"Now whatever can that have been?" Oleron mused as he stood surveying it. . . . "I give it up. Whatever it is, it's settled my work for to-day, I'm afraid—"

He folded the object up carelessly and thrust it into a corner of the kitchen; then, taking pans and brushes and an old knife, he returned to the sitting-room and began to scrape and to wash and to line with paper his newly discovered receptacles. When he had finished, he put his spare boots and books and papers into them; and he closed the lids again, amused with his little adventure, but also a little

anxious for the hour to come when he should settle
fairly down to his work again.

III

It piqued Oleron a little that his friend, Miss Bengough, should dismiss with a glance the place he
himself had found so singularly winning. Indeed she
scarcely lifted her eyes to it. But then she had always been more or less like that—a little indifferent
to the graces of life, careless of appearances, and
perhaps a shade more herself when she ate biscuits
from a paper bag than when she dined with greater
observance of the convenances. She was an unat-
tached journalist of thirty-four, large, showy, fair as
butter, pink as a dog-rose, reminding one of a flo-
rist's picked specimen bloom, and given to sudden
and ample movements and moist and explosive ut-
terances. She "pulled a better living out of the pool"
(as she expressed it) than Oleron did; and by cun-
ningly disguised puffs of drapers and haberdashers
she "pulled" also the greater part of her very varied
wardrobe. She left small whirlwinds of air behind
her when she moved, in which her veils and scarves
fluttered and spun.

Oleron heard the flurry of her skirts on his staircase and her single loud knock at his door when he
had been a month in his new abode. Her garments
brought in the outer air, and she flung a bundle of
ladies' journals down on a chair.

"Don't knock off for me," she said across a mouthful of large-headed hatpins as she removed her hat and veil. "I didn't know whether you were straight yet, so I've brought some sandwiches for lunch. You've got coffee, I suppose?—No, don't get up—I'll find the kitchen—"

"Oh, that's all right, I'll clear these things away. To tell the truth, I'm rather glad to be interrupted," said Oleron.

He gathered his work together and put it away. She was already in the kitchen; he heard the running of water into the kettle. He joined her, and ten minutes later followed her back to the sitting-room with the coffee and sandwiches on a tray. They sat down, with the tray on a small table between them.

"Well, what do you think of the new place?" Oleron asked as she poured out coffee.

"Hm! . . . Anybody'd think you were going to get married, Paul."

He laughed.

"Oh no. But it's an improvement on some of them, isn't it?"

"Is it? I suppose it is; I don't know. I liked the last place, in spite of the black ceiling and no water-tap. How's *Romilly?*"

Oleron thumbed his chin.

"Hm! I'm rather ashamed to tell you. The fact is, I've not got on very well with it. But it will be all right on the night, as you used to say."

"Stuck?"

"Rather stuck."

"Got any of it you care to read to me? . . ."

Oleron had long been in the habit of reading portions of his work to Miss Bengough occasionally. Her comments were always quick and practical, sometimes directly useful, sometimes indirectly suggestive. She, in return for his confidence, always kept all mention of her own work sedulously from him. His, she said, was "real work"; hers merely filled space, not always even grammatically.

"I'm afraid there isn't," Oleron replied, still meditatively dry-shaving his chin. Then he added, with a little burst of candour, "The fact is, Elsie, I've not written—not actually written—very much more of it—*any* more of it, in fact. But, of course, that doesn't mean I haven't progressed. I've progressed, in one sense, rather alarmingly. I'm now thinking of reconstructing the whole thing."

Miss Bengough gave a gasp. "Reconstructing!"

"Making Romilly herself a different type of woman. Somehow, I've begun to feel that I'm not getting the most out of her. As she stands, I've certainly lost interest in her to some extent."

"But—but—" Miss Bengough protested, "you had her so real, so *living*, Paul!"

Oleron smiled faintly. He had been quite prepared for Miss Bengough's disapproval, He wasn't surprised that she liked Romilly as she at present existed; she would. Whether she realised it or not, there was much of herself in his fictitious creation. Naturally Romilly would seem "real," "living," to her. . . .

"But are you really serious, Paul?" Miss Bengough asked presently, with a round-eyed stare.

"Quite serious."

"You're really going to scrap those fifteen chapters?"

"I didn't exactly say that."

"That fine, rich love-scene?"

"I should only do it reluctantly, and for the sake of something I thought better."

"And that beautiful, *beautiful* description of Romilly on the shore?"

"It wouldn't necessarily be wasted," he said a little uneasily.

But Miss Bengough made a large and windy gesture, and then let him have it.

"Really, you are *too* trying!" she broke out. "I do wish sometimes you'd remember you're human, and live in a world! You know I'd be the *last* to wish you to lower your standard one inch, but it wouldn't be lowering it to bring it within human comprehension. Oh, you're sometimes altogether too godlike! . . . Why, it would be a wicked, criminal waste of your powers to destroy those fifteen chapters! Look at it reasonably, now. You've been working for nearly twenty years; you've now got what you've been working for almost within your grasp; your affairs are at a most critical stage (oh, don't tell me; I know you're about at the end of your money); and here you are, deliberately proposing to withdraw a thing that will probably make your name, and to substitute for it something that ten to one nobody on earth will ever want to read—and small blame to them! Really, you try my patience!"

Oleron had shaken his head slowly as she had talked. It was an old story between them. The noisy, able, practical journalist was an admirable friend— up to a certain point; beyond that . . . well, each of us knows that point beyond which we stand alone. Elsie Bengough sometimes said that had she had one-tenth part of Oleron's genius there were few things she could not have done—thus making that genius a quantitatively divisible thing, a sort of ingredient, to be added to or to subtracted from in the admixture of his work. That it was a qualitative thing, essential, indivisible, informing, passed her comprehension. Their spirits parted company at that point. Oleron knew it. She did not appear to know it.

"Yes, yes, yes," he said a little wearily, by-and-by, "practically you're quite right, entirely right, and I haven't a word to say. If I could only turn *Romilly* over to you you'd make an enormous success of her. But that can't be, and I, for my part, am seriously doubting whether she's worth my while. You know what that means."

"What does it mean?" she demanded bluntly.

"Well," he said, smiling wanly, "what *does* it mean when you're convinced a thing isn't worth doing? You simply don't do it."

Miss Bengough's eyes swept the ceiling for assistance against this impossible man.

"What utter rubbish!" she broke out at last. "Why, when I saw you last you were simply oozing *Romilly;* you were turning her off at the rate of four chapters a week; if you hadn't moved you'd have had her three-parts done by now. What on earth possessed you to move right in the middle of your most important work?"

Oleron tried to put her off with a recital of inconveniences, but she wouldn't have it. Perhaps in her heart she partly suspected the reason. He was simply mortally weary of the narrow circumstances of his life. He had had twenty years of it—twenty years of garrets and roof-chambers and dingy flats and shabby lodgings, and he was tired of dinginess and shabbiness. The reward was as far off as ever— or if it was not, he no longer cared as once he would have cared to put out his hand and take it. It is all very well to tell a man who is at the point of exhaustion that only another effort is required of him; if he cannot make it he is as far off as ever. . . .

"Anyway," Oleron summed up, "I'm happier here than I've been for a long time. That's some sort of a justification."

"And doing no work," said Miss Bengough pointedly.

At that a trifling petulance that had been gathering in Oleron came to a head.

"And why should I do nothing but work?" he demanded. "How much happier am I for it? I don't say I don't love my work—when it's done; but I hate doing it. Sometimes it's an intolerable burden that I simply long to be rid of. Once in many weeks it has a moment, one moment, of glow and thrill for me; I remember the days when it was all glow and thrill; and now I'm forty-four, and it's becoming drudgery. Nobody wants it; I'm ceasing to want it myself; and if any ordinary sensible man were to ask me whether I didn't think I was a fool to go on, I think I should agree that I was."

Miss Bengough's comely pink face was serious.

"But you knew all that, many, many years ago, Paul—and still you chose it," she said in a low voice.

"Well, and how should I have known?" he demanded. "I didn't know. I was told so. My heart, if you like, told me so, and I thought I knew. Youth always thinks it knows; then one day it discovers that it is nearly fifty—"

"Forty-four, Paul—"

"—forty-four, then—and it finds that the glamour isn't in front, but behind. Yes, I knew and chose, if that's knowing and choosing . . . but it's a costly choice we're called on to make when we're young!"

Miss Bengough's eyes were on the floor. Without moving them she said, "You're not regretting it, Paul?"

"Am I not?" he took her up. "Upon my word, I've lately thought I am! What do I get in return for it all?"

"You know what you get," she replied.

He might have known from her tone what else he could have had for the holding up of a finger—herself. She knew, but could not tell him, that he could have done no better thing for himself. Had he, any time these ten years, asked her to marry him, she would have replied quietly, "Very well; when?" He had never thought of it. . . .

"Yours is the real work," she continued quietly. "Without you we jackals couldn't exist. You and a few like you hold everything upon your shoulders."

For a minute there was a silence. Then it occurred to Oleron that this was common vulgar grumbling. It was not his habit. Suddenly he rose and began to stack cups and plates on the tray.

"Sorry you catch me like this, Elsie," he said, with a little laugh. . . . "No, I'll take them out; then we'll go for a walk, if you like. . . ."

He carried out the tray, and then began to show Miss Bengough round his flat. She made few comments. In the kitchen she asked what an old faded square of reddish frieze was, that Miss Barrett used as a cushion for her wooden chair.

"That? I should be glad if you could tell *me* what it is," Oleron replied as he unfolded the bag and related the story of its finding in the window-seat.

"I think I know what it is," said Miss Bengough. "It's been used to wrap up a harp before putting it in its case."

"By Jove, that's probably just what it was," said Oleron, "I could make neither head nor tale of it. . . ."

They finished the tour of the flat, and returned to the sitting-room.

"And who lives in the rest of the house?" Mis Bengough asked.

"I dare say a tramp sleeps in the cellar occasionally. Nobody else."

"Hm! . . . Well, I'll tell you what I think of it, if you like."

"I should like."

"You'll never work here."

"Oh?" said Oleron quickly. "Why not?"

"You'll never finish *Romilly* here. Why, I don't know, but you won't. I know it. You'll have to leave before you get on with that book."

He mused a moment, and then said:

"Isn't that a little—prejudiced, Elsie?"

"Perfectly ridiculous. As an argument it hasn't a leg to stand on. But there it is," she replied, her mouth once more full of the large-headed hat pins.

"I can only hope you're entirely wrong," he said, "for I shall be in a serious mess if *Romilly* isn't out in the autumn."

IV

As Oleron sat by his fire that evening, pondering Miss Bengough's prognostication that difficulties awaited him in his work, he came to the conclusion that it would have been far better had she kept her beliefs to herself. No man does a thing better fir having his confidence damped at the outset, and to speak of difficulties is in a sense to make them. Speech itself becomes a deterrent act, to which other discouragements accrete until the very event of which warning is given is as likely as not to come to pass. He heartily confounded her. An influence hostile to the completion of *Romilly* had been born.

And in some illogical, dogmatic way women seem to have, she had attached this antagonistic influence to his new abode. Was ever anything so absurd! "You'll never finish *Romilly* here." . . . Why not? Was this her idea of the luxury that saps the springs of action and brings a man down to indolence and dropping out of the race? The place was well enough—it was entirely charming, for that matter—but it was not so demoralizing as all that! No; Elsie had missed the mark that time. . . .

He moved his chair to look round the room that smiled, positively smiled, in the firelight. He too smiled, as if pity was to be entertained for a maligned apartment. Even that slight lack of robust colour he had remarked was not noticeable in the soft glow. The drawn chintz curtains—they had a flowered and trellised pattern, with baskets and oaten

pipes—fell in long quiet folds to the window-seats;
the rows of bindings in old bookcases took the light
richly; the last trace of sallowness had gone with
the daylight; and, if the truth must be told, it had
been Elsie himself who had seemed a little out of
the picture.

That reflection struck him a little, and presently
he returned to it. Yes, the rom had, quite accidentally, done Miss Bengough a disservice that afternoon.
It had, in some subtle but unmistakable way, placed
her, marked a contrast of qualities. Assuming for
the sake of argument the slightly ridiculous propo-
sition that the room in which Oleron saw *was* char-
acterised by a certain sparsity and lack of vigour; so
much the worse for Miss Bengough; she certainly
erred on the side of redundancy and general much-
ness. And if one must contrast abstract qualities,
Oleron inclined to the austere in taste. . . .

Yes, here Oleron had made a distinct discovery;
he wondered he had not made it before. He pictured
Miss Bengough again as she had appeared that afternoon—large, showy, moistly pink, with that quality
of the prize bloom exuding, as it were from here;
and instantly she suffered in his thought. He even
recognised now that he had noticed something odd
at the time, and that unconsciously his attitude,
even while he had been there, had been one of criticism. The mechanism of her was a little obvious;
her melting humidity was the result of analysable

processes; and behind her there had seem to lurk some dim shape emblematic of mortality. He had never, during the ten years of their intimacy, dreamed for a moment of asking her to marry him; none the less, he now felt for the first time a thankfulness that he had not done so . . .

Then, suddenly and swiftly, his face flamed that he should be thinking thus of his friend. What! Elsie Bengough, with whom he had spent weeks and weeks of afternoons—she, the good chum, on whose help he would have counted had all the rest of the world failed him—she, whose loyalty to him would not, he knew, swerve as long as there was breath in her—Elsie to be even in thought dissected thus! He was an ingrate and a cad. . . .

Had she been there in that moment he would have abased himself before her.

For ten minutes and more he sat, still gazing into the fire, with that humiliating red fading slowly from his cheeks. All was still within and without, save for a tiny musical tinkling that came from his kitchen—the dripping of water from an imperfectly turned-off tap into the vessel beneath it. Mechanically he began to beat with his fingers to the faintly heard falling of the drops; the tiny regular movement seemed to hasten that shameful withdrawal from his face. He grew cool once more; and when he resumed his meditation he was all unconscious that he took it up again at the same point. . . .

It was not only her florid superfluity of build
that he had approached in the attitude of criticism;
he was conscious also of the wide differences between her mind and his own. He felt no thankfulness that up to a certain point their natures had ever
run companionably side by side; he was now full
of questions beyond that point. Their intellects di-
verged; there was no denying it; and, looking back,
he was inclined to doubt whether there had been
any real coincidence. True, he had read his writings
to her and she had appeared to speak comprehend-
ingly and to the point; but what can a man do who,
having assumed that another sees as he does, is suddenly brought up sharp by something that falsifies
and discredits all that had gone before? He doubted
all now. . . . It did for a moment occur to them that
the man who demands of a friend more than can be
given to him is in danger of losing that friend, but
he put the thought aside.

Again he ceased to think, and again moved his
finger to the distant dripping of the tap. . . .

And now (he resumed by-and-by), if these things
were true of Elsie Bengough, they were also true
of the creation of which she was the prototype—
Romilly Bishop. And since he could say of Romilly
what for very she he could not say of Elsie, he gave his
thoughts rein. He did so in that smiling, fire-lighted
room, to the accompaniment of the faintly heard tap.

There was no longer any doubt about it; he hated
the central character of his novel. Even as he had
described her physically she overpowered the senses;
she was coarse-fibered, over-coloured, rank. It became true the moment he formulated his thought;
Gulliver had described the Brobdingnagian maids-
of-honour thus: and mentally and spiritually she
corresponded—was unsensitive, limited, common.
The model (he closed his eyes for a moment)—the
model stuck out through fifteen vulgar and blatant
chapters to such a pitch that, without seeing the reason, he had been unable to begin the sixteenth. He
marvelled that it had only just dawned upon him.

And *this* was to have been his Beatrice, his vision! As Elsie she was to have gone into the furnace of his art, and she was to have come out the
Woman all men desire! Her thoughts were to have
been culled from his own finest, her form from his
dearest dreams, and her setting wherever he could
find one fit for her worth. He had brooded long before making the attempt; then one day he had felt
her stir within him as a mother feels a quickening,
and he had begun to write; and so he had added
chapter to chapter. . . .

And those fifteen sodden chapters were what he
had produced!

Again he sat, softly moving his finger. . . .

Then he bestirred himself.

She must go, all fifteen chapters of her. That was settled. For what was to take her place in his mind was a blank; but one thing at a time; a man is not excused from taking the wrong course because the right one is not immediately revealed to him. Better would come if it was to come; in the meantime—

He rose, fetched the fifteen chapters, and read them over before he should drop them in the fire.

But instead of putting them in the fire he let them fall from his hand. He became conscious of the dripping of the tap again. It had a tinkling gamut of four or five notes, on which it rang irregular changes, and it was foolishly sweet and dulcimer-like. In his mind Oleron could see the gathering of each drop, its little tremble on the lip of the tap, and the tiny percussion of its fall, "Plink—plunk," minimised almost to inaudibility. Following the lowest note there seemed to be a brief phrase, irregularly repeated; and presently Oleron found himself waiting for the recurrence of this phrase. It was quite pretty. . . .

But it did not conduce to wakefulness, and Oleron dozed over his fire.

When he awoke again the fire had burned low and the flames of the candles were licking the rims of the Sheffield sticks. Sluggishly he rose, yawned, went his nightly round of door-locks, and window-fastenings, and passed into his bedroom. Soon, he slept soundly.

But a curious little sequel followed on the morrow. Mrs. Barrett usually tapped, not at his door,
but at the wooden wall beyond which lay Oleron's
bed; and then Oleron rose, put on his dressing gown,
and admitted her. He was not conscious that as he
did so that morning he hummed an air; but Mrs.
Barrett lingered with her hand on the doorknob and
her face a little averted and smiling.

"De-ar me!" her soft falsetto rose. "But that will
be a very o-ald tune, Mr. Oleron! I will not have
heard it this for-ty years!"

"What tune?" Oleron asked.

"The tune, indeed, that you was humming, sir."

Oleron had his thumb in the flap of a letter. It
remained there.

"*I* was humming? . . . Sing it, Mrs. Barrett."

Mrs. Barrett prut-prutted.

"I have no voice for singing, Mr. Oleron; it was
Ann Pugh was the singer of our family; but the tune
will be very o-ald, and it is called, 'The Beckoning
Fair One.'"

"Try to sing it," said Oleron, his thumb still in
the envelope; and Mrs. Barrett, with much dimpling
and confusion, hummed the air.

"They do say it was sung to a harp, Mr. Oleron,
and it will be very o-ald," she concluded.

"And *I* was singing that?"

"Indeed you was. I would not be very likely to
tell you lies."

With a "Very well—let me have breakfast," Oleron opened his letter; but the trifling circumstance
struck him as more odd than he would have admitted to himself. The phrase he had hummed had been
that which he had associated with the falling from
the tap on the evening before.

V

Even more curious than that the commonplace dripping of an ordinary water-tap should have tallied
so closely with an actually existing air was another
result it had, namely, that it awakened, or seemed
to awaken, in Oleron an abnormal sensitiveness to
other noises of the old house. It has been remarked
that the silence obtains its fullest and most impressive quality when it is broken by some minute
sound; and, truth to tell, the place was never still.
Perhaps the mildness of the spring air operated on
its torpid old timbers; perhaps Oleron's fires caused
it to stretch its own anatomy; and certainly a whole
world of insect life bored and burrowed in its baulks
and joists. At any rate Oleron had only so it quiet
in his chair and to wait for a minute or two in order
to become aware of such a change in the audito-
ry scale as comes upon a man who, conceiving the
mid-summer woods to be motionless and still, all at
once finds his ear sharpened to the crepitation of a
myriad insects.

And he smiled to think of man's arbitrary distinction between that which has life and that which has not. Here, quite apart from such recognisable sounds as the scampering of mice, the falling of plaster behind his panelling, and the popping of purses or coffins from his fire, was a whole house talking to him had he but known his language. Beams settled with a tired sigh into their old mortices; creatures ticked in the walls; joints cracked, boards complained; with no palpable stirring of the air window-sashes changed their position with a soft knock in their frames. And whether the place had life in this sense or not, it had at all events a winsome personality. It needed but an hour of musing for Oleron to conceive the idea that, as his own body stood in friendly relation to his soul, so, by an extension and an attenuation, his habituation might fantastically be supposed to stand in some relation to himself. He even amused himself with the far-fetched fancy that he might so identify himself with the place that some future tenant, taking possession, might regard it as in a sense haunted. It would be rather a joke if he, a perfectly harmless author, with nothing on his mind worse than a novel he had discovered he must begin again, should turn out to be laying the foundation of a future ghost! . . .

In proportion, as he felt this growing attachment to the fabric of his abode, Elsie Bengough, from being merely unattracted, began to show a dislike of the place that was more and more marked. And she did not scruple to speak of her aversion.

"It doesn't belong to to-day at all, and for you especially it's bad," she said with decision. "You're only too ready to let go your hold on actual things and to slip into apathy; *you* ought to be in a place with concrete floors and a patent gas-meter and a tradesman' lift. And it would do you all the good in the world if you had a job that made you scramble and rub elbows with your fellow-men. Now, if I could get you a job, for, say, two or three days a week, one that would allow you heaps of time for your proper work—would you take it?"

Somehow, Oleron resented a little being diagnosed like this. He thanked Miss Bengough, but without a smile.

"Thank you, but I don't think so. After all each of us has his own life to live," he could not refrain from adding.

"His own life to live! . . . How long is it since you were out, Paul?"

"About two hours."

"I don't mean to buy stamps or to post a letter. How long is it since you had anything like a stretch?"

"Oh, some little time perhaps. I don't know."

"Since I was here last?"

"I haven't been out much."

"And has *Romilly* progressed much better for your being cooped up?"

"I think she has. I'm laying the foundations of her. I shall begin the actual writing presently."

It seemed as if Miss Bengough had forgotten their tussle about the first *Romilly*. She frowned, turned half away, and then quickly turned again.

"Ah! . . . So you've still got that ridiculous idea in your head?"

"If you mean," said Oleron slowly, "that I've discarded the old *Romilly*, and am at work on a new one, you're right. I have still got that idea in my head." Something uncordial in his tone struck her; but she was a fighter. His own absurd sensitiveness hardened her. She gave a "Pshaw!" of impatience.

"Where is the old one?" she demanded abruptly.

"Why?" said Oleron.

"I want to see it. I want to show some of it to you. I want, if you're not wool-gathering entirely, to bring you back to your senses."

This time it was he who turned his back. But when he turned round again he spoke more gently.

"It's no good, Elsie. I'm responsible for the way I go, and you must allow me to go it—even if it should seem wrong to you. Believe me, I am giving thought to it. . . . The manuscript? I was on the point of burning it, but I didn't. It's in that window-seat, if you must see it."

Miss Bengough crossed quickly to the window-seat, and lifted the lid. Suddenly she gave a
little exclamation, and put the back of her hand to
her mouth. She spoke over her shoulder:

"You ought to knock these nails in, Paul," she
said.

He strode to her side.

"What? What is it? What's the matter?" he asked.
"I did knock them in—or rather, pulled them out."

"You left enough to scratch with," she replied,
showing her hand. From the upper wrist to the
knuckle of the little finger a welling red wound
showed.

"Good—Gracious!" Oleron ejaculated. . . . "Here,
come to the bathroom and bathe it quickly—"

He hurried her to the bathroom, turned on warm
water, and bathed and cleansed the bad gash. Then,
still holding the hand, he turned cold water on it,
uttering broken phases of astonishment and concern.

"Good Lord, how did that happen! As far as I
knew I'd . . . is this water too cold? Does that hurt?
I can't imagine how on earth . . . there; that'll do—"

"No—one moment longer—I can bear it," she
murmured, her eyes closed.

Presently he led her back to the sitting-room and
bound the hand in one of his handkerchiefs; but his
face did not lose its expression of perplexity. He had
spent half a day in opening and making serviceable
the three window-boxes, and he could not conceive

how he had come to leave an inch and a half of rusty nail standing in the wood. He himself had opened the lids of each of them a dozen times and had not noticed any nail; but there it was. . . .

"It shall come out now, at all events," he muttered, as he went for a pair of pincers. And he made no mistake about it that time.

Elsie Bengough had sunk into a chair, and her face was rather white; but in her hand was the manuscript of *Romilly*. She had not finished with *Romilly* yet. Presently she returned to the charge.

"Oh, Paul, it will be the greatest mistake you ever, *ever* made if you do not publish this!" she said.

He hung his head, genuinely distressed. He couldn't get that incident of the nail out of his head, and *Romilly* occupied a second place in his thoughts for the moment. But still she insisted; and when presently he spoke it was almost as if he asked her pardon for something.

"What can I say, Elsie? I can only hope that when you see the new version, you'll see how right I am. And if in spite of all you *don't* like her, well . . ." he made hopeless gesture. "Don't you see that I *must* be guided by my own lights?"

She was silent.

"Come, Elsie," he said gently. "We've got along well so far; don't let us split on this."

The last words had hardly passed his lips before he regretted them. She had been nursing her injured hand, with her eyes once more closed; but her lips and lids quivered simultaneously. Her voice shook as she spoke.

"I can't help saying it, Paul, but you are so greatly changed."

"Hush, Elsie," he murmured soothingly; "you've had a shock; rest for a while. How could I change?"

"I don't know, but you are. You've not been yourself ever since you came here. I wish you'd never seen the place. It's stopped your work, it's making you into a person I hardly know, and it's made me horribly anxious about you. . . . Oh, how my hand is beginning to throb!"

"Poor child!" he murmured. "Will you let me take you to a doctor and have it properly dressed?"

"No—I shall be all right presently—I'll keep it raised—"

She put her elbow on the back of the chair, and the bandaged hand rested lightly on his shoulder.

At that thought an entirely new anxiety stirred suddenly within him. Hundreds of times previously, on their jaunts and excursions, she had slipped her hand within his arm as she might have slipped it into the arm of a brother, and he had accepted the little affectionate gesture as a brother might have accepted it. But now, for the first time, there rushed into his mind a hundred startling questions. Her eyes were still closed, and her head had fallen pathetically back; and there was a lost and ineffable smile on her parted lips. The truth broke in upon him. Good God! . . . And he had never divined it!

And stranger than all was that, now that he did see that she was lost in love of him, there came to him, not sorrow and humility and abasement, but something else that he struggled in vain against—something entirely strange and new, that, had he analyzed it, he would have found to be petulance and irritation and resentment and ungentleness. The sudden selfish prompting mastered him before he was aware. He all but gave it word. What was she doing there at all? Why was she not getting on with her own work? Why was she here interfering with his? Who had given her this guardianship over him that lately she had put forward so assertively?—"changed?" It was she, not himself, who had changed. . . .

But by the time she had opened her eyes again he had overcome his resentment sufficiently to speak gently, albeit with reserve.

"I wish you would let me take you to a doctor."

She rose.

"No thank you, Paul," she said. "I'll go now. If I need a dressing I'll get one; take the other hand, please. Good-bye—"

He did not attempt to detain her. He walked with her to the foot of the stairs. Half-way along the narrow alley she turned.

"It would be a long way to come if you happened not to be in," she said; "I'll send you a postcard the next time."

At the gate she turned again.

"Leave here, Paul," she said, with a mournful look. "Everything's wrong with this house."

Then she was gone.

Oleron returned to his room. He crossed straight to the window-box. He opened the lid and stood long looking at it. Then he closed it again and turned away.

"That's rather frightening," he muttered. "It's simply not possible that I should not have removed that nail. . . ."

VI

Oleron knew very well what Elsie had meant when she had said that her next visit would be preceded by a postcard. She, too, had realised that at last, at last he knew—knew, and didn't want her. It gave him a miserable, pitiful pang, therefore, when she came again within a week, knocking at the door un-announced. She spoke from the landing; she did not intend to stay, she said; and he had to press her before she would so much as enter.

Her excuse for calling was that she had heard of an inquiry for short stories that he might be wise to follow up. He thanked her. Then, her business over, she seemed anxious to get away again. Oleron did not seek to detain her; even he saw through the pretext of the stories; and he accompanied her down the stairs.

But Elsie Bengough had no luck whatever in that house. A second accident befell her. Half-way down the staircase there was a sharp sound of splintering wood, and she checked a loud cry. Oleron knew the woodwork to be old, but he himself had ascended and descended frequently enough without mishap. . . .

Elsie had put her foot through one of the stairs.

He sprang to her side in alarm.

"Oh, I say! My poor girl!"

She laughed hysterically.

"It's my weight—I know I'm getting fat—"

"Keep still—let me clear those splinters away," he muttered between his teeth.

She continued to laugh and sob that it was her weight—she was getting fat—

He thrust downwards at the broken boards. The extrication was no easy matter, and her torn boot shows him how badly the foot and ankle within it must be abraded.

"Good God—good God!" he muttered over and over again.

"I shall be too heavy for anything soon," she sobbed and laughed.

But she refused to reascend and to examine her hurt.

"No, let me go quickly—let me go quickly," she repeated.

"But it's a frightful gash!"

"No—not so bad—let me get away quickly—I'm—I'm not wanted."

At her words, that she was not wanted, his head dropped as if she had given him a buffet.

"Elsie!" he choked, brokenly and shocked.

But she too made a quick gesture, as if she put something violently aside.

"Oh, Paul, not *that*—not *you*—of course I do mean that too in a sense—oh, you know what I mean! . . . But if the other can't be, spare me this now! I—I wouldn't have come, but—but oh, I did, I *did* try to keep away!"

It was intolerable, heartbreaking; but what could he do—what could he say? He did not love her. . . .

"Let me go—I'm not wanted—let me take away what's left of me—"

"Dear Elsie—you are very dear to me—"

But again she made the gesture, as of putting something violently aside.

"No, not that—not anything less—don't offer me anything less—leave me a little pride—"

"Let me get my hat and coat—let me take you to a doctor," he muttered.

But she refused. She refused even the support of his arm. She gave another unsteady laugh.

"I'm sorry I broke your stairs, Paul. . . . You will go and see about the short stories, won't you?"

He groaned.

"Then if you won't see a doctor, will you go across the square and let Mrs. Barrett look at you? Look, there's Barrett passing now—"

The long-nosed Barrett was looking curiously down the alley, but as Oleron was about to call him he made off without a word. Elsie seemed anxious for nothing so much as to be clear of the place, and finally promised to go straight to a doctor, but insisted on going alone.

"Good-bye," she said.

And Oleron watched her until she was past the hatchet-like "To Let" boards, as if he feared that even they might fall upon her and maim her.

That night Oleron did not dine. He had far too much on his mind. He walked from room to room of his flat, as if he could have walked away from Elsie Bengough's haunting cry that still rang in his ears. "I'm not wanted—don't offer me anything less—let me take away what's left of me—"

Oh, if he could have persuaded himself that he loved her!

He walked until twilight fell, then, without lighting candles, he stirred up the fire and flung himself into a chair.

Poor, poor Elsie! . . .

But even while his heart ached for her, it was out of the question. If only he had known! If only he had used common observation! But those walks, those sisterly takings of the arm—what a fool he had been! . . . Well, it was too late now. It was she, not he, who must now act—act by keeping away. He would help her all he could. He himself would not sit in her presence. If she came, he would hurry her out again as fast as he could. . . . Poor, poor Elsie!

His room grew dark; the fire burned dead; and he continued to it, wincing from time to time as a fresh tortured phrase rang in his ears.

Then suddenly, he knew not why, he found himself anxious for her in a new sense—uneasy about her personal safety. A horrible fancy that even then he might be looking over an embankment down into dark water, that she might even now be glancing up at the hook on the door, took him. Women had been known to do these things! . . . Then there would be an inquest, and he himself would be called upon to identify her, and would be asked how she had come by an ill-healed wound on the hand and a bad abrasion of the ankle. Barrett would say that he had seen her leaving his house. . . .

Then he recognised that his thoughts were morbid. By an effort of will he put them aside, and sat for awhile listening to the faint creakings and tickings and rappings within his panelling. . . .

If only he could have married her! . . . But he couldn't. Her face had risen before him again as he had seen it on the stairs, drawn with pain and ugly and swollen with tears. Ugly—yes, positively blubbered; if tears were women's weapons, as they were said to be, such tears were weapons turning against themselves . . . suicide again. . . .

Then all at once he found himself attentively considering her two accidents.

Extraordinary, they had been, both of them. He *could not* have left that old nail standing in the wood; why, he had fetched tools specially from the kitchen; and he was convinced that the step that had broken beneath her weight had been as sound as the others. It was inexplicable, if these things could happen, anything could happen. There was not a beam nor a jamb in the place that might not fall without warning, not a plank that might not crash inwards, not a nail that might not become a dagger. The whole place was full of life even now; as he sat there in the dark he heard its crowds of noises as if the house had been one great microphone. . . .

Only half conscious that he did so, he had been sitting for some time identifying these noises, attributing to each crack or creak or knock its material cause; but there was one noise which, again not fully conscious of the omission, he had not sought to account for. It had last come some minutes ago; it came again now—a sort of soft sweeping rustle that seemed to hold an almost inaudible minute crackling. For half a minute or so it had Oleron's attention; then his heavy thoughts were of Elsie Bengough again.

He was nearer to loving her in that moment than he had ever been. He thought how to some men their loved ones were but the dearer for those poor mortal blemishes that tell us we are but sojourners on earth, with a common fate not far distant that makes it hardly worth while to do anything but love for the time remaining. Strangling sobs, blearing tears, bodies buffeted by sickness, hearts and mind callous and hard with the rubs of the world—how little love there would be were these things a barrier to love! In that sense he did love Elsie Bengough. What her happiness had never moved in him her sorrow almost awoke. . . .

Suddenly his meditation went. His ear had once more become conscious of that soft and repeated noise—the long sweep with the almost inaudible crackle in it. Again and again it came, with a curious insistence and urgency. It quickened a little as he became increasingly attentive. . . . it seemed to Oleron that it grew louder. . . .

All at once he started bolt upright in his chair, tense and listening. The silky rustle came again; he was trying to attach it to something. . . .

The next moment he had leapt to his feet, unnerved and terrified. His chair hung poised for a moment, and then went over, setting the fire-irons clattering as it fell. There was only one noise in the world like that which had caused him to spring thus to his feet. . . .

The next time it came Oleron felt behind him at the empty air with his hand, and backed slowly until he found himself against the wall.

"God in Heaven!" The ejaculation broke from Oleron's lips. The sound had ceased.

The next moment he had given a high cry.

"What is it? What's there? *Who's* there?"

A sound of scuttling caused his knees to bend under him for a moment; but that, he knew, was a mouse. That was not something that his stomach turned sick and his mind reeled to entertain. That other sound, the like of which was not in the world, had now entirely ceased; and again he called. . . .

He called and continued to call; and then another terror, a terror of the sound of his own voice, seized him. He did not dare to call again. His shaking hand went to his pocket for a match, but he found none. He thought there might be matches on the mantelpiece—

He worked his way to the mantelpiece round a little recess, without for a moment leaving the wall. Then his hand encountered the mantelpiece, and groped along it. A box of matches fell to the hearth. He could just see them in the firelight, but his hand could not pick them up until he had cornered them inside the fender.

Then he rose and struck a light.

The room was as usual. He struck a second match. A candle stood on the table. He lighted it, and the flame sank for a moment and then burned up clear. Again he looked round.

There was nothing.

There was nothing; but there had been something, and might still be something. Formerly, Oleron had smiled at the fantastic thought that, by a
merging and interplay of identities between himself and his beautiful room, he might be preparing a
ghost for the future; it had not occurred to him *that
there might have been a similar merging and coales-
cence in the past.* Yet with this staggering impossibility he was now face to face. Something did persist
in the house; it had a tenant other than himself; and
that tenant, whatsoever or whosoever, had appalled
Oleron's soul by producing the sound of a woman
brushing her hair.

VII

Without quite knowing how he came to be there
Oleron found himself striding over the loose board
he had temporarily placed on the step broken by
Miss Bengough. He was hatless, and descending the
stairs. Not until later did there return to him a hazy
memory that he had left the candle burning on the
table, had opened the door no wider than was necessary to allow the passage of his body, and had sidled
out, closing the door softly behind him. At the foot
of the stairs another shock awaited him. Something
dashed with a flurry up from the disused cellars and
disappeared out of the door. It was only a cat, but
Oleron gave a childish sob.

He passed out of the gate, and stood for a moment under the "To Let" boards, plucking foolishly
at his lip and looking up at the glimmer of light behind one of his red blinds. Then, still looking over
his shoulder, he moved stumblingly up the square.
There was a small public-house round the corner;
Oleron had never entered it; but he entered it now,
and put down a shilling that missed the counter by
inches.

"B—b—bran—brandy," he said, and then stooped
to look for the shilling.

He had the little sawdusted bar to himself; what
company there was—carters and labourers and the
small tradesmen of the neighbourhood—was gathered in the farther compartment, beyond the space
where the white-haired landlady moved among her
taps and bottles. Oleron sat down on a hardwood
settee with a perforated seat, drank half his brandy,
and then, thinking he might as well drink it as spill
it, finished it.

Then he fell to wondering which of the men whose
voices he heard across the public-house would undertake the removal of his effects on the morrow.

In the meantime he ordered more brandy.

For he did not intend to go back to that room
where he had left the candle burning. Oh no! He
couldn't have faced even the entry and the staircase
with the broken step—certainly not that pith-white,

fascinating room. He would go back for the present
to his old arrangement, of work-room and separate
sleeping-quarters; he would go to his old landlady
at once—presently—when he had finished his brandy—and see if she could put him up for the night.
His glass was empty now. . . .

He rose, had it refilled, and sat down again.

And if anybody asked his reason for removing
again? Oh, he had reason enough—reason enough!
Nails that put themselves back into wood again and
gashed people's hands, steps that broke when you
trod on them, and women who came into a man's
place and brushed their hair in the dark, were reasons enough! He was querulous and injured about
it all. He had taken the place for himself, not for
invisible women to brush their hair in; that lawyer
fellow in Lincoln's Inn should be told so, too, before many hours were out; it was outrageous, letting
people in for agreement like that!

A cut-glass partition divided the compartment
where Oleron sat from the space where the white-
haired landlady moved; but it stopped seven or eight
inches above the level of the counter. There was
no partition at the further bar. Presently Oleron,
raising his eyes, saw that faces were watching him
through the aperture. The faces disappeared when
he looked at them.

He moved to a corner where he could not be seen
from the other bar; but this brought him into line
with the white-haired landlady.

She knew him by sight—had doubtless seen him passing and repassing; and presently she made a remark on the weather. Oleron did not know what he replied, but it sufficed to call forth the further remark that the winter had been a bad one for influenza, but that the spring weather seemed to be coming at last. . . . Even this slight contact with the commonplace steadied Oleron a little; an idle, nascent wonder whether the landlady brushed her hair every night, and, if so, whether it gave out those little electric cracklings, was shut down with a snap; and Oleron was better. . . .

With his next glass of brandy he was all for going back to his flat. Not go back? Indeed, he would go back! They should very soon see whether he was to be turned out of his place like that! He began to wonder why he was doing the rather unusual thing he was doing at that moment, unusual for him— sitting hatless, drinking brandy, in a public-house. Suppose he were to tell the white-haired landlady all about it—to tell her that a caller had scratched her hand on a nail, had later had the bad luck to put her foot through a rotten stair, and that he himself, in an old house full of squeaks and creaks and whispers, had heard a minute noise and had bolted from it in fright—what would she think of him? That he was mad, of course. . . . Pshaw! The real truth of the matter was that he hadn't been doing enough work to occupy him. He had been dreaming his days away, filling his head with a lot of moonshine about a new

Romilly (as if the old one was not good enough), and now he was surprised that the devil should enter an empty head!

Yes, he would go back. He would take a walk in the air first—he hadn't walked enough lately—and then he would take himself in hand, settle the hash of that sixteenth chapter of *Romilly* (fancy, he had actually been fool enough to think of destroying fifteen chapters!) and thenceforward he would remember that he had obligations to his fellow men and work to do in the world. There was the matter in a nutshell.

He finished his brandy and went out.

He had walked for some time before any other bearing of the matter than that on himself occurred to him. At first, the fresh air had increased the heady effect of the brandy he had drunk; but afterwards his mind grew clearer than it had been since morning. And the clearer it grew, the less final did his boastful self-assurances become, and the firmer his conviction that, when all explanations had been made, there remained something that could not be explained. His hysteria of an hour before had passed; he grew steadily calmer; but the disquieting conviction remained. A deep fear took possession of him. It was a fear for Elsie.

For something in his place was inimical to her safety. Of themselves, her two accidents might not have persuaded him of this; but she herself had said it. *"I'm not wanted here. . . ."* And she had declared that there was something wrong with the place. She had seen it before he had. Well and good. One thing stood out clearly: namely, that if this was so, she must be kept away for quite another reason than that had so confounded and humiliated Oleron. Luckily she had expressed her intention of staying away; she must be held to that intention. He must see to it.

And he must see to it all the more that he now saw his first impulse, never to set foot in the place again, was absurd. People did not do that kind of thing. With Elsie made secure, he could not with any respect to himself suffer himself to be turned out by a shadow, nor even by a danger merely because it was a danger. He had to live somewhere, and he would live there. He must return.

He mastered the faint chill of fear that came with the decision, and turned in his walk abruptly. Should fear grow on him again he would, perhaps, take one more glass of brandy. . . .

But by the time he reached the short street that led to the square he was too late for more brandy. The little public house was still lighted, but closed, and one or two men were standing talking on the kerb. Oleron noticed that a sudden silence fell on them as he passed, and he noticed further that the long-nosed Barrett, whom he passed a little lower

down, did not return his good-night. He turned in
at the broken gate, hesitated merely an instant in
the alley, and then mounted his stairs again.

Only an inch of candle remained in the Sheffield
stick, and Oleron did not light another one. Deliberately he forced himself to take it up and to make
the tour of his five rooms before retiring. It was as
he returned from the kitchen across his little hall
that he noticed that a letter lay on the floor. He
carried it into his sitting-room, and glanced at the
envelope before opening it.

It was unstamped, and had been put into the door
by hand. Its handwriting was clumsy, and it ran from
beginning to end without comma or period. Oleron
read the first line, turned to the signature, and then
finished the letter.

It was from the man Barrett, and it informed Oleron that he, Barrett, would be obliged if Mr. Oleron
would make other arrangements for the preparing of
his breakfasts and the cleaning-out of his place. The
sting lay in the tail, that is to say, the postscript.
This consisted of a text of Scripture. It embodied an
allusion that could only be to Elsie Bengough. . . .

A seldom-seen frown had cut deeply into Oleron's brow. So! That was it! Very well; they would
see about that on the morrow. . . . For the rest,
this seemed merely another reason why Elsie should
keep away. . . .

Then his suppressed rage broke out. . . .

The foul-minded lot! The devil himself could not have given a leer at anything that had ever passed between Paul Oleron and Elsie Bengough, yet this nosing rascal must be prying and talking! . . .

Oleron crumpled the paper up, held it, in, the candle flame, and then ground the ashes under his heel.

One useful purpose, however, the letter had served: it had created in Oleron a wrathful blaze that effectually banished pale shadows. Nevertheless, one other puzzling circumstance was to close the day. As he undressed, he chanced to glance at his bed. The coverlets bore an impress as if somebody had lain on them. Oleron could not remember that he himself had lain down during the day—off-hand, he would have said that certainly he had not; but after all he could not be positive. His indignation for Elsie, acting possibly with the residue of the brandy in him, excluded all other considerations; and he put out his candle, lay down, and passed immediately into a deep and dreamless sleep, which, in the absence of Mrs. Barrett's morning call, lasted almost once round the clock.

VIII

To the man who pays heed to that voice within him which warns him that twilight and danger are settling over his soul, terror is apt to appear an absolute thing, against which his heart must be safeguarded in a twink unless there is to take place an alteration in the whole range and scale of his nature. Mercifully, he has never far to look for safeguards. Of the immediate and small and common and momentary things of life, of usages and observances and modes and conventions, he builds up fortifications against the powers of darkness. He is even content that, not terror only, but joy also, should for working purposes be placed in the category of the absolute things; and the last treason he will commit will be that breaking down of terms and limits that strikes, not at one man, but at the welfare of the souls of all.

In his own person, Oleron began to commit this treason. He began to commit it by admitting the inexplicable and horrible to an increasing familiarity. He did it insensibly, unconsciously, by a neglect of the things that he now regarded it as an impertinence in Elsie Bengough to have prescribed. Two months before, the words "a haunted house," applied to his lovely bemusing dwelling, would have chilled his marrow; now, his scale of sensation becoming depressed, he could ask "Haunted by what?" and remain unconscious that horror, when it can be proved to be relative, by so much loses its proper quality. He was setting aside the landmarks. Mists and confusion had begun to enwrap him.

And he was conscious of nothing so much as of a voracious inquisitiveness. He wanted *to know*. He was resolved to know. Nothing but the knowledge would satisfy him; and craftily he cast about for means whereby he might attain it.

He might have spared his craft. The matter was the easiest imaginable. As in time past he had known, in his writing, moments when his thoughts had seemed to rise of themselves and to embody themselves in words not to be altered afterwards, so now the question he put himself seemed to be answered even in the moment of their asking. There was exhilaration in the swift, easy processes. He had known no such joy in his own power since the days when his writing had been a daily freshness and a delight to him. It was almost as if the course he must pursue was being dictated to him.

And the first thing he must do, of course, was to define the problem. He defined it in terms of mathematics. Granted that he had not the place to himself; granted that the old house had inexpressibly caught and engaged his spirit; granted that, by virtue of the common denominator of the place, this unknown co-tenant stood in some relation to himself: what next? Clearly, the nature of the other numerator must be ascertained.

And how? Ordinarily this would not have seemed simple, but to Oleron it was now pellucidly clear. The key, *of course*, lay in his half-written novel—or rather, in both *Romilly*s, the old and the proposed new one.

A little while before Oleron would have thought himself mad to have embraced such an opinion; now he accepted the dizzying hypothesis without a quiver.

He began to examine the first and second *Romillys*.

From the moment of his doing so the thing advanced by leaps and bounds. Swiftly he reviewed the history of the *Romilly* of the fifteen chapters. He remembered clearly now that he had found her insufficient on the very first morning on which he had sat down to work in his new place. Other instances of his aversion leaped up to confirm his obscure investigation. There had come the night when he had hardly forborne to throw the whole thing into the fire; and the next morning he had begun the planning of the new *Romilly*. It had been on that morning that Mrs. Barrett, overhearing him humming a brief phrase that the dripping of a tap the night before had suggested, had informed him that he was singing some air he had never in his life heard before, called "The Beckoning Fair One." . . .

The Beckoning Fair One! . . .

With scarcely a pause in thought he, continued:

The first *Romilly* having been definitely thrown over, the second had instantly fastened herself upon him, clamoring for birth in his brain. He even fancied now, looking back, that there had been something like passion, hate almost, in the supplanting, and that more than once a stray thought given to his discarded creation had—(it was astonishing how credible Oleron found the almost unthinkable idea)—had offended the supplanter.

Yet that a malignancy almost homicidal should be extended to his fiction's poor mortal prototype. . . .

In spite of his inuring to a scale in which the horrible was now a thing to be fingered and turned this way and that, a "Good God!" broke from Oleron.

This intrusion of the first *Romilly*'s prototype into his thought again was a factor that for the moment brought his inquiry into the nature of his problem to a termination; the mere thought of Elsie was fatal to anything abstract. For another thing, he could not yet think of that letter of Barrett's, nor of a little scene that had followed it, without a mounting of colour and a quick contraction of the brow. For, wisely or not, he had had that argument out at once. Striding across the square on the following morning, he had bearded Barrett on his own doorstep. Coming back again a few minutes later, he had been strongly of opinion that he had only made matters worse. The man had been vagueness itself. He had not been able to be either challenged or browbeaten into anything more definite than a muttered farrago in which the words "Certain things . . . Mrs. Barrett . . . respectable house . . . if the cap fits . . . proceedings that shall be nameless," had been constantly repeated.

"Not that I make any charge—" he had concluded.

"Charge!" Oleron had cried.

"I 'ave my idears of things, as I don't doubt you 'ave yours—"

"Ideas—mine!" Oleron had cried wrathfully, immediately dropping his voice as heads had appeared at windows of the square. "Look you here, my man; you've an unwholesome mind, which probably you can't help, but a tongue which you can help, and shall! If there is a breath of this repeated . . ."

"I'll not be talked to on my own doorstep like this by anybody. . . ." Barrett had blustered. . . .

"You shall, and I'm doing it . . ."

"Don't you forget there's a Gawd above all, Who 'as said . . ."

"You're a low scandalmonger! . . ."

And so forth, continuing badly what was already badly begun. Oleron had returned wrathfully to his own house, and thenceforward, looking out of his windows, had seen Barrett's face at odd times, lifting blinds or peering round curtains, as if he sought to put himself in possession of Heaven knew what evidence, in case it should be required of him.

The unfortunate occurrence made certain minor differences in Oleron's domestic arrangements. Barrett's tongue, he gathered, had already been busy; he was looked at askance by the dwellers of the square; and he judged it better, until he should be able to obtain other help, to make his purchases of provisions a little farther afield rather than at the small shops of the immediate neighbourhood. For the rest, housekeeping was no new thing to him, and he would resume his old bachelor habits. . . .

Besides, he was deep in certain rather abstruse investigations, in which it was better that he should not be disturbed.

He was looking out of his window one midday rather tired, not very well, and glad that it was not very likely he would have to stir out of doors, when he saw Elsie Bengough crossing the square towards his house. The weather had broken; it was a raw and gusty day; and she had to force her way against the wind that set her ample skirts bellying about her opulent figure and her veil spinning and streaming behind her.

Oleron acted swiftly and instinctively. Seizing his hat, he sprang to the door and descended the stairs at a run. A sort of panic had seized him. She must be prevented from setting foot in the place. As he ran along the alley he was conscious that his eyes went up to the eaves as if something drew them. He did not know that a slate might not accidentally fall. . . .

He met her at the gate, and spoke with curious volubleness.

"This is really too bad, Elsie! Just as I'm urgently called away! I'm afraid it can't be helped though, and that you'll have to think me an inhospitable beast." He poured it out just as it came into his head.

She asked if he was going to town.

"Yes, yes—to town," he replied. "I've got to call on—on Chambers. You know Chambers, don't you? No, I remember you don't; a big man you once saw me with. . . . I ought to have gone yesterday, and—" this he felt to be a brilliant effort—"and he's going out of town this afternoon. To Brighton. I had a letter from him this morning."

He took her arm and led her up the square. She had to remind him that his way to town lay in the other direction.

"Of course—how stupid of me!" he said, with a little loud laugh. "I'm so used to going the other way with you—of course; it's the other way to the bus. Will you come along with me? I am so awfully sorry it's happened like this. . . ."

They took the street to the bus terminus.

This time Elsie bore no signs of having gone through interior struggles. If she detected anything unusual in his manner she made no comment, and he, seeing her calm, began to talk less recklessly through silences. By the time they reached the bus terminus, nobody, seeing the pallid-faced man without an overcoat and the large ample skirted girl at his side, would have supposed that one of them was ready to sink on his knees for thankfulness that he had, as he believed, saved the other from a wildly unthinkable danger.

They mounted to the top of the bus, Oleron protesting that he should not miss his overcoat, and that he found the day, if anything, rather oppressively hot. They sat down on a front seat.

Now that this meeting was forced upon him, he had something else to say that would make demands upon his tact. It had been on his mind for some time, and was, indeed, peculiarly difficult to put. He revolved it for some minutes, and then, remembering the success of his story of a sudden call to town, cut the knot of his difficulty with another lie.

"I'm thinking of going away for a little while, Elsie," he said.

She merely said, "Oh?"

"Somewhere for a change. I need a change. I think I shall go to-morrow, or the day after. Yes, to-morrow, I think."

"Yes," she replied.

"I don't quite know how long I shall be," he continued. "I shall have to let you know when I am back."

"Yes, let me know," she replied in an even tone.

The tone was, for her, suspiciously even. He was a little uneasy.

"You don't ask me where I'm going," he said, with a little cumbrous effort to rally her.

She was looking straight before her, past the bus-driver.

"I know," she said.

He was startled. "How, you know?"

"You're not going anywhere," she replied.

He found not a word to say. It was a minute or so before she continued, in the same controlled voice she had employed from the start.

"You're not going anywhere. You weren't going out this morning. You only came out because I appeared; don't behave as if we were strangers, Paul."

A flush of pink had mounted to his cheeks. He noticed that the wind had given her the pink of early rhubarb. Still he found nothing to say.

"Of course, you ought to go away," she continued. "I don't know whether you look at yourself often in the glass, but you're rather noticeable. Several people have turned to look at you this morning. So, of course, you ought to go away. But you won't, and I know why."

He shivered, coughed a little, and then broke silence.

"Then if you know, there's no use in continuing this discussion," he said curtly.

"Not for me, perhaps, but there is for you," she replied. "Shall I tell you what I know?"

"No," he said in a voice slightly raised.

"No?" she asked, her round eyes earnestly on him.

"No." Again he was getting out of patience with her; again he was conscious of the strain. Her devotion and fidelity and love plagued him; she was only humiliating both herself and him. It would have been bad enough had he ever, by word or deed, given her cause for thus fastening herself on him . . . but . . . there; that was the worst of that kind of life for a woman. Women such as she, businesswomen, in and out of offices all the time, always, whether they realised it or not, made comradeship a cover for something else. They accepted the unconventional status, came and went freely, as men did, were honestly taken by men at their own valuation—and then it turned out to be the other thing after all, and they went and fell in love. No wonder there was gossip in shops and squares and public houses! In a sense the gossipers were in the right of it. Independent, yet not efficient; with some of womanhood's graces forgone, and yet with all the woman's hunger and need; half sophisticated, yet not wise; Oleron was tired of it all. . . .

And it was time he told her so.

"I suppose," he said tremblingly, looking down between his knees, "I suppose the real trouble is in the life women who earn their own living are obliged to lead."

He could not tell in what sense she took the lame generality; she merely replied, "I suppose so."

"It can't be helped," he continued, "but you do sacrifice a good deal."

She agreed: a good deal; and then she added after a moment, "What, for instance?"

"You may or may not be gradually attaining a new status, but you're in a false position to-day."

It was very likely, she said; she hadn't thought of it much in that light—

"And," he continued desperately, "you're bound to suffer. Your most innocent acts are misunderstood; motives you never dreamed of are attributed to you; and in the end it comes to"—he hesitated a moment and then took the plunge,—"to the sidelong look and the leer."

She took his meaning with perfect ease. She merely shivered a little as she pronounced the name.

"Barrett?"

His silence told her the rest.

Anything further that was to be said must come from her. It came as the bus stopped at a stage and fresh passengers mounted the stairs.

"You'd better get down here and go back, Paul," she said. "I understand perfectly—perfectly. It isn't Barrett. You'd be able to deal with Barrett. It's merely convenient for you to say it's Barrett. I know what it is . . . but you said I wasn't to tell you that. Very well. But before you go let me tell you why I came up this morning."

In a dull tone he asked her why. Again she looked straight before her as she replied:

"I came to force your hand. Things couldn't go on as they have been going, you know; and now that's all over."

"All over," he repeated stupidly.

"All over. I want you now to consider yourself, as far as I'm concerned, perfectly free. I make only one reservation."

He hardly had the spirit to ask her what that was.

"If *I* merely need *you*," she said, "please don't give that a thought; that's nothing; I shan't come near for that. But," she dropped her voice, "if *you're* in need of *me,* Paul—I shall know if you are, *and you will be*—then I shall come at no matter what cost. You understand that?"

He could only groan.

"So that's understood," she concluded. "And I think all. Now go back. I should advise you to walk back, for you're shivering—good-bye—"

She gave him a cold hand, and he descended. He turned on the edge of the kerb as the bus started again. For the first time in all the years he had known her she parted from him with no smile and no wave of her long arm.

IX

He stood on the kerb plunged in misery, looking after her as long as she remained in sight; but almost instantly with her disappearance he felt the heaviness lift a little from his spirit. She had given him his liberty; true, there was a sense in which he had never parted with it, but now was no time for splitting hairs; he was free to act, and all was clear

ahead. Swiftly the sense of lightness grew on him: it
became a positive rejoicing in his liberty; and before
he was half-way home he had decided what must be
done next.

The vicar of the parish in which his dwelling was
situated lived within ten minutes of the square. To
his house Oleron turned his steps. It was necessary
that he should have all the information he could
get about this old house with the insurance marks
and the sloping "To Let" boards, and the vicar was
the person most likely to be able to furnish it. This
last preliminary out of the way, and—aha! Oleron
chuckled—things might be expected to happen!

But he gained less information than he had
hoped for. The house, the vicar said, was old—
but there needed no vicar to tell Oleron that; it
was reputed (Oleron pricked up his ears) to be
haunted—but there were few old houses about
which some such rumour did not circulate among
ignorant; and the deplorable lack of Faith of the
modern world, the vicar thought, did not tend to
dissipate these superstitions. For the rest, his manner was the soothing manner of one who prefers
not to make statements without knowing how they
will be taken by his hearer. Oleron smiled as he
perceived this.

"You may leave my nerves out of the question,"
he said. "How long has the place been empty?"

"A dozen years, I should say," the vicar replied.

"And the last tenant—did you know him—or her?" Oleron was conscious of a tingling of his nerves as he offered the vicar the alternative of sex.

"Him," said the vicar. "A man. If I remember rightly, his name was Madley an artist. He was a great recluse; seldom went out of place, and"—the vicar hesitated and then broke into a little gush of candour—"and since you appear to have come for this information, and since it is better that the truth should be told than that garbled versions should get about, I don't mind saying that this man Madley died there, under somewhat unusual circumstances. It was ascertained at the post-mortem that there was not a particle of food in his stomach, although he was found to be not without money. And his frame was simply worn out. Suicide was spoken of, but you'll agree with me that deliberate starvation is, to say the least, an uncommon form of suicide. An open verdict was returned."

"Ah!" said Oleron. . . . "Does there happen to be any comprehensive history of this parish?"

"No; partial ones only. I myself am not guiltless of having made a number of notes on its purely ecclesiastical history, its registers and so forth, which I shall be happy to show you if you would care to see them; but it is a large parish, I have only one curate, and my leisure, as you will readily understand. . . ."

The extent of the parish and the scantiness of the vicar's leisure occupied the remainder of the interview, and Oleron thanked the vicar, took his leave, and walked slowly home.

He walked slowly for a reason, twice turning away from the house within a stone's-throw of the gate and taking another turn of twenty minutes or so. He had a very ticklish piece of work now before him; it required the greatest mental concentration; it was nothing less than to bring his mind, if he might, into such a state of unpreoccupation and receptivity that he should see the place as he had seen it on that morning when, his removal accomplished, he had sat down to begin the sixteenth chapter of the first *Romilly*.

For, could he recapture that first impression, he now hoped for far more from it. Formerly, he had carried no end of mental lumber. Before the influence of the place had been able to find him out at all, it had had the inertia of those dreary chapters to overcome. No results had shown. The process had been one of slow saturation, charging, filling up to a brim. But now he was light, unburdened, rid at last both of that *Romilly* and of her prototype. Now for the new unknown, coy, jealous, bewitching, Beckoning Fair! . . .

At half-past two of the afternoon he put his key into the Yale lock, entered, and closed the door behind him. . . .

His fantastic attempt was instantly and astonishingly successful. He could have shouted with triumph as he entered the room; it was as if he had *escaped* into it. Once more, as in the days when his writing had had a daily freshness and wonder and promise for him, he was conscious of that new ease and mastery and exhilaration and release. The air of the place seemed to hold more oxygen; as if his own specific gravity had changed, his very tread seemed less ponderable. The flowers in the bowls, the fair proportions of the meadowsweet-coloured panels and mouldings, the polished floor, and the lofty and faintly tarred ceiling, fairly laughed their welcome. Oleron actually laughed back, and spoke aloud.

"Oh, you're pretty, pretty!" he flattered it.

Then he lay down on his couch.

He spent that afternoon as a convalescent who expected a dear visitor might have spent it—in a delicious vacancy, smiling now and then as if in sleep, and ever lifting drowsy and contented eyes to his alluring surroundings. He lay thus until darkness came, and with darkness, the nocturnal noises of the old house. . . .

But if he waited for any specific happening, he waited in vain.

He waited similarly in vain on the morrow, maintaining, though with less ease, that sensitized-plate-like condition of his mind. Nothing occurred to give it an impression. Whatever it was which he so patiently wooed, it seemed to be both shy and exacting. . . .

And then on the third day he thought he understood. A look of gentle drollery and cunning came into his eyes, and he chuckled.

"Oho, oho! . . . Well, if the wind sits in *that* quarter we must see what else there is to be done. What is there, now? . . . No, I won't send for Elsie; we don't need a wheel to break the butterfly on; we won't go to those lengths, my butterfly. . . ."

He was standing musing, thumbing his lean jaw, looking aslant; suddenly he crossed to his hall, took down his hat, and went out.

"My lady is coquettish, is she? Well, we'll see what a little neglect will do," he chuckled as he went down the stairs."

He sought a railway station, got into a train, and spent the rest of the day in the country. Oh, yes: Oleron thought *he* was the one to deal with Fair Ones who beckoned, and invited, and then took refuge in shyness and hanging back!

He did not return until after eleven that night.

"*Now*, my Fair Beckoner!" he murmured as he walked along the alley and felt in his pocket for his keys. . . .

Inside his flat, he was perfectly composed, perfectly deliberate, exceedingly careful not to give himself away. As if to intimate that he intended to retire immediately, he lighted only a single candle;

and as he set out with it on his nightly round he affected to yawn. He went first into his kitchen. There was a full moon, and a lozenge of moonlight, almost peacock-blue by contrast with his candle-frame, lay on the floor. The window was uncurtained, and he could see the reflection of the candle, and, faintly, that of his own face, as he moved about. The door of the powder-closet stood a little ajar, and he closed it before sitting down to remove his boots on the chair with the cushion made of the folded harp-bag. From the kitchen he passed to the bathroom. There, another slant of blue moonlight cut the windowsill and lay across the pipes on the wall. He visited his seldom-used study, and stood for a moment gazing at the silvered roofs across the square. Then, walking straight through his sitting-room, his stockinged feet making no noise, he entered the bedroom and put the candle on the chest of drawers. His face all this time wore no expression save that of tiredness. He had never been wilier nor more alert.

His small bedroom fireplace was opposite the chest of drawers on which the mirror stood, and his bed and the window occupied the remaining sides of the room. Oleron drew down his blind, took off his coat, he then stooped to get his slippers from under the bed.

He could have given no reason for the conviction, but that the manifestation that for two days had been withheld was close at hand he never for an instant doubted. Nor, though he could not form the faintest guess of the shape it might take, did he experience fear. Startling or surprising it might be; he was prepared for that; but that was all; his scale of sensation had become depressed. His hand moved this way and that under the bed in search of his slippers. . . .

But for all his caution and method and preparedness, his heart all at once gave a leap and a pause that was almost horrid. His hand had found the slippers, but he was still on his knees; save for the circumstance he would have fallen. The bed was a low one; the groping for the slippers accounted for the turn of his head to one side; and he was careful to keep the attitude until he had partly recovered his self-possession. When presently he rose there was a drop of blood on his lower lip where he had caught at it with his teeth, and his watch had jerked out of the pocket of his waistcoat and was dangling at the end of its short leather guard. . . .

Then, before the watch had ceased its little oscillation, he was himself again.

In the middle of the mantelpiece there stood a picture, a portrait of his grandmother; he placed himself before this picture, so that he could see in the glass of it the steady flame of the candle that burned behind him on the chest of drawers. He could see also in the picture-glass the little glancings of light from the bevels and facets of the objects about the mirror and candle. But he could see more. These twinklings and reflections and re-reflections did not change their position; but there was one gleam that had motion. It was fainter than the rest, and it moved up and down through the air. It was the reflection of the candle on Oleron's black vulcanite comb, and each of its downward movements was accompanied by a silky and crackling rustle.

Oleron, watching what went on in the glass of his grandmother's portrait, continued to play his part. He felt for his dangling watch and began slowly to wind it up. Then, for a moment ceasing to watch, he began to empty his trousers pockets and to place methodically in a little row on the mantelpiece the pennies and halfpennies he took from them. The sweeping, minutely electric noise filled the whole bedroom, and had Oleron altered his point of observation he could have brought the dim gleam of the moving comb so into position that it would almost have outlined his grandmother's head.

Any other head of which it might have been following the outline was invisible.

Oleron finished the emptying of his pockets; then, under cover of another simulated yawn, not so much summoning his resolution as overmastered by an exorbitant curiosity, he swung suddenly round. That which was being combed was still not to be seen, but the comb did not stop. It had altered its angle a little, and had moved a little to the left. It was passing, in fairly regular sweeps, from a point rather more than five feet from the ground, in a direction roughly vertical, to another point a few inches below the level of the chest of drawers.

Oleron continued to act to admiration. He walked to his little washstand in the corner, poured out water, and began to wash his hands. He removed his waistcoat, and continued the preparations for bed. The combing did not cease, and he stood for a moment in thought. Again his eyes twinkled. The next was very cunning—

"Hm! . . . *I think I'll read for a quarter of an hour*," he said aloud. . . .

He passed out of the room.

He was away a couple of minutes; when he returned again the room was suddenly quiet. He glanced at the chest of drawers; the comb lay still, between the collar he had removed and a pair of gloves. Without hesitation Oleron put out his hand and picked it up. It was an ordinary eighteen-penny comb, taken from a card in a chemist's shop, of a substance of a definite specific gravity, and no more capable of rebellion against the Laws by which it existed than are the worlds that keep their orbits through the void. Oleron put it down again; then he glanced at the bundle of papers he held in his hand. What he had gone to fetch had been the fifteen chapters of the original *Romilly*.

"Hm!" he muttered as he threw the manuscript into a chair. . . . "As I thought. . . . She's just blindly, ragingly, murderously jealous."

On the night after that, and on the following night, and for many nights and days, so many that he began to be uncertain about the count of them, Oleron, courting, cajoling, neglecting, threatening, beseeching, eaten out with unappeased curiosity and regardless that his life was becoming one consuming passion and desire, continued his search for the unknown co-numerator of his abode.

X

As time went on, it came to pass that few except the postman mounted Oleron's stairs; and since men who do not write letters receive few, even the postman's tread became so infrequent that it was not heard more than once or twice a week. There came a letter from Oleron's publishers, asking when they might expect to receive the manuscript of his new book; he delayed for some days to answer it, and finally forgot it. A second letter came, which he also failed to answer. He received no third.

The weather grew bright and warm. The privet bushes among the chopper-like notice-boards flowered, and in the streets where Oleron did his shopping the baskets of flower-women lined the kerbs. Oleron purchased flowers daily; his room clamoured

for flowers, fresh and continually renewed; and
Oleron did not stint its demands. Nevertheless, the
necessity for going out to buy them began to irk
him more and more, and it was with a greater and
ever greater sense of relief that he returned home
again. He began to be conscious that again his scale
of sensation had suffered a subtle change—a change
that was not restoration to its former capacity, but
an extension and enlarging that once more included terror. It admitted it in an entirely new form.
Lux orco, tenebræ Jovi. The name of this terror was
agoraphobia. Oleron had begun to dread air and
space and the horror that might pounce upon the
unguarded back.

Presently he so contrived it that his food and
flowers were delivered daily at his door. He rubbed
his hands when he had hit upon this expedient. That
was better! Now he could please himself whether he
went out or not. . . .

Quickly he was confirmed in his choice. It became his pleasure to remain immured.

But he was not happy—or, if he was, his happiness took an extraordinary turn. he fretted discon-
tentedly, could sometimes have wept for mere weakness and misery; and yet he was dimly conscious
that he would not have exchanged his sadness for
all the noisy mirth of the world outside. And speaking of noise: noise, much noise, now caused him
the acutest discomfort. It was hardly more to be

endured than that new-born fear that kept him, on the increasingly rare occasions when he did go out, sidling close to walls and feeling friendly rails with his hand. He moved from room to room softly and in slippers, and sometimes stood for any seconds closing a door so gently that not a sound broke the stillness that was in itself a delight. Sunday now became an intolerable day to him, for, since the coming of the fine weather, there had begun to assemble in the square under his windows each Sunday morning certain members of the sect to which the long-nosed Barrett adhered. These came with a great drum and large brass-bellied instruments; men and women uplifted anguished voices, struggling with their God; and Barrett himself, with upraised face and closed eyes and working brows, prayed that the sound of his voice might penetrate the ears of all unbelievers—as it certainly did Oleron's. One day, in the middle of one of these rhapsodies, Oleron sprang to his blind and pulled it down, and heard as he did so, his own name made the object of a fresh torrent of outpouring.

And sometimes, but not as expecting a reply, Oleron stood still and called softly. Once or twice he called "Romilly!" and then waited; but more often his whispering did not take the shape of a name.

There was one spot in particular of his abode that he began to haunt with increasing persistency. This was just within the opening of his bedroom door.

He had discovered one day that by opening every door in his place (always excepting the outer one, which he only opened unwillingly) and by placing himself on this particular spot, he could actually see to a greater or less extent into each of his five rooms without changing his position. He could see the whole of his sitting-room, all of his bedroom except the part hidden by the open door, and glimpses of his kitchen, bathroom, and of his rarely used study. He was often in this place, breathless and with his finger on his lip. One day, as he stood there, he suddenly found himself wondering whether this Madley, of whom the vicar had spoken, had ever discovered the strategic importance of the bedroom entry.

Light, moreover, now caused him greater disquietude than did darkness. Direct sunlight, of which, as the sun passed daily round the house, each of his rooms had now its share, was like a flame in his brain; and even diffused light was a dull and numbing ache. He began, at successive hours of the day, one after another, to lower his crimson blinds. He made short and daring excursions in order to do this but he was ever careful to leave his retreat open, in case he should have sudden need of it. Presently this lowering of the blinds had become a daily methodical exercise, and his rooms, when he had been his round, had the blood-red half-light of a photographer's dark-room.

One day, as he drew down the blind of his little study and backed in good order out of the room again, he broke into a soft laugh.

"*That* bilks Mr. Barrett!" he said; and the baffling of Barrett continued to afford him mirth for an hour.

But on another day, soon after, he had a fright that left him trembling also for an hour. He had seized the cord to darken the window over the seat in which he had found the harp-bag, and was standing with his back well protected in the embrasure, when he thought he saw the tail of a black-and-white check skirt disappear round the corner of the house. He could not be sure—had he run to the window of the other wall, which was blinded, the skirt must have been already past—but he was *almost* sure that it was Elsie. He listened in an agony of suspense for her tread on the stairs. . . .

"By Jove, but that would have compromised me horribly!" he muttered. . . .

And he continued to mutter from time to time, "Horribly compromising . . . *no* woman would stand that . . . not *any* kind of woman . . . oh, compromising in the extreme!"

Yet he was not happy. He could not have assigned the cause of the fits of quiet weeping which took him sometimes; they came and went, like the fitful illumination of the clouds that travelled over the square; and perhaps, after all, if he was not happy, he was not unhappy. Before he could be unhappy something must have been withdrawn, and nothing had been granted. He was waiting for that granting, in that flower-laden, frightfully enticing apartment of his, with the pith-white walls tinged and subdued by the crimson blinds to a blood-like gloom.

He paid no heed to it that his stock of money was running perilously low, nor that he had ceased to work. Ceased to work? He had not ceased to work. They knew very little about it who supposed that Oleron had ceased to work! He was in truth only now beginning to work. He was preparing such a work . . . such a work . . . such a Mistress was a-making in the gestation of his Art . . . let him but get this period of probation and poignant waiting over and men should see. . . . How *should* men know her, this Fair One of Oleron's, until Oleron himself knew her? Lovely radiant creations are not thrown off like How-d'ye-do's. The men to whom it is committed to father them must weep wretched tears, as Oleron did, must swell with vain presumptions hopes, as Oleron did, must pursue, as Oleron pursued, the capricious, fair, mocking, slippery, eager Spirit that, ever eluding, ever sees to it that the chase does not slacken. Let Oleron but hunt this Huntress a little longer . . . he would have her sparkling and panting in his arms yet. . . . Oh no; they were very far from the truth who supposed that Oleron had ceased to work!

And if all else was falling away from Oleron, gladly he was letting it go. So do we all when out Fair Ones beckon. Quite at the beginning we wink, and promise ourselves that we will put Her Ladyship through her paces, neglect her for a day, turn her own jealous wiles against her, flout and ignore her when she comes home wheedling; perhaps there lurks within us all the time a heartless sprite who is never fooled; but in the end all falls away. She beckons, beckons, and all goes. . . .

And so Oleron kept his strategic post within the frame of his bedroom door, and watched, and waited, and smiled, with his finger on his lips. . . . It was his duteous service, his worship, his troth-plighting, all that he had ever known of Love. And when he found himself, as he now and then did, hating the dead man Madley, and wishing that he had never lived, he felt that that, too, was an acceptable service. . . .

But, as he thus prepared himself, as it were, for a Marriage, and moped and chafed more and more that the Bride made no sign, he made a discovery that he ought to have made weeks before.

It was through a thought of the dead Madley that he made it. Since that night when he had thought in his greenness that a little studied neglect would bring the lovely Beckoner to her knees, and had made use of her own jealousy to banish her, he had not set eyes on those fifteen discarded chapters of *Romilly*.

He had thrown them back into the window-seat, forgotten their very existence. But his own jealousy of Madley put him in mind of hers of her jilted rival of flesh and blood, and he remembered them. . . . Fool that he had been! Had he, then, expected his Desire to manifest herself while there still existed the evidence of his divide allegiance? What, and she with a passion so fierce and centered that it had not hesitated at the destruction, twice attempted, of her rival? Fool that he had been! . . .

But if *that* was all the pledge and sacrifice she required she should have it—ah, yes, and quickly!

He took the manuscript from the window-seat, and brought it to the fire.

He kept the fire always burning now the warmth brought out the last vestige of odour of the flowers with which his room was banked. He did not know what time it was; long since he had allowed his clock to run down—it had seemed a foolish measure of time in regard to the stupendous things that were happening to Oleron; but he knew it was late. He took the *Romilly* manuscript and knelt before the fire.

But he had not finished removing the fastening that held the sheets together before he suddenly gave a start, turned his head over his shoulder, and listened intently. The sound he had heard had not been loud—it had been, indeed, no more than a tap, twice or thrice repeated—but it had filled Oleron with alarm. His face grew dark as it came again.

He heard a voice outside on the landing.

"Paul! . . . Paul! . . ."

It was Elsie's voice.

"Paul! . . . I know you're in . . . I want to see you. . . ."

He cursed her under his breath, but kept perfectly still. He did not intend to admit her.

"Paul! . . . You're in trouble. . . . I believe you're in danger . . . at least come to the door! . . ."

Oleron smothered a low laugh. It somehow amused him that she, in such danger herself, should talk to him of *his* danger! . . . Well, if she was, serve her right; she knew, or said she knew, all about it. . . .

"Paul! . . . Paul! . . ."

"*Paul! . . . Paul! . . .*" He mimicked her under his breath.

"Oh, Paul, it's *horrible!*" . . ."

Horrible, was it? thought Oleron. Then let her get away. . . .

"I only want to help you, Paul. . . . I didn't promise not to come if you needed me. . . ."

He was impervious to the pitiful sob that interrupted the low cry. The devil take the woman! Should he shout to her to go away and not come back? No: let her call and knock and sob. She had a gift for sobbing; she mustn't think her sobs would move him. They irritated him, so that he set his teeth and shook his fist at her, but that was all. Let her sob.

"*Paul!* . . . *Paul!* . . ."

With his teeth hard set, he dropped the first page of *Romilly* into the fire. Then he began to drop the rest in, sheet by sheet.

For many minutes the calling behind his door continued; then suddenly it ceased. He heard the sound of feet slowly descending the stairs. He listened for the noise of a fall or a cry or the crash of a piece of the handrail of the upper landing; but none of these things came. She was spared. Apparently her rival suffered her to crawl abject and beaten away. Oleron heard the passing of her steps under his window; then she was gone.

He dropped the last page into the fire, and then, with a low laugh rose. He looked fondly round his room.

"Lucky to get away like that," he remarked. "She wouldn't have got away if I'd given her as much as a word or a look! What devils these women are! . . . But no; I oughtn't to say that; one of 'em showed forbearance. . . ."

Who showed forbearance? And what was forborne? Ah, Oleron knew! . . . Contempt, no doubt, had been at the bottom of it, but that didn't matter: the pestering creature had been allowed to go unharmed. Yes, she was lucky; Oleron hoped she knew it. . . .

And now, now, now for his reward!

Oleron crossed the room. All his door were open; his eyes shone as he placed himself within that of his bedroom.

Fool that he had been, not to think of destroying the manuscript sooner! . . .

How, in a houseful of shadows, should he know his own Shadow? How, in a houseful of noises, distinguish the summons he felt to be at hand? Ah, trust him! He would know! The place was full of a jugglery of dim lights. The blind at his elbow that allowed the light of a street lamp to struggle vaguely through—the glimpse of greeny blue moonlight seen through the distant kitchen door—the sulky glow of the fire under the black ashes of the burnt manuscript—the glimmering of the tulips and the moon-daisies and narcissi in the bowls and jugs and jars—these did not so trick and bewilder his eyes that he would not know his Own! It was he, not she, who had been delaying the shadowy Bridal; he hung his head for a moment in mute acknowledgment; then he bent his eyes on the deceiving, puzzling gloom again. He would have called her name had he known it—but now he would not ask her to share even a name with the other. . . .

His own face, within the frame of the door, glimmered white as the narcissi in the darkness. . . .

A shadow, light as fleece, seemed to take shape in the kitchen (the time had been when Oleron would have said that a cloud had passed over the unseen

moon). The low illumination on the blind at his
elbow grew dimmer (the time had been when Oleron
would have concluded that the lamplighter going
his rounds had turned low the flame of the lamp).
The fire settled, letting down the black and charred
papers; a flower fell from a bowl, and lay indistinct
upon the floor; all was still; and then a stray draught
moved through the old house, passing before Oleron's face. . . .

Suddenly, inclining his head, he withdrew a little
from the door-jamb. The wandering draught caused
the door to move a little on its hinges. Oleron trembled violently, stood for a moment longer, and then,
putting his hand out to the knob, softly drew the
door to, sat down on the nearest chair, and waited,
as a man might await the calling of his name that
should summon him to some weighty, high and
privy Audience. . . .

XI

One knows not whether there can be human com-
passion for anæmia of the soul. When the pitch of
Life is dropped, and the spirit is so put over and
reversed that that only is horrible which before was
sweet and worldly and of the day, the human relation disappears. The sane soul turns appalled away,
lest not merely itself, but sanity should suffer. We
are not gods. We cannot drive out devils. We must

see selfishly to it that devils do not enter into ourselves.

And this we must do even though Love so trans-
fuse us that we may well deem our nature to be half
divine. We shall but speak of honour and duty in
vain. The letter dropped within the dark door will
lie unregarded, or, if regarded for a brief instant
between two unspeakable lapses, left and forgotten
again. The telegram will be undelivered, nor will
the whistling messenger (wiselier guided than he
knows to whistle) be conscious as he walks away of
the drawn blind that is pushed aside an inch by a
finger and then fearfully replaced again. No: let the
miserable wrestle with his own shadows; let him, if
indeed he be so mad, clip and strain and enfold and
couch the succubus; but let him do so in a house
into which not an air of Heaven penetrates, nor a
bright finger of the sun pierces the filthy twilight.
The lost must remain lost. Humanity has other business to attend to.

For the handwriting of the two letters that Oleron, stealing noiselessly one June day into his kitch-
en to rid his sitting-room of an armful of fetid and
decaying flowers, had seen on the floor within his
door, had had no more meaning for him than if it
had belonged to some dim and far-away dream. And
at the beating of the telegraph-boy upon the door,
within a few feet of the bed where he lay, he had

gnashed his teeth and stopped his ears. He had pictured the lad standing there, just beyond his partition, among packets of provisions and bundles of
dead and dying flowers. For his outer landing was
littered with these. Oleron had feared to open his
door to take them in. After a week, the errand lads
had reported that there must be some mistake about
the order, and had left no more. Inside, in the red
twilight, the old flowers turned brown and fell and
decayed where they lay.

Gradually his power was draining away. The
Abomination fastened on Oleron's power. The steady
sapping sometimes left him for many hours of prostration gazing vacantly up at his red-tinged ceiling,
idly suffering such fancies as came of themselves to
have their way with him. Even the strongest of his
memories had no more than a precarious hold upon
his attention. Sometimes a flitting half-memory, of
a novel to be written, a novel it was important that
he could write, tantalised him for a space before
vanishing again; and sometimes whole novels, perfect, splendid, established to endure, rose magically
before him. And sometimes the memories were absurdly remote and trivial, of garrets he had inhabited
and lodgings that had sheltered him, and so forth.
Oleron had known a great deal about such things in
his time, but all that was now past. He had at last
found a place which he did not intend to leave until
they fetched him out—a place that some might have

thought a little on the green-sick side, that others might have considered to be a little too redolent of long-dead and morbid things for a living man to be mewed up in, but ah, so irresistible, with such an authority of its own, with such an associate of its own, and a place of such delights when once a man has ceased to struggle against its inexorable will! A novel? Somebody ought to write a novel about a place like that! There must be lots to write about in a place like that if one could but get to the bottom of it! It had probably already been painted, by a man called Madley who had lived there. . . . but Oleron had not known this Madley—had a strong feeling that he wouldn't have liked him—would rather he had lived somewhere else—really couldn't stand the fellow—hated him, Madley, in fact. (Aha! That was a joke!) He seriously doubted whether the man had led the life he ought; Oleron was in two minds sometimes whether he wouldn't tell that long-nosed guardian of the public morals across the way about him; but probably he knew, and had made his praying hullabaloos for him also. That was his line. Why, Oleron himself had had a dust-up with him about something or other . . . some girl of other . . . Elsie Bengough her name was, he remembered. . . .

Oleron had moments of deep uneasiness about this Elsie Bengough. Or rather, he was not so much uneasy about her as restless about the things she did. Chef of those was the way in which she persisted in thrusting herself into his thoughts; and, whenever he was quick enough, he sent her packing the moment she made her appearance there. The truth was that she was not merely a bore; she had always been that; it had now come to the pitch when her very presence in his fancy was inimical to the full enjoyment of certain experiences. . . . She had no tact; really ought to have known that people are not at home to the thoughts of everybody all the time; ought in mere politeness to have allowed him certain seasons quite to himself; and was monstrously ignorant of things if she did not know, as she appeared not to know, that there were certain special hours when a man's veins ran with fire and daring and power, in which . . . well, in which he had a reasonable right to treat folk as he had treated that prying Barrett—to shut them out completely. . . . But no: up she popped, the thought of her, and ruined all. Bright towering fabrics, by the side of which even those perfect, magical novels of which he dreamed were dun and grey, vanished utterly at her intrusion. It was as if at the threshold of some golden portal prepared for Oleron a pit should suddenly gape, as if a bat-like shadow should turn the growing dawn to mirk and darkness again. . . . Therefore, Oleron strove to stifle even the nascent thought of her.

Nevertheless, there came an occasion on which this woman Bengough absolutely refused to be suppressed. Oleron could not have told exactly when this happened; he only knew by the glimmer of the street lamp on his blind that it was some time during the night, and that for some time she had not presented herself.

He had no warning, none, of her coming; she had just come—was there. Strive as he would, he could not shake off the thought of her nor the image of her face. She haunted him.

But for her to come at *that* moment of all moments! . . . Really, it was past belief! How *she* could endure it, Oleron could not conceive! Actually, to look on, as it were, at the triumph of a Rival. . . . Good God! It was monstrous! tact—reticence—he had never credited her with an overwhelming amount of either; but he had never attributed mere—oh, there was no word for it! Monstrous—monstrous! Did she intend thenceforward. . . . Good God! To look on! . . .

Oleron felt the blood rush up to the roots of his hair with anger against her.

"Damnation take her!" he choked. . . .

But the next moment his heat and resentment had changed to a cold sweat of cowering fear. Panic-stricken, he strove to comprehend what he had done. For though he knew not what, he knew he had done something, something fatal, irreparable, blasting. Anger he had felt, but not *this* blaze of ire that suddenly flooded the twilight of his consciousness with a white infernal light. *That* appalling flash was

not his—not his *that* open rift of bright and searing
Hell—not his, not his! His had been the hand of
a child, preparing a puny blow; but what was *this
other* horrific hand that was drawn back to strike in
the same place? Had *he* set that in motion? Had *he*
provided the spark that had touched off the whole
accumulated power of that formidable and relent-
less place? He did not know. He only knew that
that poor igniting particle in himself was blown
out, that— Oh, impossible!—a clinging kiss (how
else to express it?) had changed on his very lips to
a gnashing and a removal, and that for very pity
of the awful odds he must cry out to her against
whom he had lately raged to guard herself . . .
guard herself. . . .

"*Look out!*" he shrieked aloud. . . .

The revulsion was instant. As if a cold slow bil-
low had broken over him, he came to to find that he
was lying in his bed, that the mist and horror that
had for so long enwrapped him had departed, that
he was Paul Oleron, and that he was sick, naked,
helpless, and unutterably abandoned and alone. His
faculties, though weak, answered at last to his calls
upon them; and he knew that it must have been a
hideous nightmare that had left him sweating and
shaking thus.

Yes, he was himself, Paul Oleron, tired novel-
ist, already past the summit of his best work, and

slipping downhill again empty-handed from it all. He had struck short in his life's aim. He had tried too much, had over-estimated his strength, and was a failure, a failure. . . .

It all came to him in the single word, enwrapped and complete; it needed no sequential thought; he was a failure. He had missed. . . .

And he had missed not one happiness, but two. He had missed the ease of this world, which men love, and he had missed also that other shining prize for which men forgo ease, the snatching and holding and triumphant bearing up aloft of which is the only justification of the mad adventurer who hazards the enterprise. And there was no second attempt. Fate has no morrow. Oleron's morrow must be to sit down to a profitless, ill-done, unrequited work again, and so on the morrow after that, and the morrow after that, and as many morrows as there might be. . . .

He lay there, weakly yet sanely considering it. . . .

And since the whole attempt had failed, it was hardly worth while to consider whether a little might not be saved from the general wreck. No good would ever come of that half-finished novel. He had intended that it should appear in the autumn; was under contract that it should appear; no matter; it was better to pay forfeit to his publishers than to waste what days were left. He was spent; age was not far off; and paths of wisdom and sadness were the properest for the remainder of the journey. . . .

If only he had chosen the wife, the child, the faithful friend at the fireside, and let them follow an *ignis fatuus* that list! . . .

In the meantime it began to puzzle him exceedingly why he should be so weak, that his room should smell so overpoweringly of decaying vegetable matter, and that his hand, chancing to stray to his face in the darkness, should encounter a beard.

"Most extraordinary!" he began to mutter to himself. "Have I been ill? Am I ill now? And if so, why have they left me alone? . . . Extraordinary! . . ."

He thought he heard a sound from the kitchen or bathroom. He rose a little on his pillow, and listened. . . . Ah! He was not alone, then! It certainly would have been extraordinary if they had left him ill and alone— Alone? Oh no. He would be looked after. He wouldn't be left, ill, to shift for himself. If everybody else had forsaken him, he could trust Elsie Bengough, the dearest chum he had, for that . . . bless her faithful heart!

But suddenly a short, stifled, spluttering cry rang sharply out:

"Paul!"

It came from the kitchen.

And in the same moment it flashed upon Oleron, he knew not how, that two, three, five, he knew not how many minutes before, another sound, unmarked at the time but suddenly transfixing his attention now, had striven to reach his intelligence.

This sound had been the slight touch of metal on metal—just such a sound as Oleron made when he put his key into the lock.

"Hallo! . . . Who's that?" he called sharply from his bed.

He had no answer.

He called again. "Hallo! . . . Who's there? . . . Who is it?"

This time he was sure he heard noises, soft and heavy, in the kitchen.

"This is a queer thing altogether," he muttered. "By Jove, I'm as weak as a kitten too. . . . Hallo, there! Somebody called, didn't they? . . . Elsie! Is that you? . . ."

Then he began to knock with his hand on the wall at the side of his bed.

"Elsie! . . . Elsie! . . . You called, didn't you? . . . Please come here, whoever it is! . . ."

There was a sound as of a closing door, and then silence. Oleron began to get rather alarmed.

"It may be a nurse," he muttered; "Elsie'd have to get me a nurse, of course. She'd sit with me as long as she could spare the time, brave lass, and she'd get a nurse for the rest. . . . But it was awfully like her voice. . . . Elsie, or whoever it is! . . . I can't make this out at all. I must go and see what's the matter. . . ."

He put one leg out of bed. Feeling its feebleness, he reached with his hand for the additional support of the wall. . . .

But before putting out the other leg he stopped
and considered, picking at his new-found beard. He
was suddenly wondering whether he *dared* go into
the kitchen. It was such a frightfully long way; no
man knew what horror might not leap and huddle
on his shoulders if he went so far; when a man has
an overmastering impulse to get back into bed he
ought to take heed of the warning and obey it. Besides, why should he go? What was there to go for?
If it was that Bengough creature again, let her look
after herself; Oleron was not going to have things
cramp themselves on his defenseless back for the
sake of such a spoilsport as *she!* . . . If she was in, let
her let herself out again, and the sooner the better
for her! Oleron simply couldn't be bothered. He had
his work to do. On the morrow, he must set about
the writing of a novel with a heroine so winsome,
capricious, adorable, jealous, wicked, beautiful, in-
flaming, and altogether evil, that men should stand
amazed. She was coming over him now; he knew by
the alteration of the very air of the room when she
was near him; and that soft thrill of bliss that had
begun to stir in him never came unless she was beckoning, beckoning. . . .

He let go the wall and fell back into bed again
as—oh, unthinkable!—the other half of that kiss that
a gnash had interrupted was placed (how else convey
it?) on his lips, robbing him of very breath. . . .

XII

In the bright June sunlight a crowd filled the square, and looked up at the windows of the old house with the antique insurance marks in its walls of red brick and the agents' notice-boards hanging like wooden choppers over the paling. Two constables stood at the broken gate of the narrow entrance-alley, keeping folk back. The women kept to the outskirts of the throng, moving now and then as if to see the drawn red blinds of the old house from a new angle, and talking in whispers. The children were in the houses, behind closed doors.

A long-nosed man had a little group about him, and he was telling some story over and over again; and another man, little and fat and wide-eyed, sought to capture the long-nosed man's audience with some relation in which a key figured.

". . . and it was revealed to me that there'd been something that very afternoon," the long-nosed man was saying. "I was standing there, where Constable Saunders is—or rather, I was passing about my business, when they came out. There was no deceiving me, oh, no deceiving *me! I* saw her face. . . ."

"What was it like, Mr. Barrett?" a man asked.

"It was like hers whom our Lord said to, 'Woman, doth any man accuse thee?'—white as paper, and no mistake! Don't tell *me! . . .* And so I walks straight across to Mrs. Barrett, and 'Jane,' I says, 'this must stop, and stop at once; we are commanded to avoid evil,' I says, 'and it must come to an end now; let him get help elsewhere.' And she says to me, 'John,' she says, it's four-and-sixpence a week'—them was her words. 'Jane,' I says, 'if it was forty-six thousand pounds it should stop' . . . and from that day to this she hasn't set foot inside that gate."

There was a short silence: then,

"Did Mrs. Barrett ever . . . *see* anythink, like?" somebody vaguely inquired.

Barrett turned austerely on the speaker.

"What Mrs. Barrett saw and Mrs. Barrett didn't see shall not pass these lips; even as it is written, keep thy tongue from speaking evil," he said.

Another man spoke.

"He was pretty near canned up in the *Wagon and Horses* that night, weren't he, Jim?"

"Yes, 'e 'adn't 'alf copped it. . . ."

"Not standing treat much, neither; he was in the bar, all on his own. . . ."

"So 'e was; we talked about it. . . ."

The fat, scared-eyed man made another attempt.

"She got the key off of me—she had the number of it—she came into my shop of a Tuesday evening. . . ."

Nobody heeded him.

"Shut your heads," a heavy labourer commented gruffly, "she hasn't been found yet. 'Ere's the inspectors; we shall know more in a bit."

Two inspectors had come up and were talking to the constables who guarded the gate. The little fat man ran eagerly forwarded, saying that she had bought the key of him. "I remember the number, because of it's being three one's and three three's—111333!" he explained excitedly.

An inspector put him aside.

"Nobody's been in?" he asked of one of the constables.

"No, sir."

"Then you, Brackley, come with us; you, Smith, keep the gate. There's a squad on its way."

The two inspectors and the constable passed down the alley and entered the house. They mounted the wide carved staircase.

"This don't look as if he'd been out much lately," one of the inspectors uttered as he kicked aside a littler of dead leaves and papers that lay outside Oleron's door. "I don't think we need knock—break a pane, Brackley."

The door had two glazed panels; there was a sound of shattered glass; and Brackley put his hand through the hole his elbow had made and drew back the latch.

"Faugh!" . . . choked one of the inspectors as they entered. "Let some light and air in, quick. It stinks like a hearse—"

The assembly out in the square saw the red blinds go up and the windows of the old house flung open.

"That's better," said one of the inspectors, putting his head out of a window and drawing a deep breath. . . . "That seems to be the bedroom in there; will you go in, Simms, while I go over the rest? . . ."

They had drawn up the bedroom blind also, and the waxy-white, emaciated man on the bed had made a blinker of his hand against the torturing flood of brightness. Nor could he believe that his hearing was not playing tricks with him, for there were two policemen in his room, bending over him and asking where "she" was. He shook his head.

"This woman Bengough . . . goes by the name of Miss Elsie Bengough . . . d'ye hear? Where is she? . . . No good, Brackley; get him up; be careful with him; I'll just shove *my* head out of the window, I think. . . ."

The other inspector had been through Oleron's study and had found nothing, and was now in the kitchen, kicking aside an ankle-deep mass of vegetable refuse that cumbered the floor. The kitchen window had no blind, and was overshadowed by the blank end of the house across the alley. The kitchen appeared to be empty.

But the inspector, kicking aside the dead flowers, noticed that a shuffling track that was not of his making had been swept to a cupboard in the corner. In the upper part of the door of the cupboard was a square panel that looked as if it slid on runners. The door itself was closed.

The inspector advanced, put out his hand to the little knob, and slid the hatch along the groove.

Then he took an involuntary step back again.

Framed in the aperture, and falling forward a little before it jammed again in its frame, was something that resembled a large lumpy pudding, done up in a pudding-bag of faded browny, red frieze.

"Ah!" said the inspector.

To close the hatch again he would have had to thrust that pudding back with his hand; and somehow he did not quite like the idea of touching it. Instead, he turned the handle of the cupboard itself. There was weight behind it, so much weight that, after opening the door three and four inches and peering inside, he had to put his shoulder to it in order to close it again. In closing it he left sticking out, a few inches from the floor, a triangle of black and white check skirt.

He went into the small hall.

"All right!" he called.

They had got Oleron into his clothes. He still used his hands as blinkers, and his brain was very confused. A number of things were happening that he couldn't understand. He couldn't understand the extraordinary mess of dead flowers there seemed to be everywhere; he couldn't understand why there should be police officers in his room; he couldn't understand why one of these should be sent for a four-wheeler and a stretcher; and he couldn't understand what heavy article they seemed to be moving about in the kitchen—his kitchen. . . .

"What's the matter?" he muttered sleepily. . . .

Then he heard a murmur in the square, and the stopping of a four-wheeler outside. A police officer was at his elbow again, and Oleron wondered why, when he whispered something to him, he should run off a string of words—something about "used in evidence against you." They had lifted him to his feet, and were assisting him towards the door. . . .

No, Oleron couldn't understand it at all.

They got him down the stairs and along the alley. Oleron was aware of confused angry shoutings; he gathered that a number of people wanted to lynch somebody or other. Then his attention became fixed on a little fat frightened-eyed man who appeared to be making a statement that an officer was taking down in a notebook.

"I'd seen her with him . . . they was often together . . . she came into my shop and said it was for him . . . I thought it was all right . . . 111333 the number was," the man was saying.

The people seemed to be very angry; many police were keeping them back; but one of the inspectors had a voice that Oleron thought quite kind and friendly. He was telling somebody to get somebody else into the cab before something or other was brought out; and Oleron noticed that a four-wheeler was drawn up at the gate. It appeared that it was himself who was to be put into it; and as they lifted him up he saw that the inspector tried to stand between him and something that stood behind the cab, but was not quick enough to prevent Oleron seeing that this something was a hooded stretcher. The angry voices sounded like sea; something hard, like a stone, hit the back of the cab; and the inspector followed Oleron in and stood with his back to the window nearer the side where the people were. The door they had put Oleron in at remained open, apparently till the other inspector should come; and through the opening Oleron had a glimpse of the hatchet-like "To Let" boards among the privet-tree. One of them said that the key was at Number Six. . . .

Suddenly the raging of voices was hushed. Along the entrance-alley shuffling steps were heard, and the other inspector appeared at the cab door.

"Right away," he said to the driver.

He entered, fastened the door after him, and blocked up the second window with his back. Between the two inspectors Oleron slept peacefully. The cab moved down the square, the other vehicle went up the hill. The mortuary lay that way.

THE ATTIC

Algernon Blackwood

(1912)

The forest-girdled village upon the Jura slopes slept soundly, although it was not yet many minutes after ten o'clock. The clang of the *couvre-feu* had indeed just ceased, its notes swept far into the woods by a wind that shook the mountains. This wind now rushed down the deserted street. It howled about the old rambling building called La Citadelle, whose roof towered gaunt and humped above the smaller houses—Château left unfinished long ago by Lord Wemyss, the exiled Jacobite. The families who occupied the various apartments listened to the storm and felt the building tremble. "It's the mountain wind. It will bring the snow," the mother said, without looking up from her knitting. "And how sad it sounds.'

But it was not the wind that brought sadness as we sat round the open fire of peat. It was the wind of memories. The lamplight slanted along the narrow room towards the table where breakfast things lay ready for the morning. The double windows were fastened. At the far end stood a door ajar, and on the other side of it the two elder children lay asleep in the big bed. But beside the window was a smaller unused bed, that had been empty now a year. And to-night was the anniversary. . . .

And so the wind brought sadness and long thoughts. The little chap that used to lie there was already twelve months gone, far, far beyond the Hole where the Winds came from, as he called it; yet it seemed only yesterday that I went to tell him a tuck-up story, to stroke Riquette, the old mother-ly cat that cuddled against his back and laid a paw beside his pillow like a human being, and to hear his funny little earnest whisper say, "Oncle, tu sais, j'ai prié pour Petavel." For La Citadelle had its unhappy ghost—of Petavel, the usurer, who had hanged him-self in the attic a century gone by, and was known to walk its dreary corridors in search of peace—and this wise Irish mother, calming the boys' fears with wisdom, had told him, "If you pray for Petavel, you'll save his soul and make him happy, and he'll only love you." And, thereafter, this little imagina-tive boy had done so every night. With a passionate seriousness he did it. He had wonderful, delicate ways like that. In all our hearts he made his fairy nests of wonder. In my own, I know, he lay closer than any joy imaginable, with his big blue eyes, his queer soft questionings, and his splendid child's unselfishness—a sun-kissed flower of innocence that, had he lived, might have sweetened half a world.

"Let's put more peat on," the mother said, as a handful of rain like stones came flinging against the windows; "that must be hail." And she went on tip-toe to the inner room. "They're sleeping like two puddings," she whispered, coming presently back. But it struck me she had taken longer than to notice merely that; and her face wore an odd expression that made me uncomfortable. I thought she was somehow just about to laugh or cry. By the table a second she hesitated. I caught the flash of indecision as it passed. "Pan," she said suddenly—it was a nickname, stolen from my tuck-up stories, *he* had given me—"I wonder how Riquette got in." She looked hard at me. "It wasn't you, was it?" For we never let her come at night since he had gone. It was too poignant. The beastie always went cuddling and nestling into that empty bed. But this time it was not my doing, and I offered plausible explanations. "But—she's on the bed. Pan, *would* you be so kind—" She left the sentence unfinished, but I easily understood, for a lump had somehow risen in my own throat too, and I remembered now that she had come out from the inner room so quickly—with a kind of hurried rush almost. I put 'mère Riquette' out into the corridor. A lamp stood on the chair outside the door of another occupant further down, and I urged her gently towards it. She turned and looked at me—straight up into my face; but, instead of going down as I suggested, she went slowly in the opposite direction. She stepped softly towards a door in the wall that led up broken stairs into the attics. There she sat down and waited. And so I left her, and came back hastily to the peat fire and companionship. The wind rushed in behind me and slammed the door.

And we talked then somewhat busily of cheerful things; of the children's future, the excellence of the cheap Swiss schools, of Christmas presents, skiing, snow, tobogganing. I led the talk away from mournfulness; and when these subjects were exhausted I told stories of my own adventures in distant parts of the world. But 'mother' listened the whole time— not to me. Her thoughts were all elsewhere. And her air of intently, secretly listening, bordered, I felt, upon the uncanny. For she often stopped her knitting and sat with her eyes fixed upon the air before her; she stared blankly at the wall, her head slightly on one side, her figure tense, attention strained— elsewhere. Or, when my talk positively demanded it, her nod was oddly mechanical and her eyes looked through and past me. The wind continued very loud and roaring; but the fire glowed, the room was warm and cosy. Yet she shivered, and when I drew attention to it, her reply, "I do feel cold, but I didn't know I shivered," was given as though she spoke across the air to some one else. But what impressed me even more uncomfortably were her repeated questions about Riquette. When a pause in my tales permitted, she would look up with "I wonder where Riquette went?" or, thinking of the inclement night, "I hope mère Riquette's not out of doors. Perhaps Madame Favre has taken her in?" I offered to go and see. Indeed I was already half-way across the room when there came the heavy bang at the door that rooted me to the ground where I stood. It was not wind. It was something alive that made it rattle. There was a second blow. A thud on the corridor boards followed, and then a high, odd voice that at first was as human as the cry of a child.

It is undeniable that we both started, and for my-self I can answer truthfully that a chill ran down my spine; but what frightened me more than the sudden noise and the eerie cry was the way 'mother' supplied the immediate explanation. For behind the words "It's only Riquette; she sometimes springs at the door like that; perhaps we'd better let her in," was a certain touch of uncanny quiet that made me feel she had known the cat would come, and knew also why she came. One cannot explain such im-pressions further. They leave their vital touch, then go their way. Into the little room, however, in that moment there came between us this uncomfortable sense that the night held other purposes than our own—and that my companion was aware of them.

There was something going on far, far removed
from the routine of life as we were accustomed to it.
Moreover, our usual routine was the eddy, while this
was the main stream. It felt big, I mean.

And so it was that the entrance of the familiar,
friendly creature brought this thing both itself and
'mother' *knew,* but whereof I as yet was ignorant.
I held the door wide. The draught rushed through
behind her, and sent a shower of sparks about the
fireplace. The lamp flickered and gave a little gulp.
And Riquette marched slowly past, with all the impressive dignity of her kind, towards the other door
that stood ajar. Turning the corner like a shadow,
she disappeared into the room where the two children slept. We heard the soft thud with which she
leaped upon the bed. Then, in a lull of the wind, she
came back again and sat on the oilcloth, staring into
'mother's' face. She mewed and put a paw out, drawing the black dress softly with half-opened claws.
And it was all so horribly suggestive and pathetic,
it revived such poignant memories, that I got up
impulsively—I think I had actually said the words,
"We'd better put her out, mother, after all'—when
my companion rose to her feet and forestalled me.
She said another thing instead. It took my breath
away to hear it. "She wants us to go with her. Pan,
will you come too?" The surprise on my face must
have asked the question, for I do not remember saying anything. "To the attic," she said quietly.

She stood there by the table, a tall, grave figure dressed in black, and her face above the lamp-shade caught the full glare of light. Its expression positively stiffened me. She seemed so secure in her singular purpose. And her familiar appearance had so oddly given place to something wholly strange to me. She looked like another person—almost with the unwelcome transformation of the sleep-walker about her. Cold came over me as I watched her, for I remembered suddenly her Irish second-sight, her story years ago of meeting a figure on the attic stairs, the figure of Petavel. And the idea of this motherly, sedate, and wholesome woman, absorbed day and night in prosaic domestic duties, and yet 'seeing' things, touched the incongruous almost to the point of alarm. It was so distressingly convincing.

Yet she knew quite well that I would come. Indeed, following the excited animal, she was already by the door, and a moment later, still without answering or protesting, I was with them in the draughty corridor. There was something inevitable in her manner that made it impossible to refuse. She took the lamp from its nail on the wall, and following our four-footed guide, who ran with obvious pleasure just in front, she opened the door into the courtyard. The wind nearly put the lamp out, but a minute later we were safe inside the passage that led up flights of creaky wooden stairs towards the world of tenantless attics overhead.

And I shall never forget the way the excited
Riquette first stood up and put her paws upon the
various doors, trotted ahead, turned back to watch
us coming, and then finally sat down and waited
on the threshold of the empty, raftered space that
occupied the entire length of the building underneath the roof. For her manner was more that of an
intelligent dog than of a cat, and sometimes more
like that of a human mind than either.

We had come up without a single word. The howling of the wind as we rose higher was like the roar
of artillery. There were many broken stairs, and the
narrow way was full of twists and turnings. It was a
dreadful journey. I felt eyes watching us from all the
yawning spaces of the darkness, and the noise of the
storm smothered footsteps everywhere. Troops of
shadows kept us company. But it was on the threshold of this big, chief attic, when 'mother' stopped
abruptly to put down the lamp, that real fear took
hold of me. For Riquette marched steadily forward
into the middle of the dusty flooring, picking her
way among the fallen tiles and mortar, as though
she went towards—some one. She purred loudly and
uttered little cries of excited pleasure. Her tail went
up into the air, and she lowered her head with the
unmistakable intention of being stroked. Her lips
opened and shut. Her green eyes smiled. She *was*
being stroked.

It was an unforgettable performance. I would rather have witnessed an execution or a murder than watch that mysterious creature twist and turn about in the way she did. Her magnified shadow was as large as a pony on the floor and rafters. I wanted to hide the whole thing by extinguishing the lamp. For, even before the mysterious action began, I experienced the sudden rush of conviction that others besides ourselves were in this attic—and standing very close to us indeed. And, although there was ice in my blood, there was also a strange swelling of the heart that only love and tenderness could bring.

But, whatever it was, my human companion, still silent, knew and understood. She *saw*. And her soft whisper that ran with the wind among the rafters, "Il a prié pour Petavel et le bon Dieu l'a entendu," did not amaze me one quarter as much as the expression I then caught upon her radiant face. Tears ran down the cheeks, but they were tears of happiness. Her whole figure seemed lit up. She opened her arms—picture of great Motherhood, proud, blessed, and tender beyond words. I thought she was going to fall, for she took quick steps forward; but when I moved to catch her, she drew me aside instead with a sudden gesture that brought fear back in the place of wonder.

"Let them pass," she whispered grandly. "Pan, don't you see. . . . He's leading him into peace and

safety . . . by the hand!" And her joy seemed to
kill the shadows and fill the entire attic with white
light. Then, almost simultaneously with her words,
she swayed. I was in time to catch her, but as I
did so, across the very spot where we had just been
standing—two figures, I swear, went past us like a
flood of light.

There was a moment next of such confusion that
I did not see what happened to Riquette, for the
sight of my companion kneeling on the dusty boards
and praying with a curious sort of passionate happiness, while tears pressed between her covering fingers—the strange wonder of this made me utterly
oblivious to minor details. . . .

We were sitting round the peat fire again, and
'mother' was saying to me in the gentlest, tenderest whisper I ever heard from human lips—"Pan, I
think perhaps that's why God took him. . . ."

And when a little later we went in to make Riquette cosy in the empty bed, ever since kept sacred
to her use, the mournfulness had lifted; and in the
place of resignation was proud peace and joy that
knew no longer sad or selfish questionings.

THE DECOY

ALGERNON BLACKWOOD
(1919)

It belonged to the category of unlovely houses about which an ugly superstition clings, one reason being, perhaps, its inability to inspire interest in itself without assistance. It seemed too ordinary to possess individuality, much less to exert an influence. Solid and ungainly, its huge bulk dwarfing the park timber, its best claim to notice was a negative one— it was unpretentious.

From the little hill its expressionless windows stared across the Kentish Weald, indifferent to weather, dreary in winter, bleak in spring, unblessed in summer. Some colossal hand had tossed it down, then let it starve to death, a country mansion that might well strain the adjectives of advertisers and find inheritors with difficulty. Its soul had fled, said some; it had committed suicide, thought others; and it was an inheritor, before he killed himself in the library, who thought this latter, yielding, apparently, to an hereditary taint in the family. For two other inheritors followed suit, with an interval of twenty years between them, and there was no clear reason to explain the three disasters. Only the first owner, indeed, lived permanently in the house, the others using it in the summer months and then deserting it with relief. Hence, when John Burley, present inheritor, assumed possession, he entered a house about which clung an ugly superstition, based, nevertheless, upon a series of undeniably ugly facts.

This century deals harshly with superstitious folk, deeming them fools or charlatans; but John Burley, robust, contemptuous of half lights, did not deal harshly with them, because he did not deal with them at all. He was hardly aware of their existence. He ignored them as he ignored, say, the Esquimaux, poets, and other human aspects that did not touch his scheme of life. A successful business man, he concentrated on what was real; he dealt with business people. His philanthropy, on a big scale, was also real; yet, though he would have denied it vehemently, he had his superstition as well. No man exists without some taint of superstition in his blood; the racial heritage is too rich to be escaped entirely. Burley's took this form—that unless he gave his tithe to the poor he would not prosper. This ugly mansion, he decided, would make an ideal Convalescent Home.

"Only cowards or lunatics kill themselves," he declared flatly, when his use of the house was criticized. "I'm neither one nor t'other." He let out his gusty, boisterous laugh. In his invigorating atmosphere such weakness seemed contemptible, just as superstition in his presence seemed feeblest ignorance. Even its picturesqueness faded. "I can't conceive," he boomed, "can't even imagine to myself," he added emphatically, "the state of mind in which a man can *think* of suicide, much less do it." He threw his chest out with a challenging air. "I tell you, Nancy, it's either cowardice or mania. And I've no use for either."

Yet he was easy-going and good-humoured in his denunciation. He admitted his limitations with a hearty laugh his wife called noisy. Thus he made allowances for the fairy fears of sailorfolk, and had even been known to mention haunted ships his companies owned. But he did so in the terms of tonnage and £ s. d. His scope was big; details were made for clerks.

His consent to pass a night in the mansion was the consent of a practical business man and philanthropist who dealt condescendingly with foolish human nature. It was based on the common-sense of tonnage and £ s. d. The local newspapers had revived the silly story of the suicides, calling attention to the effect of the superstition upon the fortunes of the house, and so, possibly, upon the fortunes of its present owner. But the mansion, otherwise a white elephant, was precisely ideal for his purpose, and so trivial a matter as spending a night in it should not

stand in the way. "We must take people as we find
them, Nancy."

His young wife had her motive, of course, in making the proposal, and, if she was amused by what she
called "spook-hunting," he saw no reason to refuse
her the indulgence. He loved her, and took her as
he found her—late in life. To allay the superstitions
of prospective staff and patients and supporters, all,
in fact, whose goodwill was necessary to success, he
faced this boredom of a night in the building before
its opening was announced. "You see, John, if you,
the owner, do this, it will nip damaging talk in the
bud. If anything went wrong later it would only be
put down to this suicide idea, this haunting influence. The Home will have a bad name from the start.
There'll be endless trouble. It will be a failure."

"You think my spending a night there will stop
the nonsense?" he inquired.

"According to the old legend it breaks the spell,"
she replied. "That's the condition, anyhow."

"But somebody's sure to die there sooner or
later," he objected. "We can't prevent that."

"We can prevent people whispering that they
died unnaturally." She explained the working of the
public mind.

"I see," he replied, his lip curling, yet quick to
gauge the truth of what she told him about collec-
tive instinct.

"Unless *you* take poison in the hall," she added laughingly, "or elect to hang yourself with your braces from the hat peg."

"I'll do it," he agreed, after a moment's thought. "I'll sit up with you. It will be like a honeymoon over again, you and I on the spree—eh?" He was even interested now; the boyish side of him was touched perhaps; but his enthusiasm was less when she explained that three was a better number than two on such an expedition.

"I've often done it before, John. We were always three."

"Who?" he asked bluntly. He looked wonderingly at her, but she answered that if anything went wrong a party of three provided a better margin for help. It was sufficiently obvious. He listened and agreed. "I'll get young Mortimer," he suggested. "Will he do?"

She hesitated. "Well—he's cheery; he'll be interested, too. Yes, he's as good as another." She seemed indifferent.

"And he'll make the time pass with his stories," added her husband.

So Captain Mortimer, late officer on a T.B.D., a "cheery lad," afraid of nothing, cousin of Mrs. Burley, and now filling a good post in the company's London offices, was engaged as third hand in the expedition. But Captain Mortimer was young

and ardent, and Mrs. Burley was young and pretty
and ill-mated, and John Burley was a neglectful, and
self-satisfied husband.

Fate laid the trap with cunning, and John Burley,
blind-eyed, careless of detail, floundered into it. He
also floundered out again, though in a fashion none
could have expected of him.

The night agreed upon eventually was as near to
the shortest in the year as John Burley could con-
trive—June 18th—when the sun set at 8:18 and
rose about a quarter to four. There would be barely
three hours of true darkness. "You're the expert," he
admitted, as she explained that sitting through the
actual darkness only was required, not necessarily
from sunset to sunrise. "We'll do the thing properly.
Mortimer's not very keen, he had a dance or something," he added, noticing the look of annoyance
that flashed swiftly in her eyes; "but he got out of it.
He's coming." The pouting expression of the spoilt
woman amused him. "Oh, no, he didn't need much
persuading really," he assured her. "Some girl or
other, of course. He's young, remember." To which
no comment was forthcoming, though the implied
comparison made her flush.

They motored from South Audley Street after
an early tea, in due course passing Sevenoaks and
entering the Kentish Weald; and, in order that
the necessary advertisement should be given, the
chauffeur, warned strictly to keep their purpose

quiet, was to put up at the country inn and fetch them an hour after sunrise; they would breakfast in London. "He'll tell everybody," said his practical and cynical master; "the local newspaper will have it all next day. A few hours' discomfort is worth while if it ends the nonsense. We'll read and smoke, and Mortimer shall tell us yarns about the sea." He went with the driver into the house to superintend the arrangement of the room, the lights, the hampers of food, and so forth, leaving the pair upon the lawn.

"Four hours isn't much, but it's something," whispered Mortimer, alone with her for the first time since they started. "It's simply ripping of you to have got me in. You look divine to-night. You're the most wonderful woman in the world." His blue eyes shone with the hungry desire he mistook for love. He looked as if he had blown in from the sea, for his skin was tanned and his light hair bleached a little by the sun. He took her hand, drawing her out of the slanting sunlight towards the rhododendrons.

"I didn't, you silly boy. It was John suggested your coming." She released her hand with an affected effort. "Besides, you overdid it—pretending you had a dance."

"You could have objected," he said eagerly, "and didn't. Oh, you're too lovely, you're delicious!" He kissed her suddenly with passion. There was a tiny struggle, in which she yielded too easily, he thought.

"Harry, you're an idiot!" she cried breathlessly, when he let her go. "I really don't know how you dare! And John's your friend. Besides, you know"— she glanced round quickly—"it isn't safe here." Her eyes shone happily, her cheeks were flaming. She looked what she was, a pretty, young, lustful animal, false to ideals, true to selfish passion only. "Luckily," she added, "he trusts me too fully to think anything."

The young man, worship in his eyes, laughed gaily. "There's no harm in a kiss," he said. "You're a child to him, he never thinks of you as a woman. Anyhow, his head's full of ships and kings and sealing-wax," he comforted her, while respecting her sudden instinct which warned him not to touch her again, "and he never sees anything. Why, even at ten yards—"

From twenty yards away a big voice interrupted him, as John Burley came round a corner of the house and across the lawn towards them. The chauffeur, he announced, had left the hampers in the room on the first floor and gone back to the inn. "Let's take a walk round," he added, joining them, "and see the garden. Five minutes before sunset we'll go in and feed." He laughed. "We must do the thing faithfully, you know, mustn't we, Nancy? Dark to dark, remember. Come on, Mortimer"—he took the young man's arm—"a last look round before we go in and hang ourselves from adjoining hooks in the matron's room!" He reached out his free hand towards his wife.

"Oh, hush, John!" she said quickly. "I don't like—especially now the dusk is coming." She shivered, as though it were a genuine little shiver, pursing her lips deliciously as she did so; whereupon he drew her forcibly to him, saying he was sorry, and kissed her exactly where she had been kissed two minutes before, while young Mortimer looked on. "We'll take care of you between us," he said. Behind a broad back the pair exchanged a swift but meaning glance, for there was that in his tone which enjoined wariness, and perhaps after all he was not so blind as he appeared. They had their code, these two. "All's well," was signalled; "but another time be more careful!"

There still remained some minutes' sunlight before the huge red ball of fire would sink behind the wooded hills, and the trio, talking idly, a flutter of excitement in two hearts certainly, walked among the roses. It was a perfect evening, windless, perfumed, warm. Headless shadows preceded them gigantically across the lawn as they moved, and one side of the great building lay already dark; bats were flitting, moths darted to and fro above the azalea and rhododendron clumps. The talk turned chiefly on the uses of the mansion as a Convalescent Home, its probable running cost, suitable staff, and so forth.

"Come along," John Burley said presently, breaking off and turning abruptly, "we must be inside, actually inside, before the sun's gone. We must fulfil the conditions faithfully," he repeated, as though fond of the phrase. He was in earnest over everything in life, big or little, once he set his hand to it.

They entered, this incongruous trio of ghost-hunters, no one of them really intent upon the business in hand, and went slowly upstairs to the great room where the hampers lay. Already in the hall it was dark enough for three electric torches to flash usefully and help their steps as they moved with caution, lighting one corner after another. The air inside was chill and damp. "Like an unused museum," said Mortimer. "I can smell the specimens." They looked about them, sniffing. "That's humanity," declared his host, employer, friend, "with cement and whitewash to flavour it"; and all three laughed as Mrs. Burley said she wished they had picked some roses and brought them in. Her husband was again in front on the broad staircase, Mortimer just behind him, when she called out. "I don't like being last," she exclaimed. It's so black behind me in the hall. I'll come between you two," and the sailor took her outstretched hand, squeezing it, as he passed her up. "There's a figure, remember," she said hurriedly, turning to gain her husband's attention, as when she touched wood at home. "A figure is seen; that's part of the story. The figure of a man." She gave a tiny shiver of pleasurable, half-imagined alarm as she took his arm.

"I hope we shall see it," he mentioned prosaically.

"I hope we shan't," she replied with emphasis. "It's only seen before—something happens." Her husband said nothing, while Mortimer remarked facetiously that it would be a pity if they had their trouble for nothing. "Something can hardly happen to all three of us," he said lightly, as they entered a large room where the paper-hangers had conveniently left a rough table of bare planks. Mrs. Burley, busy with her own thoughts, began to unpack the sandwiches and wine. Her husband strolled over to the window. He seemed restless.

"So this," his deep voice startled her, "is where one of us"—he looked round him—"is to—"

"John!" She stopped him sharply, with impatience. "Several times already I've begged you." Her voice rang rather shrill and querulous in the empty room, a new note in it. She was beginning to feel the atmosphere of the place, perhaps. On the sunny lawn it had not touched her, but now, with the fall of night, she was aware of it, as shadow called to shadow and the kingdom of darkness gathered power. Like a great whispering gallery, the whole house listened.

"Upon my word, Nancy," he said with contrition, as he came and sat down beside her, "I quite forgot again. Only I cannot take it seriously. It's so utterly unthinkable to me that a man—"

"But why evoke the idea at all?" she insisted in a lowered voice, that snapped despite its faintness. "Men, after all, don't do such things for nothing."

"We don't know everything in the universe, do we?" Mortimer put in, trying clumsily to support her. "All I know just now is that I'm famished and this veal and ham pie is delicious." He was very busy with his knife and fork. His foot rested lightly on her own beneath the table; he could not keep his eyes off her face; he was continually passing new edibles to her.

"No," agreed John Burley, "not everything. You're right there."

She kicked the younger man gently, flashing a warning with her eyes as well, while her husband, emptying his glass, his head thrown back, looked straight at them over the rim, apparently seeing nothing. They smoked their cigarettes round the table, Burley lighting a big cigar. "Tell us about the figure, Nancy?" he inquired. "At least there's no harm in that. It's new to me. I hadn't heard about a figure." And she did so willingly, turning her chair sideways from the dangerous, reckless feet. Mortimer could now no longer touch her. "I know very little," she confessed; "only what the paper said. It's a man. . . . And he changes."

"How changes?" asked her husband. "Clothes, you mean, or what?"

Mrs. Burley laughed, as though she was glad to laugh. Then she answered: "According to the story, he shows himself each time to the man—"

"The man who—?"

"Yes, yes, of course. He appears to the man who dies—as himself."

"H'm," grunted her husband, naturally puzzled. He stared at her.

"Each time the chap saw his own double"—Mortimer came this time usefully to the rescue—"before he did it."

Considerable explanation followed, involving much psychic jargon from Mrs. Burley, which fascinated and impressed the sailor, who thought her as wonderful as she was lovely, showing it in his eyes for all to see. John Burley's attention wandered. He moved over to the window, leaving them to finish the discussion between them; he took no part in it, made no comment even, merely listening idly and watching them with an air of absent-mindedness through the cloud of cigar smoke round his head. He moved from window to window, ensconcing himself in turn in each deep embrasure, examining the fastenings, measuring the thickness of the stonework with his handkerchief. He seemed restless, bored, obviously out of place in this ridiculous expedition. On his big massive face lay a quiet, resigned expression his wife had never seen before. She noticed it

now as, the discussion ended, the pair tidied away
the *débris* of dinner, lit the spirit lamp for coffee
and laid out a supper which would be very welcome
with the dawn. A draught passed through the room,
making the papers flutter on the table. Mortimer
turned down the smoking lamps with care.

"Wind's getting up a bit—from the south," observed Burley from his niche, closing one-half of the
casement window as he said it. To do this, he turned
his back a moment, fumbling for several seconds
with the latch, while Mortimer, noting it, seized
his sudden opportunity with the foolish abandon of
his age and temperament. Neither he nor his victim
perceived that, against the outside darkness, the interior of the room was plainly reflected in the window-pane. One reckless, the other terrified, they
snatched the fearful joy, which might, after all, have
been lengthened by another full half-minute, for the
head they feared, followed by the shoulders, pushed
through the side of the casement still open, and remained outside, taking in the night.

"A grand air," said his deep voice, as the head
drew in again, "I'd like to be at sea a night like this."
He left the casement open and came across the room
towards them. "Now," he said cheerfully, arranging a
seat for himself, "let's get comfortable for the night.
Mortimer, we expect stories from you without ceasing, until dawn or the ghost arrives. Horrible stories
of chains and headless men, remember. Make it a

night we shan't forget in a hurry." He produced his gust of laughter.

They arranged their chairs, with other chairs to put their feet on, and Mortimer contrived a foot-stool by means of a hamper for the smallest feet; the air grew thick with tobacco smoke; eyes flashed and answered, watched perhaps as well; ears listened and perhaps grew wise; occasionally, as a window shook, they started and looked round; there were sounds about the house from time to time, when the enter-ing wind, using broken or open windows, set loose objects rattling.

But Mrs. Burley vetoed horrible stories with de-cision. A big, empty mansion, lonely in the country, and even with the comfort of John Burley and a lover in it, has its atmosphere. Furnished rooms are far less ghostly. This atmosphere now came creep-ing everywhere, through spacious halls and sighing corridors, silent, invisible, but all-pervading, John Burley alone impervious to it, unaware of its soft attack upon the nerves. It entered possibly with the summer night wind, but possibly it was always there. . . . And Mrs. Burley looked often at her hus-band, sitting near her at an angle; the light fell on his fine strong face; she felt that, though apparently so calm and quiet, he was really very restless; some-thing about him was a little different; she could not define it; his mouth seemed set as with an effort; he looked, she thought curiously to herself, patient and very dignified; he was rather a dear after all. Why did she think the face inscrutable? Her thoughts wandered vaguely, unease, discomfort among them somewhere, while the heated blood—she had taken her share of wine—seethed in her.

Burley turned to the sailor for more stories. "Sea and wind in them," he asked. "No horrors, remember!" and Mortimer told a tale about the shortage of rooms at a Welsh seaside place where spare rooms fetched fabulous prices, and one man alone refused to let—a retired captain of a South Seas trader, very poor, a bit crazy apparently. He had two furnished rooms in his house worth twenty guineas a week. The rooms faced south; he kept them full of flowers; but he would not let. An explanation of his unworldly obstinacy was not forthcoming until Mortimer—they fished together—gained his confidence. "The South Wind lives in them," the old fellow told him. "I keep them free for her."

"For *her?*"

"It was on the South Wind my love came to me," said the other softly; "and it was on the South Wind that she left—"

It was an odd tale to tell in such company, but he told it well.

"Beautiful," thought Mrs. Burley. Aloud she said a quiet, "Thank you. By 'left,' I suppose he meant she died or ran away?"

John Burley looked up with a certain surprise. "We ask for a story," he said, "and you give us a poem." He laughed. "You're in love, Mortimer," he informed him, "and with my wife probably."

"Of course I am, sir," replied the young man gallantly. "A sailor's heart, you know," while the face of the woman turned pink, then white. She knew her husband more intimately than Mortimer did, and there was something in his tone, his eyes, his words, she did not like. Harry was an idiot to choose such a tale. An irritated annoyance stirred in her, close upon dislike. "Anyhow, it's better than horrors," she said hurriedly.

"Well," put in her husband, letting forth a minor gust of laughter, "it's possible, at any rate. Though one's as crazy as the other." His meaning was not wholly clear. "If a man really loved," he added in his blunt fashion, "and was tricked by her, I could almost conceive his—"

"Oh, don't preach, John, for Heaven's sake. You're so dull in the pulpit." But the interruption only served to emphasize the sentence which, otherwise, might have been passed over.

"Could conceive his finding life so worthless," persisted the other, "that—" He hesitated. "But there, now, I promised I wouldn't," he went on, laughing good-humouredly. Then, suddenly, as though in spite of himself, driven it seemed: "Still, under such conditions, he might show his contempt for human nature and for life by—"

It was a tiny stifled scream that stopped him this time.

"John, I hate, I loathe you, when you talk like that. And you've broken your word again." She was more than petulant; a nervous anger sounded in her voice. It was the way he had said it, looking from them towards the window, that made her quiver. She felt him suddenly as a man; she felt afraid of him.

Her husband made no reply; he rose and looked at his watch, leaning sideways towards the lamp, so that the expression of his face was shaded. "Two o'clock," he remarked. "I think I'll take a turn through the house. I may find a workman asleep or something. Anyhow, the light will soon come now." He laughed; the expression of his face, his tone of voice, relieved her momentarily. He went out. They heard his heavy tread echoing down the carpetless long corridor.

Mortimer began at once. "Did he mean anything?" he asked breathlessly. "He doesn't love you the least little bit, anyhow. He never did. I do. You're wasted on him. You belong to me." The words poured out. He covered her face with kisses. "Oh, I didn't mean *that*," he caught between the kisses.

The sailor released her, staring. "What then?" he whispered. "Do you think he saw us on the lawn?" He paused a moment, as she made no reply. The steps were audible in the distance still. "I know!" he exclaimed suddenly. "It's the blessed house he feels. That's what it is. He doesn't like it."

A wind sighed through the room, making the papers flutter; something rattled; and Mrs. Burley started. A loose end of rope swinging from the paperhanger's ladder caught her eye. She shivered slightly.

"He's different," she replied in a low voice, nestling very close again, "and so restless. Didn't you notice what he said just now—that under certain conditions he could understand a man"—she hesitated—"doing it," she concluded, a sudden drop in her voice. "Harry," she looked full into his eyes, "that's not like him. He didn't say that for nothing."

"Nonsense! He's bored to tears, that's all. And the house is getting on your nerves, too." He kissed her tenderly. Then, as she responded, he drew her nearer still and held her passionately, mumbling incoherent words, among which "nothing to be afraid of" was distinguishable. Meanwhile, the steps were coming nearer. She pushed him away. "You must behave yourself. I insist. You shall, Harry," then buried herself in his arms, her face hidden against his neck—only to disentangle herself the next instant and stand clear of him. "I hate you, Harry," she exclaimed sharply, a look of angry annoyance flashing across her face. "And I *hate* myself. Why do you treat me—?" She broke off as the steps came closer, patted her hair straight, and stalked over to the open window.

"I believe after all you're only playing with me," he said viciously. He stared in surprised disappointment, watching her. "It's him you really love," he added jealously. He looked and spoke like a petulant spoilt boy.

She did not turn her head. "He's always been fair to me, kind and generous. He never blames me for anything. Give me a cigarette and don't play the stage hero. My nerves are on edge, to tell you the truth." Her voice jarred harshly, and as he lit her cigarette he noticed that her lips were trembling; his own hand trembled too. He was still holding the match, standing beside her at the window-sill, when the steps crossed the threshold and John Burley came into the room. He went straight up to the table and turned the lamp down. "It was smoking," he remarked. "Didn't you see?"

"I'm sorry, sir," and Mortimer sprang forward, too late to help him. "It was the draught as you pushed the door open." The big man said, "Ah!" and drew a chair over, facing them. "It's just *the* very house," he told them. "I've been through every room on this floor. It will make a splendid Home, with very little alteration, too." He turned round in his creaking wicker chair and looked up at his wife, who sat swinging her legs and smoking in the window embrasure. "Lives will be saved inside these old walls. It's a good investment," he went on, talking rather to himself it seemed. "People will die here, too—"

"Hark!" Mrs. Burley interrupted him. "That noise—what is it?" A faint thudding sound in the corridor or in the adjoining room was audible, making all three look round quickly, listening for a repetition, which did not come. The papers fluttered on the table, the lamps smoked an instant.

"Wind," observed Burley calmly, "our little friend, the South Wind. Something blown over again, that's all." But, curiously, the three of them stood up. "I'll go and see," he continued. "Doors and windows are all open to let the paint dry." Yet he did not move; he stood there watching a white moth that dashed round and round the lamp, flopping heavily now and again upon the bare deal table.

"Let me go, sir," put in Mortimer eagerly. He was glad of the chance; for the first time he, too, felt uncomfortable. But there was another who, apparently, suffered a discomfort greater than his own and was accordingly even more glad to get away. "I'll go," Mrs. Burley announced, with decision. "I'd like to. I haven't been out of this room since we came. I'm not an atom afraid."

It was strange that for a moment she did not make a move either; it seemed as if she waited for something. For perhaps fifteen seconds no one stirred or spoke. She knew by the look in her lover's eyes that

he had now become aware of the slight, indefinite
change in her husband's manner, and was alarmed
by it. The fear in him woke her contempt; she suddenly despised the youth, and was conscious of a
new, strange yearning towards her husband; against
her worked nameless pressures, troubling her being.
There was an alteration in the room, she thought;
something had come in. The trio stood listening to
the gentle wind outside, waiting for the sound to
be repeated; two careless, passionate young lovers
and a man stood waiting, listening, watching in that
room; yet it seemed there were five persons altogether and not three, for two guilty consciences stood
apart and separate from their owners. John Burley
broke the silence.

"Yes, you go, Nancy. Nothing to be afraid of—
there. It's only wind." He spoke as though he meant
it.

Mortimer bit his lips. "I'll come with you," he
said instantly. He was confused. "Let's all three go. I
don't think we ought to be separated." But Mrs. Burley was already at the door. "I insist," she said, with
a forced laugh. "I'll call if I'm frightened," while
her husband, saying nothing, watched her from the
table.

"Take this," said the sailor, flashing his electric torch as he went over to her. "Two are better
than one." He saw her figure exquisitely silhouetted
against the black corridor beyond; it was clear she

wanted to go; any nervousness in her was mastered by a stronger emotion still; she was glad to be out of their presence for a bit. He had hoped to snatch a word of explanation in the corridor, but her manner stopped him. Something else stopped him, too.

"First door on the left," he called out, his voice echoing down the empty length. "That's the room where the noise came from. Shout if you want us."

He watched her moving away, the light held steadily in front of her, but she made no answer, and he turned back to see John Burley lighting his cigar at the lamp chimney, his face thrust forward as he did so. He stood a second, watching him, as the lips sucked hard at the cigar to make it draw; the strength of the features was emphasized to sternness. He had meant to stand by the door and listen for the least sound from the adjoining room, but now found his whole attention focused on the face above the lamp. In that minute he realized that Burley had wished—had meant—his wife to go. In that minute also he forgot his love, his shameless, selfish little mistress, his worthless, caddish little self. For John Burley looked up. He straightened slowly, puffing hard and quickly to make sure his cigar was lit, and faced him. Mortimer moved forward into the room, self-conscious, embarrassed, cold.

"Of course it was only wind," he said lightly, his one desire being to fill the interval while they were alone with commonplaces. He did not wish the other to speak, "Dawn wind, probably." He glanced at his wrist-watch. "It's half-past two already, and the sun gets up at a quarter to four. It's light by now, I expect. The shortest night is never quite dark." He rambled on confusedly, for the other's steady, silent stare embarrassed him. A faint sound of Mrs. Burley moving in the next room made him stop a moment. He turned instinctively to the door, eager for an excuse to go.

"That's nothing," said Burley, speaking at last and in a firm quiet voice. "Only my wife, glad to be alone—my young and pretty wife. She's all right. I know her better than you do. Come in and shut the door."

Mortimer obeyed. He closed the door and came close to the table, facing the other, who at once continued.

"If I thought," he said, in that quiet deep voice, "that you two were serious"—he uttered his words very slowly, with emphasis, with intense severity—"do you know what I should do? I will tell you, Mortimer. I should like one of us two—you or myself—to remain in this house, dead."

His teeth gripped his cigar tightly; his hands were clenched; he went on through a half-closed mouth. His eyes blazed steadily.

"I trust her so absolutely—understand me?—that my belief in women, in human beings, would go. And with it the desire to live. Understand me?"

Each word to the young careless fool was a blow
in the face, yet it was the softest blow, the flash
of a big deep heart, that hurt the most. A dozen
answers—denial, explanation, confession, taking all
guilt upon himself—crowded his mind, only to be
dismissed. He stood motionless and silent, staring
hard into the other's eyes. No word passed his lips;
there was no time in any case. It was in this position
that Mrs. Burley, entering at that moment, found
them. She saw her husband's face; the other man stood
with his back to her. She came in with a little nervous
laugh. "A bell-rope swinging in the wind and hitting
a sheet of metal before the fireplace," she informed
them. And all three laughed together then, though
each laugh had a different sound. "But I hate this
house," she added. "I wish we had never come."

"The moment there's light in the sky," remarked
her husband quietly, "we can leave. That's the contract; let's see it through. Another half-hour will do
it. Sit down, Nancy, and have a bite of something."
He got up and placed a chair for her. "I think I'll
take another look round." He moved slowly to the
door. "I may go out on to the lawn a bit and see
what the sky is doing."

It did not take half a minute to say the words, yet
to Mortimer it seemed as though the voice would
never end. His mind was confused and troubled.
He loathed himself, he loathed the woman through
whom he had got into this awkward mess.

The situation had suddenly become extremely painful; he had never imagined such a thing; the man he had thought blind had after all seen everything—known it all along, watched them, waited. And the woman, he was now certain, loved her husband; she had fooled him, Mortimer, all along, amusing herself.

"I'll come with you, sir. Do let me," he said suddenly. Mrs. Burley stood pale and uncertain between them. She looked scared. What has happened, she was clearly wondering.

"No, no, Harry"—he called him "Harry" for the first time—"I'll be back in five minutes at most. My wife mustn't be alone either." And he went out.

The young man waited till the footsteps sounded some distance down the corridor, then turned, but he did not move forward; for the first time he let pass unused what he called "an opportunity." His passion had left him; his love, as he once thought it, was gone. He looked at the pretty woman near him, wondering blankly what he had ever seen there to attract him so wildly. He wished to Heaven he was out of it all. He wished he were dead. John Burley's words suddenly appalled him.

One thing he saw plainly—she was frightened. This opened his lips.

"What's the matter?" he asked, and his hushed voice shirked the familiar Christian name. "Did you see anything?" He nodded his head in the direction of the adjoining room. It was the sound of his own voice addressing her coldly that made him abruptly see himself as he really was, but it was her reply, honestly given, in a faint even voice, that told him she saw her own self too with similar clarity. God, he thought, how revealing a tone, a single word can be!

"I saw—nothing. Only I feel uneasy—dear." That "dear" was a call for help.

"Look here," he cried, so loud that she held up a warning finger, "I'm—I've been a damned fool, a cad! I'm most frightfully ashamed. I'll do any-thing—*anything* to get it right." He felt cold, na-ked, his worthlessness laid bare; she felt, he knew, the same. Each revolted suddenly from the other. Yet he knew not quite how or wherefore this great change had thus abruptly come about, especially on her side. He felt that a bigger, deeper emotion than he could understand was working on them, mak-ing mere physical relationships seem empty, trivial, cheap and vulgar. His cold increased in face of this utter ignorance.

"Uneasy?" he repeated, perhaps hardly knowing exactly why he said it. "Good Lord, but he can take care of himself—"

"Oh, *he* is a man," she interrupted; "yes."

Steps were heard, firm, heavy steps, coming back along the corridor. It seemed to Mortimer that he had listened to this sound of steps all night, and would listen to them till he died. He crossed to the

lamp and lit a cigarette, carefully this time, turning
the wick down afterwards. Mrs. Burley also rose,
moving over towards the door, away from him. They
listened a moment to these firm and heavy steps,
the tread of a man, John Burley. A man . . . and
a philanderer, flashed across Mortimer's brain like
fire, contrasting the two with fierce contempt for
himself. The tread became less audible. There was
distance in it. It had turned in somewhere.

"There!" she exclaimed in a hushed tone. "He's
gone in."

"Nonsense! It passed us. He's going out on to the
lawn."

The pair listened breathlessly for a moment,
when the sound of steps came distinctly from the
adjoining room, walking across the boards, apparently towards the window.

"There!" she repeated. "He did go in." Silence of
perhaps a minute followed, in which they heard each
other's breathing. "I don't like his being alone—in
there," Mrs. Burley said in a thin faltering voice, and
moved as though to go out. Her hand was already on
the knob of the door, when Mortimer stopped her
with a violent gesture.

"Don't! For God's sake, don't!" he cried, before
she could turn it. He darted forward. As he laid a
hand upon her arm a thud was audible through the
wall. It was a heavy sound, and this time there was
no wind to cause it.

"It's only that loose swinging thing," he whispered thickly, a dreadful confusion blotting out clear thought and speech.

"There was no loose swaying thing at all," she said in a failing voice, then reeled and swayed against him. "I invented that. There was nothing." As he caught her, staring helplessly, it seemed to him that a face with lifted lids rushed up at him. He saw two terrified eyes in a patch of ghastly white. Her whisper followed, as she sank into his arms. "It's John. He's—"

At which instant, with terror at its climax, the sound of steps suddenly became audible once more—the firm and heavy tread of John Burley coming out again into the corridor. Such was their amazement and relief that they neither moved nor spoke. The steps drew nearer. The pair seemed petrified; Mortimer did not remove his arms, nor did Mrs. Burley attempt to release herself. They stared at the door and waited. It was pushed wider the next second, and John Burley stood beside them. He was so close he almost touched them—there in each other's arms.

"Jack, dear!" cried his wife, with a searching tenderness that made her voice seem strange.

He gazed a second at each in turn. "I'm going out on to the lawn for a moment," he said quietly. There was no expression on his face; he did not smile, he did not frown; he showed no feeling, no emotion—just looked into their eyes, and then withdrew round the edge of the door before either could utter a word in answer. The door swung to behind him. He was gone.

"He's going to the lawn. He said so." It was Mortimer speaking, but his voice shook and stammered. Mrs. Burley had released herself. She stood now by the table, silent, gazing with fixed eyes at nothing, her lips parted, her expression vacant. Again she was aware of an alteration in the room; something had gone out. . . . He watched her a second, uncertain what to say or do. It was the face of a drowned person, occurred to him. Something intangible, yet almost visible stood between them in that narrow space. Something had ended, there before his eyes, definitely ended. The barrier between them rose higher, denser. Through this barrier her words came to him with an odd whispering remoteness.

"Harry. . . . You saw? You noticed?"

"What d'you mean?" he said gruffly. He tried to feel angry, contemptuous, but his breath caught absurdly.

"Harry—he was different. The eyes, the hair, the"—her face grew like death—"the twist in his face—"

"What on earth are you saying? Pull yourself together." He saw that she was trembling down the whole length of her body, as she leaned against the table for support. His own legs shook. He stared hard at her.

"Altered, Harry . . . altered." Her horrified whisper came at him like a knife. For it was true. He, too, had noticed something about the husband's appearance that was not quite normal. Yet, even while they talked, they heard him going down the carpetless stairs; the sounds ceased as he crossed the hall; then came the noise of the front door banging, the reverberation even shaking the room a little where they stood.

Mortimer went over to her side. He walked unevenly.

"My dear! For God's sake—this is sheer nonsense. Don't let yourself go like this. I'll put it straight with him—it's all my fault." He saw by her face that she did not understand his words; he was saying the wrong thing altogether; her mind was utterly elsewhere. "He's all right," he went on hurriedly. "He's out on the lawn now—"

He broke off at the sight of her. The horror that fastened on her brain plastered her face with deathly whiteness.

"That was not John at all!" she cried, a wail of misery and terror in her voice. She rushed to the window and he followed. To his immense relief a figure moving below was plainly visible. It was John Burley. They saw him in the faint grey of the dawn, as he crossed the lawn, going away from the house. He disappeared.

"There you are! See?" whispered Mortimer reassuringly. "He'll be back in—" when a sound in the adjoining room, heavier, louder than before, cut appallingly across his words, and Mrs. Burley, with that wailing scream, fell back into his arms. He caught her only just in time, for she stiffened into ice, daft with the uncomprehended terror of it all, and helpless as a child.

"Darling, my darling—oh, God!" He bent, kissing her face wildly. He was utterly distraught.

"Harry! Jack—oh, oh!" she wailed in her anguish. "It took on his likeness. It deceived us . . . to give him time. He's done it."

She sat up suddenly. "Go," she said, pointing to the room beyond, then sank fainting, a dead weight in his arms.

He carried her unconscious body to a chair, then entering the adjoining room he flashed his torch upon the body of her husband hanging from a bracket in the wall. He cut it down five minutes too late.

THE GHOST HUNTERS

ALLEN UPWARD
(1905)

The Story of the Green House, Wallington

In undertaking to relate some of my experiences in connection with the purchase and sale of haunted houses, I desire to make it clear that I have no theories to put forward on the subject of what is called the "occult."

I was successful in this class of business, but some of the adventures I went through were of such a character that I dared not continue. My nerves are fairly strong, but there are some things which I never wish to face again.

I was first tempted to dabble in this unlucky class of business by the Green House, Wallington.

My partner, Mr. Mortimer—our firm is Mortimer & Hargreaves—mentioned to me one day that he had had a client in to see him who was very anxious to obtain an immediate offer, at almost any price, for a house situated in what was then the rural district of Wallington.

"He says he cannot sell the house because people think it is haunted. It is all nonsense, of course;

but the people in the neighbourhood have got the idea firmly into their heads; and now if any tenants come they are sure to hear of it directly, and get frightened. The result is that he has lost tenant after tenant, and now the reputation of the house is so bad that he cannot sell it."

"What sort of a house is it?" I asked. "And what will he take for it?"

"He says he will take anything—£500 if he can't get more; though the house cost £1,500 to build. You had better see the man yourself."

I therefore dropped a line to Mr. Giltstrap, the owner of the Green House, requesting him to go down with me to see the property.

On the way to Wallington I put some questions about the house to Giltstrap, whose manner was rather reserved. He assured me it was in thorough repair, but he seemed reluctant to answer when I asked him about the ghost.

"Is there any story about the house? Anything to account for its being haunted?"

"No, no. What story should there be? It's a modern house—hardly been built ten years."

"And how long has it been your property?"

"I bought it as soon as it was put up."

"And how long has it been haunted?"

Mr. Giltstrap frowned as though he disliked to hear this word.

"The house has been talked about for some years now—four or five."

His disinclination to speak was so evident that I did not care to pursue the subject.

We got out at Wallington Station, and as we passed a house agent's on the road Giltstrap said abruptly:

"I must step in here and get the keys. Wait a moment."

As a house-agent myself, I could understand that he did not wish to introduce me to the local man, lest it should lead to any dispute about commission. But my curiosity about the Green House was so strong that I could not resist the temptation to walk in after him.

I was just in time to hear the owner say curtly:

"I have called for the keys of the Green House, if you please."

The local agent was evidently a man in a small way, for we found him seated at a desk in the outer office, in his shirtsleeves. He gave a cross look at Giltstrap, and a suspicious one at me, and then rose and reached down the keys from a nail.

"I haven't been able to find a caretaker yet," he said with a touch of malice. "They say you must pay them for living in such a house."

Giltstrap reddened at this speech, which was calculated to put off an intending purchaser. He glared first at the agent and then at me, snatched the keys without a word, and hurried out.

The Green House was a modern, red-brick one, standing in a road with several others, and certainly not looking at all the kind of place to have a supernatural legend attached to it.

As soon as we got inside I saw that the house was partly furnished. Giltstrap explained that he had been trying to get someone to come and occupy it rent free for a time in order to live down its reputation.

I asked if there was any room particularly connected with the ghostly rumours.

After what struck me as a momentary hesitation, he led me upstairs into what was clearly the principal bedroom, overlooking the front garden and the road outside.

"Is this where the ghost walks?" I asked as I glanced round the empty room. The paper on the walls was in good condition, and the ceiling had been newly white-washed.

The owner of the Green House was plainly annoyed by my insistence.

"There is no ghost, and it does not walk anywhere," he said irritably. "But the people who sleep in this room complain."

"What do they complain of?"

He fidgeted and again showed some reluctance in answering.

"Oh, nothing except some nonsense or other. They say they do not sleep well, and they dream things. Fancies, you know—fancies."

"Well, what sort of fancies?" I persisted. "If they dream, they must dream of something."

Giltstrap glanced up at the ceiling, and swiftly withdrew his eyes with a nervous tremor. I was now firmly persuaded that he himself had been the victim of some spectral horror, though he was anxious to conceal it for fear of frightening me off.

"Perhaps I had better not tell you anything," he said, after considering a moment. "There is a great deal in the influence of suggestion, so it is said. If I were to tell you what the people who have slept in this room have seen, or dreamt they have seen, that might be enough to make you dream the same. Whereas, if a sensible man without any notions came and slept here, he would most likely never be disturbed."

I thought there was something in what he said, and did not press him further.

There was a staircase outside leading to a second floor, and I moved towards it.

"Oh, do you want to see the other rooms?" Giltstrap snapped, as he prepared to follow.

"I want to see everything," I said decidedly.

Upstairs I found another room which had been left unfurnished. The prospect from the window showed me that it was situated over the haunted chamber.

"Is there something wrong with this room, as well?" I demanded.

"The servants don't like sleeping in it," was the grudging admission. "It does very well as a box-room."

I saw that it was useless to try and extract any more information from Giltstrap. After a thorough inspection, I decided that the house would be well worth £1200, apart from its evil reputation. I went back to town with the owner, and bargained with him on the way.

I was very anxious to secure an option to purchase the Green House at the end of a month, during which time I was to occupy it, but this proposal the owner obstinately refused.

"I want to sell it outright or not at all. If you live in it a month and have no trouble, I shall then be able to ask a reasonable price."

Anxious to secure a bargain, I gave way, and got out at Victoria the owner of the Green House, at the price of £500.

When I told my partner the next day what I had done, he declined to commit himself.

"I shall know whether it is a good bargain or not when I hear what you have sold it for," he observed grimly.

My next step was to secure some attendance, and to send down some furniture for the two empty rooms round which the mystery appeared to cling.

In the course of the negotiations I had occasion for the services of my lady secretary.

I was accustomed to discuss business matters with her, and as soon as she learned the character of the present transaction, she surprised me by displaying an unusual interest in it. She even volunteered her assistance.

"I wonder if you would mind my going to see the Green House, Mr. Hargreaves? I am very much interested in psychical research."

"Do you mean that you really believe there is something in it?" I exclaimed in dismay. I had grown to look on Miss Sargent as a young lady of great intelligence, and I was not very well pleased at the idea of taking the ghost seriously.

"I know that there are things in Nature which ordinary rules do not explain," was the grave answer. "I have seen things myself which could not be accounted for by natural means."

This was rather alarming. I recalled the strange, uneasy manner of the late owner of the Green House, and asked myself whether he had not been a secret believer in some occult happenings.

"I am what is called a sensitive," Miss Sargent proceeded to explain. "I have a peculiar faculty for seeing any abnormal manifestations."

A thought struck me.

"Would it be possible for you to go and pass a night or two there?" I inquired. "I don't mind telling you that if the apparition, or whatever it is, can be exorcised, I hope to sell the house at a considerable profit; and I should be glad to pay a small commission."

Miss Sargent appeared to welcome the suggestion. She was a good girl, the chief support of a widowed mother and three little sisters, and I knew she would like to earn something for them.

The question was referred to her mother, who arranged to come with her, it being understood that I should form one of the party. I engaged a respectable woman to come in by the day, and, on the evening agreed upon, we went down together to take possession of the haunted house

Miss Sargent and her mother were installed in the haunted room, and I decided to occupy the attic overhead.

After a pleasant supper the two ladies retired at about eleven o'clock. I sat up a little later, smoking a cigar, and contrasting the cheerful evening I had just passed with the lonely ones I was accustomed to in my West-end chambers.

Towards twelve I went upstairs, intending to go to bed. But whether it was the sensation of being in a strange house under such circumstances, or a secret apprehension of which I was hardly conscious, no sooner did I find myself in the room I had chosen than I was seized with an overmastering reluctance to get into the bed.

I took off my coat merely, rolled myself well up in the blankets, and tried to go to sleep. I am an old traveller, and have never experienced any difficulty in sleeping in my clothes in trains, or under similar circumstances.

But on this occasion the attempt was hopeless; I lay on the bed literally shivering, and not from cold. I neither saw nor heard anything, I was not alarmed in the ordinary sense, and yet if I had known there was a murderer lurking in the room ready to spring on me and stab me the moment I closed my eyes I could not have felt more wretchedly afraid.

Suddenly I heard a low moan—the moan of a creature in mortal terror, drawn out till it became a muffled scream.

I flung off the blankets, raised my head, and listened with a beating heart.

The moan was repeated, coming distinctly from underneath me. In an instant I had grasped the truth. It came from the room below.

I sprang from the bed, and, without stopping to put on my coat, lit the candle I had brought up with me, and flew downstairs.

As I reached the first floor landing the moan was repeated in a more terrible key—the key of horror instead of terror. At the same moment the door of the haunted room was thrown open, and Mrs. Sargent appeared on the threshold, with a cloak thrown over her shoulders, and a look of fear and distress on her face.

"What is it?" I gasped.

"It is Alwyne!" she cried in answer. "She is seeing something horrible in her sleep, *and I can't wake her!*"

Without stopping to consider questions of etiquette, I dashed into the room. The gas had been turned full on, and by its light I saw the girl lying stretched on a couch at the foot of the bed, her features frozen into the expression of one who looks upon some horrid sight, while from her parted lips there issued those appalling sounds which wounded like the stabs of a knife.

I caught her by the shoulders and shook her, without making the slightest change in her swoon-like condition.

"Water!" I called out to the mother, who stood wringing her hands, too dazed to act.

The water was brought, and I dashed half a glassful in the face of the sufferer. At first it had no more effect than if she had been dead.

Then came a startling change.

The moans suddenly ceased, the victim opened her eyes, which showed the dull glassy stare of a somnambulist, and sitting half up, she commenced muttering so quickly and indistinctly that it was difficult to catch the words.

"The-blood-the-blood-the-blood-the-blood-dripping-dripping-dripping-dripping-from-the red-leak-in-the-ceiling-the-red-leak-the-red-leak-in-the-ceiling-in-the-ceiling-dripping-on-*me*-dripping-on-ME-dripping-on-ME!"

The words rose into a wild shriek as her blank eyes were turned full on the ceiling overhead, the ceiling between her room and mine.

Involuntarily I looked up. The ceiling did not show the slightest mark. As I had noticed when I went over the house with Giltstrap, it was newly whitewashed— I thought I now knew why.

But the moment was not for reflection.

"Help me to carry her out of this—quick!" I called out to the mother.

Between us we lifted up the unconscious girl and carried her out of the accursed room, and into one adjoining, where we laid her on the bed.

Hardly had she passed the doorway of the haunted chamber when the dreadful ejaculations began to die away, and the rigidity of the features to relax. In a short time the trance condition passed away into a deep sleep, and I was able to leave Miss Sargent to her mother's care.

When she woke in the morning, her mother told me, she remembered nothing whatever of what had passed in the night. She was barely conscious of having had a bad dream. At her own request, I described to her at breakfast what had occurred, as minutely as possible. She was profoundly impressed.

"I am certain," she declared with conviction, "that what I saw represents something that actually happened in this house. Dreadful as it sounds, I firmly believe that somebody has been murdered in that attic in which you slept, and that his blood did drip through the ceiling of the room below, as I saw it last night."

Reluctant as I was for many reasons to entertain such a suggestion, I dared not neglect it altogether. I determined at all events to do whatever could be done to solve the mystery.

As soon as Miss Sargent and her mother had left the house, in which the elder lady would not hear of their passing another night, though her daughter did not seem in the least afraid, I went straight to a builder's in the neighbourhood, and engaged him to send some men to examine the flooring between the two haunted rooms.

The builder received my order with marked interest.

"I knew there was something the matter with that house," he observed. "It ain't likely that tenant after tenant would come away scared without something was wrong. Why, do you know, sir, in the last five years, since Mr. Giltstrap gave it up, I've whitewashed one ceiling in that house *nine times!*"

"Then Mr. Giltstrap once lived in it himself, did he?" I exclaimed.

"Seeing that I built it for him, I can say he did," was the answer.

"And why did he leave it?" I demanded, fairly roused.

But the builder could not or would not satisfy my curiosity on that head.

"Mr. Giltstrap was a good customer of mine; he always paid me regular; and I ain't got nothing to say against him."

The builder's interest led him to accompany his men, a carpenter and a plasterer, to the scene of action.

I pointed out the place on the ceiling, as nearly as I could judge it, from which the ghostly dew had appeared to fall.

The men took measurements, and then, proceeding to the attic above, located a spot under the bed in which I had tried to sleep.

The bed was quickly removed, the flooring stripped off, and in the space between the joists there was exposed a mass of lime.

Both the men, as well as their master, were quick to declare that the lime could not have been left there when the house was completed.

"That lime has been put there for no good," the builder asserted. "If you want some things hidden away and destroyed, there's nothing better than what lime is when it's fresh. It burns as well as fire, and makes no smoke."

"You mean a dead body?" I said shuddering.

"I don't say nothing about that," the builder answered, pulling himself up. "It ain't for me to say what that lime's been used for. All I say is it wasn't me that left it there, nor yet my men."

The two men began clearing the stuff away. The volatile element had evidently evaporated long ago. As they struck downward with their tools, one of them went through the plaster of the ceiling below, and a shaft of light came up.

An exclamation from one of the men followed. I bent down and peered into the cavity.

On a large beam which here crossed the floor I saw a deep black stain, the stain of long-dried blood!

A moment after the carpenter stooped suddenly, groped about with one hand amid the woodwork, and drew forth to the light a small sharp stiletto, rusted with the same dismal stain.

Nothing more was found. I gave the builder an order to entirely renew the flooring between the two haunted rooms; and from the time that was done, there has never again been the slightest complaint from any occupier of the property.

I let the Green House almost immediately to a respectable tenant, a retired school master, who changed its name; and before a year was out I was able to dispose of it to a purchaser at the price of £1,250, a sum which enabled me to compensate Miss Sargent for her trying experience.

* * * * *

The most extraordinary part of the story remains to be told.

The report of what had taken place having got abroad in Wallington, the local police came to me to obtain the stiletto, which I had been careful to preserve. By its means they were enabled to unearth a crime which had gone unsuspected till that hour, and to extort a confession from the murderer.

Into the details of this terrible case I do not mean to enter. It is sufficient to say that the victim had perished while asleep in the attic, and that his blood had actually soaked through the ceiling into the room below, which was that of his murderer—Giltstrap!

The Tapping on the Wainscot

The mysterious incident which I am going to narrate is one which seems to have a particular interest for those who study occult phenomena.

According to some who have discussed it with me, it throws an important light on the conditions which prevail in the world of spirits, and the limitations to their action.

However, I do not care to say anything on the subject myself. My object is simply to set down facts, and leave others to draw their own conclusions.

It was about a year after the affair of the Green House, Wallington, already related, when our firm received instructions from the solicitors of Sir Henry Weetman to dispose by auction of his family mansion, Hailesbury Manor, Sussex.

I was told that Sir Henry was a distant relation, who had recently come into the title and estate on the death of the last baronet, and preferred to live abroad. The furniture and effects had been sold already by a firm of auctioneers, well known for their sales of that kind, and the house and estate were to follow.

I went down with a clerk to view the place, and found it to be a very handsome old Jacobean mansion, with valuable oak wainscot in all the principal rooms.

The caretaker who showed us over it was a dear old lady who had been housekeeper to the last baronet, and was evidently heartbroken at the prospect of the old family seat passing into the possession of strangers.

"Sir Christopher—that's my late master—would turn in his grave if he knew what was being done with the old place," she lamented. "And I shouldn't wonder if he did know."

I was busy directing the clerk in taking measurements of the more important rooms and did not pay much heed to this obscure intimation.

In due course we reached the first floor, and the housekeeper conducted us into a great, square room with a huge fireplace, and two windows commanding a view over the park.

I was surprised to find that this room had not been stripped so completely as the ones downstairs. It still contained a magnificently carved oak bedstead, a four-poster, equal in size to the bedroom of a modern flat.

"This is the room Sir Christopher died in," the old lady said impressively. "He died in that bed. King Charles I. once slept in it."

"And why hasn't it been removed like the rest of the furniture?" I naturally asked.

"It is fixed to the floor, for one thing," was the answer. "And Sir Henry thought it would fetch more by leaving it where it is. But I believe he would have it taken away now if he knew what I know."

Mrs. Musgrave, as the old housekeeper was named, nodded her head and pursed up her lips, after the manner of old ladies when they have a secret which they are longing to tell, but which they think it due to their dignity only to part with under pressure.

"Why, what is it you know?" I asked, with an interest by no means feigned.

"Perhaps I ought not to speak of it," the housekeeper returned, with a glance at my clerk.

I sent the young man into the other room, and repeated my question.

"Well, sir, it may be that I ought not to be the first to mention it, but it's being talked of in the village, and if you didn't hear of it from me you'd hear of it from somebody else, most likely." Mrs. Musgrave lowered her voice: "This house is haunted, sir."

Remembering my late grisly experience, I did not reply as lightly as I might have done once to such a statement.

"Haunted? How? In what way?"

"You may believe me, or you may not, sir," Mrs. Musgrave said with deliberation, evidently in no hurry to come to the point. "There are some who can hear it, and some who can't. Some say it's only fancy, and others that it's the spirit of Sir Christopher. But all I can say is, I wouldn't pass a night in this room again, not if you were to offer me fifty pounds."

This was not very pleasant hearing. If a report of this kind were current in the village it would be pretty sure to reach the ears of any intending purchaser, and perhaps choke him off.

An old family ghost, or the tradition of one, is sometimes considered an attraction to a venerable country seat. But any really unpleasant phenomena, particularly if of quite recent date, would be a very decided drawback in most people's eyes.

"Can you tell me exactly what you did hear?" I asked.

"It is a tapping, sir, a tapping on the wainscot just over there," she pointed to the wall opposite the foot of the bed. "I was lying asleep in the bed, sir,—for when the house was stripped, and Sir Henry went away, I thought there would be no harm in my sleeping here, and I wanted to say I had slept in the same bed as King Charles. But it's my belief that Sir Henry must have heard the tapping himself, and seen something as well, that frightened him; and that's why he was so anxious to clear everything out of the house, and leave it."

I listened, hardly knowing what question to put next. At last I inquired:

"Do you suggest—is there any reason to suppose—that there was anything wrong about Sir Christopher Weetman's death?"

The question took Mrs. Musgrave by surprise.

"Wrong, sir? What should there be wrong? I'm sure the poor gentleman couldn't have died more peacefully. Miss Alice and I were with him the whole time."

"Who was Miss Alice?"

"His daughter—at least, his adopted daughter. She had lived with him since she was a baby, and he made no difference between her and his own flesh and blood." Mrs. Musgrave's voice changed again, as she added: "And in my belief it's on her account that Sir Christopher walks."

"Why?"

"Because when Sir Henry came down he turned her out of the house with nothing but the clothes she stood in. Sir Christopher hadn't made a will, and he came into everything as the heir. Miss Alice had to go to London and take a situation as a waitress."

I mused in silence, Could there be any thing in that strange suggestion? Was it not more likely that the old housekeeper's indignation at her new master's conduct had made her fancy that the ordinary noises of an old mansion by night were a protest on the part of the dead?

"And have you heard the tapping since?" I asked.

"I hear it every night!" was the startling answer. "I have shifted my bed to half the rooms in the house, but it makes no difference. Wherever I am, the taps come; and then they move along the wall and by the staircases and the corridors till they reach this room and stop there!"

"Have you followed them?" I exclaimed, astonished.

"I did the first time—now I daren't," the housekeeper answered. "But I got Jim Bateman from the lodge to come up one night, and he heard them, and followed them, and they led him to the same place. And now he would no more cross the threshold of the house after dark than he would fly."

It was clear to me by this time that, whether fact or fancy, the story called for investigation.

I am not naturally nervous, and in spite of the disagreeable memories of the last haunted house I had spent a night in, I determined to face whatever there was to face in Hailesbury Manor.

Accordingly, I arranged with Mrs. Musgrave to make up a bed for me the next night but one. Not in the haunted room itself, that I did not feel disposed to risk, but so as to enable me to be at hand when the mysterious tapping began.

I was careful to say nothing in the office meanwhile, and, above all, to keep the matter from the ears of my lady secretary. Miss Sargent had solved the mystery of the Green House for me, but she had done so at the cost of an experience to which I could not think of exposing her a second time.

On the appointed evening I returned to Hailesbury with a small dressing-bag, prepared to stay the night.

The housekeeper had prepared a bedroom for me on one of the upper floors, not far from her own. But as she told me that the ghostly tapping usually began about midnight, I decided to sit up for it, and persuaded her to do the same.

We had supper together in a room down stairs, the old lady getting it ready herself. Not a girl in the village, it appeared, could be induced to remain in the house after sunset.

After supper Mrs. Musgrave nodded off to sleep in a rocking-chair before the fire, while I lit a cigar and waited in some excitement for what was to come.

The room in which we sat was wainscotted, like all those on the ground floor. Every time a coal dropped from the fire, or a window-frame rattled, I fancied the mysterious summons had come, and started nervously in my chair.

I believe it is not merely fancy which causes us to hear so many more small noises in a house at night than in the day time, but that there is some scientific reason for it. Be that as it may, everyone must admit that the sense of hearing is more acute in the darkness than in the light.

As twelve o'clock approached I deliberately turned the lamp out, keeping a candle and some matches by my side.

Hardly had I done this when I received a shock which nearly made me jump out of my chair. It was a tap—loud, sharp, and imperative—on the door of the room.

In my agitation the habitual phrase, "Come in," rose to my lips, and I uttered it. At the same moment my companion woke with a start, and stared about her wildly in the dim firelight.

"Did you hear It?" she asked in an awestruck whisper.

"Yes. Did you?"

As she nodded in answer, the tap sounded a second time, seeming fainter and further off.

I rose to my feet, and lit the candle.

"Are you going to follow It?" the old woman breathed.

"Yes; will you come?"

She shook her head.

"I dare not. Give me the matches! Don't go till I have lit the lamp, for my sake!"

I lingered, my own nerves becoming affected in sympathy with hers, while the frightened woman clutched the box from my hand, and struck a match, which she applied to the wick of the lamp.

At the same moment I heard the Tap for the third time, low, and fading away in the distance.

I strode to the door of the room, opened it, and passed out into the passage, leaving the door ajar.

The ghostly Tap sounded again far away in front of me, at the foot of the great staircase.

I strode after It, with quickening steps and throbbing pulses, carefully screening the candle flame with one hand. It moved on up the stairs, seeming to fly before me, and I almost raced to catch up that beckoning sound.

Along the main corridor overhead I was drawn, straight to the door of the death-chamber.

As I crossed the threshold, and the huge four-poster loomed up in the shadow, the character of the ghostly sound underwent a change.

Instead of a single tap, travelling with the speed of a terrified man fleeing from pursuit, it became a hurried knocking, moving round the room behind the wainscot as if in search of something. I could have sworn that Someone or Something *was feeling its way along*.

The daunting sounds arrived at the middle of the wall opposite the foot of the great bed, and became stationary.

Once—twice—thrice—that awful tap broke the silence, louder and more menacing each time.

And then all at once the flame of the candle turned blue and went out, leaving me in the stillness and the darkness, with the feeling that I was *not alone*.

How I got downstairs again I can hardly remember, but I am not ashamed to say that never was sight more welcome than the lamp light streaming through the open door on to the passage as I rushed towards it.

Mrs. Musgrave gave me a glance, and screamed:

"You have seen It?"

"No, no," I said, "but the light went out, and I had no matches."

I related my experience in a few words, and then made a confession.

"I cannot sleep in this house to-night, Mrs. Musgrave. I must go down to the village and try to get into the inn."

To my relief she offered no opposition. I fancy I was not the first person who had left her at the same hour for the same reason.

Not even in the morning did I feel inclined to return to the haunted house. I went up to London by the first train, and, going straight to the office, asked Miss Sargent to come into my room, and told her everything.

She listened with intense interest, not interrupting by so much as a movement till I had come to the end.

Then she said with grave decision:

"You must let me go down and spend a night in that room, Mr. Hargreaves."

"Don't think of such a thing!" I ex claimed. "I should never permit you to run the risk of such a shock as I had last night."

"It is a matter of necessity," Miss Sargent replied firmly. "It is a matter of duty. I cannot doubt that the tapping on the wainscot has a meaning. It is a message from the dead."

"A message! I don't understand."

"I don't profess to understand it myself at present. But I do not believe that it is an ordinary case of what is called haunting, where a spirit appears to be bound in some way to a particular spot. Neither do I believe that the object of this manifestation has been to drive the new owner of the house away, or to render it uninhabitable."

"Then what do you suggest?"

"I feel sure there is a reason for the taps always coming back to one particular place on the wall of that one room."

A light seemed to break on her mind as she spoke, and she added quickly:

"I should not wonder if there were something hidden behind the wainscot, perhaps a will or a paper of some kind."

I recalled what the housekeeper had told me about the adopted child of the dead man, turned adrift so heartlessly by the heir to his wealth.

"Pray Heaven you are right!" I ejaculated fervently. "I will go down again and have the wainscot removed. But, mind, this must be kept a strict secret. If Sir Henry Weetman or his solicitors heard what I was doing, I might get into serious trouble."

Out of gratitude for Miss Sargent's suggestion, I invited her to be present at the opening of the wainscot. I had confided my hopes and intentions to Mrs. Musgrave, who was intensely excited at the prospect of justice being done to her beloved young mistress.

"To think that I should never have guessed what it meant!" she cried. "And I thought I understood it better than anyone else, too."

"Did you think there was any reason for the tapping on that particular spot, then?" Miss Sargent asked.

"To be sure I did. That is just where Miss Alice's picture used to hang, so that Sir Christopher could see it every morning when he woke. Sir Henry had the picture sold with all the others, and I thought that was why Sir Christopher couldn't rest in his grave."

I saw a look of disappointment steal over Miss Sargent's face.

"It may be that Mrs. Musgrave is right," she said thoughtfully. "Very often the spirits seem to have very little motive—or what seems very little to us—for what they do."

"Well, we shall see," I responded, not willing to give up my hope on the poor orphan's behalf.

I had brought down an expert cabinet maker from London, and he went to work quickly and neatly. A great space of the wall was stripped of its wainscot, and we searched anxiously for any sign of a hiding-place behind. We searched vainly. To the bitter disappointment of all three of us there was not even a vestige, not so much as a scratch on the wall, to indicate that anything had ever been concealed there.

To complete our discomfiture the cabinet maker gave it as his opinion that the wainscot had never been disturbed since it was put up in the reign of James I.

"I was right, you see, Miss," said good Mrs. Musgrave sorrowfully. "It's the thought of Miss Alice's picture that keeps Sir Christopher out of his grave."

She spoke as though the deceased baronet were an invalid suffering from sleeplessness at night.

Miss Sargent shook her head, but said nothing. She seemed to be reflecting deeply.

We left the cabinet maker with strict instructions to replace the wainscot, so as to leave no trace of his operations, and went downstairs.

Half-an-hour later, as we were sitting at lunch, Miss Sargent suddenly spoke.

"You must let me sleep in that bed, Mr. Hargreaves. I am a clairvoyant in sleep, as you know, and I may see something which will explain the mystery."

We both returned to town in the afternoon to make our arrangements. The following day we came down again, prepared to spend the night.

None of us intended to go to bed. The four-poster in the haunted room had been furnished with blankets and pillows to serve as a bed for the clairvoyant. Mrs. Musgrave was to install herself on a sofa before the fire place, in which a fire had been lit, and I was to sit up in the next room, ready to come at the first call.

Miss Sargent, who fortunately possessed the power of falling asleep at will, retired to her strange couch a little before eleven, accompanied by the housekeeper, whose excitement promised to keep her awake.

As for myself, I cherished no wish to sleep. I had provided myself with lights, cigars, and a book to read, but I am bound to confess that I found it impossible to get interested in it.

An hour later I heard a low tapping on the door of my own room. Not a little startled, I sprang up, only to find that the sound this time was free from any element of mystery.

The old housekeeper had come to summon me.

"Will you come and see the young lady?" she said. "I think something is the matter."

I felt myself turning cold.

"What do you mean? Has the tapping begun?"

The answer surprised me.

"No, that is what frightens me. This is the first night I have not heard it for four months. But I think Miss Sargent sees something."

I led the way into the haunted room. There was not a sound to be heard, and the lights had been put out by the clairvoyant's desire. But she was sitting half up in bed, her eyes fast closed, and yet appearing to stare with the most deadly fear at the opposite wall.

Suddenly a sharp cry broke from her, followed immediately by the same frantic rush of half-articulated syllables which had so alarmed me on that night in the Green House. "Leave—it—alone—leave—it—alone—leave—it—alone—put—it—back—put—it—back—put—it—back—*Ah, he's taken it!*"

With these last words, uttered loudly in distinct tones, the sleeper's eyes suddenly opened, and she gave a fearful shudder.

Tap! tap! tap!

If ever I have heard any sounds in my life I heard those knocks by an unseen hand on the wainscot at which we all gazed, unable to stir till the knocks ceased.

It was too much for the nerves of any of us to bear. I caught the half-fainting girl in my arms as she threw herself from the great four-poster, and the three of us did not breathe again till we were safe in the house keeper's little sitting-room downstairs.

There, after she had rested and taken a soothing draught prescribed by the housekeeper, Miss Sargent related her vision.

"I saw a picture hanging on the wall, the picture of a young girl, about seventeen, with blue eyes and very light golden hair."

"Miss Alice!" the old lady interrupted.

"Two men came into the room, and moved about. I could not see what they were doing. Presently, one of them, who was in his shirt-sleeves, and looked like a workman, approached the picture, and raised his hands to take it down."

"One of the auctioneer's men, my dear," was Mrs. Musgrave's murmured comment.

"At that instant I saw suddenly, appearing from nowhere, in front of the picture, a corpse."

"A corpse!" we both ejaculated in horror.

"Yes, a dead man, in a winding sheet, with his head swathed in white bandages. The corpse seemed to try to thrust back the living man. He went on without noticing it, and took down the picture, I can hardly describe how, but just as though the corpse were not there. The dead man seemed to try to detain him, but he walked off with it. Then I awoke."

A cry burst from the poor old housekeeper.

"It was my poor master," she moaned, "trying to save Miss Alice's nice picture."

The other said nothing, but bent her brows as though profoundly dissatisfied with this seemingly puerile interpretation of the mystery. I watched her with expectation. I had come to look on Alwyne

Sargent as a woman of more than ordinary powers of mind, apart altogether from her extraordinary occult faculty, and I confidently anticipated that she would not let the matter rest there.

"The picture must be replaced," she said, after a long interval of meditation. "We cannot leave things as they are. At all costs the picture must be found, and hung up there again, if it is only for one night."

"I should think that could be managed," I said, though I did not much relish the idea.

I saw that Miss Sargent wanted to make fresh trial of her clairvoyant powers, with the picture in its place, and I dreaded the injury which these agitating experiences seemed likely to do her.

However, I shared her feeling that the mystery must be probed to the bottom. The very next day I called on the auctioneers who had charge of the sale at Hailesbury Manor, and asked them to let me go through their books. I told them nothing except that I had been asked to recover a family portrait included in the sale by oversight.

They were very obliging, and with their assistance I found that a picture catalogued as "Portrait of a Girl" had been sold for £12 to a gentleman living at Sydenham.

I went out there the same evening, and saw the purchaser, who was a Common Council man of the City of London, and evidently given to speculating in pictures, with which the house was crowded.

He saw his advantage, and drove a rather hard bargain with me, but in the end he agreed to let me have the picture to show to the client whom I pretended to have in the background, on my paying a deposit.

Then he led me upstairs to a small smoking-room, where I saw the picture hanging in an obscure corner.

With hands trembling with excitement, I took hold of the frame to lift it off the nail. As I did so, the nail itself gave way, and the precious portrait crashed to the ground, the frame coming in pieces.

I fell on my knees with a cry of dismay, when I was astonished to see, among the broken portions of the frame, a blue foolscap envelope indorsed in shaky handwriting— *"Will of Sir C. Weetman, Bart."*

The will gave the whole of his property to his adopted daughter, Alice Weetman.

Human nature is a curious thing. As soon as I had made out the contents of the document thus miraculously discovered, and he knew that the picture was that of a young lady who had come into a great fortune, the owner insisted on my accepting it as a free gift for the fortunate heiress.

It now hangs, in its carefully restored frame, in its old place at the foot of the historic bed; and the tapping on the wainscot in Hailesbury Manor has been heard no more.

THE SECRET OF HORNER'S COURT

I had by this time acquired quite a reputation in business circles as a buyer and investigator of houses reputed to be haunted.

The transactions I made were usually very profitable, since, as the agents were unable to either let or sell the ghost-ridden property which they desired me to purchase, I was able to secure it on favourable terms.

Miss Sargent, my lady secretary, who possessed the gift of clairvoyance, was of great assistance in probing mysteries connected with haunted mansions.

Not long after the fortunate ending of the adventure at Hailesbury Manor, I was approached by one of the leading firms of house-agents in the West-end with reference to another haunted house.

Horner's Court, as this place was called, had been on the books of the firm for many years, but they had been unable to find either a tenant or a purchaser for it on account of its reputation.

The partner who called on me described it as a well-built eighteenth-century house, situated in a northern county, on the outskirts of a famous forest. Two dukes lived in the immediate neighbourhood, so that the house ought to have fetched almost a fancy price from one of that numerous class who appreciate high Society.

But, for some reason or other, no one seemed willing to take to the place.

I listened to all Mr. Roseveare had to say, and asked if he could tell me anything definite about the prejudice or superstition which affected the house.

He shook his head.

"I can tell you nothing. It was placed in our hands by the trustees of the estate—I don't even remember whether they are acting for a minor, or how the property stands."

"Nor who occupied the house last, I suppose."

"A widow, I believe; a woman of rank—Lady Something or Other. She gave it up on her marriage to a second husband. Perhaps it is haunted by the ghost of the first," Mr. Roseveare added jocularly.

I smiled out of politeness, though I had ceased to look upon these subjects as matter for jest.

A business discussion followed, and it ended by my securing an option to buy the property on such nominal terms that if I could rid it of its disagreeable character I stood to make a very substantial sum indeed.

As soon as the understanding was reached, I called in Miss Sargent, and dictated its terms for her to type.

Mr. Roseveare was evidently struck by her name.

"May I venture to ask if this is the young lady who discovered the secret of the Green House?" he said respectfully.

I introduced him formally, not very well pleased with his presumption. Naturally, I did not wish the most valuable assistant in our office to be too friendly with a rival firm.

"What a perfectly charming girl!" was his exclamation, as Miss Sargent quietly withdrew to make her transcript. "I quite envy you, my dear sir."

"We find Miss Sargent competent, and loyal to her employers, and we do not look beyond," I returned, intensely annoyed.

Mr. Roseveare said nothing in reply, but he smiled in a way which I found it hard, as a business man, to bear.

"Well, I will send you round a copy of the agreement as soon as it is ready for signature," I said, as a broad hint for him to go. I was determined not to give him another chance of annoying my secretary.

"I am afraid you will not send it by Miss Sargent," he retorted rather vulgarly and maliciously, as he put on his hat and departed.

As I foresaw would be the case, Miss Sargent lost no time in applying for permission to aid me in investigating the mystery of Horner's Court.

The happy issue of our last adventure of the kind made it difficult for me to raise any objection. I had come to see, moreover, that, however great the strain upon her in her clairvoyant state, her experiences seemed to have no after effects of an injurious kind.

Accordingly, I arranged with her that if, on arriving at the scene of action, I found that there was any suggestion of an occult influence at work, I would summon her at once.

I went down two days later, the agreement with Roseveare & Grimston having been signed meanwhile, not without some further remarks by Mr. Roseveare which it would be childish on my part to record.

I arrived at a wayside station towards dusk on an autumn day, and was driven for miles along a misty road strewn with yellowing leaves, till I saw in front a great iron gate thrown back and rusting on its hinges.

Through this opening the dog-cart drove, and brought me along an avenue of black and naked trees to a gaunt house that stood and frowned at its own reflection in a dreary, reed-grown pool.

I caught my breath at the sight—I could not tell why—and when I had dismounted from the dog-cart I stood on the weather stained steps in front of the door, and felt a sense of reluctance at the thought of pulling that great, iron bell-handle and passing under that forbidding doorway.

With a shiver I mounted the steps and rang. The door was opened by a man—a man of a lowering, distrustful countenance, which told me at the first glance that it would not be his fault if a tenant were ever found for Horner's Court.

It seemed to me that I should learn more from this man if I concealed the true character in which I came, and let him suppose that I was acting for another.

Handing him my bag, I let him take me through the dark and dreary hall, lit only by a solitary candle, into a vast dining-room, almost equally dark and cheerless.

Some logs had been heaped in the grate, and as we came in a woman was putting a match to the small twigs underneath.

She looked up at me with a nervous glance of dread, and in that look I read that she knew the secret of Horner's Court—and that she would never dare to tell it to me.

Very few words passed between us, and those chiefly about supper. I bade the man show me my bedroom, and he took me up to a room on the floor above—a room whose windows looked directly on the dismal pool.

"Is this the haunted room?" I asked, with an affectation of levity which I was very far from feeling.

The man raised his head and stared at me.

"No, sir, it ain't. That room's the other side of the house, and if you take my advice you won't go near it except by daylight."

For that night, at all events, I was glad to accept his warning.

At dinner, if the rough meal set before me could be so called, I was waited on by the forbidding retainer, whose manner checked all attempts to draw him into conversation.

I could only glean that he had come to Horner's Court as a caretaker on the departure of Lady Maria Cruikshank, as the last tenant was named by him. No doubt the berth was an easy one, and he would resent having to make way for a new occupier. Inwardly I made up my mind to dismiss him as soon as possible.

He was obscure, intentionally obscure, I thought, on the subject of the supernatural visitings.

"I never seen nothing myself, so I can't say," he intimated darkly. "But I seen the faces of them what has seen something, and that was enough for me."

"And your wife, has she seen anything?" I asked.

"Don't you get speaking to Mrs. Stokes about it," he broke out abruptly. "She's half crazy already, and it wouldn't take much more to drive her clean off her head."

I sipped my glass of port in silence. Stokes had brought up an old cob-webbed bottle from the cellar, where a few yet lingered from former times. I filled another glass and gave it to the man.

"Drink that, and tell me what your wife has seen, if you don't want me to question her."

Fixing suspicious eyes on me, he lifted the glass and slowly drained it to the last drop.

"She *says*—well, she says as how she have seen a child."

"A child!"

"Aye. Leastways the sperrit of one, I reckon she means. Happen you don't believe in they sperrits, sir?"

His curious eyes sought to read mine. I shook my head.

"Is there any tradition connected with this house? Any rumour of a crime or tragedy?"

A sullen flush, I thought, rose on his countenance—it might have been the wine.

"Crime? Did you say crime, sir? No, there ain't never been no crime committed in Horner's Court. Lady Maria Freer and her like aren't the sort what commits crimes, are they?"

He spoke with a certain rude insolence which somehow seemed put on deliberately.

"Just now you called her Lady Cruikshank," I said thoughtfully, casting my eyes down, as though I disdained to question him.

His secret fears came uppermost, and got the better of his rudeness.

"She married Colonel Cruikshank when she left here," he said, fawning all at once.

"How long was she here before that?"

"I don't know."

It was a lie, of course, and, like most of the lies told by ignorant cunning, a useless one. Ladies of high rank—and the style of this one showed that she could not be less than an earl's daughter—are easily traced.

A night spent in the haunted house told me nothing more. Surely the shivering miasma of the stagnant pool beneath my window was the evil influence that wrought against the place? When I rose in the early morning and saw the wreaths of dank mist enfolding the walls like a white shroud, I asked myself if any other ghost were needed.

So at breakfast I said aloud, and half unconsciously:

"I will have the pool drained."

The gloomy man overheard me, and a look of anger came into his eyes. No doubt he feared that his reign was near its end.

"There's nought wrong with the mere," he muttered.

I looked him in the face.

"I shall return here in three days' time. Send your wife to me. I have an order to give her."

He looked at me as if he would have liked to disobey, but dared not, and shuffled out of the room.

When the woman appeared she was trembling, and her eyes were steadily turned to the ground.

I rose to my feet.

"Take me to the haunted room," I said briefly.

I would not trust the husband with my intention. The woman, thus taken unprepared, shuddered, but made no protest. She led the way upstairs to a remote wing overlooking a small garden.

The room was rather sad in its neglect, but not depressing. On the walls I saw some coloured prints, such as are sold at Christmas time with the illustrated papers.

"Who used this room in Lady Maria's time?" I asked, stealing a glance at the distressed creature.

"I don't know."

It was the husband's answer, no doubt repeated by his order.

"The house is haunted by a child's ghost. This looks as if it might have been a nursery," I prompted.

The woman turned very pale, but made no motion.

"Had she a child? And did he die here, in this room? And were there any circumstances—dark and dreadful circumstances?"

I was proceeding earnestly when all at once the woman threw up her hands, and, uttering low moans, tottered out of the room.

I passed her in the corridor, and stopped to whisper in her ear—for I knew not where her husband might lurk:

"I shall return here with a lady who can read the secrets of the dead. Have this room ready for her to pass the night in, and prepare the adjoining room for me."

I thought she would have taken my words as a threat. But she lifted her eyes to mine imploringly, and I just heard her breathe, "Thank Heaven!"

When I went down to Horner's Court with Alwyne Sargent, we did not go alone. An experienced nurse accompanied her, and I brought down, in the disguise of a valet, one of the shrewdest and most determined officers of Scotland Yard.

A "Peerage" had disclosed that Lady Maria Cruikshank was sister to the Earl of Gaysthorpe, and that her present residence was in Florence, Italy. Private inquiries added the information that she was the mother of one son, by her former husband. The boy was now seventeen, and travelling with a tutor.

When we arrived at Horner's Court, the caretaker received us with the same discourteous air. His wife, he told us, was unwell, but a woman had come up from the neighbouring farm to attend to us.

The police officer, by virtue of his supposed position, assumed the right of penetrating into the servants' quarters of the mansion. I followed Miss Sargent and the nurse upstairs, whither the woman led them.

The first glance round the room prepared for their reception showed me that it was not the one which I had formerly explored.

Yet it was like it. Even the very pictures seemed the same. Only, when I passed into the next room, and saw it artfully heaped up with lumber, did I feel sure that the substitution was intentional.

I questioned the woman, who told me truthfully enough, I have no doubt, that she knew nothing of the interior arrangements of the house.

I considered what it was best for me to do, and came to the conclusion that it would not be wise to let the man Stokes know that I had detected his deceit. He might have other tricks in reserve, for it was evidently his object to throw every obstacle in the way of our discovering the mystery of Horner's Court.

I let the woman believe that I was satisfied. But as soon as I found myself alone with the other two, I told them how things stood.

We arranged that when the time came to retire, a bed of some kind should be rigged up for Miss Sargent in the true haunted room. The nurse did not intend to go to sleep, but to keep watch over the clairvoyant.

The detective, whom we had left downstairs, was informed of my discovery, and concurred in what had been arranged. His manner showed him to be sceptical of Miss Sargent's powers, but he had come already to the conclusion that Stokes was hiding some secret of a highly doubtful character. He agreed, with some apparent hesitation, to share our watch.

The caretaker seemed to hover uneasily through our part of the mansion as long as he dared. As we sat in the dining-room we heard him locking and bolting the great hall door with infinite precaution.

"That man is certainly afraid of something," the police-officer remarked.

"Whether he really thinks the house is haunted or not, he dreads some accidental discovery."

After this search we all went upstairs. Miss Sargent's couch was made up for her in the room half-choked with lumber. The nurse carried in an arm-chair for herself, to sit beside the sleeping girl. The detective and I took seats into the corridor, ready in case the man we both suspected should come prowling along in the night.

The detective, Mayhew, declares that he saw nothing, was aware of nothing strange or uncanny happening that night. But he says that he saw me shiver and turn pale without visible cause.

All at once I heard a sound from the other side. Before I could gather what it was, I felt my hair stir and rise, and at the same moment the door was softly opened.

Alwyne Sargent stood on the threshold, her face drawn with wonder and dismay, and her eyes fixed in the unseeing gaze I had learnt to know and dread.

Behind her I discerned the figure of the nurse with finger uplifted.

"Do not wake her, for your life!" she warned me. "The shock might endanger her reason. We must follow where she goes."

By this time Mayhew had risen to his feet, an expression of amazement on his face.

The somnambulist stepped out into the corridor and moved slowly down it in the direction from which my fear had seemed to come.

The three of us stole after her on tiptoe, scarcely daring to breathe.

She led the way without hesitating downstairs into the hall. There she halted for a moment, as though uncertain which way to turn. But her hesitation was quickly over; she turned away from the main door, and made her way first into a drawing room, and thence into a conservatory with a glass door at the end leading into the grounds.

There was barely light enough for us to follow her without stumbling against the furniture and the wooden shelves in the glasshouse. But the sleeper moved on surely, without a mistake.

She reached the glass door some way in advance of us, and we heard her turn the handle. Then there was a low, desolate cry, and she shook fiercely at the unyielding door.

Mayhew and I darted forward. The door was locked, and the key had been taken away.

"This is some of that rascal's work," the detective muttered. "May I break the lock?"

By this time whatever scepticism he may have felt had evaporated in the excitement of the quest, and he was as eager as myself to see the end.

"Yes, break it," I said.

He dashed his foot against the flimsy door, and it burst away from its fastenings.

The shock produced no effect on the somnambulist, but she put out her hands and groped as though to ascertain if the obstacle had been removed. Then she heaved a sigh of relief, and passed out on to the lawn.

Turning to the right, she followed a winding path, which led down to the edge of the stagnant pool. I quickened my steps to come up with her, determined at all costs to prevent her falling into the water.

As if conscious of my intention, she hastened on till her walk became a run. I sprang forward, and was just in time to throw my arms round her as she reached the brink and threw out her hands in a gesture of supplication or despair.

Then, even as I held her rigid form, I did not hear, but I *knew of* a splash far out in the middle of the water, and a deep, silent ripple that slowly passed across the surface of the pool.

Neither of our companions saw or heard anything.

After an instant's agonised struggle, the somnambulist awoke in my arms, crying hysterically.

The nurse advanced hastily, and took her from me, soothing her, and turning her steps back towards the house.

As we neared the conservatory door the police-officer uttered an exclamation and darted forward.

He told me afterwards he was certain he had seen the face of Stokes peering out with a look of no common fear. But the man was not to be found.

"I will have the mere dragged the first thing to-morrow," I declared. I remembered now the aversion shown by Stokes at my former proposal to drain the dismal pool.

The rest of the night passed off without incident; but in the morning the woman who had been waiting upon us came and made the surprising announcement that the caretaker was nowhere to be found.

Both he and his wife had fled from the house and from the neighbourhood without a word of explanation; and neither of them has ever been heard of since. It was only possible to suppose that the man had been drawing a secret allowance so long as the mystery of Horner's Court remained undiscovered, and that what he had seen on this night had convinced him that the game was up, and that he would be safer out of the way.

As soon as the necessary appliances could be obtained, the pool was dragged opposite the spot where the somnambulist had stood.

Horrible to relate, the drag brought up the skeleton of a child of about seven years of age.

As soon as the detective Mayhew saw this tragic evidence, he made up his mind that a serious crime had been committed. The subsequent investigation was conducted by him, and I need only tell briefly its result.

Inquiries in the neighbourhood brought out that Lady Maria Freer was the mother of a boy of seven or eight at the time of her engagement to Colonel Cruikshank. The Colonel seemed to dislike the boy; and his mother, who was a heartless Society woman, left him entirely to the care of servants, while she gave herself up to hunting and other amusements in the company of her future husband.

On her second marriage she had quitted Horner's Court for the honeymoon, not to return. The little boy did not appear at the wedding, and it was given out that he had been sent on in the charge of a governess to the place which his parents had chosen as their future residence.

Armed with this information, the detective called on the trustees of the late Mr. Freer, whose heir the boy was.

From them he learnt the important fact that under the provisions of the will the whole income of the estate during the boy's minority was payable to the widow. On the boy's coming of age, or death during infancy, her income was reduced to the widow's third.

Lady Maria was regularly receiving the full income from the trustees, who had not the faintest suspicion of anything being wrong.

Mayhew, who felt pretty sure that the story of the lad of seventeen and the travelling tutor was a myth, obtained a letter from the trustees to Lady Maria Cruikshank, calling for the immediate production of the heir, and went to Florence to deliver it in person.

The wicked mother, thus taken unawares, showed more fear than remorse. She made a confession, which the detective was content to accept as probably near the truth.

The boy had died in the room at Horner's Court; and if his death had not been wholly due to neglect, at least his life might have been prolonged by the care and devotion of a mother who really loved her child. Unwilling to lose the greater part of her income, to which she owed the prospect of a second husband, the heartless woman had concealed the state of her son's health from everyone but the two Stokes, and when the poor child died, she had paid Stokes to dispose of the body in the pool in front of the house. Her plan was to draw the income of the estate up to the last moment, and then send a certificate of her son's death from some foreign place where a doctor could easily be bribed.

The trustees forbore to prosecute, but I am glad to say that they firmly refused to pay another penny to Colonel Cruikshank's wife till the whole of the sum she had fraudulently obtained had been stopped out of her lawful dower; and when last heard of the pair were living in abject poverty.

Horner's Court has become the residence of the High Sheriff of —shire.

THE TWO ROSES

It would give needless pain to members of the family who are still living in the neighbourhood if I were to go into the circumstances in which the ancient seat of the Hedges, of Essex, came into the market.

It is only necessary to say that the solicitors from whom my firm received instructions to find a purchaser for the estate were not acquainted with the family history, and could tell us nothing definite on the subject of the incidents, real or imaginary, which had given an evil reputation to Bewley Hall.

They were only able to inform us that one entire wing of the building, constituting the most ancient and characteristic portion, had been shut up for a great length of time, so long, indeed, that no one seemed able to remember when it had last been inhabited.

I discussed the matter with Miss Alwyne Sargent, the young lady employed in our office, who had already given me such valuable assistance on similar occasions.

She possessed the gift of clairvoyance and had proved of incalculable assistance in explaining away mysteries connected with several residences.

These were notably the Green House, Wallington, Hailesbury Manor, and Horner's Court.

I had already become well known as a dealer in haunted property, and made a satisfactory profit on my transactions, buying the premises cheap, and selling at a profit when the mysteries were cleared up.

I was reluctant to expose her to the risk of another nervous shock, although she herself was quite eager to take her usual part in our joint investigations. I thought, however, it could do no harm for her to come down with me to make some preliminary inquiries.

None of the furniture and effects had yet been removed from the mansion, and there was a farm bailiff occupying rooms with his family in the servants' quarter, so that it was easy to arrange for a visit.

The rather senseless difficulty of a chaperon for my lady clerk was disposed of by my sister Jane, who surprised me by requesting that she might make one of the party. Jane had not previously met Miss Sargent, but she had heard me speak of her once or twice, and appeared anxious for some reason to make her acquaintance.

I was a little disappointed to find that Alwyne did not seem equally eager to meet my sister. In fact, she went so far as to say that she felt nervous at the prospect. I could only assure her that my sister Jane was a most unassuming, ordinary person, quiet, shrewd, and observant, and, moreover, devoted to me. But this information did not allay Miss Sargent's apprehensions, which seemed to increase as the moment for our departure drew near.

The ceremony of introduction took place on the platform at Liverpool Street. Both ladies, I thought, were more carefully dressed than seemed necessary for a purely business journey, on which we were to meet no one of any consequence. I caught a look of surprise on my sister's face as Alwyne came up, and she took the first opportunity to whisper to me, almost in a tone of reproach: "Jack! you never told us she was a beauty!"

"Miss Sargent is a valued member of our clerical staff," I replied severely. "Her looks are no concern of ours so long as they do not interfere with her faithful discharge of her duties in the office."

Jane looked dissatisfied, but she did not venture on any further remark. During the journey down she watched the poor girl as closely as a cat watches a canary bird through the bars of its cage. Fortunately Miss Sargent soon got over her first nervousness, and exerted herself to conciliate my sister with such good effect that by the time we reached Saffron Walden we were all chatting like old friends. Jane rather embarrassed me by forgetting the business relationship between Miss Sargent and myself, and referring to me repeatedly by my Christian name, so that I was rather glad that my partner, Mortimer, was not present.

We found Bewley Hall to be an ancient manor house of the Elizabethan type, built of red brick, which was mellowed by age, and overgrown in many places with ivy and climbing plants. The principal feature was a large and lofty hall, on much the same design as the London Guildhall, but on a smaller scale. It was stone-paved, and was panelled halfway up the walls with very valuable old oak.

The hall, I must explain, separated the two wings or halves composing the mansion. The modern portion, which had been in constant use up to the death of the late owner, had been built on to the great hall at its lower end. The haunted wing, if it should be so called, was connected with the upper end.

Here there was a daïs, also paved with stone, stretching from side to side of the hall. The door into the ancient wing opened off one side of the daïs, and on the opposite side was another smaller door, like a postern, which we found led into a little rose garden behind the house.

The only other feature that I need dwell on was a gallery, which the bailiff's wife, who showed us over the place, called the musicians' gallery. It overlooked the daïs, facing the door into the rose garden, and when we went upstairs we found it was approached by a corridor that traversed the whole length of the haunted wing.

The woman who acted as our guide was very uncommunicative, partly, I believe, because she really had heard very little, and partly because she fancied that she would lower herself in our eyes by betraying any interest in the lore of superstition.

When I asked her if she could tell us anything about the ghost, she tossed her head in disdain.

"I don't know of any ghost," she declared, "and I don't hold with any talk about such things. It's only the labourers that believes in them hereabouts."

The social cleavage thus indicated forbade further inquiry. The bailiff's wife informed us, however, that the disused part of the mansion had been shut up long before she was born, and she made a great deal of difficulty about letting us spend the night in it.

"It's all dust and cobwebs," she explained to me. "Everything there is exactly as it was left a hundred years ago and more, I should say. Your ladies couldn't possibly put up with the dirt and the damp."

We explored the wing under her guidance, and its appearance served to confirm her account. The old hangings clung mouldering to the walls; ancient weapons grown rusty with neglect were suspended along the sides of the corridor; in the bedrooms old

four-poster beds were covered with the embroidered
quilts of another age, and the robes and brocades of
a past generation still filled the closets.

Even my staid and demure sister could not resist the temptation to rummage in some of the cupboards and examine the decayed fineries they contained, while I felt no less strongly attracted by the
fine specimens of seventeenth and eighteenth century arms. I found that one superbly mounted pistol
which I took down from its place actually had the
left barrel still loaded, though the priming had long
since disappeared.

Alwyne approached me as I was examining the
pistol, and I showed her the flints still in the ham-
mers. She regarded the weapon with peculiar attention, taking it in her hand with a meditative, musing look.

"I wonder how the other barrel came to be dis-
charged," she said.

So far we had been able to glean nothing from the
impenetrable obstinacy of our guide. After selecting
our rooms, which the woman reluctantly promised
to provide with some bedding from the other part of
the house, we came back into the great hall.

I have already mentioned the daïs which occupied one end, with the two doors opening off it.
Across the daïs there extended an ancient table, long
and narrow, made of a single beam of oak.

Someone threw out the suggestion that we three should dine at this seigneurial board, in imitation of the olden time.

When I requested the bailiff's wife to make the necessary arrangements, she exhibited some slight dismay.

"Of course it's for you to do as you wish, sir," she said. "But perhaps your ladies don't know that this is the table that has the bloodstain on it."

We seized eagerly upon this allusion.

"What bloodstain?—where?" we demanded, crowding round the black and venerable board.

The woman pointed to the end of the table nearest to the door into the rose garden. Surely enough the wood seemed to have a darker tinge at one particular spot. The mark was about the size of a man's hand.

"Is there a story about this stain?" I asked, hoping to get upon the track of the ghostly legend of the Hall.

But the woman could not, or would not, be drawn.

"It's an old secret in the family, I've heard, how the stain got there. I don't rightly call to mind what it was, but I do think there was a murder in the Hall. Some say it was a hundred years ago, and some two hundred, and the murderer was Sir William Hedges.

"But anyway the table hasn't been used from that day to this, and the family never would have it touched."

Miss Sargent showed herself intensely interested in this account, scanty as it was.

"Who knows that there may not be some sympathetic force concentrated in this particular spot," she said reflectively. "I think that instead of our dining here, and possibly disturbing the magnetism of the table, it will be better for us to try to hold a séance here at night."

Although my recent experiences had cured me of a good deal of scepticism with regard to the occult, I still draw the line at ordinary spirit-rapping. I hinted as much to Alwyne.

"That is not exactly what I meant," she explained. "I am not a medium in that sense. I merely believe it possible that if I can establish a magnetic rapport with this table I may feel some direction given to me which will help us."

My sister, I could see, was a good deal puzzled by this mystic language. In the end, however, Miss Sargent had her way.

We dined and spent the first part of the evening in the modern side of the building, and then adjourned about ten o'clock to the dark and echoing hall.

We placed ourselves round the end of the table, which bore the faded mark of blood, and extinguished the candles we had brought with us. It was a bright moonlight night, and the white rays that streamed in on us through a huge mullioned window filled the hall with shadows that were startling in their distinctness.

Whether because of this brightness, or from any other cause, our sitting had no immediate results. If Miss Sargent were susceptible to any influence, magnetic or otherwise, this was evidently not the right occasion for it.

After a quarter of an hour passed in silence, she rose suddenly from the table with a sigh, and announced her intention of retiring to sleep.

"It is only when I am asleep that I seem to be sensitive," she remarked. "I do not know how it is; this spot fascinates me, and yet if I sat here all night I don't believe anything would happen."

I allowed the two ladies to go upstairs by themselves. The old hall fascinated me by its emptiness and silence, and I paced up and down on the paved floor smoking a cigar, and pondering a certain question which my sister's attitude towards Alwyne had forced me to look in the face.

How long was I going to allow Alwyne Sargent to hazard her nerves, and possibly her brain, in these uncanny experiments? I asked myself the question, no longer as it concerned the clerk in our office on whom I depended, but as it concerned the girl who, stubborn old bachelor as I was, had actually made me think it possible that I might do worse than part with my freedom.

I wish it to be distinctly understood that there
was no foolish nonsense in my mind when I thought
of Alwyne. I judged her calmly in the light of reason. She appeared to me a good daughter, a good
sister, and a thoroughly agreeable companion—in
short, an ideal wife for a sensible businessman.

I took out of my pocket a rose which she had accidentally dropped in the garden, and which I had
picked up, and forgotten to return to her. I was in
the act of raising it to my face when suddenly I
heard a sigh.

I turned round quickly—I was standing just below the daïs at the time—and saw the door of the
haunted wing slowly swing open to the width of a
couple of feet, as though it were being opened just
enough to let someone through. At the same moment I was conscious of a subtle change in my surroundings, which I can hardly describe, except by
saying that I felt as though I had fallen asleep, and
awakened again in a different life.

The general aspect of the ancient hall remained
the same, and yet somehow everything in it looked
slightly less distinct, as though the faintest possible
veil had been drawn between me and the objects
at which I looked. The moon was not less bright,
and the shadows it threw were not loss black than
before, but nevertheless both light and shadow had
become less real, so to speak.

At the same time I was conscious that the change was as much in myself as in the objects round me. I seemed to breathe less vigorously, and to be deprived for a time of the power, or rather of the will, to move or take any part in what was about to happen.

The door opened as far as I have said, and then stopped. I gazed with the most intense curiosity to see who was coming in. But no one appeared. Only I could have sworn that someone or something *had* slipped through that open space, and was gliding softly across the daïs towards the end of the table which bore the faded stain.

I turned my eyes, following the course of the unseen visitant, till it had reached the fatal spot. And then, to my astonishment and horror, I did see something. I saw a rose, a rose of the palest yellow or white, lying as if it had just been laid down by an invisible hand, on the exact spot marked by the stain of blood.

I stood still for a few moments, expecting something to follow. Then, as I again turned my eyes in the direction of the door, I saw it close again as gently as it had opened, and without any visible agency. How long I stood in a manner enchanted, gazing from the closed door to the white rose lying on the board, I cannot say. It seemed half-a minute: it may have been half-an-hour.

Then I was aroused by a sound which clearly belonged to the world of reality. It reached me from
above, and on looking up I saw that a figure had
appeared in the musicians' gallery, which I have described as overlooking the daïs.

At first sight I could have imagined that this figure was only a phantom of the brain, in keeping
with the extraordinary illusion which I had just experienced. But as it moved forward to the front of
the gallery I recognised that it was Alwyne herself.

She appeared to have come out of her sleeping
room, unnoticed by my sister, and to have found her
way into the gallery while in that somnambulistic
state which I had witnessed on previous occasions.
On the way she had assumed a curious disguise, in
the shape of a heavy riding cloak, which she must
have found among the ancient relics scattered about
the old wing.

Clad in this garment she reached the balustrade
of the gallery, and peered down at the mysterious
rose. She stood like that, in an attitude of the most
intent watchfulness, for some minutes. Then I saw
her drop suddenly down on the floor of the gallery, concealing herself behind the balustrade, and
shrouding all but her face beneath the folds of the
cloak.

Unable to understand the cause of this singular
manoeuvre, I gazed round the hall for some change

that might account for it. The face of the somnambulist was turned in the direction of the door into
the garden. I watched this door steadily, half expecting to see it open as the other door had appeared to
do. But this time the spell which had governed my
faculties ceased to operate, and I neither saw nor
heard anything happen below in the hall.

It was different with the figure crouched in the
gallery above. After an interval of time, which must
have corresponded closely with that required for
someone to enter from the rose garden and make his
way to where the rose had been lying, I saw Alwyne
rise slowly to her full height, cast aside the thick
cloak, and extend her hand in the direction of the
fatal spot.

The next instant there was a click, followed by a
spark, as the flint of the pistol which she had been
grasping struck against the rusty pan. At the same
moment her hand loosed the weapon, which fell
crashing on the pavement below.

It was the very pistol which I had idly examined
in the course of the afternoon!

The noise, or the accomplishment of her purpose,
put an end to the sleepwalker's trance. She made a
natural movement of surprise, looked all about her,
and caught sight of me.

"Where am I? What has happened?" she called
out breathlessly.

I told her in a few words what I had seen.

"You came out into the gallery, wearing that cloak, and hid yourself behind the balustrade, after looking at the white rose on the table. Then at the end of a few minutes you stood up and fired in that direction. You have just dropped the pistol on the floor of the hall."

I was startled by Alwyne's response.

"But that rose—the rose on the table—is not white. It is *red.*"

I looked, and as surely as I am writing these lines the rose which I had seen lying there white in the moonlight had changed to the colour of blood-red.

Certain by this time that my senses were deceiving me, I made two steps of it to the spot.

The rose had gone! I swept my hand over the place where it had lain as I cried out to Alwyne: "There is nothing here!"

"I can see it still!" she replied.

"Come down, for Heaven's sake, or let me come to you; and get a light," I shouted back, thoroughly unnerved.

She moved back slowly from the gallery, first casting the cloak once more about her shoulders. I went and opened the door of the wing, and presently she came in sight, descending the stairs with a lighted lamp.

She passed her hand across her forehead as she observed:

"I am afraid the strain of these experiences is beginning to tell on me. Even now I am hardly sure
whether I am awake or asleep."

I led her out on to the daïs. This time there was
no room for doubt. Neither white rose nor red was
any longer there to tease the fancy. The old oak
board lay in the moonlight, black and smooth as
when we had seen it first.

Late as it was we could not forbear questioning
each other as to the experiences of the past half
hour. I described to Alwyne what I had seen or imagined, and pressed her to explain her own part in the
strange episode.

Unfortunately, she could remember nothing of
what had passed in her somnambulistic state. She
could only guess that she must have been imper-
sonating in a dream the principal actor in that grim
tragedy which the old hall had witnessed a century
or more ago.

We were interrupted by the appearance of my
sister Jane, whom the sound of the falling pistol
had roused. Something in the expression of my sister's face induced me to whisper hastily in Alwyne's
ear:

"May I tell her you have made me a promise?—
and will you keep it?"

With the nature of that promise, and its subsequent fulfilment, the reader has no concern. There,
as far as we knew, ended the story of Bewley Hall.

But in due time I found a purchaser for the estate, for whom the romantic associations of the old Hall were the principal attraction.

He exerted himself to trace the history of Sir William Hedges, and succeeded in getting into communication with a member of the family, a rather remote descendant, who was induced to supply the following particulars:

Late in life, that is to say after he had passed his sixtieth year, Sir William took an old man's fancy for the daughter of his parish clergyman, a girl of scarcely seventeen. Rosamund, as she was named, showed the greatest reluctance to marry the knight, for no reason that she was willing to assign, except his great age.

Her father and mother, dazzled by Sir William's wealth and his promises on behalf of their daughter, forced her into the match, and in due course she went to live in the Hall as Sir William's wife.

But, unknown to her parents, and of course to her new husband, Rosamund had secretly given her heart to a penniless young gentleman of the Greville family, living some twenty miles away. Unable to bear the prospect of losing each other altogether, the lovers agreed upon a method of communication, which they meant should be wholly innocent.

Once in every month, when the moon was at the full, young Greville was to ride across to Bewley Hall by night, and obtain entrance through the door of the rose garden, of which Rosamund provided him with a key.

Rosamund, on her part, was to descend into the hall, after her lord had fallen asleep, and place a white rose upon the table as a token that all was well, and that she still preserved her fidelity to her first love. On entering the hall and finding the white rose there, Greville was to take it away with him, leaving a red rose in its place, as an answering pledge.

For some months the lovers kept up their romantic tryst without discovery. But at last there came a night when it had rained hard during the day, and unwittingly the lover brought in some of the mud of the rose garden on his boots, and left it on the stones of the hall.

As ill-luck would have it, Sir William woke that morning early, and came down before his household was astir. He noticed the mud-stains, and the red rose upon the table, and, following up the scent, discovered the hoof-prints of Greville's horse outside.

Firmly believing the worst, the knight swore to be revenged upon his unknown rival, and from that time he set himself to watch night after night for an opportunity of surprising him. When the appointed night came round again, Sir William, who was as usual watching, while feigning to be asleep, saw his wife rise from his side, take a white rose in her hand, and go down into the hall.

Leaving the bedchamber directly after her, the knight armed himself with a loaded pistol, and went and hid himself in the musicians' gallery, to see what would follow.

He failed to see his wife, who was already returning upstairs again. But before Rosamund had made
the discovery of her husband's vigilance, the door
of the rose garden was opened, and young Greville
stole in, with a red rose in his hat-band.

He was in the act of stretching out his fingers
to pick up the rose left by his sweet heart, when
Sir William fired. The ball pierced the lover's heart,
and he fell forward, his blood gushing over the white
flower, which it dyed to the colour of that one he
had been going to replace it with.

Immediately Lady Hedges, who had that moment
found her husband's place vacant, ran shrieking out
into the gallery, and flung herself headlong down
beside her lover's corpse, breaking her neck against
the ground.

This awful catastrophe served to unsettle the reason of its author, whom the law refrained from pun-
ishing. He caused the Hall to be shut up, and when
he died many years after, he so ordered it by his
will that none should reopen the ancient building,
nor profane the scene of the tragedy with any sort
of pleasure or diversion, as long as the Hall should
remain in the hands of his descendants.

The above narrative, I need not remark, exactly
fits in with the experiences I have just related, and
which the reader is at liberty to accept or reject, as
he may please.

The Haunted Woman

A month after the romantic adventure of Bewley Hall, I received the most extraordinary letter I have ever had in my life.

It was from a lady, and the envelope was marked *Private*. This is what I read:

The Abbey, Abbotsbury.

Dear Sir,

I have seen in the Journal of the Psychical Research Society an account of some extraordinary discoveries made by you and a young lady named Sargent in connection with occult phenomena in old family mansions; and I am writing to ask you in confidence if you or she would be willing to come down here and see if you could do anything to put an end to a manifestation which has been going on for a considerable time.

I ought to explain that I am the only person in the house who has seen anything, and I have not mentioned it to anyone but my own maid, who can be trusted. I am *most anxious* that my son, Captain Throgmorton, should not hear anything about the matter, and therefore it is essential that no one should know why you are coming down. Some excuse will have to be thought of to account for your visit. My son is a widower, and has never recovered from the shock of losing his wife, and therefore you will understand that I must make it a point that on *no account* is he to be troubled.

I write to you in the greatest anxiety and distress of mind, and shall be prepared to pay liberally for your services and those of Miss Sargent, for which I shall be most grateful.

Trusting you will treat this matter as one *strictly* between ourselves,

I remain, Yours truly,

(Lady) Maria Throgmorton.

P.S.—In replying, please do not use an envelope bearing the name of your firm, as the letter-bag is opened by Captain Throgmorton.

Had I listened to my first impulse, I should have written back firmly, declining to have anything to do with a matter which called for concealment, and especially when I was asked to visit a house under a false character.

Unfortunately, before replying, I showed the letter to Alwyne, whose curiosity was immediately aroused to the highest degree.

"I am certain there is more in this than meets the eye," she declared. "From the way this lady writes it is evident that she thinks there is some connection between what she has seen and her son—something which she is afraid to tell us. We must go down and find out at all events what the situation is, even if we go no further."

The moment I heard her talk like that, I bitterly regretted having shown her Lady Throgmorton's letter. I knew Alwyne's courage too well by this time to have any hope of frightening her off from an adventure because it threatened to have some risk. The only argument I could think of was an appeal to the conventions.

"I could not think of letting you enter the house of people we know nothing about under a false name, or in some concealed character," I said determinedly. "I might consent to do such a thing, but my wife is different."

"I am not your wife yet, you tyrant," Alwyne retorted with a sly smile. "If you show the cloven hoof like that I shall look out for some kind, good-natured husband who will not trample on me. But there is no need that I should take a false name, or do anything else that you don't like. Why shouldn't this lady advertise for a companion in the *Standard,* and I answer the advertisement, and go down on trial?"

I felt that I was no match for Alwyne's ready wit. She found a way out of every difficulty as soon as I stated it.

"Well, at all events, I shall insist on going down first, and finding out something more about these people," I said. "How do you suggest that *I* should manage?"

Alwyne considered for a minute.

"There is no reason why you should not go down in your own name, too," she said at length, "unless Captain Throgmorton has heard of you. You might find out that from Lady Throgmorton. I should think the simplest plan would be for her to send for you to advise her about some alteration in the house—those old places are always wanting repairs. Unless she can persuade her son to let it—he seems to be the master. You had better ask her for more information first."

The upshot was that I answered Lady Throgmorton's letter as Alwyne wished. At the same time I looked up the family in the *Landed Gentry.*

The first result of these inquiries was the discovery that Lady Throgmorton was merely the captain's stepmother. She was the widow of one of our Ministers abroad, who had received the G.C.B., and Captain Throgmorton was his son by a former wife. Apparently, however, the stepmother and stepson had always been on the best of terms, and the widow of Sir Nicholas had remained on in the Abbey as its mistress until the captain's marriage, which had taken place about a year ago.

I could not learn anything about the wife's death, but it was clear that Lady Throgmorton had now resumed her old position.

At all events, she wrote back to me, saying that there was no need for me to drop my right name, and accepting the suggestion as to letting the house.

In due course I received a letter in her handwriting, but signed Arthur Throgmorton, in which I was formally invited to come down and see the property.

It was with very much more excitement than I usually feel on such occasions that I drove up to the main entrance of the Abbey, through an avenue whose yellowing leaves seemed ominous of some catastrophe.

I was first taken up to a comfortable bed room on the second floor, and given some tea. Half-an-hour later, the footman who attended to me came back, and asked me to follow him down to her ladyship's room.

I could see from his manner that Lady Throgmorton had given orders that I was to be treated with all possible consideration.

The room into which he conducted me was one of a suite on the first floor, evidently appropriated to the mistress of the house. The furniture was almost new, and I hardly required to be told that the rooms had been prepared to receive the bride of Captain Throgmorton; they now seemed to have been relegated to his stepmother.

The appearance of my client startled me. She was a woman of fifty, still strikingly handsome, but disfigured by a too lavish use of cosmetics. She had assumed an artificial pose on a couch, beside which stood a table covered with smelling-bottles and such articles. As I entered, she raised a gold and tortoiseshell lorgnette to her eyes, and gave me almost a hostile scrutiny.

Behind her stood her maid, a tall, thin woman with pinched lips and half-shut eyes, who never moved nor spoke except to answer some question from her mistress or to hand her some scent or drug.

The sight of this rouged and laced-up figure, with its blackened eyelids and prominent nose, and the silent shadow in the background, made me feel as if I had stepped into the atmosphere of some place like Homburg or Ostend, instead of an English country house.

"Sit down if you please, Mr. Hargreaves. And speak softly, if you will be so good. My nerves are absolutely destroyed—Madeline, the essence!"

The silent maid chose one of the bottles, and began dabbing her mistress' forehead, taking care not to disturb the powder.

"The experience I have gone through has been most frightful," Lady Throgmorton continued. "Every night it has been the same. I cannot sleep without taking enough chloral to kill anyone unaccustomed to it. And when I do go off—I *dream!*"

She gave a shudder, and raised a bottle of salts to her nostrils. Even where I sat I could detect the odour; in fact, the air of the room was thick with scents.

I waited for her to explain the nature of her experiences.

"Every night since I have been back in these rooms it has come to me," she went on. She seemed to have a difficulty in speaking out plainly. "It is an apparition—or at least it seems to be one—the apparition of my son's wife."

I thought it time to ask a question or two.

"Will you tell me a little more about the circumstances," I said. "When did Mrs. Throgmorton die? And how?"

She darted a fierce glance at me as I put the concluding question.

"She died six weeks ago, of pneumonia, in the room I am now occupying. After her death my son could not bear to sleep in it, and I thought it best to return to these rooms, which had always been mine."

"But if this apparition disturbs you there, why not try the effect of sleeping in some other part of the house?"

"Because it would be impossible to give any reason for changing again so soon. The servants would be inquisitive, and my son might suspect something." She hesitated before adding: "Someone else might take my place, and see what I have seen."

"I suppose you are afraid that if Captain Throgmorton heard of this it might distress him?" I hazarded.

Again she fixed me with a threatening glance.

"Captain Throgmorton must *never* hear of it," she responded. "The shock would kill him." She looked round at the maid for a moment. "We are afraid that he has not been quite right in his mind since his wife's death."

I could not conceal my consternation at this intelligence. I began to feel thankful that Alwyne had not come with me to such a house.

Lady Throgmorton saw that she must tell me something more.

"He would not believe that she was really dead, for a long time. Then he had a special coffin made for her, in the hope that she might come to life again. And he has told me that Eleanor would have appeared to him, if she really were dead, to assure him that she still remembered him in the other world."

I considered these extraordinary statements in my mind before replying.

"And are you sure that it would not be the wisest course to let him know what has happened, and give him the chance of seeing whatever you have seen?"

Lady Throgmorton turned to the woman behind her, and made her administer a dose of some restorative, before she answered this question.

"I dare not run the risk. If he saw what I see every night it might unhinge his mind altogether. The apparition is—" she paused, and seemed to pick her words—"is not a natural one. It is—strange. And—and horrible."

A convulsion passed across her face as she made this declaration. The rouge cracked on her cheeks, and the pearl powder went in flakes.

The maid interfered suddenly, addressing herself to me.

"I think you had better leave her ladyship now, sir. It will be bad for her to talk any more."

I rose, murmuring some polite expression of regret, and got out of the room as best I could.

It seemed to me that I had got entangled in some very alarming mystery, and that the only prudent thing for me to do would be to quit the Abbey as soon as possible, and not return.

I passed the time before dinner in strolling through the grounds, as if in discharge of my commission to inspect the premises.

At the meal I met the master of the house for the first time. He was not a very young man—some age between thirty-five and forty—and his manner was subdued. But he appeared quite able to perform the duties of a host, and talked to me in a reasonable and businesslike spirit about the arrangements for letting the Abbey.

"Neither Lady Throgmorton nor myself find it a very cheerful place just at present," he said. "In fact, I am seriously uneasy about my mother's state of health. She has been accustomed to the bright society of foreign capitals, and the quiet, lonely life we lead here has got upon her nerves. I ought to take her to Paris, I expect, or the Riviera."

I did not venture to make any direct reference to his dead wife, nor did he make any nearer allusion to the subject.

The only other thing of importance he had to tell me was that Lady Throgmorton would give me all necessary instructions.

"She has always managed everything here," he explained, "and I think it is a distraction for her just now to have the reins in her hands again. As for the shooting, it is not up to much, and the steward can tell you more about it than I can."

Nothing that I saw of Captain Throgmorton was inconsistent with his being in full possession of his reason. But there are such people as monomaniacs, able to take their part in the world without giving any indication of eccentricity apart from their particular craze, and, of course, I could only suppose that my host was one of them.

But for the fact that the letting of the Abbey promised to be a piece of genuine business, I think I should have declined to have anything more to do with this family. As it was, I did not like to break with a client, and on my return to town I found Alwyne so keenly interested, and so determined to probe the matter to the very bottom, that I unwillingly gave way.

She went, as she had proposed, in the character of a prospective companion. I found it impossible to go with her, and could only urge her to wire me in case she felt the slightest uneasiness, and to come away instantly if things took an unpleasant turn.

I waited with the greatest anxiety for her report, which reached me on the second morning after her departure. I need only extract the important passages:

"I arrived safely, and had what I suppose I must call a friendly reception from Lady Throgmorton. I did not see the Captain, as Lady Throgmorton's meals were served in her own boudoir, and I took mine with her.

"I felt a great dislike for the maid, Madeline, who seemed to me to resent my coming. I fancied that she was playing on the fears of her mistress for some purpose of her own, and did not relish the idea of my doing anything to relieve them. In fact, I thought it quite possible, at first, that the apparition was the result of some trickery on her part.

"I wish I could think so still. I wish I had never seen what I saw last night, and what I am afraid I shall never be able to forget.

"When I say that I have seen it, I do not mean to be positive that it was an objective manifestation. My experience may have been purely subjective; that is to say, I may have been in sympathetic rapport with Lady Throgmorton, so that her vision was communicated to me.

"That seems all the more probable because the maid, who has slept with Lady Throgmorton since these experiences began, declares that she has never seen anything.

"Whichever it was, nothing would have induced me to face such a manifestation had I been warned of its character. But, as you know, I always consider it necessary that I should be told nothing in advance, in order to avoid the possibility of suggestion.

"Lady Throgmorton struck me at the outset as a hysterical subject, just the sort of woman to be the victim of a nervous delusion, and therefore I did not much expect to find any reality in her experiences.

"A bedroom had been prepared for me adjoining her own, but it was arranged that I should actually pass the night in a bed in her room, which was usually occupied by the maid. Madeline was to take the bed in my room in exchange.

"I will not dwell upon the figure presented by Lady Throgmorton at night, without the paint and the powder which disguised her in the day. She had a table beside her bed for her sleeping-draughts and salts, and I noticed that she lay huddled on the very edge of the bed, as though to have her medicines within easier reach.

"I wanted to have all the lights extinguished, but she insisted passionately on having a night-light, and as she assured me that she had had one burning every time the apparition visited her, I could not very well object.

"Nothing happened till we had both been in bed for more than an hour. Lady Throgmorton seemed unable to sleep, and kept fidgeting with the bottles beside her, while I lay with my eyes half shut, watching the shadows on the ceiling, and listening to the restless movements of my unseen companion.

"I was just dozing off when suddenly I heard an agonised gasp, almost a shriek, from the other bed.

"In an instant I was wide-awake, and sitting up to look round.

"The first thing that met my eyes in the dim light was Lady Throgmorton, stretched out stiffly in her place, with her head thrown back on the pillow, and her eyes fixed in a glassy stare, like a person undergoing a cataleptic seizure.

"I followed the direction of her eyes without seeing anything more for the first few moments.

"Then, as I withdrew my eyes from wandering about the room, to return to where she lay breathing convulsively, I saw the cause of her terror.

"There was another person in the bed beside her.

"I have said *in,* but I ought to have said *on.* The figure which met my sight was that of a woman prepared for burial. She lay stretched out in the rigid attitude of the dead, her face and form wrapped tightly round with white linen grave-clothes.

"My heart nearly stopped beating at this silent invasion of the bed of the living by the dead.

"But the worst was still to come.

"While I watched, an awful change came over the spectral corpse. The linen wrappings appeared to decay by swift stages, and finally to fall away and hang in shreds from the appalling Thing—for all humanity had left it—which they had concealed.

"What I then saw I can hardly bear to think of, much less to describe.

"And imagine this horror seen lying side by side with a living woman who seemed to know it was there, and to feel the dreadful pollution of its touch!

"I hardly know what I should have done if the sight had lasted a moment longer. But with the full revelation of its unutterable loathesomeness the Thing vanished—vanished from its place without any apparent movement, leaving me with the sickening dread of seeing it as suddenly return.

"Common feeling compelled me to go to the assistance of Lady Throgmorton. I had hardly set foot on the floor when she began trembling all over, and calling out the name of her maid.

"The woman, who had evidently been expecting a summons, opened the door immediately, and came in. She darted an inquisitive look at me, a look of distrust and even of alarm I fancied it, as she passed to the side of her mistress, to whom she began giving things out of the bottles.

"I busied myself in lighting a pair of candles on the mantelshelf. As soon as Lady Throgmorton was able to speak I heard her demand anxiously:

"'Has she seen it? Did you see anything?'

"I turned towards the bed, and found mistress and maid waiting for my reply with apprehension.

"'Yes, Lady Throgmorton. At least, I have seen something, which I expect is what you have seen. A dead body, lying beside you on the bed.'

"She uttered a groan as she nodded her head in confirmation.

"'And—and did anything happen to it?' she asked in a whisper.

"I could not suppress a shudder as I answered: 'It assumed an appearance of decay.'

"Mistress and maid exchanged glances of intelligence.

"'I was right, you see, Madeline,' the lady said. And then she added, to my intense surprise: 'It has grown worse night after night. The first time I saw it, the shroud remained intact. Since then the change has gone on regularly.'

"There was only one thing to say, and I said it.

"'In my opinion you ought not to pass another night in that bed, nor in this room. Whatever be the real nature of this experience, it is clear that the only chance of its ceasing is for you to leave off sleeping here.'

"In Lady Throgmorton's pitiable condition I hardly liked to question her on the subject of the spectre. But the idea had already presented itself to my own mind that the ghastly figure which was haunting her could only be that of her son's late wife, and the horrible changes it had undergone seemed to correspond with the decay of the actual corpse.

"Having been assured that there was no chance of anything more occurring that night, I went back into my own room, leaving the maid to take my place.

"This morning I have had a long talk with Lady Throgmorton, in the absence of her maid. She has told me quite frankly that she considers the apparition to be that of the late Mrs. Throgmorton. She intends leaving for London to-day, on her way to Paris, and the Captain goes with her. She has pressed me very strongly to remain behind, and to pass at least one more night in the haunted room; and as I wish to ascertain whether my own experience of last night was objective or subjective, I think I shall consent.

"But I dare not make the experiment alone, and as Lady Throgmorton is strongly opposed to any of the servants being made acquainted with the mystery, I have promised to ask you to join me here for the purpose.

"Please wire."

So ended the report, with the exception of some personal messages of no interest to the public.

I need not remark on the courage of this brave girl in consenting to remain alone in a house where she had had such a frightful experience. I wired immediately to say I should arrive by the next train, and I was as good as my word.

I found Alwyne installed as Lady Throgmorton's deputy, in charge of the house and servants, who were all under notice to leave.

We decided to sit up till the hour at which the sepulchral figure would appear, if it appeared at all. In good time we moved into Lady Throgmorton's room, extinguished all the lights except the solitary nightlight, and sat watching for what might happen.

A surprise awaited us.

We were ignorant of the exact minute at which the previous manifestation had occurred. But midnight came and passed without the slightest sign of anything uncanny.

I was just saying to Alwyne that I thought it useless to wait longer, when the silence of the night was broken by footsteps advancing suddenly along the corridor. In a moment the door was burst open, and we beheld on the threshold Captain Throgmorton, with a lighted lantern in one hand, and a revolver in the other.

"Explain the meaning of all this," he demanded sternly, as we sprang to our feet.

I was at a loss what answer to make to him. But Alwyne was quick to assert herself.

The Captain was evidently not prepared for this retort, which at once subdued him.

"I will apologise, of course, if I am in the wrong," he said, speaking more quietly. "I came down here because my stepmother's action in leaving you here seemed to me eccentric. I felt more and more uneasy as I got further from home, and finally, after seeing her off to Paris, I decided to run down here again and make sure that all was right. I have only just walked over from the station, and seeing a light in this room, I suspected something wrong."

He glanced round the room as he spoke with a mixture of curiosity and emotion.

I thought it was now time for me to speak.

"I trust my name, and the reputation of my firm, will be a sufficient guarantee that everything that has passed in your absence has been entirely in accordance with our instructions from Lady Throgmorton, to whom you may recollect you referred me. If you will now come with me into another room, I will tell you what those instructions were."

Captain Throgmorton took us downstairs into his library, and there I told him the entire story, as I have told it here, only omitting for his own sake the hideous detail of the change which had followed the first appearance of the spectral corpse.

"To-night we have seen nothing," I said in conclusion. "I think, therefore, you may rest assured that the whole thing is a diseased imagination on the part of Lady Throgmorton, due to the state of her nerves."

The Captain listened with the closest attention, wincing more than once at the references I had made to his dead wife. At the close he said:

"I am infinitely obliged to you for telling me this. It is true that I had a special coffin constructed for my late wife, but it was in discharge of a solemn promise to her, as she entertained a morbid dread of being prematurely buried. I may add that I engaged a medical man to visit the vault every day for a week, when he reported to me that changes had taken place which rendered it utterly impossible to doubt the reality of the death."

The reluctance with which he made this statement slowed me that he knew what the doctor had seen. The changes were those which Alwyne had seen in the vision of Lady Throgmorton.

"Do you think there is any possibility that Lady Throgmorton may have heard of these visits?"

It was Alwyne who put the question. The Captain shook his head.

"I think not, Miss Sargent. Naturally I did not wish such a thing to be known, and I pledged the doctor to secrecy."

He frowned as he added:

"It is a very serious thing if my stepmother has been representing that my intellect is disordered, as you say. I must consider what is my best course; but I think I shall have to follow her abroad, and perhaps to take the doctor with me."

We separated for the night with mutual expressions of regret. In the morning Captain Throgmorton, opening the letter-bag as usual, found in it a telegram addressed to Alwyne.

It proved to be from Lady Throgmorton, who was staying at a hotel in the Avenue Friedland, and contained these words:

"I have seen if here. Come immediately."

On reading this extraordinary dispatch, not one of us any longer doubted that the sender's mind was unhinged.

Captain Throgmorton at once sent a groom for the doctor, who arrived in the course of an hour.

When the doctor had been placed in possession of the whole of the facts—and this time I did not think it right to suppress anything—his manner became exceedingly grave.

"I will say nothing till I have seen Lady Throgmorton," he declared. "But I agree with you, Captain, that we ought both to go to Paris by to-night's boat."

Before leaving, Captain Throgmorton and I exchanged promises, one of strict secrecy on my part, and on his own to communicate to me the final outcome of the affair.

That promise was never kept.

A brief note, so brief as to be almost discourteous, informed me that Lady Throgmorton had been confined, with her own consent, in a private asylum in the Department of Seine-et-Oise, and that is the last I have ever heard from the Throgmorton family.

The truth was revealed to me in a singular manner, some years after, by the last person from whom I ever expected to learn it—Lady Throgmorton's maid.

Having learnt that this woman had presumed to give my name as a reference, I found her out, and threatened her with proceedings. By way of excuse she pleaded that the death of her mistress had thrown her on the world without friends, Captain Throgmorton having refused to assist her because he suspected her of complicity in his wife's death.

That death, she now assured me, was the work of Lady Throgmorton, who was unable to endure the loss of her position as mistress of the Abbey, and of certain family jewels which went with the estate.

It had been brought about, or at least hastened, by means of a drug which subsequently arrested the decomposition of the corpse.

The doctor, it appears, had already been struck by some unusual symptoms in the case, and again by certain unexpected signs in the decay of the body. On being informed of Lady Throgmorton's visions, or hallucinations, his suspicions were given definite shape, and a full confession was extracted from the wretched woman before her reason finally gave way.

Shortly after the somewhat abrupt conclusion of this adventure, a quiet wedding took place, and Alwyne Sargent became Alwyne Hargreaves. I do not think any explanation of my conduct in marrying my secretary is due from me, as a business man. Alwyne had materially assisted me to attain the prosperity I now enjoyed, and it was only right that she should share it.

Our Continental honeymoon helped to restore her health, which had been considerably impaired by the shocks to which she had been so frequently exposed.

I have now given up dealing in haunted property, and my wife will never in the future, I trust, be called upon to exercise her extraordinary gift of clairvoyance.

COACHWHIP PUBLICATIONS
CoachwhipBooks.com

ANCIENT
HAUNTS

The Stoneground
Ghost Tales
by E. G. Swain

Tedious Brief Tales
of Granta and Gramarye
by Arthur Gray

COACHWHIP PUBLICATIONS
COACHWHIPBOOKS.COM

THE SUPERNATURAL
STORIES OF MONSIGNOR
ROBERT H. BENSON

THE LIGHT INVISIBLE
A MIRROR OF SHALOTT

COACHWHIP PUBLICATIONS
COACHWHIPBOOKS.COM

TALES OF FRIGHT
AND FANTASY BY
E. F. BENSON

COACHWHIP PUBLICATIONS

CoachwhipBooks.com

COACHWHIP PUBLICATIONS
CoachwhipBooks.com

CATS OF SHADOW,
CLAWS OF DARKNESS

Stories of Were-Cats, Ghost Cats,
and Other Supernatural Felines

COACHWHIP PUBLICATIONS
CoachwhipBooks.com

COACHWHIP PUBLICATIONS
CoachwhipBooks.com

DANCING SHADOWS

Tales of the Supernatural
by Bernard Capes

COACHWHIP PUBLICATIONS
CoachwhipBooks.com

STRANGE
HAUNTS

STORIES BY
F. MARION CRAWFORD &
H. B. MARRIOTT WATSON

www.ingramcontent.com/pod-product-compliance
Lightning Source LLC
Chambersburg PA
CBHW030739030726
47497CB00001B/53